Válter Filipe Nogueira began developing his own voice by writing poetry during adolescence. Later, he would go on to accumulate an array of professions, which would drive and fuel his writing. At the University of Évora he studied Literature and Arts, exploring video, theatre, and performance.

About his present little is known…

À Daniella qui a fait ce livre enfin publié.

Válter Filipe Nogueira

A Spiral of a Dream – The Medium

Austin Macauley Publishers
LONDON * CAMBRIDGE * NEW YORK * SHARJAH

Copyright © Válter Filipe Nogueira 2024

The right of Válter Filipe Nogueira to be identified as author of this work has been asserted by the author in accordance with sections 77 and 78 of the Copyright, Designs and Patents Act 1988.

All rights reserved. No part of this publication may be reproduced, stored in a retrieval system, or transmitted in any form or by any means, electronic, mechanical, photocopying, recording, or otherwise, without the prior permission of the publishers.

Any person who commits any unauthorised act in relation to this publication may be liable to criminal prosecution and civil claims for damages.

This is a work of fiction. Names, characters, businesses, places, events, locales, and incidents are either the products of the author's imagination or used in a fictitious manner. Any resemblance to actual persons, living or dead, or actual events is purely coincidental.

A CIP catalogue record for this title is available from the British Library.

ISBN 9781035850112 (Paperback)
ISBN 9781035850136 (ePub e-book)
ISBN 9781035850129 (Audiobook)

www.austinmacauley.com

First Published 2024
Austin Macauley Publishers Ltd®
1 Canada Square
Canary Wharf
London
E14 5AA

Cover Art by Duarte Parreira

Table of Contents

Book 1: The Undecided   13

Prelude   15

   Chapter 1: The Last Miracle on My Land   17

   Chapter 2: Strange Coincidences   23

   Chapter 3: Life Is a Test of Effort   35

   Chapter 4: The Factory of Lights   52

   Chapter 5: Our Lady of Health   73

   Chapter 6: Scholarship   97

   Chapter 7: Between the Alentejo and the Aegean Sea   121

   Chapter 8: Neither There nor Here, Neither Here nor There   140

Book 2: The Promise   153

   Chapter 1: The Returned   155

   Chapter 2: A Renegade University Resident   180

   Chapter 3: The Guest and the Host   201

   Chapter 4: The Ping and the Pong   218

   Chapter 5: Man Is a Wild Animal   234

   Chapter 6: A Sad Life in Vista Alegre   250

Book 3: Garraia   281

   Chapter 1: In the Preface to the Garraia   283

   Chapter 2: Grey September   300

   Chapter 3: Internship   314

The Medium

Book 1
The Undecided

Prelude

Literature imitates life, but life never plagiarises the art that each one has in living, our protagonist will say, somewhere, later...

Let's admit, first, that this book has its own existence. Second, let it be clear that this literary work is not a reflection of the author about himself, nor less, that he has dwelt on some of my days. On the contrary, the following narrative is concerned primarily with its main intervener, as well as, in part, with other characters who will follow him along his spiriform journey.

I am just one of the narrators. However, don't count on too many judgments from me. My role is similar to that of an omniscient narrator, who stands at a distance, observing. I am what is called a deux ex machina. If you prefer, I am that kind of narrator who you don't really know where he comes from or what he is doing in the story, but who always knows much more than what he says...

What I intend to say, or, to warn you, is that the boundaries we will cross are fluid. Rather than explaining and substantiating the reason for the protagonist's action or trying in vain to justify the character of his friend Marcus, as a clear example of chance, without motivation, let us be content, rather, with what is immediately sufficient. Since, generally, at the end of a book, we understand everything else.

I alert you that, for the time being, there will be no miracle either. It was a mistake by the author, an anachronistic error, caused by the spiral in the narrative of his main character. Since, in the same place, in Fato, two distinct moments will in fact occur in the cycle that this literary work obeys.

For now, the reader will be more informed and enlightened about how the beginning of this book corresponds, more precisely, to the middle of the hero's story, which we will follow, throughout an expedition that will last more or less 9 years. In which, we will accompany, sometimes more closely, sometimes more reserved and distant, the aspirations, the desires and the adventures of a set of lives, relatively stationary in the spiral of a dream.

Often the truth of a thing, or the lie of that thing, is a reality composed of more than two halves. Let's understand that, unfortunately, some existences simply never obtain a dignified environment that allows them to reach an honourable end. Either because the environment in which they live affects them determinately, or because when they reach the midpoint of the narrative that their lives write in space and time, the force of the inaugural breath that they had, no longer suffuses their candle with the same intensity.

Dear reader, dear reader, in media res! After all, one's existence is not primarily contained in its end, nor in its beginning. But mostly, somewhere in the middle of the glass half full and half empty that we are. After this brief introduction, I will disappear.

Returning, eventually, later, if, and when, necessary!

Chapter 1
The Last Miracle on My Land

(January 2012)

I am temporarily back in the valley of the village of Avelar. I have returned not to my mother and stepfather's house, but to a decrepit dwelling that my mother inherited. Meanwhile, my brother is growing up very fast. Me? I am going, I don't know where. But I'm sure I go back to the beginning of the circle, to the beginning of the spiral. Which takes me backwards! It takes me back to the moment when I witness the vehicle moving and carrying those inside it, who are also moving away from me. And, consequently, I, too, am moving away from me and separating from this self of mine. Which, in turn, is gradually metamorphosing into a tiny planet, the size of a tiny Pluto, withdrawing, little by little, from my universe.

It is still too early to be night. But it is already too late for it to still be day. Nevertheless, I still reach that small point, which gets further and further away. Until it disappears completely. Like a black hole, like a ring of fire, still burning at the bottom of the horizon. Yet, if I close the windows and pull down the blinds of my gaze, I can still see her. But not only her, but also her mother, the cat, and all the boxes and suitcases that fit inside the car that is consecutively alienating itself from me at the end of each afternoon. Following the road until it is lost in the sea of ether. Slowly sinking into the ocean of my dreams.

She returned to her parents' home. She was fed up with Évora. Besides that, she would be tired of being paid so little and having to work so hard, so that her social balance in Alentejo would be inverted. She would also be stuffed, bored, having to wait for me to finish my degree and that this would somehow change the course of our relationship. Just as, also, my mother is waiting for me to finish my degree for good, and for me to necessarily change my path sooner or later.

Fearing that if I don't, the events that clearly stubbornly crystallise the invisible shape of my destiny will transform me negatively forever.

Now I am walking through the centre of the village of Avelar. Without knowing where I should go on, nor where I concretely have to go. I don't really know what to do here! In the centre of the village, there is not much to see, nor is there much to do. I feel tired of existing. Without knowing if what I see in the sky of my imagination, can be called a real veil, or if, perhaps, it would be more appropriate to say, that it is one of the unreal layers with the diapason and vibration that my illusion has, and that composes the compass of my fantasy atmosphere.

Still, I go on my way, looking for something that I know for certain that I will not find here. My friend Marcus, is also looking for a path and for something that he will not find, in his case, on the outskirts, or in one of the corners of his mansion. I thought about calling him. But hypothetically, Marcus is busy untangling the threads that make up his current novel thought. However, I wonder: where is he now? What is he himself doing? After all, for two friends who have known each other forever, what thickness does the wall of time have in the division of space, and the place in the house, where each one is?

The days in January advance, without me knowing yet which way I am going. It is cold inside. Now I can't talk myself into giving up. Not least because the first decision I made was to let go of everything I thought I knew before. I abandoned everything that I supposed I thought I knew, for the purpose of being born again, or at least reborn for one last time.

Potentially, it would be necessary for me to die first, so that I could then be born again. But what was really urgent for me, more than being able to resurrect or be reborn from the ashes, was to be amazed. And, more than a miracle happening to me, what I needed was not only to attend and witness that wonder, but to participate in that portent, which would have such a great volume of meaning, that it would be something as colossal, as the last miracle in my land. At the very least, its impact would make me someone quite different, in the world and time in which we live. Because, as is well known, there are simply no more great things, like miracles, that happen in the way they used to.

I rose as quickly as I could on the second day of my stay in the Avelar valley. I got up so early that the morning screen was still off. I could not see where the ceiling containing the dawn of the sky began and ended. I felt alive and determined. I left the house and walked up Rua Nova. I walked up the street knowing that I was inaugurating something new. Probably, I was restarting a new path. Maybe starting again, a long and slow process.

I heard the symphony of the morning rising, playing endlessly outside and inside of matter. Where there is not one stage, not one specific space to echo its music on the edge of the pendulum of time. The morning page had illegible handwriting. Its ink appeared written in the midst of its imperceptible nature. I could, however, see and read his writing as I walked up Rua do Castelo and passed beside the cemetery.

I continued up Rua do Castelo, where there is not, nor was there ever a castle. Perhaps, it has been erased from the place and from the pages of history. I climbed, and climbed, and continued to climb a long way that led me to walk along the altars and the scaffolding of the mountain. I kept climbing, again and again, up the same mountain. Until I reached a small bridge, which levitates over the complementary route number eight. I fearlessly crossed to the other side and continued walking for a few more kilometres. Then, I had to climb up the mountain bump again, until I found Fato, a small mountain village; and it was in Fato, that I would have had a vision, a revelation of me and my world, as well as, a vision of me with that world that lies beyond.

Although, what I wished was to have witnessed or been affected by a divine miracle. However, the oracle I had access to was indeed a supreme moment. Because, after passing the locality of Fato, I kept going down and running incessantly, behind every curve and counter-curve. Going round and round until the end of that path took me to the Fragas de São Simão, where, there, I dipped the soles of my spirit and washed the back of my soul, rubbing the boards of my body in the water of the Ribeira de Alge.

When I dived in, I prayed for a miracle, but I was not heard. Yet, I felt rejuvenated; maybe I had been born again, because when I looked into the mirror of the water of the Ribeira de Alge, I didn't recognise my face. What I saw was a heavenly essence moving in the water. It was not a miracle, but possibly a sign.

I again had to continuously climb the steep and absolute bump of the mountain. Its ascent would lead me up such a long ascent that it would continue beyond the golden plains of the Alentejo, and go beyond the boulders and peaks of central Portugal, which is a region that lies, at the centre of the world. The further I descended into the valley of the village of Avelar, the further I got away from the mountains. The more I recognised, however, where I had gone and what had happened to me.

I hadn't been tutored in geometry, either, I hadn't talked to Marcus about his arithmetic operations or his abstractions, or his usual theses that occasionally included a recent conspiracy theory developed by his persecution mania. More than having studied for my degree in Languages, Literatures and Cultures, I had re-learned the meaning of being, being able to be as authentic as the hills and the streams. More than being happy or being thwarted by the system or forced by a mother's will or discouraged by a father's abstention, I had conceived a path that I would have to keep climbing. And the more I climbed it, the more I would be initiated down that same path.

I got home by walking down Rua Velha. I had found a direction. Which was still a very indefinite itinerary. Nevertheless, what I discerned and concluded was that no matter how many are the tracks and how many are the paths, only one direction contains the key that will allow me to go through and open the lock on the portal of the dream, thus summing up the only path that I truly have left to take. Although I did not yet understand the message of tomorrow concretely, I knew that the next day, I would get up as early as the sun would awake.

When I lit the fire in the wood stove and released its heat, I felt the blessing of its generosity, warming not only the flesh of my body, but also the clothes of my spirit. Simple tasks, such as: washing the dishes, putting them away in the cupboard; are not complex daily routines. They are simple acts of daily faith. The detergent makes little bubbles of foam, the firewood pops, the flames crackle, and these are also good practices of faith.

The broth of this morning's sun is contrarily as warm as the colour of the moon perched in the middle of tonight's cooling night sky outside. Yet it is important to feel the embrace of the morning and the dawn. As much as the warmth of the wood stove, which stays lit during the night and caresses the belly of my legs without needing to touch them.

I obediently got up the next day. Before the sun was awake, I was already up. When I jumped out of bed, Buddha had not yet decided to leave the comfort of his father's palace. Still, God's favourite angel had not rebelled, and already I had aired and made my bed. Ignoring still, in which part of the book the last miracle I so desperately seek inside and outside of myself will occur.

Each life is a singular constellation of algorithms, a combination of assumptions, of chances, of moments that are like comets. They pass by us so quickly that we have no time to notice them and their brief existence. The world I was probing was still a hypothesis, still the search for the path and the miracle that would happen somewhere in the middle or before the middle of the book.

Man is an obstacle to the nature of man! We continually climb the same mountain each day and gain nothing, lose nothing. We continually climb and descend the same mountain and the same mountain terraces, and we gain nothing in the creation of man and lose nothing in the evolution of man.

Spaceships orbit between a layer of the atmosphere of the past and a layer of the atmosphere of the present, flying for millennia and millennia at the speed of light, until they reach the sky of the future. Getting lost in vain attempts to consecutively make the same nostalgic trip. Insisting on travelling the same trajectory when the circuits of the past do not connect, making impossible any attempt to return home.

I persuaded my mother to let me stay alone in the old dwelling, which is extremely close to her hair salon. The previous owner of the house that my mother inherited had a temper. In her more or less bitter end, she only had the compassion and timing of my mother, to whom she left some land and some vegetable gardens, next to the house, where she once enjoyed her time. Doing what she loved, which was, essentially, moving the earth with the slick of her hands. Making furrows in the earth like the airplanes that tear the belly of the sky. Or, simply, cultivating the earth with the manure of animals. And, instead of reading, first watering the flowers in her garden, and, instead of writing, like me, first picking the fruits that continue to grow on the trees that remain alive after her departure.

After I had washed the dishes, I went out onto the terrace that had the light of the street lamp on. While I was looking at the stars and the more than obvious signs planted on the face of the sky, and the arms of the night adulated my face, I wondered if my oldest friend, Marcus Emanuel de Monsalude e Matalorga, was also looking at the same sky, seeing the same stars and searching for the way to Santiago that would point him in the direction of a longed-for return home.

We all got lost at one time in the labyrinth of our world. Wasting too much time trying to get out of the perception we had of it. Abandoning, however, very slowly the interpretation that has the dimension of our small place in the cosmos, which we occupy within a larger universe.

Each one explores in his own way, the awareness he has of that timeless world. Which is made to his measure and to his scale. Living in it and within it. Yet, each of us does not gain, nor lose a single day in this world consciousness, that each of us has and dreamt of. I go on, sometimes going up, sometimes going down, and still having to go up. Climbing the same mountain each day, until the road takes me to a new trajectory, or else something or someone has changed direction, or else the wind, today, runs differently.

Chapter 2
Strange Coincidences

(February 2012)

The village and the moun that surround the Avelar valley were left behind. Even further behind were the Fragas de São Simão, the December nights of last year, and the first days of January of this year, in the house that my mother inherited. Night was falling fast, and I watched that whole process of transformation from day into night, through the car window, as a passenger.

I was sitting in the van that Pascal's father bought him. Looking through the rear-view mirror of the time machine, watching the day kiss the night. The day, which was more and more his only lover.

Pascal was sometimes looking at the road, sometimes leaning over to look at me. His left arm was dangling over the back of the door. With his right he mimicked relaxed. Describing his weekend to me. Today, after lunch he went to visit his girlfriend in Chão-de-Couce. On Saturday, he rehearsed with the two or three cover bands, where he drummed his bass. From the way he gestured with his arm, I could tell that his girlfriend was similar to the village of Avelar, and that she, too, was lagging behind.

Feeling at ease, he shared with me his possible decision to leave at least one of the bands where he played in the local bars where cocktails and live music were served. He justified himself that he was only doing this to earn money and to furnish his sound studio. He told me, however, that he needed not only money, but also time. He told me, with conviction, that time was money. That was his little drama. But one day he would finish his degree and shove his diploma in a drawer. And he would dedicate himself entirely to his true passion. His girlfriend in Chão-de-Couce and the village of Avelar would definitely be left behind.

While Pascal was talking and driving to the house of the colleague with whom he had also agreed to give a ride, I vaguely remembered the moment, much earlier, when Pascal had mentioned to me, still in Évora, that someone from our region was also studying there. We were not in the habit of meeting regularly. When we did meet, it was by chance of someone who lives in the same city and goes to the same places. Or, by mere chance, they come from the same place.

Pascal kept talking and I kept asking questions, just for me. Wondering what the shape of the unknown face, which would have the future, seen by me, in the rear-view mirror of the time van.

The rain had been threatening to fall since we left the baby blue pier of the Avelarense sky. The closer we got to the expectation of the greyness in Alvaiázere, the more the sky matured that it was going to rain. The closer we got to the place where we would catch our countrywoman, the more my expectation of meeting someone tremendously impactful spoke louder than my interest in the groove of the subject Pascal was so animatedly discussing with me.

And, lo and behold, we arrived. Pascal parked and I immediately felt the sensation that I had been there before. Although, not exactly a déjà-vu! Still, yes, I had indeed been there before. In an adolescent time. Before I entered higher education. In fact it was a strange coincidence. If not, then it was an ugly, ugly coincidence. It was the same mental picture from another time. The mother in her housewife's uniform and the father, perpetually, gloomy. With his depressive moustache. And that colleague, his daughter, had neither the face of Venus nor the face of Aphrodite.

There was no enigma, no mystery. I recognised those faces. I remembered perfectly what the portrait of that family looked like, which in essence had not changed at all. It was certainly an ugly coincidence, quite honestly, very unattractive. Our fellow countrywoman was, after all, a face from my past. It was a familiar face that I had never dreamt would reappear, when Pascal warned me that we still had to stop by our colleague's house. Yet, perhaps, nothing could be more symbolic and remarkable than the moment when she got into the car and it finally started to rain.

The three of us were already in the van that was the same size as the time machine. Listening, apparently, to the same music. Listening to the sounds that are conjoined at a given moment and that are close during the short period, which has the curve of time, and that, we only partially realise later, how what we say echoes and how what we do sounds.

There are notes that sound differently in the melody that is played in our head and that we only pick up on. Although, I, Pascal and our colleague, are going and doing, supposedly, all the same way.

Pascal's fingers wandered to the volume button on the radio. Then, having intuitively discovered it, he tried to press the button for the next music track. In that interval, we move from the music track to the track of the landscape that plays itself out in us. Until the kiss between night and day finally takes place and the night is left alone, waiting for its next kiss.

When we arrived in Évora, Pascal parked in the parking lot of the Verney college, which is next to the house, where he rented a room. Our countrywoman walked to her house.

Pascal's life was a simple and efficient existence. I would park myself in Pascal's kitchen and stay awake through the night. Then, in the morning, the next day, I would proceed with my very complicated quest for the grail of the Southern dream. Round and round and round the dream spiral. Pascal would just have to go upstairs to his room on the first floor and fall asleep. I would have to stay on the couch in the living room and wait. Until it was morning and night kissed the next day's face.

While I was waiting, I was looking at the stopped clock that hangs under the stairs in Pascal's kitchen. It is another one of those cases, where when the clock stops, nobody wants to stop for a second to change the battery.

I was looking at the stopped clock and thinking about the indefinite moment, which had the bridge that went from my past to my present. I tried to mentally grease a string that would explain the origin of it, shortly after breaking. Originating, another timeline. which I was, in parallel, continuing in my head, to draw the curves and arcs of this new arabesque.

Then, after I heard the doors creaking and listened to the noise of the unsettling truth that houses tell at night, I fell asleep. Only to wake up a few minutes later from the dream I was dreaming. More or less awake, more or less asleep, I drew aside the curtain of the window of that kitchen-room and peered through the wicket of my dreams. I awoke, however, suddenly. The round clock was still.

When I finally fell asleep again, I no longer knew if I was awake, or if I was just dreaming. Or, if I was just continuing to live in a state just like someone eternally, in suspense. Living I, the case of the hanger. And yet, unlike the kitchen clock that was stopped, my oneiric clock was going through the spiral of time, the spiral of Évora and the spiral of the South.

When morning rose, I left. I left without saying goodbye to Pascal. Dragging my own weight and the weight of my bags alone. It was not easy to leave, much less was it to arrive. First, that I would cross town, Pascal had already graduated and already our countrywoman had married and was the mother of two twins. Then, in the meantime, I, a few years and aphorisms later, would arrive in my new room.

I removed the ironed clothes and hung each piece on the hangers of the closet and randomly distributed the rest among the drawers. The bedroom floor was crooked, but I didn't mind. Someone came into the house and shortly after, left. I paid no attention. Soon after, someone came back in. Then knocking on my bedroom door. I waited for a moment, and only then opened it. It was the landlady. I waited for her to start talking, calculating that she would come to explain to me why she had changed her mind yesterday about renting me a room. My mother had to convince her by cell phone to keep what had previously been agreed upon.

First, she told me that I had left some poems in my old room. Referring to the alcove I had once. After commenting on the beauty contained in them, she justified herself, "You know, I was afraid that the other tenants might influence you and that the boy might get lost!"

The old woman, Maria de Fátima, looked at me, her wrinkles open and her eyes sprayed with black mascara. Her hair, partially dyed in mourning, was caught with a pompom. Only, the root of her hair was a glacial colour. She was not a character from a film noir, more like a curly character from the Southern dream. Dressed in a long widow's shawl. Both when she rented me in the past, a room, upstairs, and now, in the present basement she is dressed in black and I bet she doesn't know the words to any Johnny Cash song.

***

He returned to the same Maria de Fátima house. This time, to sleep on the ground floor. In a room much smaller and more cramped than the one he had slept in the first time the landlady rented him a room on the first floor of the house she had divided into three. He will only meet his new roommates late in the afternoon of the following day. They will only be introduced to you in the following chapters. Also, the task of revealing when and how he met the old landlady, Maria de Fátima, will be left for later. It will be left for the end. Not exactly for the chronological end of the book, but for the narrative end, which is in the third part, the last of this work. Where we will know what made up the myth, and when and why he lived, for two distinct times, in Travessa do Diabinho.

This would be his twelfth change of house. Counting since he arrived in Évora in the summer of 2008 and we are currently in February 2012, yes, this is the twelfth change of house in four years.

Perhaps, Marcus, his great friend, would be able to add up the strange coincidences in the destiny of our protagonist... Perhaps, if Marcus Matalonga would subtract the haunting inconveniences of the protagonist's existence he would eventually manage to justify the bizarre simultaneities of the sidereal events in the narrative, as well as, explain to us, in parallel, a set of actions that concern more other characters. We are content, at this point, to agree that chance and motivation are not exactly the shoe that both puts on our foot and wears the glove of our hand.

The eternal cage of the repeating wheel rests more on the protagonist's story than on its author or on the spiralling events of the other narrator, the narrator-protagonist. For my part, I think it makes the protagonist someone even more ridiculous and absurd, rather than tragic. But the cage is only eternal, for those who do not learn their last lesson. When the disciple no longer needs the master and learns the last lesson, perhaps he will be freed from the illusion created somewhere by a magic trick. Or, then, the omitted illusionist will only be considered as a seller of demagogy and disillusionment. Perhaps, Marcus Matalonga would better explain what is not at all attainable for me to say.

Right now, Marcus, is a recluse in his world, in a world in ruins. Our protagonist had no opportunity to tell him what was happening to him. They did not talk, neither about the end of his courtship, nor about what would be yet another house move. Curiously, to a house in which he would have already lived. Which made him suspect that it was another "strange coincidence." Was it? I am only one of the narrators, and I would say no.

When our protagonist met Marcus Matalonga, he had not yet entered higher education. It was only, after one more shift at the (Road) Signs Factory. When he would come home and write another shift of poetry and then go to the Triângulo coffee shop, which was in the centre of the village of Avelar. It was on one of those days, in one of those routines, that he would meet Marcus Matalonga.

First, he would notice the voice that said very assertively, "all the great friendships we develop are strange and convenient coincidences..." Only later, our protagonist would glue the voice to the face who was relatively close to his table, accompanied by some people who were also unknown to him.

When our protagonist began to enjoy the friendship of Marcus de Monsalude e Matalonga, a change in his perception of the world promptly occurred in him. And, let it be clear at the outset, that Marcus' sphere of the world and his existence, at that time, were still intact.

It was to Marcus that our hero, or anti-hero, confided the dream he had, right after the national exams for access to higher education. It was a dream that began with him contemplating a monumental portal. When he awoke, the closest thing he found in the pages of a history textbook to what he had just dreamt was the engraving showing Hadrian's Arch in Athens. Moreover, the figure of a master appeared in his dream, holding the sun in one hand and the moon staff in the other. This figure not only knew where his disciple was heading, but also urged him to come to him.

After hearing the impacting account of this dream, Marcus urged that he should have as his only option the University of Évora and, when our protagonist asked him if he should study Performing Arts, it was Marcus who told him no. He recommended that a literature course would be more suited to his personality.

You must be wondering...where is Marcus right now? Where will he be on this Monday in February 2012? Boating on his friend's favourite river? On the Zêzere River? Going upstream, downstream? Sailing again and again in an aimless boat his father had left him? Or is he swinging in a chair? Still questioning the cowardice of his father, who had fled to Brazil? Controlling, in South America, the businesses he keeps in Africa and other parts of the world? Leaving behind a lot of debts and a son who had gained a lot of doubts, that so far Marcus has not been able to settle?

But no! Marcus would not go on a boat, upstream or downstream. Nor had his father left him any boat. However Marcus would be locked up in his mansion, encloistered, enclosed, in the prison he had built himself. Manufacturing yet another impossible thesis, because he had nothing else to do. Building a *justification brick so that the mass of his being could stick to the wall of his non-existence. Thus, separating him even more from what he once was.*

Marcus, who believed blindly in the strange coincidences that are found during the brief decades of a lifetime, would begin to doubt and question everything after his father bankrupted his textile factory in the village of Avelar, which was very popular. And not only in the central region of the country.

Later, upon his parents' divorce, death knocking on his maternal grandparents' door would further implode his constant cloistering in the old mansion he had inherited from his grandparents. Sleeping by day and circulating at night through his vast garden, which is as extensive as a public botanical garden. After all that, Marcus simply did not believe in anything else, nor in coincidences, nor in strange coincidences, whether they were convenient or not.

It is the second month of the year 2012, on a cold Monday afternoon. The landlady has left. She has gone to another section of the house. Our anti-hero, perhaps still hero, is lying in bed in his new room. Remembering the Latin inscription he wrote in his diary this year *"citius, altius, fortius,"* and he laughs. For knowing, that he didn't arrive first and that he wasn't fast enough. Regretting, for not reaching with his arms the high ceiling of the supreme court of the gods and men who both accuse and defend him, that his life has not yet come that far or that close to what he desires and dreams of.

***

I got my lunch and dinner tickets from the machine that is stationed in the stairwell of Espírito Santo College. I can assure you that the food in Verney's cafeteria is still tasteless. I don't need to sample it to know that it tastes the same every year.

Then, without a minute to lose, I called Diego before noon. He didn't answer! Maybe, he was at home petting the dog. While, Tininha was ironing. And, the two of them, each in their own way, were mentally preparing to go to work at *Spettus*. I tried once more, but there was no answer either. It was probably still early…they were probably still asleep. Both of them, clinging to the pages of the novel they were developing with each other.

The next day I learned that Clarice was going to be my professor again. This time, in the chair of Portuguese Literature of the twentieth century. Perhaps this was a favourable coincidence for me. So, I walked reasonably optimistically past the lounge bar and restaurant, *Spettus*, to talk to Diego. By the time I found him, I didn't know, however, exactly what and why I needed to talk to him.

Having cooked around there the last months of my life to pay for university and a once shared authorship life, that in that present instant, I recognised no connection with my former place of work, nor with the friends and acquaintances of that islet past. Except, the necessity of having worked in the morning and afternoon. Leaving out, the uselessness of having gotten drunk on night shifts, drawing weekend alchemy scratches in the bathroom. Almost always catching a ride home with Tininha and Diego—Tininha having to drive, because Diego had been caught driving with alcohol in his blood. And all of that, at present, was simmering in my head.

Diego smiled. He greeted me. I don't know if in the role of friend or as a dedicated bartender. He was a friend, possibly moving diligently behind the counter. Offering me a drink and then taking money from the till. Giving me the exact amount, which the house was shorting me. And, that's how I got the bills done. Thanks to Diego and not Pheasant, my former employer's scammer!

That was probably why I went there. Then leaving *Spettus* and going to have lunch at Verney's canteen. Leaving behind friends who had been my co-workers, or leaving behind great friends who had been good co-workers, or not at all.

I decided to go ahead with my appetite to the cafeteria to swallow the frog that was on today's menu. When I got back from the cafeteria to Espírito Santo College, I realised that the city was the size of the university. I sat in a room next to the small cloister and watched the launching of the book *Haunted Words* by professor Maria Eduarda Lima.

I then had the opposite feeling, that the university was the size of the city and that I hadn't left the same place. And, although I was sitting in that classroom, I was wandering around. As if I were passing on a street or through a city square and greeting someone, who was an acquaintance of mine.

I got a pleasant surprise when I learned that the professor who would teach the chair of Contemporary Culture had given up teaching and was somewhere wandering around Africa. He had abandoned everything. Just as Rimbaud had done. Perhaps it was more of a strange coincidence that Clarice was teaching the chair. However, for me, it was not a strange coincidence, it was only timely.

In the evening, I went to Pólo dos Leões to watch the performance piece *War and Crisis*, or was it *Crisis and Wars*? Or, neither one thing nor the other? Still, I am quite sure that it was a master's project in dramaturgy and staging, by a student at the university. A certain Henrique Raposo, whom I did not know, nor had ever heard of. I read the pamphlet placed at the entrance. Then I walked around the performance itinerary that had been set up.

Finally, I entered the dark room, where an audience was already seated. I sat down. But shortly after, I stood up. I don't know if it was because I got bored with myself or if I was bored with the program.

I immediately returned home. I kept going straight. Trying not to deviate from which was my path. Even if I had to jump over buildings or go against walls much more intransigent than me. Like for example: those of the Évora prison. During this onslaught, I thought of my friend Francisco that I haven't seen for too long. Too long not to talk to someone who is so close and is not so far away, but who is getting more and more distant. I even thought about all those acquaintances of mine who were supposed to be my friends and who left Évora without saying goodbye to me. Some of whom I didn't mind in the least that they left the South and dream of the South.

I also didn't forget Miguel Murtinho, who would be sad forever. For one day having lost Cármen. It didn't matter if it had been for a black and not for a white. It could even have been for a grey face. What bothered him was that it had been for an evangelical. Although, what really embarrassed him, and would force him, somewhere in Lisbon, to have to live this lethargy of a love that had gone astray, was that he had simply won Cármen's love once and had just lost it. And there was no one to blame but himself.

I went on towards my room. I continued along the greenway, going straight ahead. Thinking about the race I never did. Remembering when I tried to run in my first year in Évora and gave up. Returning resigned to the residence. Now, as I pass by the Bento Jesus Caraça residence and cross the iron bridge and go down the wooden stairs, I think about it. And, I think about what I never was. I also think about what I will never be, and that everything, everything, is somehow interconnected.

Time is a box that we put off to open tomorrow. When we open the box that it was yesterday, there is nothing left inside. All that's left is the weight of the vacuum we feel, for not having opened what was still alive inside the box right away.

Francisco disappeared from Évora. Just as, one day, all my friends disappeared from Évora, and from the spiral of a dream, without me immediately realising how much I will miss them in the future and during the short concept of humanity. For, then, what is the end? What is the future concept of humanity? Man is an obstacle to the nature of man. And, we men are the present, a present without a future. After all, what is the future? What is the end for the ghosts of the past, who dress in the present, with the spirit of the man of the future?

There was no Literature and Film class. Professor Tadeu simply didn't show up. He didn't even warn me that he was going to miss it. Very soon, I will be twenty-six years old.

I met with Cíntia, who still expects me to do something as grand as I once seemed destined to do. She now has a position in the student council and wants me to collaborate with her on the activities she has scheduled for this semester.

After meeting with Cíntia and sipping coffee with her, I moved on to the palate of belief, that there was someone I would definitely be missing, as well as, there would be something I would be prevented from meeting, or discovering. Whether it was the idea of that thing, or the button of a person's revelation through that thing. To be persistent, to keep supposing on a last miracle would be insufficient. The obstinacy of a life can last as long as the breath of a day, as it can have the longevity of an ephemeris. But how long does the wick of the flame of perseverance, which burns in the fire that slowly goes out, remain lit?

Maybe, I want to leave Évora! Maybe, I just want to move to the last address, where I can live my dream, the dream of the South. Maybe, I just want the road to take me in another direction. However, I have yet to finalise what brought me to Évora. What was not, exactly, the conclusion of my course, but the mission of finding the middle: the middle of the mountain. More precisely, the middle that lies between the middle of the sky and the middle of the earth.

Yes, Cíntia still believes in me. Although, she doesn't know about the flammable fire that my body ignites, burning in my mind. Nor does she know what this fire is, that consumes me and so impulsively extinguishes itself. And then, I am left with only the silence of the ashes, in the fireplace of my spirit, to be cleaned.

No, she doesn't know how I can catch with my hands, the fire of reason, with which I wrote those verses, that later I would burn, on the balcony of an apartment in the Avenida dos Heróis do Ultramar at the beginning of a great storm that occurred between the autumn of 2010 and the winter of 2011.

Perhaps, I once wanted to write about the glorious tragedy that is the rise and fall of the man who burned his fire verses, in the fire of his own hell. Perhaps I burned most of my poems on the balcony of a building, in the purgatory paradise where I once lived. And now that I no longer live there, I recognise that the fire with which one writes, may not last forever, and that I may have lost the fire with which I wrote. Worse, I may lose my only talent at any ephemeral moment.

Coming to me, at this very moment, that dream I had much later, when I arrived in Évora: I was passing by the Santa Clara bridge. Which stretches over the Mondego River, in Coimbra. And a girl with long, wavy hair was telling me that I was going to lose my genius. Probably, I will never lose it, because it was never mine to earn. Maybe, all this is just a dream. Maybe, all of this is part of living the dream. Eventually, I will wake up later, from the nightmare of being condemned to run in more or less concentric circles and having to stay in Évora, until I find the middle of the dream in the spiral of the South.

Cíntia smiles with the beautiful Western serenity of a young woman. The mole above her upper lip also smiles at me. Like a seventeenth-century lady, who doesn't wear powder. That too obvious birthmark of hers adorns her, naturally. Demonstrating to me that a woman does not always need pearls in her ears and diamonds on her fingers, to be a woman of flesh and blood.

At this, a carefree herd of students walked halfway up the slope, entering the main gate of the university. They carried more notebooks than dreams under their arms. Meanwhile, Mr Emídio, the owner of the cafe *A Tuna*, sent his wife to get him another coffee while he quietly read the sports newspaper. Greeting me, "So, Poet!"

And I articulate back, "That's life!"

Meanwhile, Cíntia keeps reminding me of when she copied me in the Literary Critic exam. Laughing a lot. When she remembered that Professor Tadeu had given her a higher grade than the one he had given me. Then, jumping to the step of the memory she still had about the incredible coincidence of her living, where I had also lived in another moment. Then talking to me about that myth that had been formed about me. That, before, I had been her neighbour on Travessa do Diabinho, I had supposedly lived in my owned ruined castle. Then she would quickly fly off, over the top of her interest to the pollen of the next subject.

"Do you know if Professor Clarice was married to Professor Manel José?"

"Our aesthetics teacher?" I asked, playing stupid.

"Yes. That's the one."

"I don't know," I answered. Although I knew perfectly well, from her own account, that Clarice had been married to Professor Tadeu when she was younger.

Finally, we talked about when she fell in love with our classmate, Jacó Belo. With whom Cíntia had a tremendous disappointment. It wasn't our classmate Jacó, with whom I once went to the beach! It was Jacó who was even more absent from classes and the course than I was. Appearing and disappearing. And later, reappearing in sunsets and eclipses incredibly longer than mine. Neither, however, was as mysterious as I was. After all, neither of them had lived in a castle, like me! It was only Jacó, who deceived her with a friend, who, after all, was not such a friend. That was Jacó and not the other who, for reasons unknown to me, would abandon the course once and for all.

I still met Cíntia at the end of the day, at the São Vicente square. She was with her mother, who had come to visit her in Évora. They walked with the humility of two oriental ladies. They did not touch the keys of the ground with their feet. They walked with the feminine courage of those who see themselves reflected in the mirror of the shop windows, in a world on sale, for people increasingly without gender. They, however, were still two women: mother and daughter. Two beautiful forces of nature, two magnificent concepts, Yin and Yang, mother and daughter; both, descendants of Jung.

Chapter 3
Life Is a Test of Effort

(March to June 2012)

It was a pleasantly warm day. More and more clouds were moving away from the winter sky, and the next season was drawing nearer and nearer. The flowers that had already awakened were uninhibitedly sunbathing in the neo-romantic style garden. The landlady laid out her clothes on a string and left them to dry by the garage. That served exclusively as a storage room. The flamingos and other firebirds, as well as the birds of the Southern dream, would land beyond the backyard wall, bordering the greenway, where tired souls run, gasping that life is a test of effort.

"So boy! Are you going to college?"

"Yes, I will."

Besides the previous confession of the poems she had found forgotten in the desk in my old bedroom, the second revelation was that she never married the husband who left her the house. She had always been the mistress of a married man twice her age. Who would nevertheless choose to leave his wife and children to be with her.

"You know, my child, I was young… I didn't mean to! But…"

After the adversative conjunction came the truth serum. When we hear that bell, we know that what was left behind is neither interesting to hear nor to answer. Before, my landlady said that she had come to this husband's house, to be just another servant. Later, she justified herself that it was he who had first fallen in love with her. Maria de Fátima's last point was that although she had not been able to sprout children in her belly, they were both very happy. I calculated that she had changed her mind to rent me the room, only, and because my mother had touched her motherly heart, the mother she could never be.

"I was a very humble woman, from a very poor family. I would never have gotten a house like this if it wasn't for my husband," Old Maria de Fátima said. She had divided the house in three, occupying the front part, the one facing the avenue, during the mornings and at lunchtime, which was when her nephew came to have lunch with her. Then, in the afternoon, she would go home to her sister and nephew. Because after she was widowed, she decided to move in with them.

"What a good boy! Do you know I still read those poems? The ones you left here! How is the boy able to write such beautiful and deep things? It fills my soul!" She said, dressed from head to toe in mourning. Adding the old pious woman, "Never forget your mother! Always be her friend! Don't waste your time on my account. Go! Don't be late."

I said goodbye and started my walk when I saw Sebastião, Sebastião dos Santos Silva, who had been my classmate. He was walking up the stairs of the villa next door. I had recently seen him coming this way. Disappearing, then, suddenly. He disappeared, and I didn't know where he had gone. Today, he didn't see me and I didn't call him either. I don't remember seeing him around here when I first lived here. Eventually, because his parents were already separated, and possibly, at that time, he would have been living with his father. Now he must have come to visit his mother and brother.

I went to the university escorted by an academic determination, which focused mainly on the happy coincidence of Clarice's presence this semester. I clearly felt a greater degree of enthusiasm that she was once again within the sphere of my existence.

We bumped into each other, shortly afterwards, in the corridors of the old Jesuit school. It was as if we were being called, invited, to meet each other. There are certain moments and certain events and certain happenings in our lives that we are not prepared to understand how big they are. Like, I, for example, only understood much later what Marcus had announced to me and what the dimension and importance of his prophecy was.

Clarice was as happy as I honestly was, to be able to see her once again. We briefly confided in each other the emotion that are the sleeves of the thought that we were each wearing.

Then I went to the bar at Espírito Santo College. While waiting for the afternoon classes to start I remembered the moment when Marcus predicted his prophecy to me. I remembered the occasion when we went for coffee to a place relatively close to where he lived. Which he increasingly preferred, to the detriment of all the other cafés scattered throughout the rest of the world and the rest of the village. Marcus had come to pick me up by car from the Avelar valley. We were taking the complementary route number eight, even before we reached the tunnel, when Marcus told me: "I don't know if you already know or, if you've already been informed…" Then he fell silent.

Meanwhile, we entered the tunnel and he remained silent. We came out of the obscurity that the tunnel held and he remained circumspectly quiet. Advancing towards the beginning of the bridge—as if the moment needed a longer pause and even more suspense than the previous moment—and it was precisely in the middle of the bridge that he uttered his vision, "Nothing will ever be the same again!"

It was the vision of the crisis! Even before anyone knew that we were beginning the cycle of a great world economic crisis, Marcus—the angel of annunciation, the martyr saint, was already unveiling to me the light at the end of the tunnel. He was the mediator, the arch of the bridge, which connects the end of the tunnel to the edge of the mountain that lies beyond. Marcus, the messenger angel who had predicted from the beginning of the tunnel to the end of the bridge, the end of a world, the end of his world.

With the extinction of his world would also be included, in parallel, the shaking of mine. I would feel it later, because I was the friend who was closest to his universe. However, he did not clarify to me what his final path would be like. He didn't even enlighten me about the fate that would exactly befall us, after we reached the notion of his foreboding.

When we crossed the bridge, Marcus pointed out to me that he and his father were in a broken relationship. Marcus thought it morally reprehensible that his bankrupt father had fled to Brazil, leaving not only debts behind, but leaving the good name of the family dishonoured.

Marcus' mother, consequently had filed for divorce. Marcus was left residing *ad infinitum* in a small village located at the entrance of the town of Figueiró dos Vinhos, finding there his exile and the mansion he had inherited from his maternal grandparents. Marcus Emanuel de Monsalude e Matalonga, the cherubic angel, the obtuse and antiquated seraph of the crisis, who lives agonising and announcing the decadence of the global post-modern world!

When that night we reached the end of the bridge and climbed the rest of the mountain, Marcus became another Marcus. Never again would I find the early version, which I had known, before my entry into higher education. The bridge we had just crossed was now the walkway of a time and a world that had collapsed. We could no longer reach the other side, nor could we be what we were at the summit of that world and time.

We ascended to the mountains and cut through the Figueiró dos Vinhos sign, when Marcus finished, "The insolvency of my parents' company will not only mean the bankruptcy of my family. It will also mean the collapse of myself and this notion that I have of myself. I will no longer know who I am. Only, I will have a vague and faint memory of what I was. I have yet to know exactly how far I am from the end. Then, yes, the great waiting will begin. Because let's face it, I am already living the beginning of the great wait. I am only allowed to wait for my end. Maybe you don't understand now…but maybe in the near future. Maybe then you will realise that nothing can ever be the same again… In any case, I ask you to be discreet. And for now, let's keep this conversation just between us. I prefer that you hear it from me… When you hear others talking…you already know what really happened…"

If, for me, life is a test of faith and also a test of effort, of the persistent effort we make to believe every day that we can, against everything and everyone, achieve something in this life by implementing one dream or another, for Marcus, he would be part of the others, of those who are destined to suffer, condemned to wait, and can never want or intend to dream.

Meanwhile, Clarice appeared at the bar. She headed for the line. She didn't order what she wanted. She simply demanded. Then, from the full tray, she looked around for a table and spotted me. Although there were empty tables or tables full of her colleagues, she, however, sat with me.

We spoke as a student interested in the teacher and a teacher interested in the student. Apparently, Clarice was still wondering what my intentions for her actually were. She wanted to know exactly what I wanted from her. Defining, eventually, what we could each expect from each other.

In the afternoon the class was thrust into the great Hall of Acts. We were all forced to attend the award presentation and hear the jury speak.

Although it is not yet 7 pm, the sky has the face of night. One day, people will abolish the change of clocks, and there will be no more lost time. We will live in a world with no sense of time, and no one will remember anymore the world and the time that was lost.

The ceremony has begun. Someone announces that the three clarinet pieces for Stravinsky will not be played, because one of the young musicians in the music course has fallen ill. The director of the School of Social Sciences, Professor Álvaro Mendonça walked to the rostrum with vigour, the floor vibrated. He moved with the same vigour that had enraptured me when he was in the Cultural Studies classroom. Confronting the students with questions like, "but what do you really think you know? Do you think you know or do you know because you thought? Because you read? Because you wrote? Because you reflected and reflected again?"

Then followed the lukewarm speech by Professor Ferreira Gomes. Who talked a lot, a lot, nervously. Believing very, very much in his human importance. With that making me believe that students seek to find their teachers in schools, when they should be researching, probably, elsewhere.

That moment defined how bloated he was. Ending up stranded between the walls and the ears of an audience that had no genuine interest in him or his speech. He discoursed in the same way he taught, not captivating. Most of the students eventually left the great Hall of Acts, thinking that they were once again in their classroom and that there was something more important going on outside. There was certainly another place, another event, much, much more important, where one should be and where one had to go.

The Modernism Congress, in Porto, was off. It was too much for my mother to send me even more money to go to a Literature Congress. Perhaps, I don't follow the motto "honest study with long experience mixed in," from my *alma mater*, which was although first the motto of Luís de Camões. Perhaps, I have no real interest in any study that is honest. Perhaps, I am never loyal. Eventually, I'm just strongly self-interested and absolutely dishonest and frontally disloyal. Perhaps my university is not a company of knowledge, but a community of interests, of favours and schemes. Which are as useful to me as they are to others.

I, too, ended up leaving in the middle of the ceremony. I didn't have any important commitments, nor did I really have to go anywhere that was relevant to me. However, I was unable to stay until the end of that kind of liturgy. I had gone to the ceremony, I had gone to class, and that convinced me that what I had to do was done, at least for today.

When I got home there was a lively nursing party going on. The young nurses were strange bats, who, instead of hanging upside down from the ceiling of my subconscious, were flying around Maria de Fátima's house in their black capes.

They fluttered back and forth in the hallway. Chirping instructions and chirping orders to the fledglings—the other bugs.

I didn't have to leave the house to be tempted by the idea of the world, all I had to do was leave my room and go into the kitchen and past the dining room, where the sangria bowls were full and multiplying as much as the fungus on the walls. My appearance in my pyjamas and robe was irrelevant to the revellers.

My roommate, the mechanic, sat in his overalls drinking sangria, with the student ladies, the future nurses of the national health system, orbiting around him. He, who was quietly drunk, laughed, however, moderately at the screams, roars and roars of mostly women. He also laughed at the humiliations inferred by the young future nurses. Provided through childish games and the demonstrations of student power that basically involved drinking, cursing, and crawling on the floor. He would eventually go to bed shortly thereafter. Carefree and even more intoxicated. Not showering, not brushing his teeth. Lying on the bed in his overalls. Taking off only his boots. But leaving his socks on so his feet wouldn't get cold during the night.

My other housemate was the aphonic nursing student who was hysterically pacing back and forth. Rushing to get nowhere in particular. Surely, he would not find a cure for the world's great ills. Nevertheless, he kept moving back and forth incessantly. With his glasses running down the tip of his nose. Talking under the influence of the alcohol that had accumulated in his blood. In a frenzied state, he used opulent gestures, so that more toasts could be made.

His hoarseness didn't prevent him from encouraging others to drink. Mercilessly demanding that more songs be chanted in chorus. No matter how much no one could sing or how much no one could remember a single lyric. He was barfing with the rest of the strength he still had in his voice. He was barfing for no reason at all, with the so-called bugs. Then, a little later, he would shout in the air. Squealing, squawking. Probably already completely dominated by the spirit of Bacchus.

Still, not satisfied, he ran from one side of the house to the other. Moved by the propeller of the bowls of bloodletting, which went straight to his belly. He filled each empty glass he found, until the liquid spilled out onto the floor. Laughing out loud, as one of the critters scrubbed the floor, cleaning up that mess, after they had crawled to him. Laughing even louder, for being able to see that transformation of the young freshmen, into bugs, happen at his feet.

The young women and future nurses also assumed the form of the human animal. Continuing that game of make-believe, although the animals had had enough of that game and no longer wanted to be treated as such.

Isabel, the upstairs neighbour, was also a nurse. She slept in the room I had once rented. I knew little else about her. She left early. Either because she had her boyfriend waiting, or because she had to go to her internship at the hospital the next morning. The female pack was still bellowing shrilly at the freshmen, especially the boy bugs.

Demanding, finally, that they simulate for their contentment, something of a sexual nature. Insinuating that what they wanted, they could only have after November, and that in the meantime, they were the student ladies. "Eyes down, bug!" They said assertively, at least once in their lives.

I went back to the room disappointed. The pack of mammals had never heard of the myth of the last living poet. Perhaps, he was asleep. Or, then again, perhaps, only hibernated. Maybe he never existed! Maybe I wouldn't believe him either, if I had never, before, heard of the last living poet, as something larger than life; which only happens in these great myths of mankind.

The small crowd of bats and the pack of other mammals were drinking in every room of the house. They were blustering in the bathroom and protesting between my door and the door to future nurse João's room. Vomiting their torpor in the neo-romantic garden that seemed somehow unfinished and that could be seen from the bedroom window of the inebriated Nilson, who couldn't even sleep without the overalls of his profession.

A few days later, I had lunch with Clarice, in the back of the Sé. More precisely, in the space they call *Jardim do Chá (Tea Garden)*. Besides the unlicensed restaurant there is also an association that includes: yoga, meditation, alternative medicine and one etc., that includes vegetarian food. In addition, they make tapestry and pottery there. All included in the same menu. The place, however, brings back horrible memories to me...

Clarice was curious to know who I lived with. But I indicated to her that I didn't yet know my housemates well enough, but that I was optimistic about the peculiar and promising balance between the trio we formed. I described to her first, Nilson, who was a mechanic at the beginning of his profession. Tall and as long as a eucalyptus tree. Finally, I profiled João, a nursing student, from Moura, Alentejo, with a square and defined jaw. Wearing glasses to see as much near as much far.

Since professor Clarice had a class to teach after lunch, she left soon after. We agreed to have lunch again next week. I got up and shook her hand and she left. Stalking alone on the cobblestone street that led from the back of the cathedral towards the Espírito Santo College. Her snowy colour made her an easily appetising target for the King Star. Dazzling all the layers and steps her skin had.

I sat down and drank the rest of my orange juice, continuing under the shadow of the hornbeam tree and the shadow cast by the cathedral. Sónia Faria was nearby. She was sitting under the sun. Staring at me continuously. Certainly, condemning me. She was, in Évora, one of Débora's closest friends. I believe she had recently broken up with Tiago Ruivo. Strangely enough, she had an affair with Mário Silva's brother before or after, or in between. Was she currently depressed? I can't say. I don't even know how Mário's brother met Sónia. Did they meet through me? Apparently, everything is known sooner or later.

I stretched out for a long time. She continued to crucify me with her gaze. I had met Sónia through Débora. Naturally, I was seen by Sónia's tired look or by the stories Débora had once invented about me.

It was Sónia who had made the lunch. That's why she was there. However, I didn't understand why she kept looking at me like that. It bothered me how her presence was equally absent. Yet she continued to stare at me. Possibly casting spells at me. Whispering inward, and me hearing nothing of what surrounded that sinister to ancient practice. Eventually, she would be condemning me in an afternoon fire, which she herself would light and which would burn invisibly at my feet. Only she could see it, and only she could put it out.

I complimented her lunch and quickly left. She devilishly rotated her head, moving her terrifying antennae. She probably would have heard before I even spoke to her! It was the illusion of a witch eluding me, not being there, not being anywhere. Entering and leaving through a portal that was inaccessible to me.

The next day I met up fortuitously with Clarice. She was requesting a book from the Public Library that she required in her program. I wondered why she didn't buy the books of her own academic program. Now that she didn't have a rented house in Évora, she probably wouldn't want to bring with her the weight of books she had in Lisbon.

"Simão! I just suggested you for a research fellowship. What do you think about it? Professor Tadeu accepted my decision. But you should know that he considers you crazy, and also Professor Manel José, who is a good friend of his, shares the same opinion."

"Crazy?" I asked incredulously.

"Yes, 'crazy' was the word he used. But it doesn't matter. I believe in you, Simão. Don't let me down!"

Professor Tadeu was the only professor who was more disinterested in his students than his students would be in him. He was the only professor who, besides including books written by him in the bibliography of his subject program, made a point of selling them directly to the students at the very first class of the semester. He was someone only interested in the teaching profession and had no interest in being anyone's teacher. Besides these little quirks of his, he was equally concerned about what the cleavages in the front row of the classroom had to say to him.

I met the next morning with Professor Vasques, who was one of the people responsible for the project with which I would eventually obtain a research fellowship. As we talked, I understood why certain people bore me when they talk without passion about subjects that only interest them. There was nothing new or authentic in what he told me about his field of study. In which he had already accumulated more than two or three decades of study. His commitment was solely to keep his life as a cabinet professor unchanged, as he had always known it. He was comfortable in the armchair of his work where he sat comfortably every day.

According to Clarice, life is a test of effort. So, I have to make a real effort to listen to it. If I seriously want to achieve anything during this existence of mine. Because he who doesn't make an effort takes nothing. Also, because, more and more, he who makes an effort, also does not ensure, nor guarantee that he is acquiring something that is precious and valuable, only, for himself.

Perhaps, I see and find in Clarice the mother that I no longer see or find. Moreover, my mother is increasingly dependent on the comfort and inconvenience that marriage has caused in her nature. Perhaps, because Clarice is someone so demanding reminds me of my mother. Maybe, Clarice doesn't love me unconditionally like my mother. Maybe, no one ever loves me as much as my mother's love.

The promise that I was once is becoming more and more the symbol of a project that is constantly postponed. Perhaps I am no longer the same me, and am now only the representation of that ideal me. I will no longer be an uncut diamond. At most, I am a stone, a stone with an unsound figure. The rare crystal that was the myth of the last living poet, who is lost, searching for the cave of the dream of the South, perhaps, will no longer make sense. Eventually, because I am more and more a hybrid figure, a grotesque creature, a gargoyle, that fell from the Church of Graça, stumbling on the silver sidewalk.

Fortunately, as fate would have it, after my tedious meeting with Professor Vasques, I came across Professor António Benedito Pio on Avenida Leonor Fernandes. He was going in the opposite direction to me. He was so delighted to see me, as I was to meet with the Master again. After I pointed out to him the house where I lived, the Master revealed to me that we lived extremely close to each other. And so, we started to meet regularly for long walks along the greenway. They were usually as long and long as the conversations at Master's house lasted.

When the Master didn't have much time, I would stop by his office in the College of the Espírito Santo and we would sit simply staring into the silence and studying it together. Occasionally the Master would lecture me. As if it was a one-on-one class and I was his number one disciple.

When it rained during the weekend, I would go to the Master's house and find the Master equipped with his oiled suit. On those days, we would read in the garage occupied by the books that Master did not consult regularly. The newer books resided in his office and in the library in his living room. Still others lived in the Lisbon house that Master had purposely for the more emancipated books. The Master had no car, and no driver's licence. However, he did have half a dozen cats. Curiously, the Master defended that cats are animals and that animals don't need to be baptised with names or have any other kind of collars.

The Master's cats came and went as they pleased. Some of them would sometimes stand at the garage entrance, contemplating the rain that fell on the winter floor. When the rain stopped, some of them would run up to the roof, while Master and I each leafed through the motif of our respective book. At those moments, the Master was absorbed in his reading and I imitated him. In the middle of the evening, the Master would pour some tea. At that moment, Master was sparing with words, invariably expressing himself through direct gestures, and I mentally and spiritually emulated the pragmatism of Master's gestural language.

Once Master let me accompany him to the supermarket. He carried bags inside his pockets. So that he would have a place to put his purchases later.

Nobody had yet talked about reusing and already the Master knew what to do and how to proceed. He constantly gave me examples through the mirror where his actions spoke. His actions were great lessons, as long as, or longer than, the walks we both often took along the greenway.

On one of the last walks where I was waiting for the Master, on top of the little bridge, which is after the traffic circle of the Nau, I was looking down contemplatively. Seeing someone who was quite identical to me running against the wind. The same in the opposite direction, on the other side of the greenway, but not running against the wind. This someone, also, so similar to me, was running against time.

Before those two people running on the greenway crossed under the bridge, I intuitively looked away. I turned with the flexibility of a splendid acrobat on myself and realised that on the sidewalk on the left side of the bridge, there was someone also exaggeratedly similar to me. I, who was on the right bank, saw another me, who was also on the other side, on the right bank of the bridge. I was somehow another me, both on the other side of the bridge, and on this side.

Such a vision made me soar, levitate. I could effectively see higher than my height and beyond my size. I was able to watch that very moment when those two people, who were extremely similar to me, were running along the greenway. Each running in the opposite direction to the other.

Simultaneously, on top of the bridge, two other people were crossing each other. They were also people who were incredibly wearing a face very similar to mine. Each of them following indifferently along the opposite bank and in the opposite direction on their way.

In this revelation, which I call the vision of the bridge, I realise: they are all one and they are all a part of myself. Nevertheless, my light body remained fantastically still in the air, contemplating the other four. Until, suddenly, a fifth, even more faint self-dissociates and moved away from me. Pulling away to appreciate and to enjoy, quietly, the ecstasy of that moment.

But when something in me began to recognise that the one watching from above is also another part of my being, just as much as that other small part of myself that has dislocated from me, then the whole sixfold unfolding breaks. Because my observing-self did not allow that self of the conscious to keep that vision projected beyond the mind together, and so everything faded away. And, soon after, the Master appeared. He was still far away when he raised his hand.

Nilson came home and sat on the couch. After he turned on the television, he stood staring at the aquarium on the screen. He lit, minutes later, a pot cigarette. I recognised that specific smell before I left my room and sat down next to him to talk about the day's events. We talked with the legs of those who run through a multitude of topics. Anyway, we talked like two housemates, chattering away, about the most common and most ordinary things, especially about the things that lie between the glory of oblivion and the torpor of melancholy and the euphoria of a certain moment.

Nilson is still a learner in his profession. He is a simple man, with simple ambitions: to continue stopping by the café after work; one day to buy a house and get married, or get together; and later, who knows? Maybe to mate in the house he bought. Finally, to decide between having dogs or having cats, and on which side of the marquee to have the parakeets and the canaries. All very elementary things. Nothing too complex, because life's complicated enough as it is. Of course, he'll be happy forever, and of course he'll always have the same job. Yes, of course!

Each one leaned back on the sofa, articulating about everything and about nothing. It was another one of those conversations where you play chess without moving the pieces. The pieces move by themselves on the board. It was a conversation written in the manner of Charles Chaplin. No script was needed. Until he told me, "I had a girlfriend named Débora…"

And I froze for a few seconds, only then I answered, "I also had a girlfriend whose name was Débora!"

They had ended their relationship a year ago. It was as if today he had lost his great love and until today, he had not found another one that would make him forget. I had only lost my innocence and a great deal of naivety, which, fortunately or unfortunately, I will certainly never recover.

Nilson doesn't know who my Débora was, I never knew who she really was either. However, we both suspect that Nilson's Débora cannot be the same Débora that I never knew entirely. In fact, we both agree that there are more Déboras than ever. As many as there are poisonous mushrooms picked in the woods, as many as there are fungi on the ceiling and on the walls of Maria de Fátima's house. Without, however, being sure if the fungus one sees is a Débora or if what one sees is just a bacterium.

To the mechanical world of Nilson's universe and mine, was added the muscular and athletic world of João's cosmos. I let myself be infected and contaminated. We went from a duo to a string trio that kept vibrating and resonating and that kept turning itself on what was the best harmony to play together.

I quickly stopped being enclosed in my room and started living more and more with João's world and Nilson's atlas. Each decision to share my time with each of them transformed the tone of the music of my day. The choice of the note of spending time with João, moved me away from the staff of time spent with Nilson. Just as, the compass of time played with Nilson, relegated me from the interests I had alone.

The option of the three of us spending time together gave a particular musical moment, which was played only by the ensemble, in a harmony that sounded like something very familiar. João's discipline was just as important to me as Nilson's freedom and carelessness. Meanwhile, I was carving a new image in myself that made others see me from the perspective of someone who meets someone they know, but who looks completely different to someone else. Those who crossed paths with me now discovered that there was something more than they had known before.

Because more than the diet of days, more than the constant exercise of the mind, more than the restriction of the spirit and the beauty of all parts and the symmetry with the whole, what matters, after all, is not the search and demand for the absolute and for perfection, but rather, the search for harmony and balance.

***

João went to Moura. Nilson had stayed in Évora, to spend Saturday afternoon at the kart track. In an event programmed by his company. His two work colleagues went with him: Joaquim and Ricardo. Joaquim was a shy guy, who had a younger brother, however, much more strangely shy than he was. It must have been a family thing. Ricardo had an ascendancy over Nilson, which Joaquim clearly did not have The three of them called each other Master or Zé, followed by their first names. Still, all of them were masters of nothing. I, who was not part of their circle, was as if I was, because I was the object of great esteem and admiration.

It had been during the academic week, that the couches from the living room came to the patio. To sit closer to the smell of the flowers from the landlady's neo-romantic garden. Thus, making her garden another room of our living room.

When I leaned the ladder against the wall and climbed up, João and Nilson climbed up too. Bringing with them a small table. Afterwards, it became a habit to sit on a concrete bench watching the girls in tight shorts running along the greenway. It was as if we were watching yet another commercial on TV. When I would take the ladder and tell them, "Let's watch the reality programme," João and Nilson would take the small table in the living room and some beer bottles and come after me. We would go around the maze of bushes and flowers, so that the three of us could watch another episode that had the reality of another afternoon.

Another of our hobbies was playing a sport that I had invented. It basically consisted of throwing plates over the wall. The goal was to get the shallow plate across the greenway. The longer the plates took to fall, the greater the volume of clapping and points to be received for the thrower. It was a hobby that supposedly impressed both Nilson's friends and co-workers, and João's friends and course mates. Everyone wanted to throw a plate, until the event ended abruptly, because there was nothing left of the set of dishes previously provided by the landlady, the event organiser.

Even so, during the academic week, on a night out that brought together João's course mates and Nilson's work colleagues, we learned that the last poet was still in Évora and that he was still alive. Inexplicably, for João and Nilson, I who was once just their housemate, in the emptiness of the crowd, became someone they all knew. I was the last living poet; I was still the last living poet.

They were amazed when in the middle of the empty crowd a beautiful stranger walked by and kissed me. I was surprised too, but I didn't reveal my amazement. It was possibly part of the source of the myth. However, João and Nilson jumped, squirmed, and squirmed, while they wondered what it was. As if there was an oil field or a gold mine in me. They were now convinced that I was someone with a very rare power. Naturally, they believed that if they stayed close to me, they could also share in the influence that my ability had. They didn't know, however, that when queens lose their wings, the males die soon after.

It was also since the week of Queima das Fitas that we started socialising with Catarina, a freshman nurse, who began to seduce and pursue João even more. She didn't remember me. I remembered her well. She had waited tables at the restaurant and lounge bar *Spettus*. She was the goddaughter of my former employers, who now were spending more and more time with us at Maria de Fátima's house. Nilson said that Catarina was our D'Artagnan. João insisted that she was just a friend. I just thought that the world is too small for the weight of the ants and that the weight of humanity is much less than the weight of the importance that each ant has.

Very mysteriously, João has told me, in these last two months, more than once, about a book. However, until today, he hadn't shown me the cover or revealed the title. He confessed, though, that he hid it under his mattress so that Catarina would not find it, nor know what it was about.

The last few weeks have possibly contributed to the fact that when today I said goodbye to João and Nilson to go spend the summer in the Avelar valley, Nilson cried and hugged me as if I was going to die very soon. Probably lamenting my condition of the anti-hero that I am, or the tragic hero that I once was. João imitated him. Hailing me as his friend and his great ally. Roaring and howling that the last living poet still lives.

Although, there was no evidence, no clear sign that miracles and myths still exist in the post-modern world. Nor that there was clear evidence that love always triumphs, or that symbols are never consumed and never expire. After all, life is not only a test of faith, it is also a test of effort.

In the meantime, the grant became void. The research project was not funded. I was told that the crisis in the world was to blame for the lack of funds for such an undertaking. Professor Tadeu and his friend and colleague, my aesthetics teacher, Manel José, will eventually continue to consider me crazy. Denying my genius.

Still in one of the last weeks classes where Professor Amélia stuttered and my colleague Mélanie blatantly mocked her, manipulating the rest of the class to ridicule her, I found myself beset by that impulsive morality of mine. The same one that Nietzsche used to stop a coachman from continuing to beat a horse that was exhausted and would no longer accept the trot. Quite determined, I stopped the bullying towards Professor Amélia, who was not guilty of stuttering. I thought that as a student and citizen, it was my responsibility to stop it. However, the teacher didn't want to listen. Rather, she preferred to ignore it. Only later did I realise that she wasn't just a stutterer after all!

Anyway, at the end of the class, my classmate Mélanie wanted to fight me. She gathered her 'girls' who made a circle around me. Suddenly I was surrounded and outnumbered. I couldn't run away! Nor could I hide! Who was I to trust and want to impose the justice of men? After all, isn't the statue of justice a blind woman with double standards?

In that moment of great distress, I thought of pushing Mélanie down the cloister and running. To save myself! If any of her friends got in front of me, I would stick a finger up her nose. If any of them dared to come after me, I would turn around and squirt her tits mercilessly. If that didn't work, I'd have to fight them on equal terms. They would pull my hair and I would do the same.

If it didn't work, I'd have to fly out of there. In the extreme, we would all roll around on the floor of the Espírito Santo cloister. Fighting each other, rubbing against each other. Feeling love and hate. Feeling everything at the same time.

Me against all of them! All lying on the floor, rolling around. The violence in this case of mine is particularly exciting. Nevertheless, the pleasure, Marcus is doubly right: altruism is a completely unfashionable concept, and women are doomed to the nature of being women. Regardless, of the empowerment that they want to be something else.

Anyway, my good intentions had gone against me. Yes, I managed to get away with it, that's for sure! However, I clearly felt vexed, embarrassed. So much so that I walked under the cloister, sticking my head into my shell. With the feeling that I was the one who had looked bad in the picture. Ah! And, at the end of this semester, I was denounced by a colleague, during an exam, for allegedly cheating. Anyway! But Professor Clarice, my friend and mentor, preferred to take my word for it, rather than the word of the person who accused me.

At this point, Pascal and I have already passed the walls...we are leaving Évora. We are leaving one circle and going around another. All of them almost concentrically fitting into the labyrinth of the Southern dream. Pascal takes me home. He carries the weight of my books to Avelar, which travels with me in the trunk of my countryman's van. My countryman doesn't seem to mind the weight of knowledge my books occupy. Nor that it travels with me. As long as I, of course, give him afterwards, my share of the money, to help with the gasoline.

Although it is now twenty-one hours and thirty-three minutes, we can still clearly see the day leaving and the night coming on. We are heading towards the Avelar valley. I will spend the summer at home. This will be my first starry summer spent in the village of Avelar, since I came to study in Évora.

Pascal is guiding and braking with the weight of my knowledge and the sapient weight of my books. It leads me through the night sea that has its intuitive guidance. Following the path of the stars inherently lit on the map of the sky. Going with the window open and the music playing on the car radio. We talk about how music is the soundtrack of a life and how nostalgic we are for a particular song that played at a certain time. And that everyone, without exception, remembers at least one song that accompanied them for more than a certain moment.

Pascal then invites me to visit his studio. Which he built himself with the help of his father. When he talks about his sound studio, his eyes shine. They lit up as much as the stars in the sky and the fireflies lit at night in the countryside. In the archaeology of his enthusiasm is the evidence that life is about effort, the effort we make to achieve our dreams, and that our dreams are not only made of inspiration, but are also made by the sweat and perspiration of continuous work, which leads us sooner or later to complete the work, or the simple task we set ourselves.

Évora, will magically disappear into the horizon. A drunken Nilson will still be staring at the TV, thinking: what a beautiful aquarium! But without understanding how the fish had disappeared. He will certainly be joined by João. Exceedingly sober. However, he too will be staring at the TV aquarium and at Nilson's screen.

And was there, or wasn't there, a book hidden under João's mattress? A book that no one knows what it is about. The validity of its existence and the truth of its age are unknown. Perhaps, it is a book where one can read that life is not just a simple trial of effort, but that the spiral of each life is part of the sun and the moon, which reflect more or less the round shape of our illusion.

Perhaps, it is in there, somewhere, at a stretch, that the strongest overcome the weakest more often. But in the end, the strongest don't always beat the weakest. And, in an Olympic cluster of days and months and years and obstacles, barriers, that we must ceaselessly jump over and over again, life is a trial of effort, and to live is to keep going on, and to never, ever give up.

Chapter 4
The Factory of Lights

(July to August 2013)

On that torrid afternoon when I went out to look for a summer job, the sun was so close to me that the warm air was toasting my student shell. First, I walked six kilometres to the first place on my short list. It was almost certain! However, I was told to stop by later. So I walked another seven kilometres to try to get a job somewhere else. Just in case I couldn't find a job in the first place I went to. Then I walked a few more kilometres back home, still not sure of anything.

Walking was part of my *modus operandi*. Crossing a part of the Serra do Mouro and seeing the Alto da Serra quarry would probably also be part of my method. Wasting time, I don't think, was included in my process. However, my mother refused to give me a ride and I was even more annoyed by her maternal attitude. Feeding an anger, possibly of the Freudian kind.

Perhaps, I was encountering the same obvious lack of clarity and the same absence of reason that I encountered in having to peregrinate, successively, with the company of my library through the spiral itineraries that each house move forced me to.

It was after transporting my books from Évora to Avelar in the trunk of Pascal's van and lodging them on the shelves in my old room that I seriously wondered about all the useless effort that was soon or later a price to pay.

For the second time that I had to cross the Alto da Serra, I amused myself by kicking all the stones that I found along the way. Without once feeling any remorse. Amazingly, halfway up the mountain, under a blue sky, I came across with an eagle peering through its periscope. At first it seemed to me that it was lost. Although, I soon concluded that I was the one who had been shipwrecked. And that it was me, and not the eagle, who needed help.

Again, I had to walk and go through another scorching afternoon. Furthermore, once again I had to carry the wedge in my pants pocket. That day, I already knew that I was not part of any system. It was simply my mother and the universe making life difficult for me. I no longer found in me the belief to write an extraordinary chapter this summer. It was just another subsistence segment, readable in the paragraph of a book the size of my existence.

Regrettably, the life of this book of mine is becoming more and more confused with the existence of its protagonist. Regardless, the result of my work can only harm or aggrandise its author.

On the scorching afternoon of that extremely hot day, I was promptly told yes. The next day I went to work. The mother of my boss gave me a ride. It wasn't the dream factory, however, it was the light factory, where the metallic hoops are designed, in which the lamps are encased, and in which the lights are grilled, which will remain lit at one party or another, during one or another summer night.

It was in the light factory that those scattered glows were produced, similar to the stars hanging from the ceiling of the universe and identical to the lampyridae, still burning in the fire in which our childhood memory burns. It was the factory of decorative lights for summer parties and Christmas celebrations. And it was there that I would have to work during my summer vacations, where I would learn to appreciate the beauty of the metal arches that emulate the triumphal arches of the history of classical antiquity, in the era of modernity and post-modernity.

After my first day of work, I went jogging around the Atlético Clube Avelarense field. While I was running, some boys my age were playing ball on the synthetic turf, using only half of the playing rectangle. I recognised most of them. I didn't, however, have any friendly relationship with any of them. Who I was to them had long since dropped out of the Avelar valley.

For the first few days, I got a ride with the factory owner's mother. Interestingly, it was his father who had passed the light factory on to him. He did this after divorcing her. Exchanging her for another woman who was not yet old enough to be a mother. The factory owner's mother was showing less and less of the sympathy she would have for me. This made me sympathise more with the father than with the factory owner's mother.

Soon after, I started to diversify the recipient of my ride. Exactly, in the same place, where once I used to ask for it. When I was working at the Road Signs

Factory, a year before I went to Évora to study. It was, precisely, there, where I used to hitchhike every day to work.

I hitchhiked with all kinds of people who agreed to stop. I did it so that I wouldn't get so bored working at the Signs Factory and every day I could meet someone new that would allow me to discover new ideas about the world in which I lived, but about which I still knew very little. It was a time when I believed that each person was a door with access not to a house or a stairwell in a building, but to a unique and unforgettable journey.

My mother was still inexplicably angry with me. A storm of nerves flew over her head. There was always more than a sea of anger, in which she unconsciously wanted to drown me. She often argued with me, as if I were to blame for all her natural disenchantment. The factory owner's mother also started to pick on me. I didn't think it was really about me. Maybe it was because I was the guy who was new there and would only be there temporarily.

In the meantime, I had to take it! I had to keep working and listening to the factory owner's mother who constantly complained about my inefficiency. Hammering my head with the high-pitched timbre of her voice that so evidently contrasted with her body type that was shaped exactly like a sack of potatoes.

The days rolled by like dice from a board game being thrown onto the board of my daily life. Nevertheless, I continued to exercise, to read and write, and to clip my toenails. Regardless, my work schedule was absolutely unpredictable and so irregular as an irregular verb.

Meanwhile, I started to gather the documentation for the scholarship. I talked on the phone with Ms Júlia, who works at the social action services of the University of Évora. We were two old acquaintances who were accomplices and therefore spoke cordially on the phone. I, in fact, was not a student like the others. I didn't have a student life, nor an academic existence equal to that of the other students.

However, I had the book of an unwritten life, and I also had the book of an open existence. Both were being written and lived uninterruptedly by me. Every day was a new page that started blank. There were always new paragraphs to live and new chapters that hatched, bringing with them a cast and a plot of possibilities, of everything and nothing being able to happen simultaneously.

Today, the sun had not yet risen and I had already jumped out of bed. Shortly after I touched down with my feet, the factory owner's mother called to let me know that I wouldn't have to go today. I jumped back into the sheets with the same initial enthusiasm and motivation. Around one o'clock in the afternoon sharp, I argued with my mother. Not knowing why we were arguing and what we were arguing about once again. I think it was because my mother wanted me to be just like the other children. Only, I honestly don't know how I can be equal to other mothers' children.

The next day I went to work. When I arrived at the road to Ansião, after having climbed the dirt road and stopped on the way to the gas station, I wished that, instead of going to work, today would be one more class that I could miss. However, I arrived and automatically opened my thumb! And, unfortunately, someone stopped immediately and I got in, tremendously, dissatisfied with my luck.

I had the following weekend off. It was during this very short period that I rediscovered a small wonder of Portugal: Nova Rapoula! Which was, of course, in Rapoula. Where a world of memorabilia and fantasy coexisted with the reality of the world. Its founder was Gaudêncio Mendes Lopes. One could read on the inauguration plaque, now obsolete.

It felt good to be out there. Although, it was the same old human intention of making something decrepit in something that sounded recent. Just like what was done with Novo Banco. Which came after the old and decrepit Banco Espírito Santo went bankrupt. It was an old world invented and formatted to look like something new. Apparently, something that is not so young easily becomes another name.

For me, Nova Rapoula was indeed a fascinating place. There I could contemplate the iron locomotive parked forever in the melancholy of time. She knew she didn't have to go any further. I envied her momentarily and felt sorry that instead of being flesh and bleeding, I couldn't be iron instead, and that I too would one day rust.

There was also a small and rustic keep around there, which looked like the tower of King Vamba's castle of Ródão. Through the battlement, I could see a ring that was covered by the indifference of the vegetation. Further away, a stream was passing by making its way. It didn't care about the ring or me. The stream and the whole place were sealed off by the green mortar of cedars, which separated the New World from the rest of the world. Oh, and before I forget… Inside the rustic tower, there was a small, dusty museum, where an ancient loom stood out…

In the late afternoon, the New Rapoula is illuminated by the sun god, who shines on that rectangular parcel of paradise. I go forgetting where I am and to which place of destiny I will be forcefully pushed. The narrow mirror reflection of paradise is accompanied by the music of the wind as it kisses softly on the lips of the muses that were sitting on the treetops and on the summits of the Cercal and Abrunheira mountains.

After my tour of Nova Rapoula was over, I went running around late Sunday afternoon. I ran until the early evening of the end of July. Even before returning home, I ran one last lap around the full moon.

The next day, I woke up not remembering the dream I had. I awoke with a terrifying impact. With the feeling that I had been underwater for too long and had finally emerged. Feeling relieved, of course, to be able to breathe after being submerged for so long in the cave of my dream. Nevertheless, I got up full of energy.

I jumped out of bed, satisfied to know in advance what was going to happen during the day. The divorced mother of the sun-drenched factory owner was going to scream at me in her high-pitched voice. She would put her frustration on me and I would consent. Because it was a matter of a few more days before I left the factory and started working outside.

Today would be a routine and tiring day. However, I felt satisfied. The tiredness of work was an invigorating balm. My spirit felt renewed because another day of work had been won and I had gone running around the Avelarense field. This made me feel not exactly more accomplished, but even more tired and ready for bed.

I woke up the next morning with a bizarre dream. Once again, I could not conjure up the taste of the spice that was contained at the bottom of the dish in my dream. I was left only, with the atrocious impression left in my mouth of what I had dreamt. The only thing worth mentioning from that day was the girl who drove past me on the road to Ansião. Hesitating whether to give me a ride or not! Yet she left me behind, thumb outstretched and heartbroken. I would see her again the next day. My thumb would be outstretched again, in case she changed her mind, because she likes junkyards and things that are more or less smashed and more or less damaged.

***

It was 5:25 in the morning. The day had barely dawned. I was already running through the fog. Stealthily making my way through the morning shroud like a dreamcatcher. Following with the idea of the shortcut I knew and with the conviction that the wild and desolate places are honestly the most beautiful. The boss would give me a ride, and for my oh-so-unjust happiness, he was also, equitably, late. Today was the day to leave the factory and go to assist in the assembly. This task would not be completed until one thirty in the morning.

And where had I ended up? Not Mount Olympus, because there were no goddesses there, but it was relatively close to Montijo. Where the most beautiful maidens stroll in the garden of Eden, in a hidden paradise between the Tagus River and Alcochete.

The bulls had not yet been dropped. The only thing that showed, for now, was the sand under my feet, which had been spread over the village floor, so that at night the bulls wouldn't slip. The wooden walls surrounding the houses, which were painted in shades of crimson, made the streets into long, narrow arenas. Alcochete was a party and there was a whole world celebrating.

With the most beautiful creatures from morning to night waddling to the sound of a bolero that Marcus wouldn't hear. He wouldn't even allow others to hear it in his presence. Only he would listen to Ravel's bolero, but only after criticising his work. Declaring that it was not on the level of the great classical music composers. It would clearly be an event Marcus would never attend.

I am one of those assumed aficionados of women. I also like bulls, but not exactly to see them being skewered. I like women and horses more. Some women have the soul of a horse. Invariably, all horses have sensitive and delicate souls. However, not all women have equestrian souls.

The factory owner's mother is a soulless equine who came to meet us at the Festas do Barrete Verde and Salinas, driving her private car to the town of Alcochete. Today, enigmatically, she was not only more civilised, but also charming to me.

She followed us from early afternoon until late evening to jointly give birth to all of us. That's probably why she came. Also, she wanted to turn on the light, with us, when the night started. After our work was done, we slipped backstage. I could peek into that cocoon where those obliterated heroes and those unusual technicians live, who are hidden behind the big spotlights, pulling the curtain of the next day's theatre down or up, depending on the perspective.

One day I will return to Alcochete, to come and see the party one last time with the lights on. I will dance on top of the arches of the bridge that goes to the quay, with someone who loves me as much as the stars hanging from the ceiling tonight. I will come on a humble boat from the Atlantic, or I will clandestinely swim across the bed of the Tagus River! With the lights of the summer party illuminating my way back to the saltpans of the village, from where you can see Lisbon.

A few hours after I lay on the bed in the dormitory of the Pousada da Juventude, I was already in Setúbal, feeling the warmth of the sun browning the ring of my skin and breathing in the salty odour that permeated the air. The day was still breaking and I was already exhausted.

I spent the morning with a colleague, who looked much older than the years his age had accumulated. Perhaps because he had no five or six teeth. On the other hand, he had enormous strength. Greater than that of Heracles. And, if I wanted to be considered an Achilles who was not afraid to get his hands dirty, nor afraid to twist one of his heels, I would have no choice but to fight the monster of work, alongside him. Because, if anyone could bring him down, it was Fernando Arnaldo, the toothless one. Who spoke the same way he worked, without ever measuring the weight of a word at the end of a sentence.

After we had unscrewed the repeating bulbs and removed the hanging bows from the poles that had been buried in the ground, we had to throw everything onto the van. Then, it was just to roll up a few kilometres of wire, leave Setúbal, and sail in a van to Seixal, with Fernando Arnaldo at the helm.

Although, it all fit on the same day's raft, it seemed that this adventure of ours had more than one day. Eventually, because we moved to another city and to another life that had the city. I didn't have much to do. Being a simple helper, I could think about what to write and what to write about, which was essentially what I did. Those who worked with the crane had much less time to blink one thought or another.

I took the opportunity to go and buy something to bite with my great appetite for living. The strong will that my diet had, leaned towards to satisfy my thirst and hunger with fruit. Because man does not live by bread alone, but by bread and why not, a slice of melon?

I fearlessly made my way to the shadow of the hypermarket accompanied by my yellow flowered vest. There, I was completely ignored. It was as if I was invisible. I walked down the aisles of the hypermarket and it was as if I didn't exist! Nobody looked at me. Nobody dared to see me.

I brought a melon under my arm. I immediately sliced it with Mr Emídio's razor, the electrician. With diabolical precision I passed a slice to each of my colleagues. Including Mr Emídio who was afraid he wouldn't be able to catch it in the air. Each slice was a piece of the rugby ball that had to be caught irremediably at first try. Because it was a play that would decide a championship. Oh, what pure ecstasy it was to be in a game with the outcome open with one minute to go. With everyone scrambling to get their melon slice.

The soldiers fighting on top of the crane, banging their helmets on the safety box, and all the rest of the team and company of workers crouched in the trenches gave me a hail of cheers. They shouted in chorus: "Long live Saymon! Long live Saymon!" Simone wore a flowered yellow vest and was also entitled to wear a helmet. Simone, Ximenes, Salmão, Simeão: everything was easier for them than saying: long live Simão!

I would spend the rest of the afternoon pushing up poles more than five metres high and sticking them in holes drilled in the ground. These were the poles where the hoops were fixed with the lights of the lamps that were lit when the day died and his widow came covered with a mourning shawl. It was somewhere in between that moment that Fernando Arnaldo, a toothless man, and I would leave Seixal behind. We would wade through a sea that was more than a tunnel of darkness.

However, we would only go through the Ribatejo streets of the town of Benavente after surfing the highways and routes that take us everywhere and nowhere. Absolutely nothing was visible when I jumped out of the truck. I didn't know where the darkness of the ground began and where the light from the truck ended.

We quickly moved the pieces with different metal shapes, where the light strings were wrapped, onto the truck box. The week's work was thus concluded. When we finished the collection, a pit of darkness engulfed us, and the truck box of the night.

We had dinner in a restaurant where the kitchen was supposedly already closed. Unfortunately, we were still served. Not even the poor pudding looked good or tasted good. Fernando started the meal by chewing a piece of bread. Spitting out the olive stones onto a saucer. He used to come there when he passed through the town of Benavente.

For him, it didn't matter if the bread was from today, or if it was from last week. He would happily eat whatever was put in front of his plate. If necessary, he would swallow the olive stones and spit the bread out onto the floor. He was indifferent. But when I gave him my pudding, he looked at me with devotion. Sipping it in one gulp. As if the pudding were a solid refreshment that he could drink in one gulp. Very satisfied, he wiped his mouth with the napkin of his arm.

It was after two o'clock in the morning when we reached the valley of the village of Avelar. I jumped out of the van, still moving. And Fernando Arnaldo followed the rest of the trip alone on the complementary route number eight.

Whistling happily until he reached the flowery town of Figueiró dos Vinhos. Listening to the radio at maximum volume. Ploughing in the boss's van like a Portuguese sailor who once would drive his fifteenth century caravel. He would even go beyond the old mansion that my distinguished friend Marcus Matalonga inherited from his grandparents. He would enter the town of Figueiró dos Vinhos with the windows of his van and his mouth wide open. He would enter the house to sleep alone in bed. He had no wife, no children and five or six teeth missing.

The next day on my day off I saw the overtly happy Paulo, the boss. I had never seen him so exuberant. The last time I had seen him like this was last week. On one of the nights, we stayed overnight at the Pousada da Juventude and he went to a club. Taking a small entourage with him. Most of the company had gone to bed in the dormitories of the inn after dinner. My comrades in arms were left to criticise the boss and his small entourage. They thought I had fallen asleep and, therefore, each one in turn made his own pronouncements. It wasn't out of spite; it was because they had nothing else to do.

Nevertheless, Paulo, the boss, today, was happier than the child left in him. He had gotten his little toy back. The toy was the biggest truck I had ever seen. It had been made in America and was finally fixed up. It came with the trailer hooked up. And it was Paulo, the boss, who, in the industrial area, was reversing. So that the truck could enter the factory and deposit material on top of it, to be later transported elsewhere. All that movement was full of noise and excitement. It was like a cargo ship arriving at the pier to dock, and everyone was waiting to watch that majestic moment.

While the boss backed up, I was standing at the back of the truck. Listening to the sound of the backward gear that had been engaged by him. It was quite peculiar, that regressive timbre. It became the apotheosis of a glorious return. However, it was only the unusual noise of the transmission working, mixed with the noise of the industrial machinery and the shouts that contained the indication of my colleagues in the rear, such as: "Come! Come!" Convinced that the truck was an airplane that would have to be buoyed as it triumphantly passed through the factory gate, which, nonetheless, was not the triumphal arch. Despite that, the boss blew the truck's horn as if a huge feat had been achieved.

In my mind, the truck was the sperm whale, the great white whale. I felt like shouting to the guys: call me Ishmael or Melville! But I didn't. I just received the heavy rods and the metal hoops, as well as the rest of the pieces and utensils. Stacking everything on top of the truck. So, call me a coward instead!

***

I passed through the Alentejo too fast. The heat was chasing us everywhere. The sweat of work dripped down my face. While, the marble stone in the history of time poured white dresses into the body of the buildings. I could not, however, see calmly and for a long time, the inner Alentejo that I so sought to reach or, simply, to see. Except, when it was possible to do so during the journey to the Estremoz fair. When entering the city to go to the boarding house where we slept on the floor, or during the breaks for lunch and dinner when we went to the restaurant. Or, again, when Fernando Arnaldo and the rest of the colleagues would stop to go to the coffee shop and I would duck out, trying to find that Alentejo that makes up my dream.

For a few minutes I contemplated the keep of the castle of Estremoz and looked north to the Serra da Ossa. Speculating where the artificial caves of the ancient hermit monks could be found! Wishing that the square I saw could fit on me, so that I could take not only the Church of Santa Maria, but also the statue of Queen Saint Isabel. Wishing to bring the whole cluster of the white city with me, to accompany me forever on every journey home. That is, in every vain attempt that has the hope that every prodigal son can return to the mother house.

The speed with which we go through the spiral of days grinds away the linear memory of the places we once saw. It erases the names of the people and the smells of the things we witnessed in passing in those places. I fear that sooner or later, this day will be just a paragraph too short. Perhaps, if I took more than a second minute in the interior Alentejo, there would be more than one paragraph and there would be at least one chapter with the body of a latifundium.

After completing our work, we returned to the centre of the country. I returned, concluding that some classes only meet in the movies. Because in the reality of a working day, they rarely, if ever, cross paths. Consequently, I wondered if my rise before entering higher education did not coincide with Marcus' decline. After all, if Marcus' world had not collapsed, would our lives have intersected?

The sun was boiling the morning we arrived in Meirinhas. Meirinhas is a parish in Pombal that is on the side of the road. The parish church is of a contemporary style. Basically, it is an ugly temple. As a rule, churches designed in the twentieth century are always hideous examples of what more recent architecture has produced. Mário, my colleague at the Ponte de Ferro residence, used to say, usually pulverised with rage, or just influenced by his older brother Tiago Silva, that all churches should be torn down. I think it would be enough just to demolish the ones that were built after the twentieth century.

Some places are special. Their inhabitants occupy in their own way the story that has the narrative of that place. But there are places that change, not because we want them to, but because the people in charge of them want them to. After all, it is easy to understand the will of the history of time, but it is hard to understand the choice of the time of history in certain people and in certain places.

Meanwhile, a child is prevented by his mother from climbing onto the bandstand! Across the street, surprisingly, Luís Vaz de Camões and Fernando Pessoa greet me. Dom Sebastião is in the middle of them both. Each one is begging me to join in the fun and quit my summer job. However, I refused. Because, in the meantime, there would surely be at least one philharmonic band parading through the streets in the evening. And fireworks going off into the night.

Also you would hear the folkloric rancho, the bagpipe players, popular music, and advertisements for the region's companies and brands coming systematically from a fixed column on the street in the square where the kermesse stands were erected by local residents and Portuguese emigrants scattered around the world. Missing home and the summer party that takes place every year in Meirinhas.

Ah, Meirinhas! Meirinhas is not just another parish. In Meirinhas, there is a patron saint and a summer festival. There is a party full of crowds and confusion. And there is a crowd full of confusion about the definition of what is a church fair and what is a festival committee, which doesn't even contain a third of religion.

After lunch I lifted the long ladder and climbed to the top of the electricity poles, on which there were neither princesses nor dragons. But only the danger of ordinary mortals' lives, the ugliness of the electric cables, and a panoramic view of those who passed below the tip of my feet, blowing up the ladder that had more rungs than I had lives. I felt like a bird. Perched on the side of the road not knowing how to use my wings.

It was with that feeling that I stood contemplating the metabolism of oncoming traffic, with no time to stop, no time to even look up or sideways. It was literally at that moment that I admitted to myself that I still didn't know if I had truly experienced it all. But as I descended to the bottom of the ladder, I realised, clearly, that what I saw from above was the same little question mark that had my uncertainty, which I now saw the same down here.

More days passed by me, while I went through the desert leaves of the night. Reading in a cheap boarding house in the dim light, or reading and re-reading while on the move, in one of the vans with a crane, or in the truck that moved to an unknown Portugal, to a country beyond my comprehension and imagination.

And, the more I went through that multitude of days and the starry pages in the summer night sky, the more the feeling of duty done, went through me, as well as, the feeling of my hands becoming rougher and my spirit becoming more and more indifferent.

***

The convent appeared out of nowhere. It was a great black iceberg, a massive and imposing block that suddenly appeared to me. After miles and miles of highways, service stations, toll booths, and other islets around the sea of asphalt that kill the romanticism and sense of adventure of a great trip, behold, that enormous convent blackened by the passage of time imploded on our horizon. A megalomaniacal apparition of another time erupting in the history of post-modernity, with that imposing black iceberg, refusing to melt.

That black building contrasted with the white city of Estremoz. It was another Portugal! It was a mystical Portugal, where the last portals that still resist seal their entrance. When on my horizon, the convent erupted, I immediately realised how much I still didn't know the world, and that it was much bigger than the one Marcus regularly showed me on the maps that belonged to his very rare collection. After all, the current knowledge I had would in the future be completely redundant.

Rogério drove the company van like an expert. Although he didn't know exactly where he was, he remained relaxed and carefree. He had the intuition that it was more or less that way. And that was all he needed to navigate the sea of asphalt.

We were gradually getting away from the convent and the carousel of traffic circles in the centre of Mafra. Driver Rogério was still confident that the right direction was more or less that way. His father had taught him to drive trucks and cranes before he had even learned to crawl. I was sedated by the driver's devotion to his family, which was even greater than his dedication to his job.

Maybe, because my father basically didn't care about me, and, all I knew about him was more or less where he lived and what I was told about him… Probably, it was that, it was the fact that Rogério was a young father, who loved his family above all things, and that, eventually, touched me as deeply as one of Beethoven's symphonies, but not only, also because he was an authentic and genuine guy.

He was a truck driver during the week and at the weekend he managed the cranes at the light factory. He had three young daughters and no other passion than his family, no other skill than driving. He drove with his hands and feet: cranes, trucks, with and without trailers, and anything else that had wheels and an engine. He was my colleague Rogério, a fat guy. Nevertheless, he was almost as imposing as the iceberg of the Mafra Convent.

There were three of us in the van, which was heading closer and closer to the blue Atlantic. Me, Rogério, and Amílcar. It was Paulo The Boss who sent him to our work team. It was Paulo The Boss who sent each group of missionaries to a certain point in the Portuguese world. And it was boss Paulo, and not God or himself, who chose that he would come with us.

Meanwhile, Rogério already knew where we were. The colleague who came with us, a little older than me, was constantly fiddling with his cell phone with the insane expectation of receiving a message at any moment. But the message never came. And, he, a balding boy, still in his youth, would have to keep anxiously waiting.

Rogério, after finding our pick-up point, quickly decided that the best thing to do would be to go for lunch at a restaurant overlooking the Atlantic blue, in

Ericeira. We were in the West! And the Portuguese west, besides the dark blue Atlantic Ocean, also has a small rural world within it

"Maybe we'll still go to the beach?" Rogério asked, laughing with his belly.

"Right! To breathe in the sea iodine!" I answered.

"What do you say, Amílcar?" Rogério asked our colleague. Who was a little inhibited.

"I think it's better not," he replied, very embarrassed.

"It's not even noon and we're already eating lunch. Way to go!" I said.

"And Paulo's buying us lunch!" Roger added, rubbing his belly.

"Maybe we..." Amílcar stammered. "Maybe we should go, before...we...maybe we should have gone...still in the morning...to do the collection," said Amílcar, choking and hesitating.

"But is he afraid or what?" Roger asked, turning to me. Then turning towards our colleague, "Are you going for the fish or are you going for the meat?" Turning again towards me, "Look, now, he doesn't talk!" He turned back to face Amílcar, "Tell me what you want, to go to work. You're in such a hurry that you don't even choose, or let us order our lunch."

"I'm going for the fish!" I said.

"So, I'm coming too!" Said Rogério. Then he complained. "Hey, man! Choose! So, you can go to work! Isn't that what you want?"

Amílcar got up from the table in the meantime. Hesitating whether or not to wash his hands in the bathroom. He walked with the same reticent manner in which he spoke.

"He is such a nerd," said Roger, as soon as Amílcar awkwardly got up from the table. Trying to find the bathroom in the seafood restaurant. Walking hesitantly. Then looking very surprised in the direction of the aquarium, full of crabs that meditated, walking back and forth.

After lunch Rogério jumped on the crane, like one of those potbellied but still sufficiently agile domestic cats. Soaring into the sky, floating, in a kind of sudden vision equal to the sacred heart. Descending abruptly, shortly afterwards like an angel or a holy apparition. But landing on the ground like the demon of temptation, like another one of those angels fallen from heaven in a tumble.

The crane was a magic elevator that went up and came down, Roger was the great illusionist who pressed the good and evil button. And, Roger, that great balancing cat, when he got out of the safety box did a somersault. He then climbed into the van like a real circus performer. His trucker belly gave him the superpower of balance. He was possibly the last man Zarathustra had predicted.

Roger was possessed and was laughing more and more wildly. I was laughing too. Jumping up and down on the sidewalk. Amílcar held his hands together. Squeezing them very fearfully. Praying a low river, in which he sank his deepest fear. Then, with no other solution, he looked up to the sky, trying to get the invisible face of his faith to appear to him.

I meditated briefly on the words of the prophet, "the higher a thing is in its kind, the rarer is its success." Meanwhile, Roger incarnated into a skilled monkey. For he returned for the second time, swiftly climbing down from his metal tree. Perching from branch to branch, and then accelerating full speed into his boss's truck. Going to the end of the completely deserted street to make another magnificent skid. Skidding inside the empty enclosure where the annual pilgrimage in honour of the Holy Incarnation is celebrated.

Amílcar continued to pray his rosary very softly. Convincingly clasping his hand in each other's, pointing to the sky. I would jump from the sidewalk to the road, and from the road, again, to the sidewalk. And, just as the music bands and theatre companies return to the stage only to receive once again the applause of the audience, the conductor Rogério monkey would repeat his success.

At first it might seem that Roger was really leaving, and that he meant it. But promptly, after the suspense had a enough pause, he backed up once more. Stopping *in extremis*, only when he reached our side. Stalling by the side of the kerb, asking Amílcar, "Are you afraid or what?"

Pulling the van closer and closer to Amílcar, who was now running away in distress. First, he ran backwards, then he ran forwards. But the van ran even faster, sticking even more closely to Amílcar, who began to skate from accelerating so much. He could never hide from the machiavellian van. It was like one of those chases they make us watch on television.

Amílcar, however, gave up running, not knowing what else to do with his life. Deciding, finally, that the best thing would be to stay still and not move. But the perfidious van continued to run around Amílcar until the joke was broken shortly afterwards. Not because it was already over time, but because Roger, the balancing clown, miscalculated the distance and crashed his front wheel disastrously into the kerb.

"Then, having emerged, the tightrope walker who walked on a suspended rope, this one was chased by a clown who made him fall!" I drank in the prophet's words and took another philosophical swig in the liquid of the abstract, "I lived. No doubt, too long on the mountain, I listened too much to the streams and the trees…"

After quenching my thirst with the words of the prophet, I spoke up, "Calm down guys! This is nothing! This was nothing. Let's all tell the same story."

I would tell them, unmoved and serene. As if nothing really serious had happened. For a second, Amílcar blushed with relief, realising that he wasn't going to die today after all. Rogério listened to me carefully. Thinking that I had said something very right. He just shook his head up and down.

Meanwhile, the other fellow missionaries arrived from their pilgrimages and dismounted from their evangelising vans shortly after. They were furious. We had not preached the will of the boss Paulo to anyone. Not in the afternoon, not in the morning. But then again, we live in the same argumentative world, in which one lives and one dies, rightly and wrongly.

I don't know if the boss, Paulo, esteemed his employee more than the others, or if he just needed his services badly. He readily shrugged his shoulders when Rogério told my side of the story. Nevertheless, realising the true version of the story, by knowing the character in question, he could have contested it. But strangely enough he accepted it. Without once cursing.

The real heroes are fathers of families. Acrobats and tightrope walkers who walk on a thin rope, through which stretches the whole social and family system, condemned to be and to die Portuguese. But true heroes don't need to be sung about, to be heard their deeds and the events of their odyssey that is constantly tinged by the twists and turns of the epic road that accompanies the march of these great gladiators, who are men of flesh and blood, with a big trucker's belly and a long little finger nail. Not only because, yes! But because they have the right, after all, they are the real heroes, and because, above all, they are fathers of families!

The young truck driver and trapeze artist father transported me and my colleague Amílcar home. It was already dawn. He fell asleep several times on the way. I gave him slaps so that he would open his eyes and wake up. Holding the steering wheel when the car ran away to the other lane, where he followed the beautiful dream that he himself was driving.

"Hey, man, I was having such a good dream. Did you really have to wake me up? But then I can't sleep? Let me sleep just a little longer!" Pleaded Rogério.

Amílcar had asked to be dropped off at a specific place. It wasn't supposed to be near his house. It was in a deserted area. We dropped him off and left. Roger took off in the opposite direction, after the quick and clumsy goodbye given to us by Amílcar, which according to Rogério, clairvoyant in these matters, showed that he was clearly compromised.

Then Roger dizzily, made a U-turn, turned off the car lights, and did a slight time delay. And, just then, a car could be seen coming. Stopping next to Amílcar. At this, Rogério started the engine quickly, and then drove very slowly past the car and Amílcar. Turning, Rogério, the high beams and commenting to me, "I don't know what all this was about! If he couldn't have told us that his girlfriend was going to be waiting for him there!" Claimed the big pasha, who kept turning the wheel back and forth.

Then, after leaving me at home, he zigzagged away, at two hundred and something per hour, the last great Portuguese hero.

***

I took advantage of the day off to enrol for the fifth or fourth time and sleep through the rest of the light that I still hoped would burn in the day lamp. Nevertheless, I was forced to go to my mother and stepfather's house. That was where the welcome dinner for my grandmother's brother was to take place. The Portuguese uncle from Brazil who had brought all his Brazilian children. Despite that, his children had not brought the grandchildren of the Portuguese uncle from Brazil. My Brazilian cousins were mixing their samba with their family's fado in the sister country that fit in my mother's backyard.

It might sound like I was listening to a real family, but rivers flow to the sea and not the other way around. So, I couldn't understand the extent and contradiction of that bubbling current in me. Maybe it was sleepiness or an unwillingness to talk about my fado with the rest of the family to the sound of the pagode brought by the sons of Portuguese Uncle Zé from Brazil. I turned my back and abandoned the farce of the evening. Shortly after I arrived, I walked back to the old house.

My summer job would still require one last trip to Montemor-o-Novo. Specifically, on the hottest day of the year. And, once again, I would get to know the Alentejo beyond Évora. However, not being there. Nor staying there for a long time.

We awaited new orders while sleeping in the early afternoon sun. Everything that had to be done had already been accomplished. The poles were buried in the ground and the rest of the work was finished. Now, it was time to wait. As Marcus had to wait. Waiting patiently in the unnoticeable ground of his personal misfortune. His calamity is, nevertheless, more abstract than easily condensed into something tangible and concrete. At this hour, this very instant, Marcus will still be asleep in one of the thousand rooms at his disposal. After finally waking up, he will eventually play on his grand piano for hours on end. With the cobwebs expanding all over the mansion.

Meanwhile, Marcus will smoke another cigarette, not caring about the ash that will be falling mercilessly to the floor. It will be irrelevant to him whether there are more cobwebs today than yesterday. He will also be indifferent to whether the branches of trees blend with the jungle of bushes in the oasis of his garden. He will walk through the tangled web of the forest and sit on a stone bench contemplating the bucolic lake next to the garden.

Then he will look up at the night sky and throw ideological stones against boredom and against that rectangular pond with the rounded edges that his grandparents had built, using the power of the mines of the Ribeiro Travesso farm. Finally, he will read one more book. For dessert, he will devour a dictionary or an encyclopaedia, before the sun heralds a new day.

But now I was the one who was waiting. And I did it under the sunny shade, me and my summer colleagues. Each of us was burning equally inside, delirious with forty-odd degrees. Confusing the cool shade of the trees, with the canopies of the women passing on the avenue.

Some smoked a cigarette with their eyes closed, others slept with their eyes open and their caps on their heads. Still others told ordinary stories, whistling melodies that flew towards the sky. Landing, in the end, on the noses of the slightly reclining dreamers.

One of Paulo's new boss's employees asked me to lend him money. I immediately told him I didn't have it to lend. I didn't feel like losing the money that I literally earned with the sweat of my labour. You see, when you are asked for money in this kind of situation and you give it, you never see it back. Which would clearly be the situation.

Still, two, three days ago, I was following along with Fernando Arnaldo, the toothless one. We were flying along the highway at night. When the van we were in suddenly gave signs of breaking down. Fernando Arnaldo, the toothless, skilfully managed to move the van to the Palmela service station, where we had to stay.

A few meteorites and minutes later, from the cell phone, Paulo boss, yelled at poor Fernando Arnaldo. I remember, now, that moment, when old Arnaldo wanted to contest what Paulo, the boss, was so unfairly accusing him of. Fernando Arnaldo opened his mouth and closed it, exactly as the garbage truck does. Then, in a strange spasm he would move his old chest forward, and then, zap, backward. At first, I thought that there was an electronic device in the back of the bench that was propelling his body like that. This resulted in an involuntary contraction that repeated itself. As naturally as the heartbeat. Continuously going forward and then backward. Simultaneously opening his mouth, and then automatically closing it.

When the call ended, Fernando Arnaldo complained to me about how he was treated by his boss. I was still, however, much more interested in working on this book, than that night docked at the Palmela service station having to listen to that story. Nonetheless, I heard the whining Fernando Arnaldo telling me, "I, I, I…who serve him, and who, who, who help him as I can and can't! What, what, what, what more can I do?"

He looked even older and more tired. He searched exhaustively for the pack of cigarettes until his despair found it in one of his pockets and he could finally light a cigarette. Repeatedly he blew out his disquiet. Then he still paced back and forth around the perimeter of the gas station. Smoking indifferently, relatively, near the gas pumps. I continued to read and write under the artificial light lamp, as if it were something so natural, someone reading and writing and thinking in a gas station, not to kill time, but to quench the thirst for knowledge that has the water of the source of his life.

The sounds of automobiles in the post-modern night were rapidly crossing the endless sea of the highway. The distant stars blurred with the overhead light of the airplanes. Making me believe that there were more airplanes in the sky than stars currently shining.

We were two worker soldiers in the trenches of the gas station. Waiting for reinforcements and for the first-aid kit that would only appear when another day of work began. But it wouldn't show up until mid-afternoon, and to my delight I would end up being able to read another book and write another four or five lines and think about something that will have no practical resolution for my life.

Finally, it has come to an end, my last day of work for my summer job. I am now in the trunk of boss Paulo Guimarães' van. I sat on top of a toolbox. I am reading and shaking. All at the same time. My summer colleagues stay behind, to fulfil the rest of their contract. Mine is already over.

Paulo the boss is arguing with his mother while driving. In between he asks me, "Is everything okay there?"

And, I, too, answer with the same question—not realising that the boss Paulo, nor the mother who is now scolding, can see me from the other side of the van. So, they cannot read the expression of irony that I carry with me in the trunk.

Paulo, the boss, drove on and on, yelling at his mother. And the mother continues the rest of the way trying in vain to keep up with her son in the argument. In the end it is the mother's son who wins the heated argument.

August has also come to an end. The summer is also naturally coming to an end. I am gradually recognising that I will never be able to return home this or any other summer. In the valley of the village of Avelar my return home will no longer reside, nor will I live. Therefore, I will no longer be able to wait to one day see the postcard of a sunset on the beach of adulthood. There will not be for me a single summer party, or a single trip to the beach. There will remain, only, the memory of the light factory. Flashing intermittently in me, decorating the memory of this summer when I was once again separated from my little brother and from my mother's arms.

I passed through Mafra, through the Portuguese west that is painted by the blue of the Atlantic. I crossed Alcochete, Setúbal and Seixal. I crossed Bidoeira de Cima from one side to the other and still passed through Alentejo, only to return there later. I didn't go to see Pascal's sound studio. But when Marcus called me, we went back to where we used to go. We passed, in the late afternoon, through the tunnel, from the complementary route number eight. Entering, in the early evening, only, when we passed the bridge to the other side.

Telling me insistently, Marcus, that I was overly tanned and thin. I don't know what bothered him more, whether it was that I was ostensibly thin, or that I presented myself to his eyes, overly tanned. Then he moved on to his favourite summer hate: the eucalyptus trees!

"They are a plague!" He said, repeatedly, and added, "And mimosas are also another plague." In conclusion, the sentence to be applied. "But why don't they burn for good? Why don't they all burn at once? It would be like nipping it in the bud!"

He would continue his sermon. "You look around and what do you see? All you see is eucalyptus and more eucalyptus. And more eucalyptus! There is nothing! Nothing at all! Nothing but mountains and mountains with nothing but eucalyptus. The whole Pinhal Interior Norte is just one eucalyptus. There are not two or three oak trees, not a single cork oak! As if this were not enough, they plant even more eucalyptus. In two or three years everything will burn down. And what do you see? Eucalyptus! Eucalyptus trees that have sprouted again and naturally multiplied…"

Four years later, on the holiday, October 5, in the year 2016, I saw Fernando Arnaldo, the toothless one. He didn't recognise me. I was with Marcus. Marcus was once again reflecting on his past. Without being able, however, to remember what he had recently done to alter whatever his present was. He kept imagining and just trying to predict what the cloud in the sky of his future would look like. Always with the same sky tone and the same gloomy, sombre chord. Very different from the one I had once heard and imagined with him when I first met him.

After having left me in the Avelar valley he returned to the mansion. Following not the complementary route number eight, but rounding the bend in the night by the old road.

Marcus seemed as resignedly absent on that October 5 holiday as he did on that late summer day in the year 2012. Now, there was no longer any doubt. Marcus was getting closer and closer to the end of his grandiose wait.

Even before returning to the Alentejo, I had to move my books that were at my mother and stepfather's house to the old house. Because my stepfather didn't want so many of my books sleeping in his house. It was confusing to him, not only because of the weight of my knowledge, but because there were so many books gathered in one place. Like me, my books also had the particularity and specificity of their own existence and could not be in one place for long.

Chapter 5
Our Lady of Health

(September 2012 to March 2013)

The landlords' son was an old acquaintance of Nilson's, who had started to take a course in mechanics with him, but who would drop out a month later to take a computer course. Not satisfied, he would again change his field of study to accounting and management. It was he who came to collect the rent money, and it was he who showed us the house his parents had to rent in the Nossa Senhora da Saúde neighbourhood. Before I, and later, João, left Évora. Because, only Nilson moved there at the height of summer.

When we went to see the house, the plates we had thrown in the spring were still a recent memory that flew above our heads. If we looked closely, we could still see them climbing the stairs of the firmament. Or else, no! They were not kitchen dishes, but flying saucers that also flew beyond the wall of the landlady Maria de Fátima, passing the greenway and gliding in slow motion beyond the neighbourhood of Nossa Senhora da Saúde. Landing in an uncertain place. Probably, somewhere on the edge of the horizon, or on the edge of the place where the three of us were now going to live.

During the summer, I called João and Nilson. They seemed even further away than I was at present from the Southern dream. There was now clearly a greater distance between me and where they were currently; something had definitely shifted. Perhaps, we could not be the same with another change of house and another change of season.

After packing up my clothes and the rest of my junk, I sat uncomfortably on the couch. Staring in frustration at the blacked-out television set. I didn't know what to do. João had not yet returned from Moura and Nilson was still working. I waited impatiently for a new semester to start. Although it wasn't the next morning, hope always lies in tomorrow. Maybe, when classes finally started, I would also be the usual me. Maybe, each of us will cultivate the seed of our habit, and that habit will grow in a pot without soil.

João hadn't arrived yet, when Nilson came to pick me up at home, after he had finished his work in the workshop. Today he was going to show me his cafe paradise. That's where he often went to drink beer, after the workshop bell rang and he knew it was time for him to quit his job. He took the opportunity to tell me about the most recent occurrence, "It's official!" He said nonchalantly. "João and Catarina are dating."

Soon after, his colleague Joaquim appeared, and only then did his colleague Ricardo arrive. Ricky was his favourite. Not that he had indicated it to me. But we recognise by how we are treated, and how others are treated, whether we are more or less important. In the world and in human relationships, not everything is democratically equal. There is no mistaking it.

I went with them to reconnoitre another mystery place, where Nilson and his colleagues went every Wednesday. It was Lopes' tavern. Everything fits there. From his teacher who explained to him the mechanics of things, to Ramos, who was a salesman and lived in Garraia, to Vilela who is currently unemployed and has a chameleon as a pet. And, who, on top of the unpaid monthly house rent, has a wife and two daughters who are still little. Nilson's friends and acquaintances are collectible figurines. They are the cromlechs of a place, menhirs that gather around a balcony in Évora, characters from an Évora story, which are not, however, part of the history of Portugal. There is nothing admirable about that court. They are geeks that I or anyone else has in their notebook.

Lopes is just Mr Lopes, who, besides owning the cafe, owns a lady heatstroke he has on his face and a portentous bulge he has in his belly. The morbid effect of the wine heat is communicated to him directly by serving others.

Joaquim, Nilson's least loved colleague, after his work in the workshop, went to work in the workshop he had on his parents' hill, which was somewhere near Degebe. Nilson's other colleague, Ricardo, his favourite, went to Viana, Viana do Alentejo. He would also make almost the same trip. Before, he would pass by the house of his beautiful girlfriend who was a single mother. His parents were not Francis' parents. To them, it was indifferent whether the girl was blue or pink. What mattered to them was if they were both happy.

Nilson and I returned to the Senhora da Saúde neighbourhood, waiting for his best man to pass by afterwards. To fuel him up, with the light numbness that had its usual consumption.

When his best man arrived, he sat down at the oval kitchen table. He was not a very polished guy. However, he was cordial enough. Second, on Nilson's label, he was a sensitive former drug addict. He had chronic depression and was taking daily pills that the doctor had prescribed for him after his mother's death. Nevertheless, the doctor's prescription had not stopped him from attempting suicide more than once. Although, not once was he successful.

His wife was a tender girl with green eyes, who said hello to Nilson and me when we went shopping together at the Pingo Doce hypermarket.

"His wife likes him very much. But he is a head freak. They have a daughter. And that calmed him down!' Nilson said, shrugging his small moral shoulders. Anything that was exaggerated in others was too much for his conservatism, a native of the lower border region and the fossils of Mação.

When it was just the two of us sitting and talking on the sofa in the living room, the bony and trifling figure of the godfather, with bushy eyebrows, full of wrinkles of anguish and marks left by days badly lived, still appeared reflected in the irises of Nilson, who was staring in astonishment at the television, camped in the centre of the living room furniture. Until he opened the blindfold of the restlessness that truly bubbled up in his spirit and began to cry.

It was usual for him to shed tears. Essentially, he shed tears for three reasons: first, because he was afraid that he would not be hired at the end of his first contract. Secondly, he cried because his parents quarrelled more and more often, and because his mother threatened to divorce the father. Finally, he cried because he no longer had his Débora. Those were the three mechanical scenarios mounted on the cogwheel of thoughts that spun constantly through the mechanism of his mind.

After mopping up his little salt tear, Nilson went to bed. Tomorrow, however, he would be unable to remember why he cried today.

**

My housemate, João, arrived in the meantime. He was a runner who had fallen behind the front pack. When he crossed the finish line, he showed however he was in a hurry. Catarina arrived soon after. She reminded me of one of the dogs of the neighbours in front of us, who are always with their tongues hanging out, barking at the cars that pass on the street.

They lick their owners' mouths, after having sniffed their own asses. With the same curiosity and excitement with which they search for the fragrance of the ground their owners walk on.

Then, after Catarina went into João's room, Nilson hit me on the arm. Laughing. Getting hiccups from laughing so hard. Commenting on the situation and relating the event that took place beyond the door of João's room. Which was next to the living room.

The only window in his room overlooked the kitchen. He had chosen last and had been poorly served. I knew the feeling of choosing and being chosen last.

Nilson continued to laugh extravagantly quietly. He laughed because in João's room we could hear the burst of fireworks that occurred after a Greco-Roman wrestling match between two or more worthy adversaries. The sounds of pain and the sweating of pleasure pierced through the walls, no matter how much we stayed away with the TV set at maximum volume. What was really happening in the room next to the living room was, however, deferred in our imagination by what was happening live, backstage in the great theatre of human life.

João and Catarina were already in the kitchen with Nilson when I finished showering. And so, they saw me walking by with the towel wrapped around my waist. Catarina looked at me as if she had never seen me before. She stared at me with such desire that she didn't disguise her dumbfounded why. Continuing reticent to stare into the mirror of my soul. João applauded my excellent physical form. Gazing also amazed, being somewhat uncomfortable by the effect caused to Catarina. Noting that I had progressed more than he had during the summer.

I continued to religiously follow the creed of my physical exercise and to obey the doctrine of the attitude that saves any spirit. Increasing, however, my difficulty in balancing on the scales. On one hand there was João's dumbbell weight, on the other hand there was Nilson's counterweight.

But something had changed! In Nilson's opinion, the change was not due to our moving house, nor to the change of season, but to Catarina's presence in João's life. As well as the consequent intrusion between the life that the three of us had on Leonor Fernandes Avenue, at Maria de Fátima's house, and the life we now had at the house we had rented from the parents of Nilson's former colleague in Senhora da Saúde neighbourhood.

A few days later, Catarina did not come alone. She brought a friend. A mystery client who had come today to learn about Nilson's repair services. Catarina had devised a future couple who could feed her own romance. João had thought of the same thing before, but to no effect.

Early last summer I went with João to the kiosk that is between the Patrocínio Hospital and the nursing school. To casually meet up with Catarina and this friend of hers, who, today, did the reverse route.

Our meeting went nowhere. Cátia Vanessa was not interested in me. However, today she was visibly interested. Not in me, but in Nilson. And Catarina was determined to pair Nilson with her or with some other friend. Sometimes she insisted on bringing another friend of hers, who, although she already had a boyfriend, didn't mind giving a leg up.

Even though Nilson seemed oblivious and uninterested in the reality of what was happening next to him, he was just pretending to be very engrossed in the fictional program playing on television.

Something had definitely changed. If it wasn't for the result of moving once again, something had changed this season, and it wouldn't just be Catarina's fault…

***

I got up and went for a run. Two hours later I came home and took a shower. Then I ordered a cab to take me to the bus station, just because today I could finally do it. I tried to read on the express bus with the natural light from the afternoon lamp. But the time bus was moving downstream, too fast for me to keep up with my ambition. I left the Senhora da Saúde neighbourhood, it was still daylight. When I arrived at Avelar it was already night, and, already, it was almost Christmas Eve.

My mother agreed to let me spend the last days of December and the first days of January alone in the old house. As long as I would spend some time with her and my brother and the rest of the family in their house. Although my stepfather refused to talk to me, it was imperative for him that we were all in the same house and in the same division of time.

Afterwards, going upstairs to my old room and being alone with my thoughts, I tried to get rid of them and fall asleep. As much as I really wanted to be with my family, I couldn't spend the evening staring at the television. Just like Nilson would do in Évora or Mação. The best thing would be to sleep. To follow the example of a hedgehog or a bear that went into hibernation at the beginning of winter. And when, by chance, it wakes up in the middle of the morning, it is still in its lethargic state. Just like me, who woke up shortly after having finally managed to fall asleep.

It was almost Christmas Eve, and I felt terribly lonely in my mother's house. Tomorrow, there will be no presents to open. Nor would there be any snow on the ground. There wouldn't even be the day after tomorrow, a night of pure magic. I felt close to something without a frame. I felt again the sensation of something in me, being dark and scary and as terrifying as the experience I had, before I left for the first time for Évora, with a light bulb bursting in my room.

I was standing on the balcony, gazing at a small fraction of Rua Nova. I was waiting for Inácio, Marcus' old butler, to come and get me. I was thinking about death and life, precisely when, at that unusual moment, an ambulance came out of the hospital, from the centre of the village of Avelar, repeatedly roaring its siren. I thought it was a life that had just been born or that, for some other reason, was on its way to Coimbra Hospital. At that same amazing moment, on the Rua Nova, in the opposite direction, a funeral van had passed. And the light bulb? The light bulb went off when all that crossed paths.

Today, it was almost, almost Christmas Eve and there wasn't that magic that we find in the movies and in the enchanting stories. Nor was there anyone to tell them around the fireplace. Nor was there anyone who could decode the faces that are hidden in the flames and the names that were written there. Fire is an idea as primitive and mesmerising as the idea of family that warms us on a winter's night or chills us by its absence of fire and flame.

I woke up again and it was not yet Christmas Eve. It was just nocturnal anxiety. I had awakened once again before the next day had even considered rising. It was still a dark night outside and, equally, inside me was a dark page. I amused myself by looking at the white of the ceiling and the solid emptiness. One can easily find the phenomenon of the aftermath that has the warm awakening, in the warm bed of our lives. It is a certain imbecilic existence said in a vulgar way: so, that's it! That's life! There's nothing to be done…

I then plunged my mind into the cotton swab of sleepiness. I tried to sleep the rest of the night. I tried to numb my body in the valley of the village of Avelar with my head on an orthopaedic pillow and the body of my life somewhere parked in Évora.

I stopped moving in bed. I was projecting the film of the past, daydreaming about it. I was lying in bed in my old room in Avelar, but analytically strolling through Évora. Walking through the map of my consciousness. Venturing into the cave of the unknown like an intrepid explorer, like a more or less hesitant speleologist searching for the stalactite motif that has its indecision. Opening a door and experiencing the sensation in that room of the house. Opening another door and entering the room of that street. Enjoying that feeling of the street also being a room, both private and public.

I am walking around Évora with my mind. Although, I'm still lying down in my old room, in the Avelar valley. I'm symbolically looking back and inside the mirror of time. I keep looking in the rear-view mirror that constantly shrinks and mirrors what is seen there. I keep convincing myself that the past has no reason to exist and that it is merely a personal creation. It is something that was once realised without me realising it on the balcony of this or any other room.

Perhaps, I never really existed and never left for Évora. Nor have I ever left the valley of the village of Avelar. Maybe, Marcus is just a friend planted in the matrix of my imagination. Maybe, all this is a dream, maybe, all this is the spiral of the dream, the dream of the South.

The rain is now falling in the middle of the night. However, you can't see the rain falling on the night floor. It doesn't matter! I have in the regime of the moment, my feet warm, and knowledge is a regime that moulds my inaction into a state of hibernation. I already think about the possibility of going to Évora early. I am already thinking of leaving. Only to lose myself in the impossible sea that fits inside the ocean of the spoon, that I use to stir my mug more or less full of faith.

I am already thinking of leaving without ever reaching the promised land. I already feel the senescence of the body as something as natural as the memory that is fading. I try in vain to climb the stairway to heaven and the higher I climb, the more I get lost in it, always remaining halfway up

Until I fell asleep and Christmas Eve finally came. Soon after, the long-awaited miracle happened. I was walking again towards the Fragas de São Simão. Asking for a sign. Not, necessarily, from God. But of a greater and more sublime presence than mine. I was walking, praying for a miracle, for a last miracle in my land.

Just as I had done at Christmas last winter, or at the beginning of the first chapter. And, lo and behold, miraculously, a drop of divine water fell directly below my left eye. This may not be the great amazement that was expected. But for me, at least, it was a believable wonder that had been revealed to me. There were no clouds, no rooftops. Nor is there supposed to be a roof hidden in the sky. And lo and behold, admirably, a drop of divine water fell. Coming from above. Spilled from the mountains of the sky.

The face of the invisible one shed a single tear, the cry of his compassion. A tear from the veil of heaven fell to the face of the earth. And, behold, at last I found the fossil of the miracle I had been looking for since I went to Évora. The cave of the miracle for which I had searched so hard since my last Christmas. And from which I had already given up hoping and believing that there was still one last portent that humanity could witness, and that it could happen in my land.

The walk to the crags of São Simão was proof that only God and babies can genuinely cry. I had been blessed. I had finally witnessed the last miracle on earth, in my homeland. I felt ecstatic to experience the pill of the divine. The result of what had the heavenly form still rested on my gentile face when I walked to the Fragas, without, however, having imported a new notion, of what this stimulating pill of good and goodness really was, just as it was still undefined to me what was bad and what was evil. It just exhorted me full of joy in the pure air that I breathed. Accepting that it was part of the endorphin of the path.

My residence will henceforth be a walking grotto. It will be a path of constant self-discovery. This is the way to the furna. To the cavern where prehistoric men took refuge from danger, entertaining themselves by telling others of their adventures with dolls made on wallpaper, on which they recorded their rock paintings figures. Although the grotto is not my home, it is the way. Because the way to the cave is the cave. And my way back home is the cavern. Therefore, the path will be my only shelter.

I had a triumphant lunch just before noon. I felt one and complete. I had found a known path that led to the unknown. In walking through the midst of nature, I found my nature. In knowing the complexion of my nature, I glimpsed God. In knowing God's vision, I knew myself and recognised myself in it.

Now, I was no longer afraid of being afraid, nor did I feel anguish for not feeling exactly satiated. Anguish was a locality, which I happily passed through. Anguish or desolation was a place like Alta da Derreada, in the municipality of Pedrógão Grande, like Fato, in the parish of Aguda, in the municipality of Figueiró dos Vinhos.

Fato is a small locality that lies before the Fragas and the chapel of São Simão and the schist village of the same name that hides between the balconies of the mountain. It was when I was reading in the distance the plaque announcing the toponym of the place, that the last miracle actually took place.

Before the day is over and it is another year, and we make one complete turn of the planet earth around the sun, I recognised that the harmony of life does not consist only in having a rich diet. There has to be a balance between physical and mental and spiritual activities, there has to be an equitable restraint between work and leisure and well-deserved rest. One has to dress with the well and the good, but without excess. We must practise bodily cleanliness, as well as regularly practise cleanliness of the soul.

A little cleanliness is enough to produce a little more lightness in the cloud that occupies the sky of our spirit. Because the compass of humanity has a contradictory and averse magnetism, for those who dare to navigate beyond the cape of pleasure and the continent of pain.

It is all part of the cycle of a common breath, the breath that we are and the world we live in and the place we find ourselves in the world. When I went to bed on the last day of the year, having taken a bath in the polyban and being grateful to be alive and in good spirits and enjoying relative health, I nevertheless consented that the universe was not better or different because we were at our best and doing our best.

However, the water flowed down the drain. The hot steam increased its density, and the thermometer in my heart was hopeful about the idea of a new idea of existence. It kept me calm and serene. After all, after a storm there is always a bonanza. Of course, after the tide is calm, it doesn't always remain calm. But I had the intuition that one day the bridge for change would appear in the middle of the horizon, and I would be able to pass to the other side, the river or sea of my interior, regardless of whether today or tomorrow it would be agitated.

I will return to Évora with the agenda of a new year in my suitcase. I will take vitamins in the pharmaceutical form of pipettes. I will be a believer and I will enlarge even more the believer in me. I will continually evaluate every step and every decision. I will still run again this morning, just to continue within the underground path that leads from the aqueduct that was born in me and extends into all the seasons of today and all the seasons of tomorrow.

I'm one athlete who goes running in the middle of the atlas. I'm just another armillary athlete who goes running in an effort race, an endurance race. Running on one of the tracks of the spiral, of the dream, with or without an audience in the stadium, it doesn't matter. What matters is to keep going.

Perhaps, my mother is genuinely the athlete I will never be. A mother capable of anything, of forgiving any fault and any crime of her son. After all, mothers are the best regime the world has.

There is no weighing the good, and no weighing the evil. For those who truly believe, there is no scale for salvation, nor for damnation. Order and chaos are just a swing that goes back and forth, depending on the wave that has its own oscillation.

After the miracle and a hot bath, I argued with my mother. It was six o'clock. The day died there. I still felt one, but now there was another part, in me, that felt divided. Was it too late to have witnessed the miracle? Probably the path of penance would not redeem the sins of my soul.

But I had been blessed, I had witnessed that little portent that occurred in the middle of the afternoon. A prodigy that no one could see and that no one would therefore know, except me, of the nature of God's touching my face.

I now recognised my new physiognomy in front of the broken mirror hanging crookedly in the bathroom of the old house. On my face, that powerful evidence had been left. A small crater had been left, after the protruding meteorite of God had fallen from the sky. After all, miracles still exist. Although, it is increasingly rare for men of flesh and blood to be able to prove the existence of something higher than their morality, whether it is equal to or higher than that of the angels, or the uncreated, who are in contact with something greater than themselves.

Everything is composed with a moral form, without, yet, being able to read at the end, how this objective morality acts in concrete. That's what the miracle told me. Thus, the importance of Marcus' ethics, which he alone will continue to profess, is lost on me. Blindly, believing, both in the morality of man, and in the moral end that will have the history of humanity.

Before, yet another departure to Évora, I stayed overnight in the old house that my mother inherited and that, possibly later, would be part of my brother's inheritance. There was a round moon in the unusual sky that night, after a day that had been almost perfect.

It had been a day with a blameless morning, which had been dressed with a sudden afternoon of fog. It seemed that it had never happened, an afternoon of foggy incomprehension, that lasted an entire day. And that no day contained a total understanding that would usually take a lifetime to achieve.

It was certainly an unusual moon, on a rare winter's night. I stood for a few minutes under the cold night sky, under the canopy and branches of the splendorous tree of truth that stands by the gate of the old house, when my flesh body felt humbled by my spirit body.

The next morning, the doubt signal began to vibrate stridently. While I waited for my mother and her delay, I thought I would not be able to catch the bus and feared I would not be able to start a new life in Évora. I gave in to temptation! I believed that it was too late and that I would not be able to catch the bus that would take me to my new life in the South of Portugal, in a sort of new world.

Despite my mother's delay I arrived on time. When the bus was already on its way. The bus driver realised it, and waited for me. He stopped the bus and I got on it. However, when I got on and sat down, I thought it was already too late to start a new life in Évora. When I got on the bus it was as if I had left my old world without one having yet been created.

Before arriving in the Nossa Senhora da Saúde neighbourhood I hatched a plan. I decided to move to the annex. I would be separated from João and Nilson by a yard. This would be enough distance for me to get away from the lives they led. I stopped by the mini-market where the landlady had her business, and she promptly approved my far-fetched plan.

My renewal was a strange idea and too abstract for the mechanical universe in which Nilson's jagged life rotated. João, on one hand, was too excited to wonder about my transformation. But I immediately renounced the world of the domestic trinity and my previous mundane life. João went to his room soon after with Catarina, and Nilson was buried in the comfort of the living room couch, and I headed for the annex, where my body cooled, hibernating, in the early evening.

***

On the 17th I dreamt about the current Portuguese prime minister, Pedro Passos Coelho, and my mother cutting his hair. This episode of Morpheus was recorded for me when I woke up. Perhaps, I subconsciously thought that I should incorporate the prime minister's austerity policy into my life. It would serve me not to fight Portugal's economic crisis, but to neutralise the crisis in my soul and spirit.

For now, I had to put to sleep the scenario of an increasingly global Portugal that ignored local people. What mattered to me now was to overcome the imposition of my own troika and enforce only that which was my will. Perhaps, my new belief was an unnecessarily fundamentalist strictness. After all, to be free, is to infringe our own constitution.

In the last event of my dream, I was pleading with an officer to let me stay in the army. I would do so, after having passed him over. Choosing, rather, to go to university. Basically, it was what I had decided during my waking state. Perhaps the dream indicated to me that it would have been better to choose exactly the opposite. But now I could not go back. What I could do was regress. If that was not possible for me, then I could only accept it and move on.

Clarice joined me at the university bar. As usual, she was impeccably prepared for the day ahead. More than I would have been able to experience today. She was from another era. She was a woman dissenting from women's catholicism, let's say, she was a protestant, because she didn't stop believing in the role and importance of valuing women, but she didn't want to stop being a woman to pass on something else.

When she sat down at my table, I couldn't help but notice that she had the same body as the abstract concept of rigour that I had dreamt in my dream about the former prime minister. Clarice, everything she thought, was a conclusion of what she had read and reflected on, what she had lived and experienced, and probably also what she had dreamt.

"Simão, I strongly advise you to look for a way to make money writing! You should try practical things. You have to know what you are writing about. And you must know how to write for which reader will read you. You must not do anything that does not have a goal, a purpose. It is extremely important that you make money from your writing! Consider money with the potential that only it offers."

I listened to her, intently. She was not a second mother. However, she was a different kind of parent.

"Basically, being creative is not to repeat formulas, or forms that already exist… Don't forget Simão! You have to know what the boss wants. Writing is not enough. You are only completely free when you know what is part of the text frame. It is important to know how to distinguish what is relevant to be in the picture and what is not at all capital to be in it. It is not enough to dump things into the form that has your vision. It takes method! It takes a register! That's the only way, that's the only way to be completely free and creative. Simão must ask himself: What is my register? What is my method?"

Then, assertively wiping the corners of her mouth, she shot back with more emphasis, "Test your limits. If you don't, you will never know who you really are. You will always be thinking about what you could have been, instead of trying to be…to have a method is not to tumble forward. Pursue every inquiry and every clue you find on your path. Look at new frames, formulate new shapes within yourself. Design not only the frame of a thought, but inaugurate the whole picture that has the revelation of what is, as a rule, beyond our gaze. Simão! Ask yourself: where do I insert myself? Do you see how it is?"

Promptly, I wrote in my diary her prescription: "Tony Judt, *Thinking The Twentieth Century*; Edições 70; Lisbon, 2013." Stating still categorically, "Read it, Simão! We must discover the treaty of our dissatisfactions. We can't go on living like this. We can't."

She left, shortly afterwards. Before getting up, in a tone halfway to apocalyptic, she commented that our cognitive models were broken and that contemporary history was a tragic page in human history.

Clarice was someone who was fully functional and definitely integrated into society. Marcus, no. He was definitely no longer that someone. He had once been a promising medical student, then the bright promise of architecture in Portugal, only to ultimately delude himself that he could stay locked up in his maternal grandparents' mansion, studying biology or palaeontology, and in between, play on the black and white keys of his grand piano. Where there is no room for any grey tone or for any tone that contains any other colour.

Thinking and believing that a few hobbies and crusades, for one knowledge or another, would be enough to provide him with all the action and all the source of a life, which would neither quench his thirst nor quench the ambition of his poor knowledge of who we are in this world so full and so abundant with illusion.

Clarice went to give a lecture. I had no lecture to give. It was four pm when I went, by mere chance, to the small auditorium of the Espírito Santo. The conference was being held—*The Academies of the Future in the twenty-first century*. I entered, driven by the propeller that was the engine of my curiosity. I sat in the audience. They were talking about sustainability and social insertion.

They were also talking about selfishness and about one or another concept that they themselves considered to be unacademic.

Skittering from the chair, in one of the first rows, was Belchior. I hadn't seen him since he insisted on offering me a book that was required reading in my course—Theory of Literature. This happened when I no longer lived at the Ponte de Ferro residence. I was living with Vânia Velez and Mariana, André Monte's and Mário Silva's girlfriends, both of whom were my former housemates and were still living there. Although, we all spent most of the time at the house of Maria de Fátima.

I used my old student residence, Ponte de Ferro, at that time, basically for washing clothes. It was during this period that I met Belchior Barreto. Who was now occupying, coincidentally or not, my old room, sharing it with my former roommate, Jacinto Jesus, known also as Lagos. Belchior, inexplicably, insisted on giving me that book. Possibly, it was cursed and he just wanted to get rid of it as soon as possible.

I accepted his gift, thinking he would promptly shut up. But he continued to talk at length about the specific nothing he had to tell me. I learned that he studied psychology. Little else did I learn. Also, we never saw each other again. Nor have we ever crossed paths since.

After the concepts of the new academy were lined up and gifts and souvenirs were thrown to the audience, the speakers continued to sell the conference with questions and answers. But what I wanted to know was how I could belong to an academy of the future, now, in the present. Except that the community of knowledge, it turned out, would not be assembled, right now. Neither in the acuity of tomorrow, nor in the transformation of the day after tomorrow. Only in the long after the long day after tomorrow.

No, it would not be for today! The academy of the future would be progressively caught up with the society of now, but only much later. Initially, I was tempted by that integration discourse. But there, supposedly, were the new holistic professors of the academy of the future, all hired by the same university of the past.

After all, the search for cooperation and knowledge sharing in the community by the Academy of Tomorrow lies in the same meanders and corridors as the university of yesterday. They are part of the same network reason, so that today's community is not yet enrolled in tomorrow's society. And eventually, it will be today's students in yesterday's university, who will be the future teachers of that future community academy? The one that will only bloom long, long after tomorrow if it doesn't wither next weekend?

At the end of the conference, without me asking him, I learned from Belchior Barreto himself that he had given up his degree in psychology and that, in the meantime, he had gone to spend a season with his girlfriend in Serra da Estrela. They had both worked in an association that helped children with adaptation difficulties. The conversation would end with him admitting that he had quickly grown tired of the experience.

I left the university uncertain about what was next for my non-existence. Simply put, after not existing, the next step would be to give up? To cease altogether? Would I sooner or later be forced to exist?

I went to the Espírito Santo library in search of more knowledge, but could not find it there in book form. I then went to the students association. There I wandered, once again, with the mere chance by which I followed the path of my day. I followed only the shadow of my non-existentialist intuition. However, it was not the shadow of a feeling of mine, it was, technically, something else. Accordingly with, the scholar, my friend, Daniel Filipe Mansilha.

Of whom I will speak very little or rarely…not because life is this or that, but because the narrative has been arranged precisely like this… And it was thus, also by mere chance, that I enrolled in taekwondo, beginning to practise the sport. Nonetheless, I resolutely maintain my hesitation, which contemplates my academic life as an indecisive student.

In the evening, I went to the Polo dos Leões to see Harold Pinter's play 'The Lover.' Played by Tomás Porto and Madalena Figueiredo, students of the theatre course. I sat distrustful and uncomfortable in the silence and solitude of the dark room and felt terribly alone in the middle of the audience. After the play I went home and swore I would never go to the theatre again.

The next morning when I woke up the first task I had was to reflect on why I had dreamt that I was running alone on the sand in last night's dream. João and Nilson were sitting on beach chairs. They were fraternising by the shore with drinks and were asking me, begging me, to stop running and join them. Something about the dream was a clear evocation of the landscape of my last summer. I also dreamt that I was reconciled with Débora. She was crying. She cried exaggeratedly.

If the dream embodied the fulfilment of a wish, there was something disconnected between me and my dream, because my wish was to never meet

Débora again, or any other Débora in the future. Probably, what we dream is contradictory to what we really feel.

Before I got out of bed and put my feet on the ground that was my reality, I concluded that true change is an internal journey. Being, inevitably, a consequence. A consequence of the world we live in…where not a single state of permanence resists it. What persists is a certain longevity in the stage of our consciousness. We only remain, ourselves, when we consistently inhabit the incongruity that our understanding of time has. Only then do we have the vain understanding of what remains unchanged in every change of house and every change of season and every small change, which aims to alter our opinion, be that change less slight or more profound.

We randomly take a book off the shelf without opening the window of our gaze. We choose so so. We decide, not to decide. We give up choosing. We choose not to choose.

Not to choose is also a decision. However, clear indecision.

We are almost, almost, at the end of the February fog, and our protagonist has fallen deeply asleep. His existence or non-existence has hibernated. Since the month of January. Yesterday, he remained indifferent, and, today, when he awoke from the March thaw, he no longer took any vials of hope. Inadaptation is a matter exclusive to souls living in hibernation, as is, perhaps, the case of our protagonist. Belchior Barreto's attention deficit, Nilson's indifference are another regime. Or, perhaps, not!

Are the Indigo Children mentioned at the Future Academies conference so different from the others? Are the children of each generation special? Or are the bambinos of the underprivileged generation no more and no less special than all the others? Is our protagonist's generation just another generation more or less in trouble? And, therefore, more or less resourceful? Or are we already in the millennium generation? Is this an even more indignant generation? Are the sons and daughters of Belchior Barreto as indignant as their father? Will Nilson be a father as resigned as the non-conformity of his generation?

At the end of January, when our main character returned to Avelar he met his friend Marcus. Marcus who denied more and more categorically that he could even think one day of changing his routine or the absence of it. At that time a trip to the usual cafe or a stroll through the usual places with Marcus was an act of penance, for those like our protagonist who were allowed to accompany him.

In the middle of January 2013, they had dinner at the Terrabela restaurant. It was a traditional restaurant and cafe in the town of Figueiró dos Vinhos, which they often revisited Two or three years after our hero went to study at the Espírito Santo College, the owner closed his establishment. Because since the crisis in Portugal was implemented, he could no longer put up with the government's misrule, nor the government of a world increasingly in crisis. He only sporadically opened his establishment to wealthy clients who secretly requested his services.

It was after the wonderful meal that Marcus unexpectedly presented his friend with a silver letter opener. Usually, Marcus would offer his loyal friend, at an absolutely unusual moment, what was already an expected gift. This veiled moment happened at the invariable interval of two years.

The first was a cavalry officer's sword; the second gift was a pipe made in a vat, carved in wood; the third was an ancient esoteric book, which had been miraculously saved from the fire that would destroy the impressive library of Alexandria. But half of the pages of the book had been torn out by Marcus himself, who insisted that his friend was not yet ready for the doctrines and practices described there.

They would end the evening discussing the subject of Inácio. Both agreed that he had reached an expressive age and that he still retained unique characteristics that made him someone much more than an ordinary butler. Let's not forget that he was, in fact, much more than that.

Marcus suggested that the end of the one who had been his preceptor from childhood to late adolescence, and who was still his instructor and advisor in adulthood, as well as his gardener and driver, and, of course, his butler, served to bring Marcus even closer to his first end. Affirming himself, that Inácio death would also be part of the great waiting that he had only to look forward to.

Marcus' abstract intelligence had no place in his friend's more practical world. That, after having witnessed the miracle and the sign of doubt having grown in him, meant that at that moment he was not interested enough in listening to Marcus, as was always the case.

Surprisingly, Marcus had spent his last months tutoring in maths, chemistry, geology, history, and one or another foreign language when he was in a good mood. All of his students were students who conformed to a certain standard. He *confessed that he was fed up with so much exposition…and that he gave tutorings only, and only, to instil something in this generation.*

He complained, however, that this generation did not want to accept the scrolls of Marcus de Monsalude e Matalonga. He refused to give his lessons in the mansion, and mostly it was Inácio, his old butler, who drove him to each student's house. Simply because Marcus didn't like to drive: neither to the nearest big cities, nor to places that were far away from the municipality of Figueiró dos Vinhos.

Our protagonist would meanwhile return to Évora and Marcus Matalonga would continue to pursue his strange way of life. Until he and his way of life extinguished him. Dying one day by the way he constantly refused to exist—never existing. Only, resisting in the trenches of his world, in which he lived practically alone. The meeting between the two friends took place at the end of January. We are now at the end of the second month, more precisely, in the foggy February of the year 2013.

***

I woke up today inexplicably remembering the main course of the dream, with newborn felines, that I had on January 11 of this year 2013. There is something very disturbing about dreaming of such small cubs. The house where I was in the dream was stuffed with cats. In fact, there were not only felines there. But my brother, my mother and stepfather were there, and also other people I didn't know. Only one of the kittens had white fur, and only one was resurrected in my dream. All the others, ominously, withered away after being born.

What made an even greater impression on me. It was that when I woke up that morning of January 11, I instinctively associated the little cub with my little brother. It was possibly a kind of metadream. Because in the subsequent sequence of this dream episode with the cubs, I saw through the reflection of a mirror, someone coming out of the shower, wrapped in a towel.

I could not see if it was me, or if it was someone else who appeared reflected in the mirror of my dream. This me or this someone was surely the more or less unconscious digestion of that moment when Catarina stared at me after seeing me coming out of the shower naked, with the towel wrapped around my waist.

I still, nevertheless, do not connect with why I dreamt of the replica of that previous moment, having included in it my dear little brother. Who is a blond angel, innocent of the sin of the world and of the sin of his older brother, who will surely be condemned for all the sin he has generated with his passage through the world.

Somewhere in me, somewhere in the space of my meditation, in the annex of my existence, in the lunch break or in the break of another meal, somewhere on the bridge that is somewhere, lies the passage to the other side of the world and to another world.

The end may not be a definite conclusion, it may only be the middle, the centre of everything that leads us to believe that it is still possible to reach the other side of the bridge in this life. Perhaps, one day, I will be able to prove this opinion of mine and realise that after all, there is always a plank of salvation in the middle, even if it is at the very edge of the end.

After I moved into the annex, João moved into my old bedroom. Confessing that he now felt he had more privacy.

I don't know if my move to the annex will count as one more, in my already long list of my many house moves. Perhaps, after finding the meaning of the Southern dream, I can steer the ship of my soul and return home one day. Perhaps, I will never truly return home. Perhaps, I will never find the south of my dream! And I will spend the rest of my time, orbiting back and forth. When we are born, the subject of returning home is a reminiscence that we understand, without having to have read Plato once. However, the more we grow up, the more we forget and let the subject die.

Earthly time passes so quickly that it is rarely possible to measure the sense of the segment of time we live in, just as it is equally difficult to account for the entire stretch of time we do not live in. But there is no exact definition for the time of each life when lived and when not truly experienced.

I got up at six o'clock in the morning. The cold of dawn embraced me with the feeling of the unprecedented repetition of yesterday's cold. We repeat ourselves to improve ourselves. We affirm that tomorrow will be as good as today, even if the translation that the interpreter makes only for us doesn't make sense.

My feet were cold and I had the perception that the same day is reproduced every day, or that something in me is repeating itself and continually resonating.

I woke up today startled by the man inside the bear's belly coming out of his hibernation state. My heart is trembling. Beating with a louder tone, for I am this man who, having awakened only now in march, had consequently missed a very important appointment with destiny.

It was an earthquake felt in my spirit. Perhaps, it was a forewarning, of a great seismic tremor that would be strongly felt by me later and that something astral would be impossible to achieve in this my carnal life. All I could aim to be, at present, was to be the arrow that was shot unluckily and hit, unfortunately, in this age. But which aimed at another era. This existence that I currently live will serve only as a refinement. So, it won't hurt, if I, at times, am an imperfect being. I just have to keep trying to be someone not so unfinished.

I woke up, today, at six in the morning. But my senses remain slightly dulled in the afternoon. Just like, a sleeping beauty who after the kiss of Prince Charming, continues to sleep indifferently.

It was after the Carnival vacations that I dreamt about the number three. It is one of the dreams that I keep repeating. As for the miracle that happened in my hometown, lately it has not repeated echoes of faith in me. I believe that it is natural to expect that every day the miracle that was once experienced will be repeated. No matter how much we fail to catch up with what or who it was that passed by in the course of our existence.

In fact, no matter how much I stubbornly believe that I am following the course of my life, it goes on regardless of my will, making its own path. No one can cheat the river of life! Only we can let ourselves be fooled. Only we! Only we can stop fooling ourselves, stop self-sabotaging and self-creeping. And, not only ourselves! But also others.

When I tidied up the drawers of my chaos, my new world had only one room. My whole life fits in the annex. By the time I finished putting the files in order on the shelf of my mind, it was March and I got the feeling that I had overslept.

***

I dreamt that I made love. When I woke up, I immediately tried to find my way back to the dream. Then, gurgling my way back, I left the annex of my unconscious and dived into the ocean of reality. Swimming from the annex where I was sleeping to Atlantis parked in the back of the main house.

In the middle of the day, I went to the university. I met with the Master in his office. After the maxim "those who search for truth do not always find happiness" had been memorised and thus ended his lesson, the Master revealed to me that before he got married and his children were born, he lived on the same street where I live now.

It was with great joy that Master recalled how strong the sun was beating down on the beams of the attic where he had lived during that hot summer, which he now recalled with great satisfaction. He remembered when he had to correct his exams on the balcony. Because it was unbearable to work during the day inside his residence.

The Master who was sometimes quite emotional, could also be rational. Absolutely rational. Such as when he told me, afterwards, that all that effort to live in less comfortable conditions not only accompanied him in the first years of his profession, but also promoted the success he would later obtain in his career as a full professor.

The month of March has long since begun on the fiction calendar I have hung on the wall. I have awakened, finally, from my state of hibernation. And, there is no other world more suitable, otherwise, I would have woken up in it.

When I woke up today, everything was clearly zoomed in on another distorted day. Anyway, to believe in miracles one must have faith. Who used to say that, once in a while, was my friend Francisco. He was the one who said that miracles cannot happen for those without faith. Therefore, for those who lose their faith, as I did, miracles disappear with the fog of memory of January and February, and it is as if that divine wonder of December last year never happened.

Meanwhile, my hair has grown so long that the root of my spirit was divided between the scalp of my discipline and the ends and the strands that fly with the freedom of the wind. Those like me who search for a moment of happiness cannot find it in just one truth. Yes, the Master is right. A house needs people, carefree happy people. Like Nilson, who is a person who dares to be simply happy, like João, who has in Catarina fountain the water of his happiness.

I live, now, alone, in an annex. I reside only with the satisfaction that has the company of my discipline. Which carries me with it through a freedom, where no one can want to understand me or even want to follow. My freedom does not accept that I am free. It is an asceticism without humanity. Perhaps, all asceticism is inhuman.

My move to the annex, created yet another wall of mass separation, between me and the space occupied by Nilson on the living room couch and the space occupied by João and Catarina in the main house. Nothing else is the same after reaching the end of a state of hibernation. We roll on a board like pieces with no direction and no destination. However, the destination and direction that a pawn takes is different from the destination and direction that a king captures, or, the direction and destination that the knight will take, or, finally, that the bishop has already taken.

Before I fell asleep again, I lit scented candles and made promises in vain. I closed my eyes and climbed a staircase without a handrail. The stairs led into a sphere of a world, where there were no more steps and where nothing could be seen but the blanket of darkness. And so it was that I fell asleep once again.

We always fall asleep, not knowing if we close our eyes forever or if we temporarily close the window of our gaze, to open another form of projection? After all, where do we go after we have not lived? Do we go to Malevich's black square? Which is so deep and so superficial that we can no longer see the colour that the art of living really has?

I slept all day and woke up with a debt greater than the debt of existing or not existing. I tidied up the expectation of my room again. The tidiness of my personal space offered me an instant sense of peace and mental tidiness. As I left the annex, I passed through the courtyard. I headed toward the back of Atlantis.

I entered the house and crossed the kitchen desert. I crossed the hemisphere of the living room and reached the hallway and opened the front door. Reaching, finally, the neighbourhood of Nossa Senhora da Saúde. Verifying that there was no longer any sun. Only, some clouds of cotton wool, levitated across the street, which was on the other side of the world.

When I closed the front door and went back inside the house, I assumed I had fulfilled my strict itinerary of exercises, workouts, diets, and now, in the late afternoon I didn't know what else to do but drink. I couldn't predict the weather of what was coming next. I couldn't read or interpret what was obviously going to happen immediately after I got drunk so quickly. Even the globe was moving, with me standing still.

I went with Nilson to the supermarket and got ready for the month. I bought two doses of quick contentment and bought yet another portion of indifference, shaped like an acorn, and didn't pay part of the rent. Nilson invited me to have dinner with him and Ricardo, his co-worker. Ricardo enjoyed my company, and Nilson greatly appreciated that Ricardo approved of my presence. This is how the world proceeds. Approving the social contract of the collective or rejecting the contact of one individual in favour of another.

Dinner was a simple *bitoque*. No fancy cutlery, no fancy napkins to wipe my mouth. Then we headed to Viana do Alentejo. To the bar owned by Ricardo's friends. We watched the rest of the night pass us by hesitantly. Without me thinking afterwards if the hesitation is ours or the others around us.

I erased in me that idea of Marcus, who invariably insisted on telling me that Christ was the way. I incarnated instead the image of a commercialised Christ. With his sacred heart burning perpetually forever. I felt in me, this cross of fire, burning, on earth as well as in the sky of Viana do Alentejo. Seen, possibly, from the top of a hill. No one would do, however, anything which would extinguish that or any orchard. Pontius Pilate, too, washed his hands. Solomon, possibly, would let the rest burn, because what no longer burns, can no longer scorch us.

It wasn't a new world, but it was a new Alentejo that I rediscovered in Viana do Alentejo. Nilson and Ricardo carried me on the litter of a profane tour, which for that very reason did not include the passage of our procession through the Church of Our Lady of Aires. But it did include a secret passage through some automobile repair shops, where I would taste a few portions of the local carnal gastronomy.

There, private parties were held. No one at this pagan-type party knew who was who. The locals participated with the outsiders in a bizarre dance extravagantly in popular taste. But with a touch of strange and exotic tone. As if folklore and electronic music were their spoonful of refinement.

A funaná played on the car stereos of high-end cars, instead of waltz number two from Shostakovich's jazz suite. Women in short dresses shook their hips provocatively. Not caring about the graphic content of the posters hanging on the walls of each workshop. They paraded unencumbered by the nuts and bolts and the oil spilled from the cars.

I stuck my head in one of Nilson's straw hats, and put on Ricardo's sunglasses to protect my spirit's eyes from the light that the darkness of the night was casting. My soul metamorphosed in that instant into the soul of a clown, who had once deceived his shadow and was now running toward a destiny from which there was no escape.

After the rally through Viana's repair shops, we sailed with Ricardo's entourage of argonauts friends, orbiting through Viana's starlit night to the bar, where the owner was also a friend and cousin of Ricardo. We went through the rest of Viana's night guided by the light of the stars. Burning with the last glow of their lives, when others die shining brightly for showing us the way to Santiago.

It was after three in the morning and the bar was still open. But now it was just for us; Ricardo's friends and cousins. The owner of the bar drank with us and ordered endless more rounds. It was Barnabé, Barnabé Moisés! Now, Ricardo's friends and cousins are everywhere. Some play darts, even if they have to go to work the next day at the sawmill or in construction. Others are coppersmiths and they talk as they think. Others are mechanics and argue among themselves about who has more strength to tighten the loose nuts left over from yesterday's morality.

Some neither study nor work. They are too young to be anything or anyone. Ricardo's friends are now my friends too. Including the beer distributor, who lives at his grandparents' house and is sitting on my right side. On the other side is another friend and cousin of Ricardo's, who I don't know the name. What I do know is that tomorrow, all three of us will be crucified by the hangover the next day. Amen!

Chapter 6
Scholarship

(April to May 2013)

I was cooped up in the boredom of my annex when I got the news that I was going to get a scholarship for the second time. I found out yesterday. During my birthday. I was also informed that the overdue amount would be immediately paid to me in a single transaction. Soon after, I talked about the poisoned gift with Zé Nilson and Zé Ricardo. I vaguely informed them of the misfortune I anticipated would happen, for agreeing to receive this long-awaited treat, which did not come from Marcus. I explained to them, allegorically, that the globe of my world could be turned upside down by turning the sea of heaven and that I could therefore go to the bottom. However, they didn't understand anything I was telling them.

 I decided to go to the barber on 5 de Outubro Street. He did me the courtesy of cutting my hair very short and shaving my beard. When I arrived in the neighbourhood no one recognised me. Catarina needed to look at me twice. I was amazingly another me in her eyes. Only, because I now had a haircut, a clean face, and money rolled up in my coat pocket.

 Plus, I had my electrifying, contagious energy and my good manners, which always seduced the most sophisticated women, as well as distinguished acquaintances, old hoodlums. and other cronies from the street. And then there were my immoral, classroom-less professors and brilliant, illiterate students that I met by a magnet of chance, and then there were people, absolutely unusual people, and people, simply decadent people. Wonderfully, decadent.

 Now I couldn't sleep. There is an hour in the early morning when most of the world goes to sleep, another part can find no place to lay its head. That other part, just wants to fly in circles and drive quickly to an unknown canyon that ends with a slow dawn. However, in the end, the magic of that beautiful dawn suddenly disappears. Never knowing whether we lived in darkness or whether we came out of it when the mists of the morning dawn were lost. Because, after the dawn breaks, the sun tears the cover of the book that had the image of heaven and of our salvation.

When the sun rises, half the world falls asleep in its vampire coffin or cardboard box. While, another half of the world gets up to go to work. Still a third or less of that will remain awake, after the sun rises. Being that small group unable to sleep for two or three days. Ceasing to realise what it was that they chased so nonchalantly and so interestedly, before the arms of the last aurora collapse them, and, finally, cradle them against their breast.

This was specifically the moment when I was to commit to my little world and spin with it. But, no sphere of the globe gives us the feeling of greatness, when we want to grab it by force. I have a simple mission: to finish my degree. Still, there is something inside me that yearns for more than completing a degree. A part of me wants to take another course, a part of me wants to follow the course of another river, a river that can both drown me with its current and save me from my own abyss. In the end, dying may not be just an end. Yes, dying, just like living, may be just another means to reach the truth of what the meaning is.

Me and Zé Nilson are spending more and more time together. Zé João is busy with his internship. Catarina comes and goes, while the sun rises and sets. Both are watches. One is probably an accessory, the other, eventually, is not only essential, but indispensable, both for me and for Zé João.

I am watching my classes and the days of others who pass by me running. I go regularly to the university pavilion, temporarily transformed into a dojo, and I also go from time to time, with Zé Nilson, to look at the picturesque paintings of the Brazilian women who serve at the counter and at the tables. For Nilson, it is part of his routine. But for me it is like going to a museum on a field trip, where the mechanics are served and the women serve by seducing.

There is no second moment like that indefinite instant when there are no words, only ecstasy and a kind of pure rapture, which one feels only during the first time, when one experiences something unheard of, something naively new. In a second moment, I always have money in my pocket and a credit card full of confidence. And, there is no second moment to create a good first impression. As Marcus would tell me. Unaware, completely, of this or any other, completely, immoral, moment of mine.

During that second moment, I didn't slow down to think. I went to the working girls with Zé Nilson. Not really knowing what was going to happen there. Feeling, promptly, sorry for the price to be paid. Not only did I regret the price I would pay later, but I also regretted the price to be paid, only to have a woman with bleached or oxygenated blonde hair sit on top of me, talking about the tattoo she got five years ago. When she was not yet forty-five. Even the act of carefully washing my foreskin didn't excite me. She put a condom on me as if she had been doing that all her life. I didn't feel special because she told me about her son who was studying at the University of Porto almost the same age as I.

As I listened to her, I kept thinking that I should have gone with her Brazilian colleague instead. Who was taller than the Eiffel tower. In fact, Zé Nilson recommended that I go with her. He told me that he had tested it and that it was good. At first, I thought he was talking about a car engine. I would have been better off spending all that scholarship money on jelly beans or something else that wouldn't taste so bitter in the end. Even when she kissed me on the cheek, saying goodbye, she couldn't convince me that I wasn't the whore.

Zé Nilson religiously goes every other week to visit his parents, just as he goes, at least every other week, to visit the nuns at the Alcáçovas convent. Sometimes he goes weekly, regardless of the fact that Cátia Vanessa often comes around the neighbourhood of Nossa Senhora da Saúde to rub her body on Zé Nilson's single bed. However, this doesn't change the discipline he has in his routine.

Nevertheless, Catarina's project to make Zé Nilson and Cátia Vanessa, a couple, has won. Because, after a second or third home date, Zé Nilson would sleep with Cátia Vanessa. Being lovingly drunk—which for the young nursing student looking for love and lovemaking, was not a problem at all. He was tall and his appearance provided more than enough indication that he would protect her for life.

In the meantime, I made the belt change. After my taekwondo graduation, I was left with the feeling that I still had a long way to go. It was still just the colour that was the beginning of what we hastily thought was already the middle arch. Because, supposedly, beyond the middle are the intricacies of the outcome of everything that happens. However, one day, at a certain or undetermined moment, before I reach the middle of my expedition, I will have to decide who I really am and I will have to choose definitively how I want to spend the rest of my time and with whom I want to share it.

During that martial moment, when I dropped my old skin and not only changed the way I feel, but also changed the colour of my belt, Zé Nilson told me bluntly that he didn't like Cátia Vanessa. He looked to me for advice. And I told him that he should be a man and tell her so. I added something like: "a man should never cheat on a woman." In the end, Zé Nilson followed the committee of my moralism. He confessed to Cátia Vanessa that he hadn't fallen in love with her after all.

But two weeks later, he repented. And he declared himself to Cátia Vanessa. Asserting that it was really love after all, and that he had been wrong before. However, my counselling proved to be tremendously helpful. My advice made Cátia Vanessa think that Zé Nilson, besides being a mechanic, was a gentleman who respected women. In the end, everything turned out well.

After sleeping with Cátia Vanessa on Mondays, Zé Nilson went to visit the ladies in Alcáçovas in the middle of the week. Almost always on Wednesdays. He continued, perhaps also, to fly, every other week, to his parents' house, returning with his clothes ironed and some meals already prepared.

Before Zé Nilson went to repair his car in the workshop that his colleague, Zé Joaquim, had at his parents' hill, and before I went with him, he had told me that one day he would take me with him to visit the place where he was born, as well as to meet the friends he had had since childhood.

But…an hour later, his car was in the elevator and I was sitting in the back seat, too, in suspension. Zé Joaquim and Zé Nilson were changing parts in the car and I was getting drunk. Zé Joaquim would stretch his arm out the window to pour me another drink and I would ask him: "Are we there yet?" For Zé Nilson, my behaviour was directly embarrassing him. It was as if he and Zé Joaquim and all the Zés of this world were always more sober and more serious than me; and that only I, only I, would be capable of making a fool of myself.

I took another sip to make myself laugh at what wasn't funny at all. Zé Joaquim wanted me in his workshop, as Zé Simão or Master Zé Simão. He didn't want me to be me! He just wanted a clown with or without face paint or someone who would wear the mask of a comedian. They, who called themselves Zé or Master Something, were not masters of anything. They weren't even masters of their own fate.

But I, I, was the clown, perversely, drunk, on top of the repair elevator, making a fool of myself. I was the clown with no paint on his face who opened the back seat window and stuck his head out. As if I was feeling the wind and the car was moving. And there was no one behind the wheel feeding the delirious dream that had that speeding trip of mine through the landscape in the garage of that reality of mine. And yet, the car was snaking along the wrong side, the more errant side of the lane. Going further and further south and I was increasingly losing my north. Leaving behind the Southern dream. And, it was zigzagging and staggering that I got out when I had to jump out of the car.

Later, at home, in the living room, Nilson told me, very gently, that he would no longer be able to take me on a weekend to his parents' home in Mação. The fear he had gained and the possible consequences of taking me with him now spoke louder than his compassion and brotherly love for a clown he was more or less friends with in the second moment, which divides this chapter with the title Our Lady of Health.

Because the third moment is 68 kilos. It included at least one holiday, more money in my pocket than saved in the bank, and excellent physical shape. Also, it included not being able to go to Nilson's parents' house next weekend, but being allowed to ride in the passenger seat, now, next to him. With Zé Nilson going full speed and driving professionally drunk. Making curves and straight lines on the go. Listening to his funaná or a repertoire that ranged from popular taste to electronic music.

He was going to work in the morning, after a few hours of rest. Me? I couldn't fall asleep that easily. However, I was going to class. But the next day, the trip made the day before yesterday no longer had the adrenaline of the trip I was trying to find today. The adrenaline of the trip that was made the day before yesterday and that was repeated, in the meantime, also yesterday and today, was increasingly lacking.

It is in a third moment that he spends much of his time at the Cafe Atlântico. Emptying what money he still has in his pocket. Stupidly trying to save his doses of euphoria and lethargy. His mother still helps him with his school fees. Unaware that he has received a scholarship for the second time. Essentially, the third moment is an out-of-control car proceeding with him in the back seat, being driven by someone else, going in the wrong direction.

Today he went jogging for two hours and drank until it was dawn, without, however, managing to get drunk. The owner of the cafe, João Paulino, opened the secret door for him, after he said abracadabra or some equivalent password. Joining João Paulino's friends club, which includes: João Paulino's brother-in-law, the butcher that owns his butchery shop and the fishmonger in the neighbourhood, the owner of the supermarket chain, the plumber who has no front teeth and many other friends and acquaintances, most of whom either live in the neighbourhood of Nossa Senhora da Saúde or lived there.

It was João Paulino's wife who drew his attention to that customer who was so polite. If his wife hadn't noticed him, João Paulino probably would never have invited him to his club of friends. Even, Simão would have preferred to continue drinking coffee at the cafe and reading his newspaper there. Without ever knowing what really happens beyond the secret door.

In a third moment our protagonist attends the path and the way of the last living poet, whose teaching could be summed up as—be too free and the wings of your freedom will cause your soul to overflow and fall into an abyss. But before the chaos and him falling into a precipice, he was accepted in the Atlântico club and cafe. Moreover, he was esteemed and respected by all and welcomed in any house, corner or street of the neighbourhood. The neighbourhood became his home and his second university. Meanwhile, João Paulino became a friend, as well as his brother-in-law.

João Paulino's brother-in-law had been a father exactly one month ago, and now, there the three of them were. Extending alkaloid, natural, crystalline conversations. Both talking too fast to understand the nature of their excitement. Two minutes ago, they had gone to buy just one more gram from a policeman who was a friend of the club. João Paulino's brother-in-law paid for it. The night comes and goes and João Paulino's brother-in-law doesn't go home to his young wife and newborn daughter.

The night comes and goes and our protagonist aspires to another line of complicity, but when he gets home, he will be alone. He will plunge into the despair that there is nothing else to do next. If not, try to sleep and not succeed. The night comes and goes and João Paulino's brother-in-law won't go home. But he will go to work in the morning at the office, at the company, which for some decency and delicacy, the name will not be mentioned, by me.

In a fourth moment will be his successive trips to Lisbon. He often goes to the capital. One doesn't know concretely, nor exactly why. He will return immediately, soon after, to Évora. For not being able to stay long in the dullness of Lisbon. However, he will get even more bored once he returns to Alentejo.

Usually, after one of those trips to Lisbon, when he arrived in Évora, he would cross the cable to the Cafe Atlântico, before returning home. In one of these moments, João Paulino idealised a future, in which our Simão Pinheiro would live his writing life to the full. He spoke as if he knew who he really was. He talked about a big house on a hill, in which he projected our protagonist, writing his work.

João Paulino even confessed to him that his father-in-law had a carcinoma. However, this did not move him as much as it moved him that João Paulino was a good father and a good husband. That's what moved him. That was probably why he admired and respected him so much. Maybe because he never had a father figure, but in compensation he had a mother who insisted on playing both father and mother. Although, shouldn't one and the other eventually be impossible at the same time?

The chord of the fifth moment was strummed with a tone of someone increasingly stunned by the desolating effect of loneliness on the flesh and blood cascading down the river of the man he was. But our Simão was still too young to be able to withstand the force of the waves breaking on the shore the next day. He could go to class and go to his training sessions without sleep and be constantly accompanied by a hangover that lasted for weeks. Nothing stopped him, not even the back pain that was growing in his consciousness.

During the vibration of the fifth moment, everything seemed to be mysteriously happening, simultaneously and synchronously, inside and outside his mind. Simão was developing a thesis in which something or someone had to suddenly collapse, possibly he or someone would die. He even thought he was already dead. But no. He didn't expire in this chapter. Maybe, he will never die. Or, maybe, we know that he will, in the end.

Maybe this book will immortalise him, or maybe not! What happened, however, was that he was selected for an artist's residency on a small Mediterranean island. This, because, in the meantime, he had crossed paths with Sebastião, the Sebastião dos Santos, in one of the university corridors. Simão went with Sebastião to attend the presentation of one more of those artistic projects financed by European funds, and that, naturally, had more than one interested student.

The introduction was made by a pot-bellied man in his late thirties, who, in addition to the pair of glasses that hung from the mountain top of his greasy nose, had a brave roman tonsure. It was that individual he would immediately recognise from one of the cafes in his beloved neighbourhood. Precisely the same, Henrique Raposo, who, last winter, exhibited his master's project at the Pólo dos Leões. After all, the Eborense world is not a small stage. In fact, there is more to it than the sea and a multitude of people.

Now, when people ask him what he is up to, he always answers, "well, nothing much! I have to go to Greece soon. But it's only two weeks. Then I'll be back." Everything would now end in the refrain of Greece and see you later!

It was not Henrique Raposo, who selected him. Who selected him was, more specifically, his partner. They were one of those modern couples who have children and live together, but never get married. Neither by church nor by registration. The other students, who were also competitors, were very disappointed that he was chosen and not someone else. After all, he was him. And that upset a lot of people.

Henrique Raposo would later comment to our Simão, the current anti-hero, that he had been warned. That he had made a terrible mistake. Repeating, to Simão, what he had been told. "He's going to cause trouble." Eventually, it had been one of his arch-enemies: Raul Cancelo, Professor Luiz Alberto Ferraz, or else, another irreproachable intellectual, who saw in him a threat to his cultural and social privileges.

In the Cafe Atlântico, Simão Pinheiro wields his sword, the sword of speech acts. The language he uses is the expression of his camouflaged social condition. Constantly elaborated and invented in dialogue with others more or less known to him. He is a fictionalised self, but one that produces monologues and dialogues with his real self, the author's self.

I must tell you, very honestly, once again, that he is definitely not me. I am clearly not the author of this book, nor am I its protagonist. I will say it again, I am only one of the narrators of this work, and that, after one more walk of Simão around the neighbourhood and the morning he was still awake and stretching, I could see that he followed like a zombie to the university. Not noticing, he, me, who was watching him intently. It was one of those mornings when he could neither sleep nor begin his work in language studies.

Simão Pinheiro was looking at the cloister of the Espírito Santo, through the window of the library, seeing all those students also hesitating, who, like him, were talking indecisively to each other. Some were young lovers holding hands, sitting side by side on the stone benches; others were just brilliant minds shining solitarily with the day sky; others were just a glowing summary of a dream, flying aimlessly to yet another station. But they were all passing through the same university, they were all passing through an age that was universal, and they would all, in the future, be part of that future without logic.

Without an option other than mathematics and computer science. Where, there will fit little more than one or another exact science. They will be part of a future and a society and a language made with even more technology. Independently, language being the memory of history, or the history of society being made, essentially, of language, of verbal language.

He would get lost that day reading Ludwig Wittgenstein's logical neopositivism. He decided, inexplicably, that he would not finish the work he had promised Professor Suzana Sofia Balaaia so much this year and in previous years. He also decided that he would stop by the Cafe Atlântico later in the day. He would arrive home around 5:30 in the morning. Wondering how it would be possible for João Paulino to return home at that same hour? To go to bed for two hours and wake up again with energy to run his business?

Neighbour Vitinho was now a regular visitor to the trio's house in the Senhora da Saúde neighbourhood. Today, before lunch, while our protagonist was exercising in the huge concrete pond between the annex and the house occupied by the duo João and Nilson, neighbour Vitinho, as if he were too far away to be heard, shouted, "Look, exercising and jerking off makes you sterile!" He then laughed to himself. Continuing the conversation with the duo João and Nilson. He had come for shrouds, or he had probably come for a pinch of salt, or a dash of olive oil. That or some other trifle would be the only reason for his visit.

That poor creature was a damned soul! Without a single talent. He was already missing a bunch of teeth and constantly lacked money for a more comfortable life. His salary and the working hours of the girl he lived with were scarce for his daily expenses. At forty-one years of age, he was a sample of someone who never wanted to be what he was today. But he also never wanted to be anything else. He had neither the confidence nor the intelligence to be anything else after tomorrow. It was Vitinho…it was poor neighbour Vitinho…

Now that I try to remember his real name, I can't. What I do remember is that our protagonist owed him money. As will be told later, possibly, by the *author narrator. That is if he doesn't forget…or if the narrative doesn't force him to forget… One thing is certain! He never demanded it back from him. Not even when they met later on the greenway by mere chance. Already, Vitinho had wrinkles in his facial expression. They were the hands of time, sounding the alarm of premature ageing. In that interval that they didn't see each other, Vitinho's neighbour had become another angel who had fallen gracefully into yet another terrible personal misfortune.*

He and the girl he lived with had split up, and he would continue with the life he had: few or no friends to help him be something else; little desire to be something other than the job that crushed him; and even less desire to pay off the bank loan that took almost all his salary, because of the house he bought and where he now lived desolately alone. Waiting for someone to buy it from him, so that he could go and live alone in a room.

The moment when things went from relatively to absolutely out of control was somewhere when he attended the premiere at the Sociedade Dramática Eborense of the play, A Primeira Morte de Florbela Espanca, by his master, António Benedito Pio. It was especially noticeable how paranoid he was that day. I was sitting three rows behind him. He was one row behind Professor Benedito Pio. From where I stood, I could see him cowering and suspicious, thinking that someone could guess what he was thinking at that very moment.

About why he was punished with an existence that had the spiral shape of a labyrinth in his spirit, from which our protagonist seems to have no way out. Which convinces him that his end can only end badly. Increasingly believing that the Southern dream he dreamt is merely an unreal dream, being something unattainable and impossible. Thus, our protagonist becomes less and less credible for being where he is.

Neither near nor far from his dream, but finding himself in the middle of an audience, pretending he is just another extra, one of those very upstanding ones. Curiously, his friend Francisco is one of those great actors who can never play the role of a bad actor.

After applauding his master and shaking his hand, he fled home wildly. Running uselessly against the current of time and wind, against those walls that have no visible form. When he woke up with one more day to learn how to die he confirmed whether he had lost any teeth. Finding relief when he ran his finger over it and could verify that none were missing after the dream he had dreamt during the night, although he could not remember the content of the dream nor most of the content he had yesterday afternoon and morning.

He left home the next day without a single reason. The trumpets of the sun were sounding as the Monday mid-afternoon, which is beyond the beginning of his adulthood, pushed him in a certain direction. He was continually being pulled by an uncertain magnet. He walked without thinking and without even wanting to look any further for a meaning, which would be able to explain to him the meaning that had the orientation of his path. It was at this moment that he found him again.

He was talking to a woman who would be in the prime of middle age. He was courting this lady lawyer. It was always more with his gestures than his words. This was how he usually represented his role as an action hero, who lives suffering inside and seducing everything and everyone. He had come to Évora to serve as a witness in a case. It was at this juncture that our protagonist suddenly came from behind and cowardly attacked him with a hug. Leaving him completely defenceless.

Both immediately returning to a compartment of the time train, which neither goes backwards nor forwards. It was already all right. It didn't matter anymore, if they had gotten upset and who had sulked and gotten angry.

They quickly forgot everything that had been left behind and remembered only that they were friends. Fundamentally, they remembered that they were the greatest of friends, and that they would always, or almost always, be for the rest of their miserable lordly lives.

It was his great friend Francisco Salvador! At this very moment, Francisco was just another graduate who had finished his course somewhere last year and was now also seeking to find and reconcile with himself by resorting to Buddhism as training and exercise. It was the way he had found to measure the weight of the dumbbell of his conscience. Trying to find, with it, the path that would lead him to the liberation of his self. But the religion of one or the affiliation of the two was a road to perdition.

The middle path led them not to the road to liberation, but to the last station. There was always a subway, train or plane that would quickly take them to Devastation, or to any other station that was part of the Death Pulse, the analytical place announced by Freud, Jung, Jim Morrison, as well as other illustrious psychoanalysts prophetically announced in the past.

"*You really are friends!*" Exclaimed the assertively attractive lawyer lady on the sidewalk court. She is very amazed and stunned by that hug that disconcerted Francis and that undid the moment when the beautiful lawyer was almost, almost seduced and almost, almost falling into Francis' web.

"*No, no!*" Our infamous anti-hero said. Adding very formally. "*I don't know this person that well,*" said our protagonist. Laughing inside with a sinking river of happiness after being reunited with his long, long, lost friend Francisco.

"*We are. We're old friends,*" said Francis, still very reticent. Never anticipating that during that coming to Évora, he could reacquaint himself with his friend Simão, or that the reunion between the two of them could even happen that afternoon. He never guessed that Simão, or if you prefer, the Poet, because, after all, that's how he was usually called, would still be in Évora, and it had never crossed his mind to receive that merciless hug. For which he was definitely not prepared.

He had been caught completely off guard. That reconciliation hug, however, made the lady lawyer lose interest in being seduced and just want to feel attracted by being able to witness the genuine reunion between two friends who had not seen or spoken to each other for a long, long time. Too long. And no matter how much Francis had plans to return to Santarém that day, they would suddenly be changed, were it not for the will of the gods, the saints, and the little angels, but not for men who think they can do anything without suffering any consequences later on.

They met precisely after the narrative of this book had already begun six chapters ago. But the chronology of this work does not obey the time of its story. As I had indicated earlier, it was planned by the author to start the book in the middle. By placing at the end the corresponding to the beginning of Simão's life in Évora. Therefore, it would be more or less programmed, what would be narrated, now, here, or later. Except, the unpredictable that cannot be controlled when it happens to be narrated.

For four days and four nights, nobody slept. Queima das Fitas took place in the open field, next to the university grounds of the Espírito Santo College. And it was in the crowd that piled up in the enclosure that Francisco crossed it, brazenly, with his penis sticking out. Then he arrived at the roulettes and asked for two imperials. Turning to his friend, the Poet, and saying: "*You see, young man! You see, it's not an urban myth. You can really walk around with your dick out and nobody will see you. More than three minutes and you are hunted! But until then you can blow off some steam! How long has it been?"

"Two and a half minutes," answered his friend, without looking at the winding clock, which his grandfather had given him.

"Yeah, time to close up the store," said Francis, very confidently, leisurely gathering the material inside.

Too much time had passed since the Poet had been with his great compadre. Too much time had passed since they had last spoken. Both were now facing the chaos of change. Change for the protagonist was a much easier task. For Francis every change was painful, the most poignant of jellyfish. Can our protagonist confirm this, both when they shared a house on the Travessa do Diabinho, and when they shared an apartment on the Avenida dos Heróis do Ultramar, Francis used to show him his dried blood. By posting the painting pain on one of the walls of his bedroom.

It was a performative painting that was disconcerting to say the least, according to our protagonist's artistic vision. But whenever something changed in Francis' life, there was always a new painting to look at again. After all, it wasn't a performance. It was the painful way! Indeed, the painful pain that one feels at every terrible change of season, or every change of opinion!

The inevitable pain that lies between the aligned end of an order of orderly things and the beginning of chaos in every kingdom that orders change. Yet Francisco sawed the skin off his arms and hurt himself, not only because he liked to show off his pain and wanted to show others the colour and texture of it, but also so that they would pity him and so that he could be allowed to feel that he himself deserved to experience a little self-pity once in a while.

Our protagonist had always known about all the times his friend Francis had cut himself superficially or mutilated himself more deeply. But now, at this moment of reunion, there were parts of Francis' life that Simão didn't know had been torn or even amputated. He even didn't know if these wounds were still open and if they were healing properly. They had been friends for too long to stop being friends now or later. It was as if one day they had to jump out of their friendship in order to save it. Francis sang, "like a force, like a force. That no one can stop, force! Force!"

It was the anthem of the 2004 European soccer championship. But it was more than that. It was the soundtrack of their friendship. Their friendship was really like a force that no one could stop, neither at the end, nor at the beginning.

However, defeat or a draw would be technically acceptable, in the middle of the meeting of their lives.

We strangely become not so strange in this world, when we are no longer alone in it. By having at least one friend with us, or by getting back a friend we have lost. Getting back a lost friend is as important, or even more important, than gaining or making another friend. No one survives alone. In the company of our constant loneliness, we can't disguise the curtains of emptiness.

Each generation is neither higher or deeper. One day, Portugal will be swallowed by the European sea of progress and collapse, the rest of the world will be just a cloud of dust drifting in the forgotten cosmos. The myth of the protagonist will die, as will the myth of his friend Francis. The myth of their friendship will not! This, in turn, will never be extinguished.

Francisco kept alive a theatrical air, of one who is on stage, but is deeply worried that the raffle he got out of him does not correspond at all with the life he dreamt of. It was still hard to see what effect the passage of time had on him. Nevertheless, Francisco Salvador was still Columbano's living self-portrait, he was still the same statue in constant pose and elegy of vain suffering. He had the nostalgia of an era that never existed. It had the sense of dismay and indignation of an entire generation that had little reason to exist.

Obviously, this did not include Marcus de Monsalude e Matalonga. While Francis was someone who wanted to exist in a way that was most favourable to him, Marcus, on the other hand, was an admittedly non-existentialist who, if possible, had never been born, let alone existed. There was, however, a more or less pessimistic flavour to the trio. Cause our protagonist was the most optimistic of the three.

They continued to nonchalantly drink wine from a stray cup from the university cafeteria, and Francis continued to stay overnight at our protagonist's house. Staying overnight in João's old room, which was now unoccupied.

Meanwhile, someone rang the doorbell. It was Belchior and his friend Francisca. Their coming had happened because our protagonist had been having lunch last month with Belchior and his former colleague—Eduardo— from the Philosophy and Psychoanalysis.

This lunch between the three happened because our protagonist had crossed paths with Eduardo Parreira, whom he hadn't seen for some time. Belchior showed up shortly afterwards, in the midst of this friendly meeting. Our protagonist ends up inviting Belchior, because Eduardo knew him. Our protagonist knew Eduardo more or less well, but he knew Belchior very poorly. The Belchior who had insisted on giving him a book. Had it not been for Belchior's sudden and forced departure, it would have been a really good evening between the three of them.

Not least because the protagonist had proved to be a good host. That day Belchior and Eduardo stayed most of the afternoon digesting the meal and sunbathing with Simão. But then, suddenly, Belchior said he had to leave. He mumbled a somewhat indecipherable justification. Eduardo ended up going too. He then had to walk home. It was quite scabrous. But considering that it was Belchior Barreto, maybe not so much.

This time Belchior returned to the neighbourhood of Nossa Senhora da Saúde in the company of his friend Francisca, who was someone our hero had crossed paths with superficially during his first years in Évora. Clearly, she did not match the first impression he had of her. Nor with the label of lesbian that Belchior, his friend, had attached to her before introducing her and bringing her to Simão's house.

Belchior was now returning to our protagonist's house, because, simply, Francis had asked him to invite someone to stop by, in order to entertain them. But it turned out to be Francis who had to entertain them. By wrapping kitchen film around his face. As if his face were broccoli. Making his friend, the Poet, believe the astonished spectators not to be scared, because it was part of a performance and it was just one of the oldest numbers of that old illusionist.

"Don't fret! He does this every day," said our protagonist, while nonchalantly wallowing in the wine that was floating in his bowl. He regretted not having invited Eduardo instead. Because Belchior seemed to him to be someone extremely doubtful. I have no doubt that he is someone who generates a lot of questions. Also, his friend Francis raises many questions. Likewise, our antihero will be the one who perhaps raises the most questions about his character. Francisca, on the other hand, will be the character that will raise the least suspicion. Perhaps, because of some naivety floating with her on the surface.

Later, Francisca wouldn't be able to get an ounce of pixie dust and that make Francis cry, rant, jump on the trampoline of the sofa. He would go to the kitchen and return to the living room with a pot on his head. Knocking on it with a knife, making the contact of the knife on the pan, his drumming.

Francis was wearing that day the same sweater as in the past. He and Poet were too friendly, dangerously, too friendly. It's as if they had many layers of skin, but no more than a change of mask. There, the two of them were drinking, day and night, night and day. With Francis, swallowing his dose of brandy. Then collecting the canister and calling his father Calé, after he had gained enough courage to do so. Warning him that it was, exceptionally, only one more day, and that he would only go the next day, because he was at the Poet's house. It was then necessary to repeat the same phone call successively, in the following days. So that Francisco would inform his father that he would only go after all...

But then, the next day, it would take another day, which would be spent, by accident or mere chance, with a former classmate of our protagonist: Sissi. Our notorious hero was too drunk to remember some of the names and faces he and his faithful squire had crossed paths with. Both of them didn't know where they had really been and what they had really done.

Francis would assert that he hadn't figured out whether Sissi wanted to get involved with one or both of them, or if she had nothing else to do. That was more or less what he had concluded. Because when Francis expressed himself, he always repeated what he had read in a book, or directly quoted a line he had heard in a black and white movie, or something simply intellectual that his friend José Pedro Viegas had said.

It may seem to the reader that I am describing someone very fake, but the truth is that there was no soul more longsuffering than his. He genuinely loved to give to his friends, as he would take back what he gave, if someone proved not to deserve his loyalty and his precious kindness. For Francisco had often been wounded by the thorn in his nature. Being betrayed by the luck he came into the world with and the luck that has the kind of character that keeps forever the friends he didn't have at birth.

Sissi, inexplicably, stubbornly accompanied them everywhere, for the entire journey that day. They wondered as you are wondering now, "What did she want anyway?"

Then it was their turn to accompany her. First, to her house and then to her room. The two of them, following, always in accordance with her directions and suggestions. However, that day would not end in an orgy. Because she didn't choose the two or either one of them. Instead of all that, she went to the Queima das Fitas, with another boy. Who came to her, shortly afterwards. Francisco and Simão would end up going drinking at the Alquimia bar, which was next to her house. Each of them repeatedly drank the rest of the liquid in the night glass. Not caring either of them to acknowledge that they had enjoyed being captured by the adventure of that day. Although, they couldn't remember everything that had happened.

Francis, now, also wanted to go with the Poet to Greece. But our protagonist considered that it would be best to go alone. Convinced that it might make him well and that he might be able to detox for good. Perhaps he thought that seeing the blue sea would exorcise him and purge him forever. When his friend Francisco finally headed for the bus station, Simão refused to escort him. As he used to do, when they shared the same apartment or house. This time, he stayed at the Cafe Atlântico shaking hands with João Paulino's known customers and friends.

After reading the newspaper, he would stay until dawn in a café where not only tea or coffee is drunk and consumed. Therefore, each one, sooner or later, will hear their own fado. Each one of them will find the fado curve, the fate that will meet him in the middle of his path. Sooner or later, Jupiter will appear, or a Nameless God, will be silent and say nothing; and each of them, sooner or later, will make his way with or without the help of saints and angels, but always with that which one friend has always given to another friend.

***

End of the school year. I don't know exactly how many times I drank coffee today. Every moment is a formidable excuse to drink coffee. The trip to the Hellenic world is coming soon. Évora will be temporarily behind. While this is not happening, I'll have another coffee. As for the scholarship, it is a buoy with almost no air left.

Sixteen hours and thirty minutes, the sun tries uselessly to beat down on the glass wall that separates us from the outside. Today, we rehearse in the complex, where we can see the inside of the arena. Meanwhile, Henrique Raposo had lost control. He usually proceeds exactly like this when someone has an opinion contrary to his own. I don't mind. They have already bought me a plane ticket and when I get to the airport, I will leave everything behind. That is, if I manage to reach the departure lounge. Until then, I maintain the expectation of salvation.

The boy who studies cinema in Lisbon was very bothered by Henrique's temperament. More than he would have been bothered by the crisis or the hunger in the bellies of the African children. After the break, he left and never came back.

I returned from the rehearsal on foot, with Henrique Raposo, who, coincidentally or not, had his office in the Nossa Senhora da Saúde neighbourhood. More specifically, in the attic of his parents' house. Basically, we were neighbours.

We both walked with the rhythm of the cotton pickers. Henrique had gained some empathy for me. However, it seems to me that he is wary of this in tune between us. He probably hesitates whether to remain my friend or to remain merely at a distance. We walked and talked about the inexplicable reason why we are the shadow of our own contradiction. The constant dance between what one writes and what one thinks, and what one then ends up actually doing. Feeling, afterwards, the invariable disappointment. When you read that what was written, never coincides with what you truly feel happened.

We walked and talked rambling about the need we have to alienate ourselves and how we need banal matters and absolutely trivial moments in order not to be singled out as a rare species and thus become not so alienated from the rest of the world. Taking the opportunity, Henrique, to ask me, on the way, why I had left, last year, in the middle of the presentation of his performance, at the Pólo dos Leões, which was part of his final work for his master's degree in dramaturgy.

Recently, I met Adriana Espinosa. She seems inexplicably interested in me. She collaborates with Henrique's association. But she is not coming with us to Sifnos at this stage of the project. Since André Monte's comment, I have been wondering if she will really like me, or if as he had suggested, I won't have any chance that she will like me one day.

It was when Francis and I went to quench our thirst at the Bar *A Oficina* that I stumbled upon André, who was at the counter. But I didn't even blink, I didn't even protest. Not a single reaction. If not, a vulgar expression like: so, you bastard, here again? Proceeding as if I had seen him yesterday. He was accompanied by his new girlfriend. Who, curiously, studied in Évora, but was born in Porto. Where he now resides. Living from the intermittent money that his job as a freelance illustrator gave him.

André had come to visit her. He was now conditioned to have to come to the South to give kisses to his girlfriend who was a native of Porto, but who ironically was studying at the university, and in the city he had deserted.

Andy had left the Alentejo because he was fed up with the world heritage that had the city's history not making room for those who lived within the walls or on the outskirts.

He fled Évora, too, because he had quickly grown tired of his domestic life. He had gorged himself on the idea that he could easily afford the life he once shared for a few short months with Vânia Velez. Working, first, part-time at the PT call-centre, so that he could then have the other half of his time dedicated to art. Soon after, however, he was forced to go to work full-time. Constantly complaining to me about what had become the beginning or the middle of his adulthood.

Possibly it was one of those coincidences of fate that happen on purpose. Or maybe not. The stage of the Eborense world is too narrow and we end up returning to the point in the dream from which we originally set out. Now Andy was returning to Évora, not to finish the course he had left unfinished, but to ask me with his circumstantial rhetoric: "your friendship with Francisco, it only brings you problems, doesn't it?" Besides, his occasional morality would bother me even more. Leaving me completely obsessed with his stupid remark, "She's not in your league. You don't stand a chance." I must have heard that or something very similar. But that deep down would mean or imply the same thing!

André was that friend who told me that I could never choose to have what I supposedly wanted most. André was probably one of those champions to whom the luck of love and gambling offered him no other option but to always win. He was one of those guys who were never abandoned, nor despised, he was one of those artists, always much desired and loved, to whom the art of love and the art of life made others unable to resist his designs. I would eventually be one of those defeated ones, to whom even the art of fighting courageously against the laws of love and the immoral laws of life would not be enough to captivate anyone.

Andy's coming to Évora had coincided with my friend Francis' extended stay, which I had just gotten back. That night, when I ran into André Monte, Francis was drunker than I was. He had gone that night to the home of his friend and former housemate, Bernardo. So that he wouldn't be even more disappointed with him and think that Francis preferred my company and my house to his company and the house he shared with Regueira, Dinis and Granja.

He left the bar without needing to grab onto the railing at the exit. He was a true Ribatejo man: he had the gift of balance and the rare talent of walking on the razor's edge without staggering.

As he walked, he would touch the edge of the path, just to make sure he was going in the right direction of the next deep stroke. Missing himself once again, not only in the present, but also with who he was in the past. But because he had passed through the Southern dream in the more than imperfect past tense, he would know by heart where to put his feet and where not to, so that he would never stumble and never stagger.

I was still the Poet, but I was a poet who no longer wrote poetry. My pals and comrades at one time still insisted on calling me the Poet, although I no longer wanted to be called or recognised by the cognomen of the last living poet.

André went back to Porto; Francis went back to his parents' house. He sat in the house like a buddha from the three hundred store. Which has become a Chinese store, but is practically the same kind of weak piece made in China. And, I, today, after another rehearsal with Henrique, walked into the house, not knowing exactly what to do with myself and the empty space, which had settled between me and my housemates. So now, the space we shared was getting wider and wider. Everything had changed places, and simultaneously, nothing had changed places.

Each day that passes by me is just another rehearsal. Tomorrow, it will be just another step of the ladder that has to be climbed to the top of the mountain. Tomorrow, it is a mountain or a ridge that surrounds the valley of Avelar and that one has to climb continuously.

Essentially, so that when we finally reach the top, we will descend it again with satisfaction and understanding. Then, of necessity, other reasons will be invented to have to climb the same mountain again. Only then, afterwards, will the last living poet die. Afterwards, there will be no more mountain that needs to be climbed.

***

"A trail of destruction will be left behind!" I said to Master Benedito, who listened to me with incomprehensible compassion. Then I asked him, "There is no redemption for a villain, is there, Master?"

"There is redemption for the villain as much as there is salvation for the hero." Then he shot a lingering laugh that went skyward and added, "Just as, there is no salvation for the villain, nor redemption for the hero." The Master was as benevolent to my vilest version, as he was at times, disciplinarian to my best version.

The afternoon sun was slowly burning the fire that had our skin. We walked with no other option but to move forward, aided only with the canes of our firm and convinced resilience.

I was just talking to the Master about how my last trips to Lisbon turned out, "This time, when I went to the capital, I had a destination to go to a concert. But I ended up not going. Because, let's say, I was overly touched by the effect of ethanol and couldn't leave Bairro Alto. I stayed all afternoon drinking with my friend Miguel Murtinho. With whom I was supposed to meet, just for a quick drink. With the intention of later going alone to that concert and having more experiences, the kind that don't add to your resume."

"But you got distracted. You ended up losing track of time…" commented Master Benedito, while he stopped to wipe his forehead.

"Yes, because then Zé Pedro Viegas came along and moved to Lisbon this year. He started another course. Something like acting in film and television. He brought a friend with him. A strange guy. Anyway, I dragged myself around until it was too late to go anywhere, and I stupidly ended up at my ex-girlfriend's house."

"Ex-girlfriend?"

"Débora, who did me the favour of leaving me last winter."

The Master stopped abruptly on the greenway. So, he could laugh. Exaggeratedly opening his mouth and thereby drinking gallons and gallons of air that left him rejuvenated.

"And then what?" He asked.

"The next day, I woke up, next to Débora and with a bad headache. Not understanding where the hell I was and how I had gotten there. Murtinho would meet me that day. Bringing a bottle of wine in each hand, telling me that this was the best prescription for my migraine. And, as we walked down the steps of the building, he confessed to me. 'Yesterday, after you left the Bairro Alto, I saw you in the subway. Didn't you see me? You were beautiful!'"

The Master stopped again, this time, to clean the lenses of his glasses that saw further ahead than I or anyone else could usually see.

"I hadn't seen him. I don't even remember how I ended up in Alvalade, in the building where Débora's mother had an apartment with rooms to rent. Débora, supposedly, had been there for a few months... I ended up staying there for four more days. Because in the meantime I met Ben. He had rented a room from Débora's mother. He was a young German man. His job is to play online poker. Then he surfs. He paid for everything. According to Débora, he had moved to Portugal because of a woman older than him, with whom he had fallen in love. But she no longer wanted anything to do with him. And, he, there, in Lisbon. Playing poker and surfing and waiting for…a miracle? He is younger than me. Twenty-four years old. But he has more money and even more innocence than I still have."

The Master stopped again, but this time, only to ask me, "But why have you gone to Lisbon so often? And why is it that when you are there, you forget what you went there to do?"

"I don't know, Master. All I know is that whenever I go to Lisbon, I call friends who no longer remember me. Some don't even remember if we had ever been friends. For some, I was someone they only vaguely remembered. For others, I was supposedly dead and buried. They were very surprised to find out that I was still alive after all. It was during one of these trips to Lisbon that I learned that Miguel got involved with Vânia Velez. She was André Monte's ex-girlfriend, who was my housemate at Ponte de Ferro.

"Fortunately, Miguel no longer complains about having lost Cármen, nor does he say that she was the great love of his life. Not least because I was already vomiting all that talk. But that's it. He no longer cares if she is in Africa with a coloured boy or if she is in Africa with a boy who has more than one colour. But he still can't stand evangelicals!"

"So, the last time you saw your ex-girlfriend was when you came to Lisbon, at my invitation?"

"No, it was before. Then, I went to Lisbon, at your invitation, and when I got out of the subway station, I ran into the grey wizard. I don't remember if I had already told you about it?"

"No. Tell me!"

"I took the last train from Évora to Lisbon, the professor must have been at the bookstore a long time ago. Then, when I arrived in Lisbon, I still spent half an hour looking for Rua Garrett. But it was after I got out of the subway that I immediately ran into a peculiar figure. A grey old man who stared at me in the most fulminating way. His eyes were on the threshold of my spirit.

"He carried in his gaze a ball of fire. He was a grey bearded man with rather large hair of the same colour. All pulled back. He walked past me, never turning away from the flame that burned in his gaze. He seemed to me to be a magician, a charmer of horses and other equally sensitive souls. Behind him came a hive of children, of whom he was certainly the shepherd."

"And then?" Asked, Master, very candidly.

"Then, I walked around Chiado, asking: please excuse me, can you perhaps tell me where Rua Garrett or the Sá da Costa bookshop is? But I was more interested in crossing paths with that strange stranger for at least one last time, rather than wanting to quickly find that street and the respective bookstore. Until I met Professor Benedito Pio and shook your hand. Do you remember?"

"Yes, of course I remember!"

"Then, having greeted you, I took a glass of wine. When I turn around, behind the ears of the unknown scholars, who were still standing, comes, triumphantly, the magician with his grey cloak. Appearing on the scene again, to my delight. Gloriously entering the door with his flock of children. Turning all that mixed toast of readers and authors to contemplate and salute him."

"Was that Barahona?" Asked the master.

"Yes, the grey wizard, it turned out, was the poet Barahona!" Master Benedito laughed. So much so, that he scowled.

I proceeded with my rant. "The grey charmer sat in the front row, from the audience that filled the bookstore. The professor was there and saw it. So, you know what happened."

"The spring of the old heterodox corpse came loose," Professor Benedito commented.

"Yes, he complained that that wasn't declamation at all. That it wasn't a tribute to António Maria Lisboa, and it was clearly heard in the middle: 'But what is this shit?' Let's go!"

Suddenly, the Master stopped very seriously to speak up. "You see, the organiser of the event never did anything again. She evaporated off the map! She completely withdrew from the scene. Imagine the consequences that that single act did not have, Simão." Then he smiled candidly at me. Continuing to walk serenely and nonchalantly. Trying, I, to keep up with the previous pace the two of us were taking.

"That afternoon, I met Raquel Guerra. I think she only became interested in me when I told her that I was the last living poet. Afterwards, she asked me very insistently what I had published and who I really was."

The Master cracked a smile again. Confessing his appreciation for her poetic work. But more than her first book of poems *Groto Sato* being a work I should include in my readings, was knowing that she buried with her late grandmother some original poems in the Caneças cemetery. Because, to me, that is poetry.

I said, complaining, "Master, she was not very pleased when she realised that I only have three poems published in scattered magazines."

"It could be less!"

"But could there be more?"

"Yes, not only deserve to have been more, but all your poems should have been published by now… Simão, maybe we should knock on the door of *ETC* Publishing…"

"Good," I replied, excited. Then I told the Master how it was like to see on a Sunday the Ervideira Rally with mechanics and auto body repairers, and with their families. I even confessed how I used to meditate on the roof of my neighbour Vitinho's car, in the street of Nossa Senhora da Saúde, where he had also once lived. Finally, there was the story of my trip to the Aires party in Viana do Alentejo and how I had unwittingly gotten into a *garraiada*. Ending up under the bleachers. Finding myself in a maze of friends who were not my own. But they were the friends of Zé Nilson and his colleague Zé Ricardo.

My final comment was to complain, to whine that, besides having been in the middle of cows and bulls, I got involved in a pilgrimage that was not mine, but with that, drawing the dew of a life that, also, was not at all the one I had dreamt of; the Master interrupted me abruptly, nevertheless continuing to walk afterwards along the greenway, "But that all this constitutes the creation of myth—the myth of the last living poet!"

And, I ran after him, thus trying again to keep up with him.

Chapter 7
Between the Alentejo and the Aegean Sea

(June to August 2013)

Adriana Espinosa, who collaborates with the *Amphitheatre* Association, insisted that I go and say goodbye to her in the public garden. To say the least, it was an unusual encounter. After I arrived, her ex-boyfriend showed up shortly after. As if this was not enough, we were also joined by her current boyfriend. The four of us sat there for some time. Apparently, all for the same reason. However, two minutes were enough for me to decide to get out of there. I got up, said goodbye, and headed for the train station. I was running away from me, from Adriana and her boyfriends. I was escaping from there. I kept travelling. I was moving on to a new adventure. But I carried with me the opinion that I would have to return, later, to the same corner of the wall where I would have to await the punishment of my world. A world where familiar faces later become an unrecognisable face. Contrasting with the semblance of what they were at a certain moment.

When I came out of the garden, the sun was hanging high. Anyway, I could feel my gourd hitting the ceiling of the sky even more. When I arrived at the station with my hangover, Henrique was already in the station, surrounded by a set of suitcases. And next to him was the parked Cândido. Smiling genuinely at me. With the smile of a black swan, which is always more honest, more loyal and more authentic than any other. Flora, with blue eyes and a porcelain face, was another member of the Portuguese group that had been selected for an artist residency in Sifnos. She studied in Lisboa and was originally from Évora. She recently requested a transfer this year to Évora.

Probably, she and I were taking inverse paths. She is also attending the same course as me. Although, her profile is different from mine. She was accompanied by her father, who looked very suspicious to me. He seemed to disapprove of me. However, I didn't feel uncomfortable. His manners spoke for him. There was no need for him to open his mouth. He was clearly suspicious of everyone and everything. Especially himself.

Before catching the plane at Lisbon airport, we stayed overnight in an apartment in Parque das Nações. In which Flora paid monthly to sleep in the living room. The group spent the night and the early morning awake. I ended up going to bed in the spare room that was usually occupied by Flora's flatmate. No one had the audacity or courage to leave the group and go there to sleep. But I did. However, when I woke up, I still hadn't managed to kill the hangover.

I brought only one backpack for my redemption trip. It had my hair dryer and a pillow in there. Basically, that was all I needed. Henrique marvelled at the size of my minimalism. In it, my most unnecessary materialism fit and I still had room left over. He was dragging the weight of his body and the weight of his luggage with difficulty. He admitted to me very spontaneously that he would like to live the way I do. Without a lot of weight and without a large volume that would occupy the consciousness of his suitcase.

The last member of the group appeared at Lisbon airport. He was accompanied by his ego, which was exaggeratedly disproportionate to his slender body and his thin moustache, which reminded me of a horrible version of the great Mexican mambo maestro, Pérez Prado, or of someone who would play the conga in a Latin orchestra in South America. He also had an earring in his ear and wore a purple bandana. He made a fuss when he saw us. He was hysterical. He flew from Porto to Lisbon. His mother would pay him for any whim.

When we arrived in Rome, I convinced Henrique to get us out of the airport and take a look at the coliseum. The rest of the group was seduced by the idea of wandering around the streets and traffic circles of Rome. Instead of staying a couple of hours at the airport, sitting around waiting. In any case, I no longer had the money in my purse to kill my hangover, nor to kill my hunger. When Flora and the rest of the group ordered slices of pizza, I had a glass of water to go with my last undeserved cup of coffee. It was the rest of the money that had survived from my scholarship.

But fortunately, the hangover wore off during my stopover at the colosseum in Rome and eased up while I waited at the airport. Finally, it disappeared when I was sleeping on my stomach in the hotel in Athens. Suddenly, it was obvious to me that the flight I had taken was not to heaven on earth, where my salvation would be. Soon after curing my hangover, my mind no longer probed for the discipline of the sea route leading to the island, or the cave, where I would prostrate before the evidence of the gold, that has the form of redemption in the heart of man.

It was already dawn when we arrived in Athens. As the morning rose, we took a bus. Then, after we found the subway station and took us with it, behold the Port Piraeus! Behold, the Aegean Sea! Behold, the ferry!

We were entering deeper and deeper into the dark blue Aegean Sea. I was looking in vain in the direction of the port that I had not reached for a long time and which was getting further and further away from my earliest memory. The sea embraced the ferryboat and I plunged into its arms. Drowning between the dark blue of the Mediterranean and the Olympic blue of the sky. Without, however, getting wet.

The ferryboat was pulled here and pushed there. Pulled this way here and pushed that way there. The dark blue of the Mediterranean merged with the sheet of the baby blue sky in an endless blue journey. I was propelled by a force greater than that which was in the vessel of the man I was.

The hours went by with me counting the waves that marched without direction. I would leave the deck, walk down the stairs to the lower deck without feeling nausea, and go to the bar, not having any money. Just so I could stare at the display cases and take notes and record who was ordering what. The sea breeze and the social breeze hit me, yet I didn't fight back.

Suddenly, at once, in the middle of an inhospitable blue sheet, the first mound of land appeared. It was only a small island, but we all jumped in unison. There was in each crew member the expectation of having found there, not only their final destination, but the great illusion of the lost paradise, in a small portion of land surrounded by white foam, and the dark blue that lies between the Alentejo and the Aegean Sea. When the boat docked, some tourists left. Those who stayed remained saying goodbye to the departing ones. It was a goodbye forever. It was a tender human farewell. It was also the Portuguese goodbye with longing for those who stayed on the other side.

I was exhausted Living inconstantly cannot be living. Is this the constant result of surviving? The ferry comes here and goes there; I come here and the boat goes there; I go there and the boat and the ferry come dancing here.

After voguing and wandering through the plains of the dark blue liquid, and pulling over to yet another tiny island of the circular archipelago where the Cyclades were sown and are apparently so dispersed, we arrived in Sifnos. We disembarked like children in search of the mother who cries for having given birth to the father of inhumanity. Us reacting like lap babies: amazed to be alive, to be burned by the sunlight and to feel it's comforting warmth burning inside us.

After the rest of the groups that would participate in the art residency had gathered, we artistically formed a long line of tourists. Each one waiting his turn to get on the bus, which would take us to the hotel half an hour later. The journey continued under the shade. It was sunnier in Sifnos than in Évora, and I did not find any crisis floating around there.

However, there were armed police in Athens, tensions and demonstrations in front of the high schools and universities harpooned on the great avenues of the past. Especially the ones depicted in the history textbooks. I saw them in passing and I also saw in passing the attempts to stifle them. But in Sifnos there is no crisis by the sea. Here, the sky is blue and the sea is also blue; in the Alentejo, the sun is golden. I am, now, between the blue of the Aegean Sea and the sun of the golden Alentejo.

After arriving at the hotel and leaving for the cultural centre of the village of Artemonas, I looked longingly at the mirror of the sea lying on the horizon. The island that stood on it was a lonely lookout post that stood far away. I realised that I was tired of myself. The sea was the portrait of someone who didn't want to see anything but the blue of the sky and the blue of the ocean. This whole journey with the blue symbol to get here…to the impact of the first experience of air travel to finally fall into me.

Maybe, if we could never leave the boat, the ferry, and simply be benignly swallowed by a blue whale! I could possibly change paths, because when I set foot on the Hellenic ground, I sensed that my trip was just a good justification for being here and for once again not finishing my degree, postponing it for another year. The sea has a certain length and propensity. And we sail the sea of life with a strange purpose. Mine would be, perhaps, to connect the golden Alentejo to the blue Aegean Sea. It would not be to debate, nor to listen to others talk about the crisis, but to know that the crisis is a merely abstract idea, especially for those who live far from it.

I recognise that I will no longer start a new life. I will no longer search for myself, nor will I be able to rediscover myself. And, I will never be able to forgive myself. Just because we travel to a new place, we don't see or see more clearly, nor do we suddenly find more peace in our lives. I feel that none of this is a fresh start.

So, I'm going to float out to sea in a little while. Maybe, I'll stick my head in the sand. Anyway, the simple things in life! Those elementary things that sometimes hang in the web of the mind. Which, therefore, weave backwards through the life of any man. Sometimes they are great causes, other times they are tiny spidery women that we crush out of aversion or out of habit? Is it the aversion of a greater love that we feel being crushed in the act?

The Portuguese group that was selected by Henrique, was now gathered on the beach: one black guy, one spoiled girl, two homosexuals; Hilário, who was cool, the other was too shrill for my taste. Finally, the worst of all stereotypes, me! There they were, all kinds of legs, temporarily buried in the sand. With their calves in the water. The waves came and didn't go. They died at our feet. It was the only moment truly spent together. Then we each liquefied into a kind of splinter group. We didn't fit together. After all, each of us was there for different reasons.

Nothing had effectively changed but the reality of the scenario. It was my fault and mine alone. It was me, who voluntarily chose to embark on a little adventure rather than step forward. But for crabs, progress is measured backwards and sideways.

In Sifnos, the program moves forward with the usual introductions. Nobody gets rid of having their name written on a sticker that has to be pasted somewhere on their chest. In the evening, the waves break and we do a wheel on the beach. It's just a game and we play the game of who's who and go to dinner. Meanwhile, we are served and there can no longer be a full-bellied revolution. Not even after dinner! It is written somewhere in the constitution of any revolution.

The next day, the flags of Europe and Greece rolled up in the morning blue. Forming a strange pair of Chinese shadows. Flora cried. Her phobia was revealed. The poor thing, she had only just realised that she was surrounded by water and that she was on an island. Just when I thought she would stop crying, she burst into sobs again. And now it's not because of the island, but because she misses her boyfriend.

The golden sun of the Alentejo warms the blue of the Aegean Sea. It blends with the blue of the sky's palette, which in turn amalgamates with the colours dyed in the clothes made in Bangladesh, and which are worn by European bodies, still young. They are bodies full of colour. Absent of grey. They are expressly joyful faces. Incapable of a ridiculous or undignified moment. They are boys and girls incapable of representing truth on the stage of reality. They are, however, boys and girls capable of pretending and genuinely simulating. Without ever coming to an honest conclusion about who they really are.

I am currently between the Alentejo and the Aegean Sea. With my head hanging in certain places and in certain regions, in which, my spirit remains in body and soul. I am lost between the Golden Alentejo and the Blue Aegean, I am between here and there, between now and what comes after, between what has never been and what will never be.

The cameraman is Mustafa; Algerian descendant. He was born in France and is part of the organisation. Mustafa arranges the microphone for the French director. Soon after, the second cicerone spoke, an old Greek academic full of energy, stood up very slowly as in a foreign film, without subtitles. He left the edge of the stage and walked away. Abandoning the scene and taking with him the scenery that he was alone. Both cicerones are versions of a Luiz Alberto, just like the one in Évora. Yes, everywhere there is a Luiz Alberto. Worse, in every corner of the world, there is a Raul Cancelo.

All the groups were presented on top of the stage. The spokesperson is always the director of each company. The spokesperson talks and the rest of the company sits on the platform of the stage or stands quietly. Each group is an event. Every event has a repercussion. And today is no more different than the indifferent event that has yesterday's paradox (Hum?).

What I achieve in the dark blue of the sea I cannot find in the sticky faces that remain attached to each respective body. Only so that each face can be named and the face of one can be glued on, with its respective arms and legs. Just as well, the sea doesn't need a face. Nor does it need a body for it to be identified. Fortunately, it doesn't necessarily need a designation like Ioli or Haikkan, so that it can later be remembered by its proper name.

After the monotonous presentations by each group, the tedious debates followed. All morning and all afternoon talking about the crisis. What is a ponderously stupid discussion, talking about people and their problems. As if, the solutions to them were merely born from statistical consultations. They are just individuals with no problems talking about people who are starving and living miserably.

Without ever, for once, being able to present a solution. It seems to me that this is more the stuff of someone in crisis, of a Europe in Crisis, and of a Europe that is only partly in crisis. In fact, my mouth is too dry to talk about the crisis. It is too hot to talk about the difference between those who accumulate fortunes and those who accumulate crumbs. For those who don't know, misery is a somewhat contagious disease. I'm sleepy just thinking that I've come to purge myself with the idea of doing theatre. In fact, what I came to Sifnos to do was probably to sunbathe on my forehead. It wasn't exactly fighting the crisis, as the boards of the stage creak at my passing.

The sun is blue in Sifnos. The sea is bottled up with a golden liquid like the cornfields of my Alentejo. The world always goes on and on, regardless of the virus that we are and all the viruses and poisons, earthquakes, earthquakes and fires that together we create. I will continue on vacation looking out to sea. Getting some sun on my head. Eating grilled fish and tasting tomatoes stuffed with rice.

I will be, today and forever, enjoying my personal misfortune. I will be perpetually forever on vacation and persisting, not caring whether I am in crisis or not. The scholarship money is gone, but the vacation continues. Now all I can do is spend and waste my time uselessly. I am now somewhere between the past and the future, uselessly killing my time. It could be worse! After all, I am on vacation. I am holding my hand to one or another girl I have met in the afternoon on the beach and at the dinner table.

Then I stay with them looking at the stars and watching the flames of the bonfire that still burn bright, in the middle of the sand on the beach, until it is dawn. Listening, far away, to the waves breaking closer and closer. They look for a continent, but come across the archipelago of the island where we lie. Indifferent, they roll with us on top of the grains of pleasure that are contained in the sand of the beach. They roll with us and the stars in the sky and the starfish. Until the sun rises and there is no more pleasure than the delight of me going back to the hotel alone, with only my pants and nothing else.

The owner of the hotel and the lady at the reception are my accomplices. They wash my clothes and teach me words in Greek. They fascinate me for the next eternity. They forgive me for the hundreds of cans of beer that I pour out by myself. I promise them that I will stay in Sifnos forever. And they answer in English: "and why not?"

The summer nights between the Alentejo and the Aegean are too long. Easily, we get lost in them. Hilário, who likes to be called Jedi, is a photographer who takes life from everything he sees. He is from Beja, but lives in Lisbon. He is a cool guy. He wears a braid, just like a Jedi from the George Lucas movies. My other colleague is the one who wears a bandana, which every day has another colour, and who usually whispers with Flora. They are the kind of people who don't discriminate against anyone. But also no one can escape their critical pink news.

The next night, an English girl with bangs drank a bottle of whiskey with me, while the drawing of the moon meditated on the canvas of the sky, with the portrait of someone who had a round face. We left the restaurant in a locomotive of people that was slowly derailing down the street. Soon after, we separated from the group and the two of us walked along the beach. Leaving behind footprints and pieces of clothing.

I was so distraught that I forgot where I was and who I was with. She went back to the hotel. But I was left floating naked on the sea raft. I don't know if she wanted more than a kiss or if I just wanted company. I don't know exactly when it was that we said goodbye and when it was that I resolved to strip off my prejudices. I don't remember. All I know is that the next day my coat was buried in the sand. I had searched for it for a long time before finding it a few metres beside the sand, where my boots remained untouched.

Early the next morning I ran on the beach with Henrique. It was his idea to accompany me. However, he gave up shortly after dragging himself for three or four yards. We walked the rest of the way to the other end of the beach. When we returned, we dived into the sea. I immediately felt at that moment that Henrique could be a brother—my older brother—from whom I could learn more about myself, about the cosmos, about Europe's crisis in Europe, and about the crisis in the world. And, above all, I could understand my crisis, in this world, in which many live it very superficially.

Usually, after breakfast a bus would stop in front of the hotel and take us to the other peak of the island and we would go to rehearse at the Artemonas cultural centre. That day, late in the afternoon a car came down the tarmac speeding and honking. It was not a bunch of lunatics! It was just a performance. It consisted of a convertible car carrying a group that was made up of elements from other ensembles that were part of the Sifnos artistic project. They stopped in front of the cultural centre of Artemonas and stole the European flag that was hanging from the top of the pole.

Francis' performance in Évora, however, was far more impressive to me. He would climb to the top and carry the Portuguese flag in his teeth. Usually, shortly after, a patrol car would pass by and applaud him. Then they would give him a ride to the police station.

In performance and in real life, it was the girlfriend of the French company's group director who did this. But she didn't climb the pole. She simply pulled the nylon rope. The parents of the young French director had a second home in Sifnos, and were probably not in crisis either.

I shit on fiction that had that definition of art. On the stage of life there is no room for those who have never experienced life, to imitate the role of someone who has actually done it. I left the cultural centre and went for coffee. I took the opportunity to explore around. I stopped here and there on a narrow street. Observing the white houses and the blue domes of the churches that are as many as there are days in Sifnos.

I also notice the nails that have been nailed into a post, which faces the square—I readily understand why the post has so often been pitted and punctured. It is where the obituary sheet of the island is posted. It is there, where you read the news of who died last week. There is nothing to do but lament that the pole will be pierced many more times.

That late afternoon, the busload of people who had gone to the Artemonas cultural centre in the morning were divided between those who stayed to watch more performances and have workshops, and those who, like me, went to the beach that was parked in front of the hotel.

After drinking my Greek coffee, I took the bus and went to stretch out on the towel. Digging holes with the tips of my toes in the sand. I got under the rest of the blanket that was sunny. Lying face up and sprawled out like a boss, I thought about what Francis' father would say: "burp *pelintra*!" And I burped, out of complicity, with Pai Calé. Then I laughed alone with the horizon, who was also on vacation.

Those who came with me on the bus were singing out of tune. Each of them connected, and interconnected by the same mantra and creed of interests. They were one group of believers who were convinced that this was not only the best world, but also the best time to be alive and to sing the hallelujah of the world and the instant you are living in. Even though this is not at all the best world, nor the best moment. However, the illusion of our life is a moving wheel and every day the bus of our existence makes small crossings. Yes, life is movement and the wheel of life is someone constantly moving.

Cândido would always go to his room early, eventually, so that he could have some privacy with himself. He refused to take a bath when Henrique and I were in the shared room. He seemed more the colour of sadness when surrounded by all those white Europeans, tanned by their parents' money and their lives that had been dictated to them by a generous amount of money.

Cândido was still a young teenager. He had finished his studies at the André Gouveia secondary school, where Eduardo had studied. He couldn't communicate with anyone in English. However, his body spoke. It communicated the universal language. Although people paid attention to him, no one was really willing to listen to him. His soul was too drunk to be interpreted correctly. He very innocently just wanted to get inside a woman and talk to her, through the language of his body. Still, no one was attracted to poor Cândido, who was paid for his trip to Sifnos. His luck promptly stopped as soon as he docked on the island.

When the girl he wanted to captivate, seduced me, his face filled with another shade of sadness. He went back to his room early, and I only returned the next day. When the alarm to wake up rang, Cândido got up to go to breakfast, becoming even more disappointed when he noticed my triumph.

The initial enthusiasm that was our companion on the first nights was lost. Generally, each one lying on his respective bed spoke spontaneously, in a dialogue more for two than for three.

"Do you remember the Flying Castle?" Henrique asked me.

"No! What was it?"

"It was a series… You have to see it!"

"Are you still there?"

"No. And you?"

"I don't know," I answered him, finally. Happy to be able to have that simple fraternal dialogue with Henrique.

The closer the performance date got, the more Henrique cared about what his fear of failure communicated to him. Consequently, he became more and more nervous. Therefore, he distanced himself from everyone else in the group. He was a completely different Henrique, or he was him without a mask. Maybe this project was too important for him. For me, it was just another chapter in the book that my life was writing. More and more I doubted that art could be more original than our own life story. More and more I believed that what was truly lived could never be fully translated, and that one could convert the illusion of the novel of our lives into pure fiction.

It was already evening when the six or seven theatre companies got on the bus back to the hotel. I was next to the Italian dancer whose stomach hurt today.

I gave her my coat when she started to shiver with cold. Valeria clasped her hands against her ballerina belly.

She was twenty-five, two years younger than me. She was born in Oristiano, Sardinia. She currently lives in Rome.

I tried to distract her. Her stomach ache was totally deserving of my male empathy.

"What will you do after Sifnos? What do you do? Do you work or study? Or do you do like me? Do you do everything and do nothing?"

"I study and work. I teach dance and ballet to children. I also work as a secretary in a gym. Besides, I am an actress in several theatre companies. Sometimes I also babysit. Essentially, I am an actress. But I also consider myself a dancer. A dancer has different ways of expressing himself and different ways of performing the same choreography. Which can enhance different kinds of expression." She smiled at the end. Convinced that she had said something very important that would pay off all my attention to her.

"Are you happy?" I asked then.

Her face quickly answered what her mouth was slow to reply. Articulating, just assertively: "next subject!" And, unexpectedly, touching gently on my face. Smiling, without offering me any explanation. Just like a woman who, when she doesn't know what to say, uses aggressive tactics. The conversation would then chalk up to the debate of whether the world can change or not.

"I believe that the world can change. It's we who don't change," she said. Then, comparing the crisis to a glass of water. Meanwhile, the bus stopped and we got off. Valeria gave me back my coat and went back to the hotel, and I headed for the beach.

At the end of that night, some of the girls in the Greek group and the French group took off their bras. I contributed to the revolution by taking off my shorts. And, while I thoughtlessly swam naked on the ground that was studded with sea urchins, the rest of the Sifnos project danced in the sand around the lit campfire. Chasing the sound of bouzouki played by the Greek musicians, who mingled with us that night on the beach. It was that night that I supposedly paddled beyond what would be reasonable.

The saga of my swims would be told to me the next day. But no one would dare, that night, ask me what I was doing when I floated on my belly up, dipping my gaze into the starry sea. No one went to ask me what I was doing there when they stopped spotting me. It's usually like that. We get worried about others, but do nothing that requires us to go out of our way. Which is more characteristic of a bad Christian than a good Samaritan.

On the last day I hung out the cab window waving an effusive goodbye. Staging the Portuguese farewell at length. Everyone was running after the cab. Including the hotel owner and the lady at the reception. It was a goodbye said in the language and tradition of the Portuguese merchants and sailors, who don't bother to mix all languages to communicate the same universal goodbye. Farewell! Adiós! Au revoir! Longing for those who stay and longing, also, for me, who is leaving.

***

I returned to Évora without setting foot in the neighbourhood of Nossa Senhora das Saúde. I arrived in the middle of the afternoon. I was now half way through my life in Évora. I was in the middle of Alentejo. Between the golden sea of the Aegean and the Alentejo blue, after having lost myself for a few days in the valley of the village of Avelar, being surrounded by hills. Hills that lie somewhere between the sea of the Alentejo and the Greek sea that is deep blue.

Henrique was waiting for me on the stairs of the *Industrial and Recreational Workers' Society*. One step further down, Adriana, was waiting beside him. Without thinking about what I was doing, I hugged her. I did so passionately. When I realised where my impulse had taken me, I impetuously hugged Henrique, too. He was very disoriented by the warmth of my gesture. Hugging him was socially too informal for our working relationship. He did it in a contrite way. As if he had never seen me before. I didn't mind. I just wanted to wrap my arms around Adriana's presence.

Then, after returning from Sifnos and spending a few days in the village of Avelar, I went back to Évora for some more rehearsals and a new trip that had Epidaurus as its destination. So, after the rehearsals at SOIR, I would leave the rehearsal room to stop by the Café Atlântico's lounge. Somewhere, in the middle of all our travels, we necessarily stop more often at certain places.

Just like now. After another return to Évora. I would stop at João Paulino's Guild. And, only afterwards, would I reach my annex. On other days, when there was no rehearsal, the itinerary was from home to the club and from the club to home.

Today, if it hadn't been for Tomás insistently banging his belly on the door, I wouldn't have gotten up startled. I definitely wouldn't have caught the plane. Nor would I fly now with Adriana at my side. I definitely wouldn't have known what might or might not happen during the trip to Epidaurus if I had stayed in Évora, sleeping sitting on the sofa in the living room.

But in the meantime, I still couldn't erase from my mind the visit to Tomás' house the day before. When I went to confirm the time of the ride with him to the bus station, I discovered the pigsty he lived in. It was the home of a pig who wore clothes and drove around in a car. The smell of clutter wafted through Tomás the pig's house, it was an odour so impossible to ignore, that it eventually became impregnated in the memory that has the clothes of that day. Tomás was a collector of dirty dishes and a stacker of unwashed clothes, as well as an accumulator of junk that was of no use whatsoever.

Within those four walls lived the dump of a lifetime. It was a collection of garbage that could no longer fit in there. Under that cramped ceiling lived a frustrated opera singer. That repeatedly told me about his passion for trains. Peacocking his knowledge of the Portuguese and European railroad map. Both were drawn in his head. Which was very impressive. But even more admirable was that he was unable to make the bed he lays in. Or simply not being able to wash the dishes after making his lunch, or washing the clothes he had worn for the past month, even if by hand.

He was separated, as well as, often unemployed. He was more of an obsessively obese guy than a morbidly one. Not, that it bothered me. What bothered me was that his arrogance was as dull or more than the fat that was essentially accumulated in his belly.

Just like Tomás and Adriana, César was selected by Henrique. César was a friend from his adolescence. Likewise, Rafael, who came from Bristol to meet us in Brussels, was a friend of Henrique's.

I walk through Brussels airport, telling jokes to the group and listing the faces that look like someone I met somewhere in the dream spiral. I walk through the airport flying with my imagination without needing a runway to land on. Adriana laughs. She thinks I'm funny. César laughs because Adriana does. Tomás's boar, on the other hand, is very disappointed that he has to laugh at my good humour.

Ever since he gave me a ride from the Nossa Senhora da Saúde neighbourhood to the bus station, Tomás has never stopped complaining and protesting, while chewing on the leftovers in his mouth from yesterday or the day before. Not even when we arrived at Lisbon airport and flew back to Brussels to make our stopover there did he calm down. Henrique is not laughing.

He is very upset about having to travel, now, not only with the burden of his weight, but also for having to carry with him the extra weight of his partner, Anabela, and the little Afonsinho, his son, who has a Mickey and Goofy hat on his head. And that, according to Anabela, his coming into the world was something that was completely unforeseen. Which made me conclude that many of the world's children are made by mere chance. Some, supposedly, are a beautiful accident. Such is the case with Afonsinho.

Meanwhile, Tomás is getting impatient at having to wait for the flight to Epidaurus. I like waiting at airports. I like to watch the planes take off and land on the runway. Also, I like to see the people passing by who don't notice me. Basically, they don't look at anybody. They are just paying attention to what is happening on the small screen of their cell phone. When it's not the cell phone it's another screen.

They are people who are sleepy, thirsty, hungry, and probably want to fuck as much, or more, than I do every other day. They are just people, like Tomás, who are very impatient for the future to arrive and for the present to depart as soon as possible from the airport where its past is landing.

Évora was left behind. The internship with Henrique and Anabela's *Amphitheatre* Association fell through. I decided to let Adriana do it. Even because I don't know if I will return next academic year to Évora. Now it's too late for me. Although, it's still morning and I've been half awake for almost seventy-two hours uninterrupted. The world never stops with the movement that the wheel of people has. If we stop, we die of boredom and not, properly speaking, from tiredness, which sometimes it costs us to pay to live.

Between today and yesterday, what I saw, especially, as I walked back and forth in the world, was etched in my mind. It is engraved in me the women in dresses, crossing on the freshly painted crosswalks on the Lisbon tarmac. Just as it was chiselled into me, the surroundings of Portela airport. Just as, before, it was imprinted on me, the bumpy, graffitied, and written walls of the city of Eborenses with the phrase, such as "culture when?"

It all stuck to the bottom of my temple. After all, what stays in our minds before we fall asleep is what counts as fuel for the dreamlike journeys we make and will make during the rest of our miserable existence.

After all, we dream about the world we live in. And that world is the size of a footprint that is roughly equivalent to our dinosaur foot. We dream of a world the size of our dreams. Because the world is the size we dream the world to be. I dream of paradise, not in heaven, but on earth. Now, paradise, for me, is in Epidaurus, and I am on my way to it.

Life takes a day, or more, of travelling. That journey doesn't always last as long as we would like. Today is already a day too long for me to fit lying down on the chairs at the Brussels airport. Anyway, some dreams are travelled alone or proudly accompanied. Anyway, some dreams are footprints the size of our dinosaur feet, they become extinct and we disappear with them.

But my problems, now, were the size of the houses I could see from the small window of the plane. I was somewhere between Alentejo and Athens. Goddess Shiva, or her cousin, lounged on the horizon and rose from her bed made by clouds, when shortly afterwards the aircraft encountered (my) turbulence and I gave Adriana my hand. No, it wasn't only because she was afraid of flying, but it was the fastest way I could hold hers.

When we arrived at night in the metropolis of Athens, we took a cab to the hotel. Inside the cab there were more suitcases than the group Henrique had assembled to go to Epidaurus. Some of them had to squeeze into their own luggage to get us all together across the large avenues and pages that were the size of a volume of the encyclopaedia of Universal History, lying among the dust on the bookshelves of Marcus de Monsalude e Matalonga. Henrique was furious with the Greek taxi drivers who deceived us once again, leading us, again, to literally walk in circles.

He was even more enraged when I disappeared the next day. It was after I had gone for a run through downtown Athens. When I climbed the suburbs back to the hotel, I got lost.

I got lost somewhere between Mount Licabeto and what I thought was supposedly next to the hotel. But as it turned out, it wasn't. I only discovered that every corner, and every urbanisation looked the same to me much later. I had no GPS, no cell phone, and to make things more difficult, I hadn't taken any sense of direction with me. Fortunately, I had no worries about getting lost and being late that morning. In fact, I knew more or less what planet I was on. What I didn't know was in which country I was exactly now.

Everything seemed to repeat and continuously reproduce itself block after block. Only, the graffiti on the walls were direction signs, which made it easier to distinguish buildings and buildings from each other. But I didn't give up circling until I found my hotel. Regardless, I had the feeling that I had already been there, just a few minutes before. It took me, quietly, two hours to reach the inn. Along the path of my own doom, I explored the streets and alleys and the maze of nature's greenery that broke through the white cement city terraces.

When I finally found the hostel, Henrique almost cried with nerves. Most of the group had, in the meantime, imagined the worst had happened. Except, Tomás, who still had chocolate cake served for breakfast hanging out of the corner of his mouth. I tried to ease the tension by joking about the situation. But I didn't have to say anything else, because Tomás began to sing a Verdi aria on the hotel balcony. Refusing to wipe the corners of his mouth first.

Meanwhile Adriana came to tell me that she had been distressed. I shrugged my shoulders and contemplated the white acropolis and an entire city civilisation where there was no longer room for anything else. For a moment, I thought I was happy to be in the middle of Athens and that it was still the middle of the morning and life is a journey and it sometimes takes longer than a day to reach your destination.

In the middle of the first night, in Epidaurus, Adriana came knocking on my door. She wanted to go see the sunrise with me. I went with her. But shortly afterwards we went back to the hotel. She didn't know what she wanted. I, too, didn't know exactly what she was really in the mood for. I don't know if she got sleepy, or if she didn't want to wait so long to see the sunrise. The next day, we went back and forth. With Adriana always impatient behind me.

When she didn't know where we were she would sulk. Then she would be embarrassed, after quickly discovering, with me, paradise in the middle of Epidaurus. A paradise that I believed I had once found in a dream.

On that day, we both carelessly threw our arms around each other. I, personally, swam in the Aegean Sea, thinking that all the dreams we dream are a fraction of the veil of the ocean, which we know only very superficially. For me, paradise was there, and the plunge of my longing was in that now, when Adriana was splashing and throwing water on me. When Adriana would dry herself on the towel and I would get out of the water, I would no longer have that vision of someone who had reached paradise.

It was after we went swimming to the other side of the shore that I thought very strongly that I had finally found the model of the dream, the dream in which I was diving into an underwater cave and when I surfaced, I found an altar. And now, there, in the middle of the rocks was a crack that possibly led to a cave. Eventually, to the cave I dreamt about.

Between dusk and nightfall, Adriana, Tomás, little Afonsinho, Henrique and the rest of Henrique's company of friends and family headed towards the site of yet another page in history. We walked on foot to the small theatre of Epidaurus. Henrique was proceeding in a certain direction and I was initially pursuing this path of his as well.

Usually, when I laughed, everyone laughed with me, following with the fate of my laughter, with more conviction than they followed in the actual direction that Henrique was going. Once, I decided to follow Henrique. But now, I would be on my own. There are men who follow no one. They follow only their dreams, because dreams are bigger stages than any ego in the universe. And between the reality of my dream and the dream of my reality, there are cosmoses of constant detachment.

On the penultimate day, Adriana wanted to be alone in the amphitheatre enclosure. She broke away from me and the rest of the group to say goodbye to something that had happened there and that she couldn't bring with her to Évora. When she arrived for dinner and sat down at the table set by the sea, she became angry. She was very uncomfortable when Rafael asked her, after she had once again sat down beside me, if she didn't have a boyfriend. Looking, first, at her, and then, at me.

The face of c-fiction is easily confused with the body that reality has, but also reality sometimes gets entangled with fiction. In fact, what we see on the cover of a book does not always correspond to what we find inside it.

But everything has a term. The horizon that we see also has one, at the end of the day, and only what we don't see or can't see contains in it an endless infinity. I went back the next day, to the neighbourhood of Senhora da Saúde. When we arrived in Évora, Adriana wanted to thank me with a long hug and a thank you for everything. Only I didn't understand the meaning of her thank you for everything.

Shortly after, her father arrived. Who was not supposed to arrive, according to her, so soon. Adriana was visibly uncomfortable with the fact that her father had caught us, hugging in the middle of the Évora bus station. It seemed to me that he had interrupted something. But I still didn't know exactly what it was, what he had interrupted.

After I put the keys in the locked door, I couldn't turn it. My landlords had changed the locks. Leaving me completely stunned by that plot that had the connivance of Nilson and João. I begged the landlady's grocery store, however, to let me stay just one more night. I made a fuss while the customers were there. And she, of course, immediately agreed to let me stay. It wasn't the fact that I had paid her rent for almost a year and had not fallen behind at all. No, it was the fuss I made in the grocery store, with her customers that convinced her.

Now everything was going to be different. That was the idea I had when I reached the end of the Vasco da Gama Bridge. It was very strange this time that the bus had taken a different route and had passed this time by the Vasco da Gama Bridge and not gone as usual, by the 25 de Abril Bridge. Maybe it was a sign! A sign that nothing could ever be the same again…possibly, it was Marcus' prophecy that manifested itself with his first great revelation…

I returned indefinitely to my mother and stepfather's house. Finding my brother talking on his cell phone with my grandmother. Realising how much my brother had grown in my absence. He had grown like a tree toward the sky. It had grown like a bonsai, which had swollen amazingly more than, when we were watching over it. My brother thought I was a hero coming from the war against the crisis in Portugal and abroad. But for him, I didn't need to have a cape or a sword, nor did I need to pretend to be something I'm not at all. It was enough to be me, his older brother.

The Avelarense Philharmonic Band now passes through the street. It is an army dressed in the same uniform that marches towards the Rua Nova. They are boys and girls in hats, who take the music elsewhere. I see lying on the bed of my old room, through the balcony window, this militia of pants and skirts going down the end of the street. I will end up, however, not being able to hear the end of all that marching that is still being played.

I haven't decided yet if I will go back to Évora. But I have asked for a transfer to Universidade Nova, in Lisbon. And I already know it was accepted. There isn't exactly an end, nor is there exactly a beginning. There is only a fickle tide. Today is just another end, the end of one wave and the beginning of another.

Epidaurus is somewhere allegorically left behind. Paradise will be forever lost. The love generated in the belly of paradise will be forever deferred. I will end up not being able to see or hear the waves that are breaking in the memory that I still have of Epidaurus' beach. I will fall sooner or later in the sand of oblivion. And what does it matter what we lose? What does it matter if we lose, if we win? Life lasts a single day's journey and everything that is important fits in a handbag.

The summer will end, the music will end. There are only three heuristic steps: the first step is the search—everything we decide depends on the number of alternatives we have.

When we have nothing, we can't really choose. Because there is nothing we can select. First, you inquire. You investigate. I more or less tried to find myself this summer. Crossing the silver aqueduct that goes from the golden desert, in the Alentejo, and passes through the sea of air to the civilisation of an Athenian blue people, who like me are also experiencing a crisis. The second step is to stop, to cease. Even if we have and can find and have more alternatives.

However, we have to end the search. Because of our limited abilities to conveniently analyse all the possibilities we actually have. At the end is the third step. The last step is the decision. The summer will end, the music will end. There are only three movements in a sonata. It's the Koch curve! Everything looks like everything and nothing looks like nothing.

Chapter 8
Neither There nor Here, Neither Here nor There

(September 2013)

I was running zig zag down the dirt road, which was descending more and more steeply, when my knee gave way again. I did not remember that it might not withstand the steepness of the descent and break more than once. I definitely did not remember that I ventured into such repeated misfortune. Just as, I ignored that it would be possible for it to shatter, to shatter even more than what was already shattered. With that, indirectly or directly altering the course of my destiny. When I got up, I didn't know where to go. I continued, the rest of the way, limping. Knowing that I could no longer repair what had happened, neither here in Avelar, nor there in Évora. It was another injury to my left knee.

I was hospitalised between my mother and stepfather's house and the old house she inherited. I stayed waiting for the arrival of autumn and veiling for a new semester to be born on the horizon. I gave up on the idea of moving to Lisbon and kept putting on weight until I could go back to Évora. In the meantime, I swallowed the mountain of my pride and borrowed, although annoyed, money from my stepfather. I now had no other choice. Basically, because I had not seriously tried to find one.

Now, there I was. Neither there nor here. Just waiting for my stepfather's money to supposedly return to the south and the dream of the South. During the time I spent between there and here and there, I was devouring books and crunching thoughts. And, in addition to the notes I was grinding to improve my writing, of course, I went to visit Marcus. Old Inácio, his butler and the last facilitator he had left, brought him to his father's factory. As he had done so many times in the past. But now in a completely different context.

I walked through the open rusty September gate and headed for the office, which was the only part of the factory that was lit. Marcus seemed to me to be higher up than reality showed me. He greeted me childishly from an adult dungeon. Surrounded by office files.

The mirror of what we see is only a bending of ourselves. I considered commenting, just for myself. Marcus sketched an incomplete smile, through the clear windows of that dust filled, cobweb-filled factory module. Considering, eventually, Marcus, just for his buds, that we are what we find around the mirror, and not necessarily what we see directly reflected in it.

I formally raised my hand as I made my way through the machines, the weaving machines, and the surviving ruins of another glorious industrial time. My return suggested a balmy breeze, in the late afternoon of this late summer. Incredibly making us return to an earlier stage, to another state of affairs. When we were still hopeful for the projects and dreams we had, before the economic crisis declared itself to the world, and long before, Marcus revealed to me that nothing else would be the same.

At the very least, we would be regressing to the period of uncertainty that would have the rest of Marcus Matalonga's life virtually non-existent. Somewhere between my first two years spent in Évora. Somewhere between 2008 and 2010. Because after that, Marcus would do nothing else. Except, hide himself in his grandparents' mansion until, now, September 2013. And, probably, and essentially, nothing or little else will change or he will do.

Marcus, who had given up world travel, was now asking me somewhat animatedly, how my artistic residence in Sifnos had gone. Wondering if I had enjoyed Epidaurus as much as he had enjoyed his latest readings that told him about Greco-Roman civilisation. He seemed genuinely interested when he inquired about my upcoming plans.

Momentarily, Marcus appeared to be coming to his senses, dropping that sad version of himself. I seriously believed that he was slowly waking up to life, and that like a vampire who had slept through an eternity he was now thirsty for the new blood that was throbbing in the veins of the world, through me.

Shortly after, Marcus called Inácio with his little copper bell. For him to come and open one of his bottles of wine, from his rare collection. Which he had decided to bring to celebrate this occasion. He went on to tell me about what he had read lately and the classical music records he had acquired. Naturally, criticising what I had recently written and read to him. Ending on his favourite topic: his non-existence.

Weaving in between one opinion or another about the abstract world he resided in. Complaining about how he will always live without ever managing to be someone effectively practical. Meanwhile, a mild September summer breeze, between late afternoon and early evening, was wafting through the decaying factory.

After the wine was released, a whole optimism was regenerated in him again that had the company of another time—that wonderful time, in which more than a decade of friendship had been founded.

Marcus took a swig of the rouge liquid and went on to talk very sceptically about how the world had become lawless and without order.

"We live in a financial Pharaoh's Wild West." Making, in the end, a spontaneously theatrical and informal gesture. It was unusual for him to make such an expansive gesture. He smiled at last, showing me his wine-stained lips.

He called Inácio again, this time to find out if his oldest piano was still in the factory. He remained leaning back in one of the armchairs abandoned there. Smoking compulsively the tobacco that had stained his teeth yellow. Giving me, once again, his critical reading of Schumann's work. One of his favourite composers these days.

As well, he took the opportunity to conclude on the vital importance of classical music. And, of course, stressing to me, that jazz was just a detour in the history of human music. He constantly maintained an inattentive air for those who didn't really know him well. Probably because he was constantly in two worlds: not being there, and not being here.

He stood up energetically. Running to what had been his first piano. Playing at my request Chopin's Farewell Waltz. Stopping halfway through to complain about how out of tune the piano was. Starting again from the beginning and stopping in the middle to protest with Inácio. Giving Inácio the order to immediately buy another piano. So that when we meet again in his father's old factory, I could be presented with a worthy interpretation of Chopin's Farewell Waltz.

Inácio, who in other times had been his most brilliant preceptor, out of love for his protégé had decided to spend his last days serving him. Being his butler and a kind of handyman. Recognising Inácio, in one of his rare indiscretions towards me, that Marcus would never know how to govern himself. Fearing that when he was gone, except for me, Marcus would have no one else…

He abandoned the piano just in the middle of the waltz that he was once again trying to play. This time, evidently, he had given up for good. Coming toward me. Asking me accusingly, "Do you know what Chopin's last day was like?"

He questioned me with his face very close to mine. Questioning me with one of his famous alter-egos. One of those he developed when he wanted to be considered as a mysterious entity. Even suggesting, very comically, that he was possessed by the spirit of an inquisitor.

I'd go along with it.—"No. I confess I don't know, Marcus."

"No? Are you sure? Think it over! Are you sure?"

"No, I don't."

"No? Well, I will tell you. What you will hear you will never find written in the pages and dungeons of history, but I will tell you with the clause."

"With the clause that it wasn't you who told me!" I added.

"Exactly, I didn't tell you anything."

"Right, Marcus."

"Well, then, where to start?"

His face lit up. It was as if his truth had another colour and another essence. And that he, he alone, would be able to alchemically sketch under the expression of a magic formula. But that in the meantime, it had disappeared, and he, the scientific magician, had realised that it was no larger than the mathematical expression that had that magic of his. He could not avoid being swallowed by this exact and rigorous reason, losing himself uselessly to it.

The factory where we were spending our soirée had been closed for two, three years. After I had gone to Évora to study, what was left of his parents' empire was gone. So, too, had Marcus' will to exist. Also, Marcus' genius had been lost. However, the inheritance left to him by his grandparents, allowed Marcus to continue neither there nor here, neither here nor there.

After finding some fabric left over from the confection, he spread it out across the floor. Muttering sarcastically, "It is a cloth that has been woven by the factory of my destiny."

After trampling on the cloth, he lit a cigarette, illuminating the darkness of the decrepit assembly line, where old machinery and some antique furniture was hiding shamefully from us. Both covered by long white awnings.

The story of Chopin's last day was for now in the background. Because his entertainment now consisted of smoking and walking in circles; concentric circles. Always similar and always identical. He walked and puffed, puffed and walked, always around and around. Always swaying on a train still powered by coal. Going from there to here and from here to there. Being neither here nor there. Neither there nor here. His hair now had cobwebs and his clothes were covered with factory dust. He looked older to me at that moment.

In fact, it seemed to me that he had instantly aged a decade. In that moment he had the life of that cigarette, which he was still puffing. I was left doubting whether it wasn't somewhere, around there, that in the meantime his first grey hairs had amazingly sprouted. He was only a few years older than me. However, he was still too young for his first grey hairs to have suddenly begun to grow.

He sat down next to me and complained like an old man about his old age. Complaining that his worst luck had once been that he was born in a cradle of gold. Complaining about the fortune that was at his side when he was born. Finally, he told me, completely disgusted, "My worst luck was that one day I got lucky."

Fundamentally, Marcus would only listen to me when what he was trying to say could not find an echo in him. When he listened to me it was to search for the password that would allow him to re-enter his forgotten old domain. It was always he who spoke, and it was almost always I, who had to listen to him.

He smoked now in disbelief. Talking continuously about his misfortune. Blaming the moral decay of humanity for his personal and social catastrophe. Going to the front gate just to raise his arms and accuse the full moon, for this and for that. Exclaiming, very loudly, that the other stars dared not contradict him! Because they also had responsibilities. And they were not few!

He would come back and bring another subject from his usual repertoire, "How is it that some guys without a trace of character, today, reach the highest offices and the highest political levels?"

His speech was an opera, an opera that was repeated and heard wherever we went. It was played, now, on the stage of the factory of another time; it was invariably transcribed, always, in the cafe that we frequented relatively close to his mansion; it would also be heard, on the radio, when we took our drives through the mountains and some of the small towns, which for some mystical reason were very dear to him. And, generally, he was the one driving, and not Inácio. Only because he was used to that specific route.

On the rare occasions he invited me to listen to a classical music record in the lounge of his library, or on the also rare walks I could take with him through the woods and walled gardens of the Ribeiro Travesso farm, I heard in between that same repeated opera. However, the spoken opera would not be heard in the other parts of the farm, nor in the other rooms of the mansion, because they were closed to me.

For Marcus, only the corrupt leader now mattered to analyse and alone dwell upon. It was as if he was speaking indirectly about his father who bankrupted the company or speaking directly to his moral mother. Who somehow allowed his family to come to that end. He was tired of existing consistently. Yet, it was his thoughts that sank him into an incoherent reality, which was a kind of pool without water, where he had no footing.

"It's social conformity! Everyone follows a certain trend. The world is going in a certain direction…which is completely wrong, in my understanding. Everyone is pulled along by the trendy wagon, thinking that if it's trendy, it's right—"

"A cup never dirties the surface, if there is a base underneath the cup," I interrupted. But I didn't get any reaction. Except the expression of one who was interrupted. Perhaps, he had not heard me at all?

He continued, "How is it that some guys with no character reach the highest levels and the highest political positions?" Repeating the same rhetorical question twice more. He did so, ignoring what he was telling me he had, unfortunately, told me more than one occasion during the evening.

Then, surprisingly, he shut up and took a sip at the end of the liquid that was still standing in the glass. He sighed as if he wanted to have drunk the rest of a hope that had meanwhile been lost. He laughed, and the echo of his laughter, laughed inexplicably too. Throwing in his despair, a loud laugh. In order to disguise his existential industrial emptiness.

As Marcus started to smoke the beginning of his third pack of cigarettes, I spoke about my desired way of life which included: having a professional occupation in my field of study; balance between my social relationships and my leisure activities. But Marcus continued his monologue once again as if he was not there and was not interested in what I was telling him.

Inferring, "Living in this environment, in this region, in this habitat…plus the lack of a decent job, plus the family, plus the complex relationships that proliferate in the modern world! Add to that the kind of education everyone has today; the philosophy that is increasingly considered a dead language; the religion of our parents that is also increasingly in disuse. Plus, the opinions of the newspapers, which only tend to increase polemics, and only polemics. Plus, our beliefs are questioned immorally by everything and everyone. It is part of the propensity to follow with a certain slant. But I refuse to go trawling and going in that direction."

Suddenly, I wanted to ask him specifically about that archaeological moment in our friendship. When we reached the tunnel of the complementary route number eight, which connects the Avelar valley to Figueiró dos Vinhos, and, he mysteriously utters that he has something very important to tell me. But only when we reached the middle of the bridge, which appeared on the horizon, did Marcus announce to me the beginning of his crisis and the beginning of the economic crisis in Europe and in the world.

He also unveiled the curtain of disturbance that had been generated within his family. And, that somehow came to dwell and occupy his being. He was clearly the most invisibly affected element.

I couldn't help myself and asked him about the expression "Nothing will ever be the same again!" That he had once used. I questioned him about what he really meant by that.

He answered promptly, "I don't think it's good to remember that kind of content. The past is the past! We shouldn't go back to it." His voice echoed through the cracks and crevices in the factory walls. It went through all the corners, where another atmosphere had built up in the ceiling, that had the factory of his world. And he asked Inácio to bring the second bottle.

When I first enrolled at the University of Évora, Marcus had returned from abroad after a sabbatical year from his architecture degree. He returned to Portugal somewhat disappointed. When he re-enrolled in the architecture course in Porto, he wasn't exactly thrilled either. He stayed in Porto for the next two years to finish his architectural course. When he completed it, he moved permanently to the mansion he had inherited from his grandparents. Being far from everything and close to nothing. Being neither there nor here.

During these last few years, I have been noticing a loss of appetite for his daily life. I also registered an exponential increase in his intellectual pleasure in satisfying himself in a world in which he clearly no longer lived. His psychic transformations, his mood swings, his constant restlessness, indicated to me an apparent irritability, more and more frequent in his personality. Resulting in his becoming more and more an inconsequential nonconformist.

Inácio arrived with the second bottle and ceremoniously poured the ointment on each body. Retreating, immediately after the task was completed. Machiavellian toasting Marcus to the bleak future that humanity would surely have in his perspective, and the balm quickly slid into his blood. Settling in his nervous system. Creating in him reactions that were sometimes startled, sometimes changing to a sudden euphoria, which quickly faded as it rose in him.

When the crisis had fully germinated in his mind, Schumann took a place on the podium of his favourite classical music composers. Schumann, who never held a place near his palanquin, now played a new prominence. Underlining the funereal form of a parallel musical canvas that resonated in his psychic life. I feared that Marcus, too, might meet an insane and gloomy end. Exactly, as happened at the catastrophic end of the composer Robert Schumann's life.

His speech was now taking on the free expression he had in his glass. His essay was increasingly exuberant and complex.

"Some systems become a school made on a planetary scale. But no system should ever be considered as important as our solar system!" He continued cheerfully. "You see, good students copy their teachers, and so they naturally become bad. In every system, the bad teachers were brilliant students who took advantage of the systems. It is exactly like that in the political system! A system that, in turn, gives rise to a new social organisational body. Now, I ask you: do you know of any model as important as the sun and the solar system? Galileo is one of those good students who ended up cowardly complying with the old ideas of his teachers. It is important that we don't forget "

His clothes still bore traces of the factory dust. As well, a small mound of cobwebs still lingered convincingly in the lock of his hair. Marcus Matalonga was now officially a nonbeliever, not only of humanity, but also an increasingly fervent believer in his own personal calamity.

The full moon was still hanging in the night sky. Illuminating the fabricated decay of his soul. We said goodbye before the day came to yield night. Marcus stood at the factory gate of another time waving at me, having insisted that I let Inácio drive me home.

But I refused. Walking down the street of the 5 Vilas, wishing that one day I wouldn't have to end up tragically indifferent like Marcus or like Zé Pedro Viegas. Thoroughly analysing my mistakes with no real ability to discern between my insistence and the stubbornness of fate. Ah! If only Marcus and the Viegas of this world could correct their *qui pro quos*, by definitively learning the lessons of the spiral of each one's dream! I could hoist, with pomp and circumstance, a flag capable of representing the edges of the chimaera. It would be something of an impact, just as if man landed on the moon for the first time.

Although Viegas is still convinced that man has never set foot on the moon. Maybe, Viegas will wake up one day and get out of bed. Maybe, one day, the father of all non-existentialists will finally get out of the basement and run away from his parents' house. After all, all men are drifting islands. Going in a certain direction. Going sooner or later, towards the final address. Then, to win or be lost in the spiralling sea that crosses into adulthood.

Ah! What would become of Viegas if he were able to lift with the weight of his knowledge, his dead weight? Who would this Viegas be? Because Zé Pedro Viegas is a Diógenes. He is a Diógenes dog that was repeatedly abandoned. He was rejected so many times that he became a renegade. A stray animal. Constantly avoided by everyone. Zé Pedro is one of these lonely dogs that is today howling at the full moon and at the cars that pass by him on the road.

The last time I saw Zé Pedro was in Lisbon. But it seems like it was long ago. At that time, he was in Lisbon studying cinema. When we met in Bairro Alto. That day he was too insecure to be cordial. He was more comfortable playing another role. With him was a friend. Who was a strangely hostile guy. One, Matias. I was too intoxicated and uninterested to hear what Viegas' friend was saying during the dinner that Miguel and I had at Bairro Alto.

Today, I definitively abandoned the idea of transferring my enrolment to Nova de Lisboa University. On the last day of the deadline for enrolment in the next academic year I decided to go back to my Évora. But I'm still doubting myself and my decision. After all, the longer I stay in Évora, the more I paradoxically move away from me. I would somehow get closer to Marcus. Also, I would stay neither there nor here. Neither here nor there. This was my current conviction.

It was intertwined with Marcus' main line of thought, which was going in the same uncertain direction as my present belief. There was no longer any point in fighting the current. Nor was it worth trying to float with it. Nor could I even aim to levitate in the river of men that flows into the sea, where in the depths of the oceans, gods and nymphs live comfortably among mansions and castles of once. I would stay neither there nor here. Neither here in the Avelar valley, nor exactly there, on the plain of Évora.

More and more, too, I am becoming convinced of Marcus' reason to believe strongly that neither in heaven nor here on earth do we find peace and love, but only the great waiting. Although, I still struggle to disagree with him. Believing or wanting to believe that our whole life consists of seeking to find the grail, which is a spiritual treasure. It is a search that has a greater meaning than discovery. After all, our understanding of waiting and death are only human notions. Even if we never find what we are looking for, the search must continue. It is indispensable. Otherwise, we are doomed to the divorce between our soul and the body that has our more or less immaterial life.

I met again with Marcus on the eve of my return to Évora. Marcus came with Inácio to pick me up at home. In the car, which had also been left to him by his grandparents, the magnates. In the back seat he reported to me that he could see the road in the distance with increasing difficulty. He refused, however, to consult a specialist.

"I can read the fine print in my books," he said, incredulous that I dared to contradict him. Continuing his obsolete argument, "So why do I have to see an ophthalmologist?" Lowering the volume of our conversation, so that in the front seat, Inácio couldn't hear us. Telling me about a dream he had recently, "I dreamt that I was sitting on a stone throne. On a high hill. Possibly on top of an acropolis. I was experiencing the advance of time. During the dream, I felt the presence of creatures that were not at all visible to me. And not even friendly! They were camouflaged by a fog that blurred with one of the layers in the atmosphere of my dream. And when I woke up, I woke up with the word protagonist on the tip of my tongue…"

I interrupted him, "In July, on the 24th, Marcus, I dreamt of a bag full of sand, which I immediately associated with my feelings for Adriana Espinosa."

"That one, with whom you travelled to Epidaurus?" Marcus asked, proving to me once again that his constant and apparent distraction was merely apparent.

"Exactly. I dreamt about her. But I know that she also dreamt about me. I know that, because she told me."

"It must mean something, dreaming about each other," Marcus sentenced.

I continued to tell him about the content of my dream, "My dream involved pieces of raw meat that were stored inside an old travel bag. I deduce that they are symbols and allegorical signs that indicate to me how slow my movement will be through the various tracks that the spiral of my reality has. Because when travelling in the hourglass, the reality of the dream has another speed. Without my being able to see, however, how fast is the passage of each grain of time that circulates from one dependency to another dependency."

"It seems to me a paradox!"

"Our journey through life lasts only one day, Marcus. And each day took us, with it, in a certain direction. Sometimes we end up confusing who is going in that same direction that only we and no one else is going."

"Perhaps, it is just a premonition. What does your intuition tell you? Maybe you should follow your intuition. If your intuition tells you that you should do something about it, then maybe you should consider doing it."

"My intuition tells me that she likes me. But that there is something in me or outside of me that will eventually ruin everything. And that in addition, there is something on her part that prevents a future relationship, no matter how much another part wants it. All this time in Évora, Marcus! What have I progressed? I read some books. Just that. Maybe I've just accumulated garbage, rubble. After all, where is the third eye? The truth wide open like a door that opens right in the middle of your forehead? It's the monkey mind, Marcus!"

"The monkey mind?" the ornery Marcus inquired, from what he had just heard.

"The monkey mind!" I repeated assertively.

Marcus was still dazzled by the expression I had used. I quoted Homer to him, to arrest him further. "As swiftly as flies, so flies the thought of a man who has travelled many lands, pending in his mind: Ah, were I here or there? And stirs the mind in many thoughts; so swift and ready was the flight of the venerable Hera."

Inácio was driving toward the usual place. The Iliad's father stopped Marcus' full attention. If I continued to develop the conversation he sought, I would be heard. Without once interrupting me. However, I wanted to tell him about the illusion of the moon and the illusion that Adriana's round face had on the moon's face. And of how my former colleague and residence, André Monte had raised in me the wall of the notion of being an impossible romance.

I couldn't resist and commented to Marcus, how beautiful the full moon was tonight. Continuing the full moon hung from the ceiling of the night, following us from the village of Avelar to the village of Figueiró, following us in a certain direction, the direction where Marcus and I were being led by Inácio.

"The closer the moon gets to the horizon, the more its size increases and any tiny distortion in the atmosphere causes it to fade," Marcus said, thinking he was helping me in some way. Then he paused for a long time. Until he gazed at the moon and exclaimed, "The moon never gives us the exact distance our eyes mimic. Limiting our eyes to closely embracing that reference of the moon in the distant sky."

I, too, paused contemplatively, but not too long, and said, "I will return to Évora, now, with a certain condition. An even more uncertain condition."

Surprisingly, Marcus didn't comment.

After having sipped our coffee, Inácio drove us to the village of Avelar to drop me off. Then, after having left me in the square in front of the urbanisation, he continued with Marcus to an uncertain part. Surely, he would cross a bridge that extends in a certain direction. Then, I could no longer tell if they were going more further, way here, or, more, further way there.

Book 2
The Promise

Chapter 1
The Returned

(September to October 2013)

I go back to the same point from which I left, but not exactly. It is the law of Eternal Return to Évora. I regress to recede. I return to a place that is known, yet now unknown to me. If I look with the regression binoculars lens, I can see myself here somewhere returning to the beginning. The beginning is a simple white building. With the university symbol embedded in the wall. Yes, I have been here before! On another night. With other faces, other visages in another feature of time. I was 22 years old! I was the famous poet bug. Now I'm 27 and time doesn't go back; so, while the clock of time goes forward, we go backwards, humanly speaking.

I left my luggage at the linguistics department office with the nice lady with a secretary's belly. I depended on her kindness. In fact, I was subject to an ingenuity of favours and loans, which was engendered from the very beginning of my stay at the University of Évora. I arranged the rest of my luggage in the cliché of my locker (for those to come, know that even today it is possible to go to number sixty-nine, and find my belongings there) and I followed the romance of the corridors of my *alma mater*, learning to modestly bite my shadow. My humble shadow, in turn, branded out the tail of my reptilian arrogance. It was increasingly obvious to me that I was repeating myself elsewhere.

Then I visited the university social services and learned that the whole system had changed. Even the building had moved! Even the top people in charge had left their jobs or had been displaced from their positions, like "doctor" Lúcia, who had lost her little domain. Such a beautiful thing, and such a rare thing, to see someone in this world lose power for power's sake.

"Mr Simão, it is no longer up to me to give you lunch and dinner tickets," she was still talking vainly.

"I understand, doctor Lúcia. Let me just, on behalf of all the students I know and who really, really appreciate you, convey a collective recognition for your work in the social services over all these years. But Mrs doctor Lúcia must be exhausted from hearing the same praise over and over again…"

It was a lie! Nobody liked her. Whenever she could, she made life difficult for every student with her personal theocracy. On the first scholarship I got, the former principal had to correct the "doctor," in front of me. Because she had made a big mistake. She had given me a much lower amount than I should have received. Besides, Lúcia wasn't a doctor at all.

After the failed meal tickets, I signed my name on the accommodation contract. When I learned that I was placed in the Vista Alegre residence, I promptly ingested a thought pill in the form of self-knowledge. I immediately felt its placebo effect. It was probably where my mind was. And my mind was, perhaps, with the snaking sensation of an aversive thought, which was creeping into me. I was not for the first time, not for the second time, but for the third time residing in a university residence.

I was clearly where I shouldn't be! I was returning to the beginning! However, the beginning was no longer a simple white building. Although, they kept embedded in the white wall the symbol of the dove, which is the symbol of the University of Évora and is also the symbol of the Holy Spirit. If I look with the binoculars through the regression lenses, I can barely see myself here anymore. But yes, I have already been here five years ago. In another night with other faces, in another physiognomy of time.

After checking into the residence, I made an effort not to stay there too long. I walked away, quickly. Before they threw the predictable question at me: "You are the Poet, the famous poet, aren't you?" The colleague in the room across from mine still tried to make conversation. But I excused myself, saying that I was late for a class. I always spoke very formally and maintained a body language that told him I wanted to keep my distance.

The lady who works at the Vista Alegre residence is the same lady who, every Wednesday, replaced Mrs Laurinda at the Bento Jesus Caraça residence, better known as Ponte de Ferro. I remember her, as I also remember that I had been here one night when the dream of the South was only the beginning of the dream. Although, I got intoxicated that night, or every night of the first year. And later part of the following one! And also, some afternoons and nights of the other one. Including, also part of this year's morning.

In which, I followed the convex curve of the spiral. Which in turn makes another curve even further out of the spiral road. Sadly, pushing me out of the dream, the dream of the South. Forever the promise of paradise, on a label also, perpetually, lost and gone! And, throughout this process I am continually in vain remembering.

The day is grey. But that's okay. I brought an umbrella. Although I never carry one with me, today, I didn't want to get wet. I didn't want Adriana to think I'm one of those stray dogs that likes to walk in the rain and doesn't mind having a wet coat or a soaked spirit. So, I bought an umbrella with the promise to keep it. Because if a single drop of water hits me, I might lose track of the reunion that will take place today at the cathedral. Therefore, during this day I will not be able to walk in the rain! Nor can I risk getting sick. At least I will have to postpone until the end of the meeting with Adriana.

I slip inside the classroom and wait impatiently. In the same way that each day drags on through the Alentejo. I go on without knowing if it is my will that goes faster than the determination of the time in which I live. I wonder if it is no longer me, but another me, who says that I am still here. Because, if it is not me who inquires, I ask myself: who is this other me? But yes! It is me who is sitting in the same place where I have sat dreaming since my first enrolment. With the same impression in both smell and touch that I am repeating myself: century after century, year after year, month after month, day after day, hour after hour, minute after minute, second after second, and that I am still somewhere in time echoing myself.

Now I am again in room 107 at Espírito Santo College. Yes, I have been here before. Reading and admiring the story that is told on the blue and white tiles that decorate the classroom. Eventually, I am returning to the same place…so that I don't get up from my chair again and leave in the middle of class, as I did the first time. I fear that the punishment that will be applied to me by the law of the Eternal Return to Évora, is that I won't be able to meet Adriana again this afternoon, in this life, nor in any other afternoon, or any other life that I may eventually live…

All I asked was that the class would end early. And I could go to Adriana. However, this is not going to happen. Life is not a dream. Nor is there a connection in heaven for my prayer to be answered. Everything I say will end up on voice mail…as much as I want time to fly, I recognise my punishment in being a returnee. Because that is what I am now: a returnee! After all, the semester train has already left, and I have never returned to Évora so late…

I stood on the first steps of the Sé stairs. With my umbrella open. Although, concretely, it was not raining there. Everything took place precisely as I had not conceived it in my head. Nothing that we said was part of the dialogue that I had written before. Because after I confessed to her that I had bought two tickets, Adriana seemed frankly disappointed. Perhaps, the climb to the top of the cathedral reminded her of something she had already done more than once with her boyfriend, or perhaps with her ex-boyfriend.

She obviously didn't want to spend too much time contemplating the city from the top of the cathedral. Maybe she was afraid of heights, afraid of slipping? Would it be better if the kissing scene took place on the sidewalk? Or would it be better if the scene of our first kiss took place by the silver aqueduct? With each of us keeping our umbrellas closed or open? We are so close to the clouds that this should be a unique moment… No? I closed my umbrella superstition and tucked it inside my armpit.

We slowly descended the spiral staircase of the cathedral. I went down without knowing how many degrees and steps of the dream of the South I was now. Perhaps I didn't really want to return to Évora and only wanted to find Adriana and the door to the cave, where the essence of the Southern dream is! The fault, eventually, is not only the law of the Eternal Return to Évora, but also the tax to be paid for my hesitant comeback to Évora. This is probably what Marcus calls "apparent retrograde motion." If only he were here, to define me who is what?

Today, when we hugged, I didn't feel the same tight knot of the human bond that we gave at the bus station, before I returned to the Avelar valley. The feeling of the reduced space of two worlds that wanted to come together, was this afternoon so far away. It is definitely not the same hug we gave when we said goodbye and were interrupted by her father, who is another kind of returnee. More specifically, a returnee from Macau.

I have no explanation for the odds. What were the probabilities that he arrived that day, just when Adriana with her tongue in my ear was whispering, "thank you for everything!"

Before I realised what her thank you meant and before I could read whether that moment was the moment for kissing, Daddy showed up! Supposedly because it didn't happen when it should have—under the roof of the bus station or in Greece underwater. Now it was too late to consummate our love.

After I lost my faith near the cathedral, we went to the convent pastry shop, *Pão de Rala*, for tea. What I had to tell her was lingering in me. I yawned suddenly. Was I bored? Tired? The tea was floating in the middle of the warm afternoon cup when I quickly made up an excuse to leave. Before the evening came and it was too late, I walked back to the residence with the umbrella under my arm. The rain was falling. But I didn't even feel it falling on me.

***

It was not yet five o'clock when the early morning alarm clock rang and I awoke with the ceiling of my shared bedroom closer to my head. Also, the deep breathing of my colleague, lying in the other bed next to me, could be heard much closer today. Shortly thereafter, I rose. Propelled by the force of belief that told me I had something to do. I, however, did not yet know what sense of duty was, today, capable of making me jump out of bed so quickly. Was it the constitution of the law of return to Évora that was already being applied to me?

Early in the morning, I took my lunch ticket from the machine parked in one of the stairwells of the Espírito Santo College. Then I went to sit on a bench in that cloister where there is a small square garden with an artificial lake. I stayed there for a few hours contemplating the water lilies. I believed in the importance of that moment that contained pieces of my silence and pieces of the buzz of those who passed by me, to go to a class to study an exact science.

Tired of contemplating so much, I got up and returned to the residence. Doubting myself now. Wondering if I wasn't a copy of what I had been. Wondering if I didn't have to relearn to be someone else again. Perhaps, that which I had been, had already worn out. And would I now have a duty to realise who I am today? Or am I just being punished? Is this the principle of being punished by the law of the Eternal Return to Évora? Could it be that all of this is a conversation, a monologue, of one who lies? Could it be that in the end, I, or he—the other me—was the only one who still didn't know anything? Could it be that life and literature are just a dream that one dreamt? And that death is also the dream of a life one has dreamt?

I was about to open the front door of the residence… I had already taken the keys out of my pocket, when I heard someone repeatedly from across the street shouting my name. Then, having turned around to see the person who was doing it so insistently I hesitated. I hesitated for that brief instant. I couldn't make up my mind. But even before his voice was heard, I had a feeling; that he was accompanied by a figure. In the throes of my indecision—between running into the house and saving myself or turning around, again, for a second of curiosity, just so I could peek at who I had already managed to identify—he was already there, next to me. Too close, so that I would now decide to ignore him! It was Belchior.

"I have to go shopping!" I excused myself. But Belchior insistently offered to accompany me. No matter how much I told him that it wouldn't be necessary, that I was grateful, he said yes! Again, I told him no, but again he told me yes! I claimed that he didn't have to bother, but Belchior was adamant that he was happy to. Making it more than explicit that it was as important, or even more important, for him to come with me, as it was fundamental, for me, that he didn't come.

The mysterious figure of my premonition that had appeared to me before Belchior had called me, now followed at my side. Besides, of course, the company of my squire Belchior Barreto. The figure that escorted us was as blurry as the afternoon mirror that was currently reflecting the early evening. And, it was as foggy as the bathroom mirror, when I took a shower this morning! The figure and I are following the path that Belchior is showing us. We are moving away from the centre of the city, and simultaneously, we are moving inside the nucleus that has the coiled shape of the screw from my dream.

I bought the items I needed and quickly headed for the supermarket checkout. At first, Belchior stood next to me. However, still at the end of the line, he asked me for my cell phone number and without any justification, disappeared into the crowd of customers. As unexpectedly as he appeared to me late this afternoon, he vanished into the early evening. I was left at the front of the line with the figure that, in turn, did not let go of my premonition.

***

I brought less suitcases on my return to Évora. The weight that I feel in my head weighs more than the luggage in my body. Some ideas have an unreal weight, but they transform the scales of our world into something real and concrete. Before returning to Évora, I tried to rid myself of the burden of my weight. Relieving the load that I have to carry with me. But, there are thoughts that are anchors that stubbornly float in our mind.

This morning, I went to taekwondo training. I went with the conviction of someone who finds it hard to change the colour of his belief. Basically, the colour of my taekwondo belt has the weight of how I feel. However, each training has a specific measurement. And you cannot measure your progress. Progress is always observed by someone who is far away from you. This is why magnifying glasses and microscopes are used to advance the science of a personal laboratory. That, or some other reason or justification that prevents me from going further. That, or some other reason or justification that fully explains why I can't see close up what I am trying to find.

Is the proof that I seek, and that I don't seem to have in front of me, the proof of this mismatch? Am I the man who threatens the tiger with his own extinction? Am I the serpent that predicts its own self-destruction? Am I the dragon that consumes himself in the fire of his own combustion? Am I the Poet who never finds salvation? How do I bite the Poet's tail that makes the tiger man live on? Let the last living poet die! Let the tail and the serpent's head of the last living poet be cut off!

After lunch, I headed to the Praça do Giraldo. Just to see Adriana, and not really, to watch her performance. When I arrived, the event was already happening. I had walked all that way and another to be able to see her. Now that I was there so close to Adriana, I was a little further away. Farther away from her and farther away from the city centre. Or the opposite! Because Adriana is more and more a place and Évora is more and more a woman that I love, above any other place. At the end of the performance, I left. I didn't say goodbye to Adriana, nor to Henrique, who was the creator of the performance in collaboration with Cerci of Évora.

I went on alone, intending to retire to my new shared room, like one of the monks living in the Cartuxa Convent. Adriana was a holy statue on the altar of love and was to be adored. However, she could never be touched. When kissed, only on the tips of her fingers or toes. Because her holy light would strike everyone twenty-four hours later.

Amazingly, halfway down the path I ran into Belchior again…this time I was too far away to be able to say that I had seen him, and too close to change course without it being too obvious. He wanted to show me the den where he lives. And where, recently, a large explosion had occurred. Curiously, not only the house, but also the Vista Alegre neighbourhood had almost, almost blown up! However, he didn't give me a single explanation as to how all that had happened. At the end of my visit to his palace of terror, Belchior invited me for a nocturnal soirée.

When I went to tell him that I would like to, but unfortunately, I couldn't, Belchior said that Eduardo would join us. So, I decided to tell him yes and headed to the Vista Alegre residence. Following my punishment, of being one more returnee. I experienced something relatively close to what a refugee child finds in a piece of world surrounded by barbed wire, with military personnel who tell him very assertively that that little piece of world does not belong to them.

Eduardo, Belchior and Francisca, Belchior's friend, came to meet me, exactly, in the room of the residence, where I was. We didn't stay there long. Francisca insisted that we should hurry. Repeating the anguish of having the car badly parked. As we were about to leave, Belchior pulled out of his coat pocket, which was too large for him, a book that he had cunningly taken from the closet of my study room. It was from the University of Évora's collection. Not only did he show me what he had done, he showed me how he had done it. I was not impressed, on the contrary. Eduardo shrugged his shoulders and smiled with careful diplomacy.

It was raining a little when Francisca made us run from the residence to her car. Belchior was excited to enjoy so much company at once. He obediently sat in the passenger seat. But more and more I could see that he was being contaminated by the agitation of his friend Francisca, who was driving faster and faster. Complaining sometimes with the driver of the car in front of her, and sometimes protesting against the rain, which was lightly hitting the front window of her car.

I was explaining to Eduardo in the back seat how I had usurped the study room where he had come to meet me. As I summarised to him the consequent transformation of that common space, which I converted into my office, Eduardo acclaimed my victory over part of the University of Évora's estate. The copilot Belchior was now cleaning the front window of Francisca's car, which had fogged up from the inside, while the impassive and serene windshield wiper was going from one side to the other. Francisca drove with the same initial haste with which she made us run to the badly parked car. Now that she was mounted on it, she was going even faster than the speed that the car was reaching at that moment.

We were going in circles through Saturday night. The whole of Évora was mistaken for the wheel of a giant roundabout spinning around us. Eduardo was telling me why he chose to specialise in clinical psychology, telling me about the end of his first year of his master's degree in psychology. He also summarised what had happened to him since we had last met in the Nossa Senhora da Saúde neighbourhood, when I was still sharing a house with Nilson and João, and had not yet travelled to Sifnos. In the end, he laughed. But he did it with discretion. Possibly remembering how abruptly the evening had ended. Simply because Belchior that day suddenly presented us with a far-fetched and abstract justification.

We finally stopped for a few minutes in the parking lot where the silver aqueduct passes. Francisca stopped beside a lone automobile. She got out of her car and Belchior went with her. Eduardo and I stayed inside the car and chatted. I took the opportunity to comment to Eduardo that the city we lived in was a very different city from the one we now saw comfortably seated in the back seat of Francisca's car.

He immediately looked at the night screen. Then turning very calmly in my direction. Then looking analytically again, beyond the window that held the brains of the night. Examining something that was inside or outside the anatomical veil that had the sky that Saturday night. I definitely could not see what he was looking at. It would certainly have a scientific colour. It would eventually be the result of a tone. Or of a set of tones, from which Eduardo extracted, only for himself, a meaning and a logical sense.

I enunciated, meanwhile, in my head a series of questions that I felt like asking him, such as: the first. "why have I never met you with a girlfriend?" The second, "are you celibate?" The third, "why do you live with your mother and brother?" The fourth, "why are you studying psychology?" Or, better! To rephrase, why do you study psychology and not philosophy? But I already knew! When Eduardo presented his candidacy, they had already closed the philosophy degree at the University of Évora. So, perhaps I would ask, "why didn't you go to study in Lisbon or Coimbra?"

But I didn't dare ask him stupid questions. Questions for which I didn't need any answers. His empathy and consideration were what mattered most to me, and he had already made them available to me. Not least because to truly know each other and become good friends, we don't need to know about personal archaeology that only concerns one's history.

Before Francisca and Belchior got back into the car, Eduardo picked his teeth. Debiting the ephemera of the October 5th holiday. This was not the first time that I had been graced with the opulence of his favourite entertainment. I then confessed to him that I felt bored sitting there. Although I enjoyed the pleasure of his company, it bored me that we were sitting in the desert of a parking lot, watching the rain fall and being washed away by the silver aqueduct.

I revealed to him that it was depressing me. And Eduardo listened to me. Without judging a single word of what I had told him. Not only did he understand me, but he openly stated that he felt the same way.

Francisca and Belchior soon after returned to the interior of the car, and we interrupted the conversation. Apparently, only so that we could continue driving around, outside the city walls. Driving Francisca, now, very calmly. Following Belchior, harmoniously, at her side. After turns and more turns we finally get out of Francisca's car, but my expectation quickly succumbs as we head towards the sinister villa in which Belchior had a rented roof.

The funereal melody of the rain played continuously. Breaking up into tiny scores that were fragmenting into exceptional musical droplets. Finally, the recapitulation of the rain sonata was heard. However, still without hope that today, October 5th, 2013, an armistice will be signed in the sky.

Belchior took the lead. He used his cell phone flashlight to illuminate his rotten front teeth. Scaring us even more when he showed us his distinctly evil laugh. I thought he had gone crazy, that he had been influenced by the evil spirit hidden in the sheet that night, when he very calmly stated that he didn't have the keys to the front door with him. However, he quickly asserted, very relaxed, that they were not necessary, because all that was needed was to push the door open. After all, he wasn't crazy… The door didn't have a lock! If in the afternoon, the house had the look of a low-budget action movie, in the night a thriller was being shown, shot by a director I couldn't find on the set.

We silently climbed the hallway stairs through the dark tunnel and were led by Belchior into the dimness of his bedroom. There was no electricity in his alcove, and roughly speaking, there was none in the other rooms either. This was the inauspicious result of the explosion, which remained unclear. Belchior lit all the candles he had and spread them around his chamber. The only window in his quarters remained partially open, and the light fog that had arisen in the street drifted into the room.

What was there and who was there lined up in one arrangement. Quickly, the astral plane and the real plane were pierced by the haze of the fog. It was during this moment that I fearlessly stuck my arm and hand out the window, to confirm if the rain I heard was still the same fatal and deadly music. I collected the sample discreetly, intent on not revealing the liquid piece of evidence I had found. Before the tiny droplet slipped from my palm, I partially clenched my hand and carefully placed it in my coat pocket. Storing it there for later analysis.

Belchior, Francisca and Eduardo sat on the mattress. I sat in the armchair, looking at the three of them sitting on the raft, which was crossing the darkness. Heading towards the sorcery contained in the mist, which was as much inside the room, as it was beyond the window. Francisca would consecutively roll the same hashish cigarette. And we smoked and twirled it repeatedly. A larger, denser haze was now floating around. Forming a single cloud of smoke. And I asked them, simulating, the voice of a spirit or a lost spectre, "Am I still here? Am I still here? Who is still here? Who is here? Who is there? Where is, here, who is there?"

Shortly thereafter, the bedroom door opened, ghostly. Revealing a disturbing noise, coming from somewhere inside the villa. Belchior's landlord's dog whined, tucked under the living room couch. Belchior promptly presented the thesis that an attic door had been left open… But he did so after Eduardo had argued that it was a draught that blew out one or another candle. Meanwhile, Francisca went fearfully to the bathroom. Groping, groping every wall along the way. Still, repeatedly stumbling in the creeping darkness.

The three of us stood by candlelight measuring the invisible room where our present fit. Each one unaware of what face our future would have and unaware of what colour the picture of our past would be painted. It was still raining. Francisca lingered in the half-ruined bathroom. It was during this period that Belchior told us what had happened. His explanation made the event of the explosion more anecdotal than tragic. It was a laugh-out-loud drama, a laugh-out-loud comedy! On his own initiative, he had started to cook food for the landlord's dog.

However, the poor wretch remembered that he had an appointment! And the poor thing was left to be cooked in the pot with the stove on minimum… Until the explosion! With Belchior's landlord's house almost completely blown up. The unfortunate Belchior's forgetfulness would kill most of the electrical appliances, and seriously injure some of the rooms in the house.

Fortunately, the starving dog stayed in the backyard and was saved! The blame, however, would not be admitted by Belchior, who calmly accused the landlord of not taking care of the dog. He concluded that if he had fed the dog, none of this would have happened.

At the end of the evening Francisca took Eduardo by car and left him at home. I walked to the student residence. It was already raining only on the roof of my mind. Passing, only, a small portion onto my clothes and the walls of my body. Besides the harmony that the rain played, there was a voice that only I now heard, a voice that told me, clearly, that I should keep a certain distance between me and Belchior. Perhaps, it was only the aria intoned by the final rain.

I ended up not being able to talk to Eduardo about the law of Eternal Return to Évora. Although, we did talk about how epic was the number of houses I relocated to. Eduardo compared my little modern epic to Ulysses' Odyssey. He couldn't, however, tell me if I was Homer or if I was not only Ulysses but also Homer.

Two days later I left the classroom, leaving the teacher ecstatic with me. I answered every question correctly. I knew everything. After all, I learned something from the books I read. Just as I learned the same from all the hours I spent alone. Essentially, I learned from all the people who are travelling salesmen! Not only of dreams and utopias, but also of chestnuts and cotton candy. Because some people are open-ended stories, they are books written by the pages of their own lives.

The simplest paragraphs of their days are events of extraordinary singular reinvention, and the nights, dressed in majestic fiction. Yet some dreams never bloom. Some of my dreams will never flourish. But they do make me genuinely know something about myself and the beauty and ugliness of those around me. Not least because I have employed successive defects and had a dozen painful professions that made me, at times, not exist.

Also, because I have made error after error, and perpetrated mistakes, and so many misunderstandings that I have naturally achieved more failure than success. And so, one day I will triumph! Because no one has ever failed as much, and repeatedly, as I have. But I am still here! Yes, I am still here, still around the dream, the dream of the South.

The residents of Vista Alegre already know who I am. My reputation must have arrived, regrettably, before me! It must have come directly to the residence.

Not needing to make a stopover in Lisbon. Like Belchior, good or bad fame doesn't need a key to enter the house.

My roommate, who is much younger than I am, tried to convince me what his space was and what mine was in the room he had occupied since last year. Now, as I was getting ready to write about what I think of him, he asked me, "if you please, turn off the light."

***

I returned to Évora as a Portuguese returnee, coming back to the same place, recognising that nothing else can be exactly the same. Not even an empire identical to what was once the homeland in his memory. Greece would probably be part of the map of the Southern dream. It would, eventually, be part of the paradise of a dream forever lost. Epidaurus, possibly, would also be part of that shipwrecked territory.

I wonder if I was, or not, in Epidaurus, the underwater cave I dreamt of, when I first came to know Évora and the cloister of the Colégio do Espírito Santo. It was precisely on that first trip to the South, that I dreamt of diving into a sheet of water, emerging in a cave, in which, there was an altar without any image. There was only a cup and two candlesticks.

When I woke up in the bus that had left Lisbon in the morning, in the summer of 2008, I was already arriving in Évora, when I identified the supposed sheet of water in Lapa da Moura, at the bottom of the São Neutel Mountain, where my grandmother lives. Perhaps Lapa da Moura is also part of the puzzle of this mysterious dream. Had I almost found in Epidaurus what I had already dreamt about? Had I almost fulfilled my dream? Where is its exact meaning? Will I find it in the Ribeira de Alge? In the stream that passes by the Lapa da Moura waterfall?

Adriana came to meet me at the university in the middle of the afternoon. She waited for me, sitting on the cloister steps. I left the classroom and went to meet her under the frontispiece of the sun and moon. Flora Raimundo followed me with her gaze. She was the same Flora who had gone to Sifnos with me and returned disliking me as much as I disliked her. After she had moved from Lisbon to Évora and I had rejected the idea of moving to Lisbon to study at the Universidade Nova, she was now my classmate in some subjects.

I sat next to Adriana, under the symbols of the moon and the sun, eternally hanging in the frontispiece of the ether cloister, of the once Jesuit college. Every cloud that crossed the blue afternoon sky was a crab in the river of life. It was a raft mattress, leaving Belchior's room and going down the river of the sky, to the river of the night! With Eduardo and Francisca rowing with their arms. And the mattress raft gliding upstream, downstream.

Until each one reaches the end of the river of life and the three of them finally enter the sea of the unknown.

Flora kept sniffing me with her gaze. As soon as she saw Adriana leaning against me, she revealed exaggerated amazement. Immediately she smothered the face of her inner self. Flora's world had, perhaps, turned upside down! But it mattered little to me, if my existence had a tremendous impact and annoyance on her. I was presently more concerned with finding an integral explanation, which would resolve the contradictory why of Adriana's actual distance from me, regardless of her bodily proximity.

As well, what I wanted was to elucidate the dream I had about her, and if possible, to understand what possible relationship it had with the other dream I had during the hot summer of 2008, when my head kept hitting the bus window, and I kept waking up and dreaming.

Because the stone-carved gate I had envisioned sleeping with, still in the village of Avelar in July 2008, I discovered it, before entering the ramparts by my own foot, immediately coming across the monumental portico of my dream, which was next to one of the entrance gates to the city. It was there, that I found, materially and immaterially, in part, the replica of one of the three arches from my dream, on the first day, when I arrived in Évora. Later I would realise that what I had dreamt of was more like the façade of the Espírito Santo College.

That portal in somnial stone, similar in Antalya to Hadrian's gate, was somehow related to the dream in which I emerged in an underwater cave, and found such an altar. Which contained only a chalice and two candlesticks. Possibly, these two oneiric experiences and the more or less recent dream with Adriana would be part of the master key, which would open my soul to the understanding of the dream chest in which she emerged. Once the lock of my spirit was unlocked, I would enter and travel through the realms that lay beyond the stone portal of the Southern dream.

My coming to Évora would certainly have to accomplish more than a mere degree. My return to Évora will also have to explain in which curve of my spiral

Adriana enters, and in which curve the symbols of the moon and the sun, encrusted in the frontispiece of the cloister of Espírito Santo College, enter. And why they are so important to me.

While swimming with Adriana at one of Epidaurus' beaches, I had a déjà-vu. It was exactly when I stepped away from her for a moment that I noticed the protruding crack in the rocks on the shore, which probably led to a sea cave. Soon after, she called me to come back to her, and we both floated on our bellies, holding hands, splashing and playing, and innocently exploring the curious contours of our bodies in the water.

Now, in Évora, we are both concretely under the star of the sun and the symbol of the sun and the carved symbol of the moon and its appearance, in the blue sky of this afternoon, with only a few clouds of cotton and white linen. The six of us form one esoteric frontispiece. Perhaps, these are not the final pieces of the puzzle that will fully or partially reveal to me the explanation of my dream. Perhaps, perhaps, there will never be a simple explanation of the dream of a struggling generation, of a generation outraged at the idea of paradise having been sadly lost forever?

Adriana and I left the cloister of the Espírito Santo College and moved closer, paradoxically, to each other. She didn't want to go to Renato's café, because she usually goes there with her boyfriend. She didn't tell me directly, but it was easily implied. I didn't mind not going… Certainly, that was part of the plot that the loom of our destiny was weaving. In the future, we would be together and could go to as many cafes as we wanted.

I didn't mind if we landed in the lily pad of a cafe far away from everything and everyone. Not least because then she could tell me what I didn't yet know, about who she had been in the past and how many lives she had lived to get to me.

After coffee, before the late afternoon slowly fell upon the two of us, we went through the golden wheat field. We walked until the veil of the sky covered the face of the night and the railway line was completely extinguished. Meanwhile, Adriana was still anxious. She grew impatient whenever she walked to a new place or when she did not quickly find reflected in the mirror of what she saw in her old safe haven.

When she ranged away from her familiar surroundings, where she usually moved, she immediately became uncomfortable. Such happened when we strolled in the sun, through the unfamiliar streets and beaches of Epidaurus.

Perhaps, the unknown was a terrible threat to her. Perhaps, she saw or felt in me, the danger of that world that is sailing through unknown waters. And that, somehow, she contradictorily recognised as living inside her.

We would then come across a stream and the ruins of a large walled property, where cows grazed their thoughts, some spotted, others smoother. We sat down on a small bridge that joined two banks and watched the water pass under our feet.

From there, I could see where I had once walked with Débora. It was the past walking with me, intertwining on the banks of the stream where the water of the present flowed. From there I could see Débora without a dress, lying on the golden wheat field. Lying on a white summer sheet that we brought from home, when we lived in Horta das Tâmaras, in a two-bedroom, next to the prison. Surely, everything is interconnected. Both the edge of the future, and the edge of the past, as well as, all the other edges that lean allegorically on the window sill of the present through which we peek.

Just as Adriana and I were leaving, I found the husky, who I had seen in another room of time with Débora, rolling around in the dry Alentejo. Now I head alone to the university pavilion. For one more taekwondo training session. I worked hard to leave Adriana and fulfil all my commitments. I worked tremendously hard to maintain the discipline of my routine. Still, when I get home, I will continue to pursue this routine of zeal.

As editor or reviewer of this book, there are junctures, which the author will have to cut out or simply omit. Perhaps, there will be a narrator who will reveal everything and who will somehow condition me…somewhere in the middle of the book, at the end or the beginning of the myth. But I, the protagonist, or the protagonist narrator do not, exactly, control what I feel, nor do I control what the author chooses to do with me at a given moment. Perhaps, an example is the afternoon of the next day, when I went to attend the Literary Criticism class, and promptly decided that I was not going to improve my grade.

I left before the break and didn't come back. Instead, I wandered the halls of the university. I looked for places in the College of the Espírito Santo, where I had never been before. I started by going up to the second floor, where the rectory is and contemplated the paintings hanging on the walls. I went through the layer of reality that had the museum's history of that time.

The air was cooler there and there was a silence identical to that found in a convent. What I saw painted on the walls of the university was somehow the annals of another time, just as it was also a more or less allegorical exposition of my world. Clearly, therein lies inexplicably the origin of my proto-history.

As I was walking down the stairs of the amphitheatre that I call Beato Salú, I ran into my classmate, Filomena, who asked me for an autograph. I wrote my name on her chest and my last name was caressed on her nipple. At the end she told me, twirling her tongue in my ear, that I was her favourite classmate and that there was no one more interesting in the course than me. Believing, possibly, that I was a guide, who would show her paradise on earth and save her from the hell that also lies in the same paradise on earth.

Then, from my walk through the halls and cloisters of the Espírito Santo College, I didn't go to the taekwondo training. But I did go to the actors' training at the Sociedade Operária de Recreio e Instrução (Recreation and Instruction Labour Society), losing the rest of the hope I had in Henrique's humanity. I was just going to be with Adriana. And, probably because of this, I am increasingly confusing the position of the moon on the stage of heaven. However, I am sure that it is the same moon that was chasing us at the moment Marcus and I were led to the usual place by Inácio. In the astral event of that instant, Marcus believed that the moon was really chasing us along the road. In fact, no matter how fast Inácio went, we could never get away from it.

After the rehearsal was over, I decided to write a play. I have decided to write about all the matters that are walled off by the invisible layers of the apex we live in. I will put them together in my mental spinning machine. Mixing the wool subjects with the polyester contents. Naturally, each piece will stain the whole. Once the program is finished, each piece is removed and stretched out on a clothesline with no logical springs.

And mattresses! There will have to be lonely mattresses, like the ones I constantly find abandoned in the streets of the historic centre. I will also include that news I read about NASA paying to lie down for a certain period of time, which is part of a study aimed at the project to colonise Mars. This is a non-return trip to planet earth—subsidised by the American businessman Elon Musk. I will incorporate all this into my script. Francis will be the protagonist. And, yes, I'm still here, and, yes, Francis has already agreed to do the play and I haven't even asked him yet.

***

I went to taekwondo training. This time, my roommate went with me. At the end of the training, he told me that he enjoyed the experience, but that he will not go anymore. Justifying himself, in the end, that it was too far for him to walk back and forth by his own foot. Then I talked to Francis. We talked on the webcam. First, due to the fact that I felt uncomfortable being in a university residence again. Then we talked about how he felt ostracised in the city of Santarém and how inappropriate it was for him to still be living at his parents' home. We also talked about how he left Buddhism forever. Returning to drugs and alcohol entirely.

Finally, a mention to José Pedro Viegas, who at twenty-six years old, had found his first job. Viegas was now working part-time like Francisco. The two were cashiers at the Pingo Doce hypermarket. And before turning off his PC camera Francis assured me, that he was going to have a vacation and he urged me, in the meantime, to schedule the premiere date of the play. I was left with the sole task of taking care of everything. Including asking Professor Luiz Alberto Ferraz whether or not we can present my play at the São Vicente Church.

Evidently, I regressed to Évora as someone returning home, entering a room of the world he knows, but who, at the same time, feels lost in a space that is no longer his. It's one more turn in the wheel of fortune, one more turn in the cycle of the circle of destiny. It is also the phases of the moon and the oscillations of the tides, the game of truth or dare, it is losing or winning. I returned to Évora not being able to return to the same place. After consecutively losing the idea that I had at the beginning of the path, it was now obvious to me that I could never win.

Late the next morning, I ran into Clarice. She seemed slightly frightened. Perhaps, she was upset by the rapidly deteriorating state of her mother's health. She was complaining that she had to immediately hire someone to take care of her mother, because she couldn't just slip away and stick her mother in a nursing home. Perhaps, she was also uneasy that she now had to wear glasses. Not yet accustomed to their presence, nor inclined to have to accept their perpetual company.

What is certain is that she was visibly irritated by the threat that her retirement could be drastically reduced by the current government. Her new pair of glasses only increased her concern about the amount of money she would receive each month. She is retiring now. Her decision consisted of the tautology of being better now than later.

She said first, almost whispering, "I'm worried about you, Simão." Taking a short pause, and resuming, without delay, what she really wanted to tell me. "Simão still has a way to go! Daniel Filipe Mansilha is already established; he has a job, a wife and a house."

"Yes, he told me he was happy to be teaching and to have moved to Oeiras."

For some reason, Clarice had felt the need to justify why she had previously made it difficult for him to defend his master's thesis. Interestingly, the last time that I had been with Daniel, he had complained about her. However, acknowledging to me that the severe rebuttal he had suffered from her, had allowed him to gain even more prestige academically. But he had only filed out such a declaration of interest, because he knew how much Professor Clarice meant to me, in the same way that Clarice had invoked her performance, in the jury she had composed in the past, because she knew that Daniel was my friend, and that I held him in equally high esteem.

"Simão you will have to find your way." She said, by way of conclusion.

With that, I pondered whether or not there was a hidden prophecy in her words, in the manner of Marcus Matalonga.

Clarice chewed slowly. Somewhat dissatisfied that she had to be the one to grind the food that was put on her plate. Taking the opportunity to recover an old topic, the subject of her first novel—which had won a revelation award. My dear mentor was still bent on selling me a copy of the book she had written twenty years ago. My admiration for her was not pinched by her mercantilist protestantism. A concept I had invented myself. However, now I don't have time left for much reference to it. One thing was certain, she did not act like the Master, who, besides offering me all his published books, always included in all of them a distinct dedication, "to my disciple and friend, Simão."

It was during dessert, that I confessed to her how I felt about Adriana. I couldn't describe to her, however, what it was that I really felt. I couldn't even tell her if Adriana was or wasn't in love with me. Clarice, after listening to me carefully, turned to the love experiences that the sponge of her life story had absorbed. In order to instruct and advise me.

Initially, she told me about her short-lived marriage to Professor Tadeu. Labelling her first partner as someone who was as intelligent as he was macho. Claiming that the signs she found before the marriage took place were more than enough for her to realise what she was getting into. Confessing to me, despite that, she was happy that Professor Tadeu had found someone who could put up with him. After having complained once again about the expiration date she had been subject to since the beginning, of her first and only marriage, she told me about her biggest mistake.

The mistake of leaving England and quitting her teaching position in the department of linguistics and literature at Oxford. And, sadly, her boyfriend was also left behind. A respected English cardiologist, who had been her great love. Based, probably, on this bitter taste of a sweet lost love, she encouraged me to tell Adriana how I felt about her. Assuming, finally, that she still couldn't have relationships with people who weren't the least bit attractive to her.

Clarice, today, seemed to me definitely aged. Eventually, her far and near glasses were to blame. But whenever she smiled her femininity revealed itself beautifully. Before she got up from the table, she said to me, "Sometimes any decision we make is always the least correct. Nevertheless, Simão, the right path is always the most complicated. Don't forget that…"

Then, already standing, she stared at me, and said, without blinking, "There are things we want to do, but viscerally we cannot. Simply because it is not in our blood mass."

And she left. She was going to give a class. At the end of this class, she would return to her house, in Parede, Lisbon. I followed her, until she went through the austere door. Disappearing like a beautiful meteorite falling on the horizon, fading away. This effect, consequently, convinced me that Adriana was really a satellite the size of the sky that had my illusion. As Marcus would say, "it's the moon's fault." Yes, I consent, it is the moon that induces me to believe that I am an inch away, when in fact we are effectively that far away from each other. And yet, what the understanding Clarice had advised me, left me even more confused and exasperated.

We were to meet after her last lesson. And, today, was the paragraph of another day. Today was the day Clarice would leave Évora and leave the University of Évora. We took a black and white picture, in front of the door of the Sala do Atos, to later remember the promise that I had been once… Then we went to lunch, because in old age and youth all time seems so little. In fact, one gets old and tired by being born every day. You get old and tired because every day the sun rises again, and with it a new day sprouts. You get old and tired while the earth makes the same revolution around the sun over and over again.

I myself get old and tired before the sun goes down.

We had lunch at the *Alguidar dos Sabores* restaurant, because it was close to the Espírito Santo College and on the way to the bus station. It was the waltz of one more goodbye. And the waltz of the distance that would remain between us and this moment, until our next meeting, would be another mentor from whom I would have much to learn in the future.

"You know, Simão, it had to be now. Otherwise, later on, I will be even more affected by the final amount of my pension."

That slender swan knew what she was talking about. She was never wrong. She was precise, rigorous, and meticulous. Once, she asked me why I was interested in her. She did it directly. Without beating around the bush. I never understood the reason for her question. But I also never understood why nothing in our past is ever entirely resolved.

"Simão has to take care of himself!" She repeated insistently.

Perhaps this was truly her last lecture. In which I should take note of her final summary. "The focus of the path we take is basically implanted in the root of what pleases us intimately." She then exemplified, as was her habit. "Take the case when, for a period of time, far longer than the energy of our body and spirit would be able to bear, we choose to continue. We carry on. Not for a moment do we think of giving up…essentially, because we enjoy what we do so much, we never feel fatigue in the arms or legs of our mind.

"Read biographies! There you will find great examples, models of how to achieve a path of excellence. I, now, am only interested in reading biographies. I am no longer interested in reading fiction. I now read only biographies. Especially of people who inspire me and from whom I can really learn something. If you are looking to progress in one area—which in your case is writing—first define what your concept of success is. We don't always understand that what we want has a very different process and definition than what each, originally, each of us has. Know what your method is. Do that, in the same way that you discover yourself.

"The more you know yourself, the more easily you will be able to identify what your real motivation is. After all, to create a work of art the artist needs to transform himself! He needs to transpose into the process what is also his being and to computerise that transmutation, which occurs first on an abstract plane and only later on a concrete and objective plane. The power to change the world, or ourselves, begins with us. The key that opens the door to change is inside us.

We have to search in the most hidden corners, we have to dig into that division of our being that we rarely show to friends who supposedly know us best.

"We have to search ceaselessly in the attic of our being, where we store the obsolete junk of our ideas and notions that are going out of date, and that no matter how much we no longer use any of it, we foolishly insist on keeping. Know what lies beyond the wall of the analytical house that is your being. Witness what you feel with what you judge your thinking. Don't live by the dictates of your senses alone. Nevertheless, chase the effect of that buzz that we feel in the shiver of our arm or the sudden punch of our stomach. But never lose yourself in the ring. Because the only opponent we can defeat or win is ourselves. Simão, don't just try to see! Look beyond, too. Understanding the parts that make it up; it is not always easier to decipher the enigma of the symphony that is our life."

She then said goodbye and walked elegantly down the vertiginous Serpa Pinto street. She still had plenty of time to get to the bus station and catch the express bus that would take her to her house in Parede. Besides, she was still young enough to change her life and live it as she saw fit. For a moment, she turned away. Realising that I had remained where she had left me. I waved to her from up the street and she held out her long, delicate, arm to say a final goodbye to me. And there, far away, she still looked bigger than the real version of her. With her, a certain belief in me was definitely gone.

The next day Adriana defended her Master's thesis and we met at her request. It was a brief meeting. She was not happy to have finished her master's degree, nor was she happy about the opportunity to soon start her internship in Henrique and Anabela's association. We stayed by the arcades, sitting on a bench talking and looking at the starry screen that mirrored those passing by the Praça do Giraldo. Then each one went back to their house. I walked with the prison of what I felt. Maybe, if I revealed to her what I felt for her, I would be free. However, maybe even that wouldn't free me.

I went down João de Deus Street, when I found a couple, in the square, cooking their dinner. Today, in the heart of the city there was an improvised kitchen. She was roasting mushrooms and cooking rice in a small pot over a camping gas stove. He was an old Scotsman with a dry wrinkled face, who strummed a guitar without much technique, and no matter how much he kept quiet or did nothing, it was easy to notice the age difference between the two of them. Night had long since come and that couple didn't mind the darkness. Nor did they mind the cold that crept under their skin at dawn.

In the middle of that atypical couple, there was a dog. Who apparently didn't know what he was doing there. Just like me! They called the dog Banana. It could have been Fig, Strawberry, but it stayed Banana. The dog, no matter what name they gave him, never leaves them. It was like he was tied to them. However, it was not chained. But it was subdued, like me. Presumably, the poor dog was sorry to leave them alone with that ideology of life that holds that freedom sometimes forces people to sleep in the street.

I ran into that strange couple again the next day. I brought them with me to the Vista Alegre residence. So that they could stay overnight at least for one night in the residence's garage, which housed a dozen paraphernalia. Although, I first had to appeal to the other residents to their duty of solidarity and universal camaraderie. They reluctantly agreed to let them stay, but, in return, the couple would have to leave before the employee arrived at the residence.

The next day, after the end of the rehearsal at SOLR, I took the longest walk to return to the residence. I wanted to tell Adriana that I had continued to dream about her. Extraordinarily, she confessed that she had also been dreaming about me lately. When I said goodbye to her, I didn't tell her that she was the same size as the illusion of the moon in my sky.

But I told her that I felt very small, because she was so close to me. But she didn't understand anything, and I continued walking back to the residence. Alone. Contemplating the moon. She was following me now, and I was also following her on her walk. Adriana's round face had the same face as the moon in the night sky.

***

Morning walks, at this moment, inside the residence in pyjamas. I am on the balcony. I hear my roommate, gnawing on the bone of his chocolate-filled cookie. Then, unwittingly, I watch the final scene. Which consists of him putting his fingers inside his mouth, licking them, one by one.

In the next room are other fellow residents. They play on their laptops, as if they were still small children who woke up on Saturday morning to watch cartoons on TV. It's the same in every room. All my housemates are in their pyjamas playing on the computer.

Unrestrainedly munching on all kinds of goodies, which include at least a little piece of chocolate. They don't take their fingers off the keyboard. No classes today. No time to waste! You have to play all day long on the computer and eat all kinds of sweets. Above all, you have to devour as many packages of crisps as possible. And, of course, at the end, push it with soft drinks. Which must contain a vast quotient of dyes and preservatives.

Francis has been repeating it to me lately: "I'd rather be a big fish in a small aquarium, than a small fish in a big aquarium." Maybe it was Zé Pedro who uttered it, in his parents' basement, where he kills his time. And Francis of course put that pearl in his pocket.

The last time he unleashed the Viegas pearl, presumably he was referring to his little elan: which includes the gang of childhood friends, headquartered in the only street in Vale Figueira…since he, in Santarém, is Calé! And there is no room for Calé's son at the top of the big landowning society. Nor in the green wheat that is the colour of the sun of my Ribatejo. He is on the other bank of the Alviela. That is, he is on the bank! And when a small river fish is caught in the sea, it is immediately returned to the river, or else it fucks up and dies.

I couldn't fish out from the balcony, the cloud passing by me…so I went to the cafe next to the residence. Shortly after, my fellow residents arrived. They came in droves to watch the broadcast of a soccer game and to read freely the polemics and crimes described in *Correio da Manhã*. Leaving finger-pointing over an unimportant scandal.

Meanwhile, I left the cafe and went, again, alone, for a short tour of my Sunday afternoon. Sunday evening had a smell of spoiled fish that crept into my hands. I could not get it out of my imagination. I walked along the Sunday roadsides with the feeling of emptiness in the stomach of my soul. The currents led me to the Alentejo desert and no one was ever seen in the desert of its streets.

I am a fish out of water. I shake myself without hope of returning to the sea and regret that I can't, today, swim with the mermaids and with my urchin friends and with my friends who are stars in the sea. I get tired today of walking once again through the desert sand that exists every Sunday in the Alentejo. Unbelievably, today, the sky is blue and tastes just like the salt of the sea.

It seems that the world has been interrupted and is closed for construction work this Sunday, and on top of that the traffic is cut off. Until the rest of the Sunday that is left of my life. In addition, everything else is limited to me. That is, that everything I want and desire can only happen on another day and in another lifetime. That's how it is! It is the law of the Eternal Return to Évora.

Two days later I met up with Adriana. We went to watch the sunset at Diana's garden gazebo. Her future mother-in-law was calling her every five minutes. Until suddenly her boyfriend arrived. And I left the stage convinced that only two could stay.

I said my line and left the place of the crime, that is, the place where I wanted to have committed the sin of love. It was a crime that I was in love with Adriana. But not being able to kill the love I felt for her was an even greater crime. I was not only guilty, I was hostage of the love I felt or thought I felt.

The sun had fully set by the time I reached the entrance of the residence and Adriana unexpectedly called me. To ask me if I liked her, more than, as a friend. I promptly answered her no. So that she would have no doubts. Then I lay down on that steep slope of the floor that accessed the basement. And I called her back immediately to confess, and she answered, "I only see you as a friend…"

I stopped listening to the rest. It started to rain in torrents. The water followed with the same slope as the ground. Draining down the drain and pulling me into it. I turned on my side as if I were lying on my bed and pulled the sheet of water over me. So that I wouldn't feel the rain falling so hard, I had that slow giddiness of the night fall on me. But it was inevitable not to feel all that rain suddenly pouring down on me.

The reason for love, after all, is to never find the reason for that feeling. I stood up, having memorised the pain I felt. I can remember everything I felt when the rain wrote on my body, that the magic of love is a certain portion of people you look for and can't find when you need it most.

The next day, my housemates showed me a photograph where I appeared completely drunk. Sleeping in my bed. With all of them around me. All of them laughing very loudly and me naively sleeping and who knows, dreaming!

Chapter 2
A Renegade University Resident

(November to December 2013)

The returnee disappeared. Inexplicably, in his place stood a university resident, in renegade form. The renegade stopped going to classes, stopped paying for housing, and started meeting regularly with Belchior. Which is also a good example of an individual who has turned into someone execrable. El Belchior does not work or study, and, similarly, he too was once a university resident. For now, he lives a *sui generis* existence, to say the least, in that unusual villa in the Vista Alegre neighbourhood that he almost blew up. As for me, last month I was just a returnee, now I am a university resident dethroned in the Vista Alegre residence.

Nilson called me at the beginning of the week just to inform me that the last electricity bill had already come. He had nothing else to tell me… As soon as I could, I went to the Nossa Senhora da Saúde neighbourhood. And, it was João and not Nilson who condescendingly opened the door for me. He was visibly uncomfortable. His glasses were falling down to the tip of his nose and he was repeatedly pulling them up.

We talked little and said a lot during all that vast silence, in which we looked at each other demurely for a few long seconds and did not recognise each other. Basically, I went in, paid, and before I left, I retrieved my toaster. I took it back more out of pride than necessity. Finally, I told him with conviction, "Goodbye, João!" And I write this "Goodbye, João!" now, in the interval of a writing workshop for dramatic text.

Meanwhile, my classmates had mostly all left the classroom. I took the opportunity to reflect during the break and couldn't get out of the same place I was sitting. The more we move away from who we are, the more we are pushed into what we essentially always will be. We spend a lifetime going to the same school only to never get out of the experience we had in it.

Almost everything I know I learned on my own. I mastered objective reality and the power of abstraction through my teaching curiosity, and still took in each daily lesson the importance of each subject being unique and absolute in the university of life. Time is my master, time and Master Benedito. With whom I will meet next week, for another walk in a straight line talk.

During the beginning of the class an exciting debate arose. In particular, with only one classmate. Damião! Or, Pantufa? Which is what some classmates call him...by his professional name. The clown Pantufa argued that the role of the stage director should be abolished. I claimed that would not always be possible. I used as my main argument, the example of a group of actors that didn't have such characteristics in themselves, would need a conductor, a maestro.

The Pantufa clown insisted adamantly and unyielding in his position. He wasn't really interested in debating, nor was he interested in fencing ideas. He quickly justified himself with his theatre company—*So-So Theatre*. Illustrating not his vision, but the religion that had been foisted on him. The heated debate grew lukewarm. The opponent refused to let himself be beaten. He had intellectually nothing that was truly of his own making to say. The civil war in the classroom dissolved ephemerally shortly thereafter.

Damião, The Pantufa clown continued with his shawl dancing awkwardly on his shoulders. In addition to his Mexican cape, he had a beret, which hid the messy arrangement of his hair. If one part was straight, another part of it was extremely curly; and if behind the nape of his neck his hair was short, in the middle it was over-lengthened. There were also two or three dreadlocks that went all the way to the end of his tail.

After class, I passed by the bus station and carved in the margins of this day's sheet the presence of those who arrive in Évora, as well as, the absence of those who leave. I wrote not with the nostalgia that I sometimes feel in my belly, but with the ink that is in the impatient look of passengers who wait and despair.

I went, not only to describe and be able to narrate the first enthusiasm of those who arrive and the helplessness of those who leave without knowing if they will return one day, but I also went to register the great expectation of those who wait beside me in the waiting room of the bus station and look away suspicious and committed to something and to someone. These are true dramaturgies that are perpetuated in each arrival and departure.

At the end of the afternoon, the next day, after my taekwondo training, I stopped by the São Vicente Church to talk to Professor Luiz Alberto Ferraz about the possibility of premiering the first act of my play, *The Guest and the Host*. The holy priest received me as a father receives the prodigal son. He immediately expressed that I was welcome in St Vincent's Church and that I should appear more often at his Eucharist. I was the sheep that had been lost and was now returning to the motherhouse, he was the Lord, the all-present, all-powerful Lord Teacher who is everywhere.

If anything happens in Évora, he is there to zealously judge what he sees and what he doesn't see. Because he was directly commissioned by the only Lord Teacher of the system that is above him, to represent him everywhere. Wherever there is a creation, in the South, he would be there. He, meanwhile, was preparing to project short films on top of the statues and altars of his church, and I rejected his invitation to attend with the rest of his cultural congregation.

When I got to my room, I learned the official and definitive result: I will not get a scholarship. Nor will I get free lunch and dinner tickets. That is the end of my little scheme in my little university world. Now I am even more renegade. For not having paid this month's housing, nor last month's! I expect to very soon be kicked out. Or simply swept out of the dorm. Maybe, this whole situation of mine has an honourable explanation, or maybe not! Perhaps, it is a happy conclusion, where I have no justification, no forgiveness.

The next day, without notifying me, he suddenly passed by the residence in the middle of the afternoon. It came and went, and came again, only to disappear soon after. At this moment, my office, that is, the room in the residence that is in the basement of the first floor, is his new hangout. The student residence has become the Belchior airport of Vista Alegre, where he makes more and more frequent stopovers.

I didn't mind that Belchior broke out or disappeared, or that he always had greasy hair, and dandruff resting on his shoulders. Nor did it bother me that his clothes were always dirty and grimy with stains, or that he simply smelled. Belchior is a renegade just as important or even more important than I am. So, I don't mind if he asks me for glasses of water as often as he begs me for a plate of food. After all, he is a *muy* respectable renegade residing in a rented room in that glorious decadent villa in the Vista Alegre neighbourhood that smells like mould.

This afternoon I went to the College of the Espírito Santo with no desire to learn. However, I had a great desire to teach and share what I knew. In practice, everything I knew, I had learned outside the university. But there was still time…so, with thirst and hunger for knowledge I headed for the bar at Espírito Santo, where once there was a laboratory.

There I met up with Eduardo, who was accompanied by a colleague. I sat down with them, having been invited to do so. His colleague was from the Algarve. He came to Évora every week to attend two days of master classes. He would then return to his parents' home. Somewhere between the beach and the hills. He was a grown man over forty years old. He was as bald as he was nice, although fatter than bald, still an extremely nice guy.

Eduardo and I arranged to meet, with the commitment to extend the rest of the conversation on next Sunday's clothesline. Then I was left alone, selecting future readings that would constitute new territory on the map of my linguistic knowledge. So that I could know where the other worlds of language begin and where the universe of my ignorance ends. It would also be part of the blueprint I wanted to show to Professor Suzana Sofia Baldaia.

Thus indicating to her where the future country of linguistics would be located. But Eduardo, before he went to tidy up the board, told me that Neurolinguistics was already on the route I had intuitively traced.

I continued for a few more minutes sitting at the university bar. Outlining an alternative route for my linguistic thesis. Some students came and went without leaving any marks on the floor. They passed by talking loudly, without, however, being able to hear the voice of their ideas and the expression of their dreams. They passed quickly, talking in a hurry. They knew where they were going and where precisely they were going to flock to.

Others knew where they wanted to go, but were unable to leave. Those would stay in the same place where they are now. They will never go where they really want to go. Nor will they ever get there. More students leave and arrive this fall/winter at the College of the Espírito Santo and enter the bar where I am sitting, while, outside, the leaves fall from the trees.

I woke up the next morning with a dry mouth. My body was sweaty. I was soaked. My body had been crying all night. I ran a marathon in my sleep. I promptly wondered if there was any colleague of mine in the Vista Alegre residence who ran, slept and dreamt as much as I do, who only knows how to run, sleep and dream. How many will cry with their bodies and know how to groan with their souls?

It is sunny in November; the cold of the present is only paradoxical. I do not feel the contradictory aspect in me. I only feel that I am a renegade university resident. More out of obligation yesterday, than out of vocation today. The sun sets on me. I don't feel the weight of the sun. I don't feel like I am still here. I don't even know if I have ever been here! In this place where I am today.

My classmates come into the classroom. Other classmates, who were once in my class, enter another room. Others are no longer here and I no longer remember the shape of their faces. Those I still remember, I will, presumably, eventually forget. I, perhaps, last, vaguely, in their memories. Like a figure that unwittingly took on the conformation of someone else. Someone, who they never knew who he really was. Knowing, however, more about me, than I will ever supposedly know.

Some leaves are piling up on the sidewalk. It's autumn in Évora, it's autumn in some streets of the world. I am crushing and stepping on the autumn leaves in Évora and Alentejo, and I hear: crash, relax, crash, relax, crash, relax. Not satisfied, I go kicking them into the middle of the road. Just as, on the other side of the sidewalk, on another street in the world, a child or an adult is doing exactly the same.

I returned to the residence. I passed by the last house Francisco lived in, which was inhabited by no one else until now. Half of what he was, was left there. The same half of the actor he aspired to be was also left there. The other half, surely, chose to stay with him.

***

Eduardo meticulously showed up at the stipulated time for dinner. He appeared just when my fellow residents already considered my stay a kind of illegal occupation. I was evidently going against the grain in their eyes. I would walk around the residence as one of those unwanted emigrants. To my colleagues, I was not only a renegade, but I was also someone who clearly did not belong there.

Eduardo's presence was yet another strange refugee event in their university lives. Only able to integrate the hazing and the group study for exams. There was only a little more room to go home to their parents during the weekend. This would include having the clothes ironed by the mothers, and the empty tupperware containers that would miraculously come full of soup and chicken stew for the whole week.

The repast was served in the basement room in which I had set up my office. There was no meat or fish dish. Nevertheless, it was a divine feast. The salt was more than enough and the wine was carefully released. It breathed in and out of the bottle, into the glass that was shaped like our bodies. We toasted to health and friendship. Then we spilled the wine moderately into our spirits.

Chewing its colour and enjoying its smell. Filled, but not satisfied, we washed our palates. All my supplies for the rest of the week and month were on the table. To be absorbed and shared extravagantly with my friend Eduardo in an ostentatiously pompous dinner. The nostalgic image of Coltrane and the sound of his saxophone was the musical dessert that we both digested with the help of the projector I requisitioned from the university. We saw and heard him projected in the middle of the stage on the residence wall, convinced that there was a resurrection window and that he was there with us.

Meanwhile, we went from a duo to a trio, because the buffoonish Belchior sprang up. He asked for wine instead of his usual glass of water. And he didn't shy away from accepting and twice repeating a plateful of food. Then Francisca arrived and we formed a quartet. Even more dissonant. Finally, Ana Maria, Belchior's girlfriend, joined us. And we were no longer an ensemble at all, but a certain group of very different people, living together in a certain Orpheus moment. In which anyone had a place to sit with us at the table.

It's already Monday. I took my time leaving the shell of my shared room after discovering what my roommate so secretly hides under his bed. His safe is nothing less than a huge plastic box, which contains no gold, jewellery or money. Only, his precious goodies are kept there. During his wait for the scholarship results, he even more religiously keeps an eye on his little box. He usually sits on the bed, sometimes looking at me suspiciously; other times, he spills his gaze to the bedroom doorway with a rather serious and thoughtful air. Fearing that someone wants to steal his precious chocolates.

In the kitchen, he asks for the scraps that others leave on the edge of the plate. After licking someone else's plate, he says that when he gets his scholarship he's going to watch Sporting play in Alvalade for the championship. But he never talks about giving back.

In the evening, I went to the hypermarket not to shop, but for inspiration. Basically, I went to collect material for my theatre play. I tried to find the main and secondary characters of the Eborense society there. Not leaving out the extras and their marginals. Those great intellectuals who are left off the stage of society and are generally seated at the door of the hypermarket. The example I picked was that of a bodhisattva wearing a bandana with his hand outstretched.

Belchior came with me and told me very enlightened, "Eh, *pá*! I prefer people who are hypocrites! I can't stand people who are unkind." Then it suddenly faded away. I wasn't shocked. I think, because I have become accustomed to his personality traits, it is easier for me not to judge the character that makes up his character.

When I got to my room, I sent correspondence to the *Student Support Division*. I begged them to grant me food aid. Not that I really wanted to receive help, because what I really wanted, and what was really important to me, was to practise the different genres and registers of writing. That's the only way a writer progresses. And the less help I had, the stronger my writing would become. That is why I urgently requested a new meeting with the Social Services. Although, I knew in advance what the outcome would be…

After I had sent correspondence, I lay down on the bed and imagined that Eduardo was in a corner of my room, sitting in a comfortable chair, giving me a free consultation. I could even hear him.

"It's impossible not to be punished, dear Simão! It's impossible to go away forever. A more benevolent action doesn't erase or forgive all the evil actions that you have constantly practised, throughout the spiral of the dream. Just because Simão left the old Scotsman and his young apprentice wife to stay overnight in the garage will not erase his unconscious past. Just that single pious act and a few other more selfless moments will not deliver him from hell, nor erase a third of his sins. Then he foolishly wanted to confess his love.

"Well…it was as foolish a decision as your roommate's need to repeatedly dip his fingers and tongue in the sugar of childhood. No! You should never have told Adriana how you felt about her. And, just because your friend Marcus, whom I have yet to meet, looked at your birth chart and gave his approval, that does not mean that he is capable of reading or interpreting a birth chart correctly.

"Nor should we consider astrology a science. Now there you are! Lying on a bed as flat as a wing of an aeroplane that doesn't work without the dream engine. And I have to sit here and listen to it? Surrounded by shelves and cabinets with pots piled up…and what's with all the cans of tuna? And why do I speak with this semantics and this syntax that is more yours than mine?"

"Oh, Eduardo, I don't know either! That's why I called on you," I said, not liking what my own conscience was telling me. Just then, someone unexpectedly knocked on my bedroom door. At first, I was startled. Thinking that someone had heard me talking to myself. But no, it was the dormitory worker who had come to announce it to me.

"Boy, there's someone who wants to talk to you," I quickly concluded that it could only be Belchior. He was the only one who appeared to me without warning.

Yes, it was Belchior. He had nothing to tell me…just, he needed to make time until his next appointment. When he was told to be at x place, he would run there. I had no desire to be with Belchior. But I wasn't opposed, today, to his passing company either. I too am a Belchior running around. Yes, I too am a Belchior running around in circles in the atlas, going round and round without knowing how to get out of the traffic circle, which still goes round and round in our heads.

Yes, I am also a poor Belchior who doesn't know which exit to take, nor which path to follow. I am a Belchior, accused by the old neighbours of almost blowing up the Vista Alegre neighbourhood. I am also that Belchior that continues and will continue at the beginning of each dark and cold night, lighting short wick candles that don't spray a great fragrance. I am right now that Belchiorinho who lives smoking the rest of a joint forgotten by someone in his ashtray. Eating bread with improvised butter and systematically tasting the flavour of running all day long from one place to another without ever achieving anything with it.

Before El Belchior left, he wanted to exchange my jacket, which has a damaged zipper, for a jacket that is distinctly large on him and which is part of the collection of clothes that he has in the closet of his room, and which belongs to his landlord's father. He seemed very happy after we made the exchange. I was also pleased. He got the jacket that Débora liked to see me wear, and I got rid of another memory that I will no longer need to wear.

I am now on the basement floor, listening to the symphony of drums that belong to the university laundry orchestra. They play the tempo of someone who is more and more a renegade, than a university resident. It is an orchestra composed only of washing instruments. They musically wash dirty laundry. I take a book out of the closet and read. I take another book out, and then another, and so on. I do literary zapping, because I have nothing else to do. That is, because nothing else, today, I feel like doing.

I missed classes and taekwondo training and, obviously, tomorrow I will not go to the acting lab, directed by Henrique Raposo. With the more than certain presence of Adriana Espinosa. I will distance myself, as the wise and the defeated do. I will distance myself like the planets and the stars do. Maybe, I will send a message to the girl I met this week when I went to take a coffee and naturally had to pay for Belchior coffee. She was with a friend and Góis, who, curiously enough, was a childhood friend of Henrique Raposo.

I had known him since we met on one of the nights at the *Sociedade Harmonia Eborense,* where we both presented an artistic project in 2010. Since then, we became fast friends. Until I left with Belchior from the café, Góis' friend didn't take her eyes off me. I, on the other hand, didn't take my eyes off her friend. Because I had nothing else to do and because I didn't feel like doing anything else but fucking. Now, she, I don't know!

***

I swim from one side of the pool to the other this Sunday. I try to forget the smell of chlorine. I doubt what I know, what I have been, and what I still aspire to be. For each stroke, my lungs inhale and exhale for not knowing why last Friday, the friend of Góis came to dinner with me at the residence. It's because after I had projected on the wall of the basement of the residence a movie session, halfway through, I decided to squeeze her tits. She didn't mind, she wasn't very interested in watching the rest of the movie.

For her sake, we had jumped right into an action scene. Her interest didn't go beyond a late-night soap opera on TV that didn't make her think much. After I convincingly squished her tits in my office, I continued to squish them in my bedroom. At the end of the fun, she went home and I turned the other way, and my roommate finally got a chance to lie down, in his own bed.

I now swim from one side to the other with no one in the pool this Sunday. I look at the indefinite blue background and recognise that the decision I made to return to Évora will make me not only more apostate, but even more of a renegade. Time is a bottomless pool. In the same deep space, you go from the Aegean Sea to the Portuguese sea, which is the labyrinth of saudade.

After going to the municipal pool, I went back to the residence and sat down in my office chair. Soon after, Belchior, without hesitation, knocked on the door.

"Hello? Hello? Are you there? Can I come in?" Belchior asked. And after five minutes he left.

He had arranged to meet there with Ana Maria, his unusual girlfriend. Who gave order to his nothing less than bizarre and unbalanced life. After the stopover, there, made by the two of them, each one went on separately.

The only difference between me and Belchior, is that my former landlord, with the approval of my former housemates, changed the lock on the entrance door. Belchior's landlord, on the other hand, believes that there is no need for a lock on the front door to enter the house. Something changes when we move to another house. We probably find out what lies beyond the shell appearance when we get a real taste of the true opinion others had of us.

Perhaps, we are forced to not only move house, but also, we are pushed to another area of residence, to possibly be closer to fulfilling the dream. With one more house relocation, I will be closer, certainly, to finding my way home and to the dream, the Southern dream, or maybe, not! Because, time always changes the places where we want to stay and in which we really, really want to stay forever.

Age has not one side of truth. Also, evil, wickedness, as well as goodness and generosity have more than one side. Not least because every human being is not exactly square. Perhaps this is why Francisco has definitively exchanged Buddhism for going to the gym. Fulfilling his four-hour shift and then religiously going to the gym to lift iron. Reluctantly returning home to his parents.

There he reads a paragraph with the cover of a book turned upside down. In the meantime, his mother Ana has made dinner. She put his plate on the table. His only task is to open his mouth. Or has Francisco changed too? Change everything! Change the world! Turn it inside out! Just don't change Francisco.

A few days later, I went to taekwondo training, although master Ruben Rebocho had no interest in my development. He was more committed to the athletes who have been practising since they were kids. Preferring, above all, those who are elastically younger than me. One of them was stabbed in the Cruz da Picada neighbourhood, where Góis' friend lives. Unfortunately, he was not able to defend himself with master Ruben Rebocho's taekwondo. Fortunately, the marks from the stitches will heal with the help of time.

After going to taekwondo training, I passed the hypermarket and ran into my fellow residents, who were following in droves. They were coming in the opposite direction to me. They had gone to buy soft drinks and frozen pizzas for dinner. Later, I ran into nurse José Carlos Caneira. We exchanged mere polite words.

I wondered, afterwards, what label would he now have stuck on me? What would my expiration date be? And what price would he have branded on my forehead? Did José Carlos Caneira recognise me from the Philosophy and Psychoanalysis classes where I was a colleague of his and Eduardo's, or did he just keep the memory of the conversation we had in the psychiatric hospital when I went to visit Débora after she was admitted there?

The next morning, I went to the Leões—the School of Fine Arts. I was quite excited, regardless of the weight of time, and the mark that age has on my soul. I left home without breakfast. Not exactly out of forgetfulness. However, the hunger and my appetite for existence was greater than the hole I had in my stomach today. Just as it was greater than the feeling of emptiness I found when I awoke today.

Still in the middle of the morning, I decided not only to write, but also to produce and stage the first act of my play—*The Guest and the Host*. I also decided to gather my friends together, and form a new theatre company. As I had previously done with the company *Sulfato de Amónio e Esse Não*, which I created in 2010, for a three-day event at the *Sociedade Harmonia Eborense*. Followed by the supplement of a one-day presentation and discussion in the university's small amphitheatre, where I was carried on shoulders. Not quite, but my brother and mother came to attend.

Although, it was not the same, if they had come and I had actually been thrown in the air, and carried on shoulders, and had witnessed the exaggerated glory of that moment, they would have understood more the myth that I voluntarily or involuntarily alone or accompanied was creating. Coincidentally, Eduardo showed up at *S.H.E.* on one of those three days. Maybe Eduardo and I are predestined to be great friends. One could say that after the glory of the moment, which in part did not happen, the circumstances of fortune did not make it easy for me. However, one could also say that it was I who did not contribute to its continuity.

In the meantime, I again answered Professor Artur Quaresma Rosado's questions correctly. I was still able to comment on whether Shakespeare's play—

The Tempest—could be considered his best. Professor Quaresma Rosado was not the only one who was delighted, my classmates also started to consider me as one of those gifted know-it-all.

Like my brother thinks that the older brother could one day go on a TV show and get paid for answering questions on *Who Wants to be a Millionaire*, or show off on *Got Talent*. But I will never go on television to answer questions that are not about my book, or any other book that I will write. That is, if I don't, in the meantime, decide to disappear. And be that, my last great performance, which unfortunately will not be on television or in the movies.

My little brother really wants me to go on TV, so he can tell his little friends that his brother is really a genius. One day he will understand that some things are as stupidly important as the excess weight you pay for at the airport. And that it matters as much what you keep as what you leave behind. And, in the end, it may actually have been worth it to refuse to pay so much for so little that contains your weight.

The prior must be tired of waiting for me to confess my sins… He has promised me that if I give him a simple synopsis, I will instantly receive his absolution. However, my path is more than an allegorical procession. In fact, my path is not a simple summary. No, my path is not just a play in which Francisco will be the protagonist. Therefore, more and more I doubt that my path will lead to the church of the prior LAF.

I am aware that all the roads in the atlas of planet earth have been traced in the cosmos and in the sky, and that all roads point to a constellation. After all, people follow paths. And, all people are, in their own way, roads, and they are all made of the same matter and mortar that is found in a star. Let's face it, all roads lead to heaven and hell. The button where each one begins and ends, has another button. Finding it is an endless adventure.

Tiago Silva, the older brother of "Miudinho," Mário, my former housemate at Ponte de Ferro, suddenly called me. Telling me that he really wanted to come and visit Évora. When what he should have promptly said was that he needed me to give him shelter. And that he couldn't think of anyone else who could help him so suddenly. I assumed he felt the need to temporarily leave Lisbon. To escape from the place where he was. That he needed to get away from his parents' home. Although, Tiago justified himself, in the end, with something purely abstract, something like, he was attracted by the magnetic energy of the city of Évora.

I can no longer remember when Miudinho finally decided what he wanted and abandoned his economics course, returning to Lisbon. Would it have been two, three years ago? Could it still have been during last year? Time goes by so fast that it seems like it was the day before yesterday that everything happened. In fact, it seems like it was yesterday that I arrived in Évora, entering through one of the doors of the city of the Southern dream…

He would arrive a few days later, on the bus express that came directly from Lisbon. Stopping only in Montemor. His interest in Évora was not that of a mystic. But that of a sorcerer. At the very least, one of those very doubtful ones. I had no doubt that Évora was indeed a special place. The doubt I had was that he might actually be someone as special as the city of Évora. The magician brought his electric guitar in a bag that he carried on his shoulder. It was more to give shape to his style than to play during the weekend on the strings of his electric guitar.

He was wearing his old leather jacket; however, his long straight hair was changed to a short hairstyle, which was shaped with the help of a wax bought in a store somewhere between the Elevador da Glória and Bairro Alto. His opening speech had its usual warm tone at the beginning, and then progressively turned into a tone that was no longer warm, but toxic. His good and beautiful manners would suddenly become frozen.

When he needed to control and manipulate those around him he would become as cold as an ice cube. The more his demand and his desire to get attention, the more he would be kept in that iceberg temper of his in I don't know how many negative degrees.

He has just arrived and already I am contrite! No, I shouldn't have offered Tiago a mattress. A mattress that isn't even mine. I shouldn't have agreed! We have reversed the roles. Now I am his host and he will be my guest. However, I cannot forget that the two times I went to Lisbon and stayed at his parents' house, it was Tiago and not his brother, Mário, Miudinho, who always provided me a good stay. But anyway, it doesn't matter if I regretted it. We now walk back to the residence. To leave his belongings. We quickly dragged one of the mattresses that was in the garage of the residence, to the basement floor, in the room where my office was, so that he could sleep there during the weekend.

Temporarily behind would be Lisbon and his current degree in history, being taken online. His twin sons, two or three years old, would stay in Tomar in the care of their mother—Filipa, who did not want to continue her relationship with him after she became pregnant. The management course would also be held in Tomar. Dropped halfway through. In a way, his younger brother faithfully copied his example.

Next to me, and at the same age as me, follows a hated Tiago without a job. And that is the real reason. And not the ones he invented to come to Évora. Maybe he just wanted to gain time? Or maybe he just wanted to spend it?

The next day, I no longer knew where I had put him. Between today and yesterday, I lost it. Something told me to remain carefree, that I would find him when I least expected it. That's what my grandfather used to tell me. "Let yourself be still and quiet because what you've lost always shows up later."

It always worked. It was similar to a sudden revelation, reminding you of the last thing you did and said; even feeling the impact of what you've lost, which you simply can't find, because it's in a different place than the one you usually leave it—and then the cell phone rings!

"Hello, Poet! Man, I don't know how I'm going to get there!"

I went to meet him. But I went slowly. I was in no hurry to find him again. I didn't care if he was lost yesterday or today. Or if he was lost forever. When I saw him, I mistook him for a tourist who didn't know how to get back to his hotel. He was quick to accuse me of the hangover that was accompanying him. Which was predictable! He fell silent when I asked him very calmly if he needed space, or if he wanted to spend some time alone to reflect.

Because I had better things to do than to put up with him. He didn't expect me to be inflexible with the child who refused to leave his adult body. He completely blurted out when I reminded him that it was he who wanted to spend the night drinking at the *Sociedade Harmonia Eborense*, while I rejected such a possibility and went back to the residence.

Because…rewinding the tape back…we had spent the end of the afternoon and the beginning of the night at João Paulino's cafe, in Bairro da Nossa Senhora da Saúde, when at midnight the apprentice magician got a slap in the face from Armando the plumber. The Catholic hand of his plumber's arm didn't like that Tiago, a drunken and unknown Lisboner, was standing there playing the fool and invoking the devil. With Latin he had memorised with the help of a website or an obscure book. Tiago winced at the conclusion of his scene with a grimace. Only the audience didn't like it at all. So much so that he received a bump on his trumpet to learn how to play his part better…giving a pirouette that made him fall to the floor.

Naturally, João Paulino recommended that I take Tiago out of there. Reassuring me that it was none of my business. Assuring me that everything was fine between us, because I was a gentleman. But that Tiago was not. The night would end there for me. But not for Tiago. Because when we arrived at Giraldo Square, Tiago went to the *S.H.E.* and I went to the residence.

But first, Tiago cried. He wailed and sobbed from the moment we entered the greenway until the moment we left, on the wooden stairs, which are next to the Ponte de Ferro residence. I had never seen him cry a tear. What annoyed me the most was not that he was shedding tears, but that he was victimising himself and blaming others for the situation he had got himself into. Not once did he take the blame. Not once did he consider that he was responsible for the consequences of his actions. He complained about everything and the same old thing. He complained that his parents had stuck him and his brother in military school.

But not once had his mother or father slapped him! Just like Armando the plumber had. Maybe if they had, none of this would have happened.

Tiago the headbanger was still weeping and wailing like a choirboy. I'd never seen a metalhead carping before. I didn't know what to do. Still, I bravely got in front of him and told him, "Either you stop crying, or I'll slap you in the face again myself!" Right and proper! He immediately stopped crying and started wanting me to go with him to the *S.H.E* to drink, but I refused.

I was afraid it was my turn. And that once I got there, it was very likely that I would get more than a slap in the face. So that's where I left him yesterday. Then going to the residence. But first I called Góis' friend to wait for me there.

He spent the rest of the morning and much of Saturday afternoon sleeping. Woke up Saturday night. We had only spaghetti for dinner, because that was the only thing I had. Belchior showed up. He brought not only hunger. But he also brought with him the curiosity to know who Tiago Silva was. He ended the leftovers we had for the next day. Initially, he said he didn't want anything. Indicating that he had already had dinner. But then he took a little bit off. Already uninhibited, he finished what was left from our dinner.

After a very satisfied and satiated Belchior had left, I commented with Tiago, about his behaviour during the past week, looking for a more or less tangible explanation.

Days before Tiagão arrived in Évora, Belchior had arranged a small *soirée* with me. He was in charge of inviting Eduardo. And since nobody showed up on the stipulated day and time, I went to his house and knocked on his door. He answered, but a long time later. Acting as if he didn't know me or didn't recognise me. I still went up the stairs to his room and, scandalised, found Eduardo there. I immediately confronted Eduardo and Belchior. Assertively stating to both of them that I had been waiting for them.

When I told them I was leaving, Eduardo accompanied me to the bottom of the stairs. Apologising and informing me, however, that he didn't know what had been planned. I soon realised that Belchior had forgotten again that another burner had been lit on the stove. Or that simply my company was only needed when he needed to make a stopover or when he was looking to repeat a plate full of spaghetti and pasta two or three times.

The abominable Mr Belchior was supposed to show up on Sunday afternoon. With Eduardo and Francisca. He had accepted the mission to entertain Tiago, who complained that I was too isolated. He could not explain to me why Belchior had a certain behaviour when Eduardo was with him and developed another when Eduardo was not.

The magician didn't offer me any magic formula, nor could he justify the motivation behind Belchior's obnoxious behaviour. After all, Tiagão was not a real magician, nor was he a professor of ethics. He just needed more attention than most. So, he didn't feel so strongly about human emptiness.

He had no interest in the laws of nature. His interest was essentially in the black magic he painted himself on the canvas of human stupidity he encountered. He was not a true adept. He was just someone interested in programming the minds of those who habitually surrounded him. Manipulating the largest group of people for his personal gain. He had strictly no perspective that would help me understand Belchior and the sphere of his world.

On Sunday afternoon, Belchior was agitated; Francisca was hypnotised by that sinister being, who quoted two or three phrases in Latin, two or three phrases that he kept repeating and that was enough to convince her that he spoke a dead language or that he spoke the language of the dead; Tiagão was entertained by the show he had quickly set up in my office stall, leaving a table lamp on to match the light in the spirit world, as well as to illuminate the astonishment on Francisca's face, which according to her, was just respect.

The fake magician's performance included drawing tarot cards and interpreting their meaning simply by relating it to the design on the faces of those present and the possible wishes and desires written somewhere on the arms and legs of his spectators, while Eduardo laughed scientifically inside.

At the end of the matinee, late afternoon fell and Tiago was invited by Belchior to sleep on a more comfortable mattress, which Belchior would be kind enough to put on the floor of his room, next to his bed.

He left for Lisbon by train on Monday. I accompanied him to Rossio Square. Then I left him and went to a class of Professor Ferreira Gomes. The explanation why I went to the French class is simple, I just wanted to see him go. The magician was thinking of staying one more day. At the farewell he again used his good manners to thank me for the weekend. And I was sorry that he wasn't always like this. I wouldn't have gone to class and I would have arranged for him to stay another day or two in Évora. Maybe on the way to Lisbon he would have grunted at the ticket inspector and had to be slapped again to learn some sense…

***

I met with the Master for another walk in his house. The Master, before closing the street door, told me that "the evolution of things and beings that were created, progress in a continuous line filled with ups and downs." When he slammed the door and locked the keys in his pocket, he concluded "knowledge is a heaven that never ends."

It was raining and cold, but the Master's suit was an impenetrable oilskin suit. Master walked dry and walked with a frankly optimistic smile, and today there was no exception. A few metres later, Professor Benedito insisted to me that the colour of the grey sky at the end of November could have another colour and another perception in my imagination, and that it was indifferent whether I closed my eyes or opened them. Then he took a deep breath and looked up, as if contemplating a world beyond the layers of colour and perception that I was also trying to gropingly observe.

He interrupted our walk again, only to tell me that it was important that I retained the Latin I had acquired in high school. Stressing once again the importance of me learning Greek. When he caught his breath, he moved forward with conviction. I was about to complain about Professor Luiz Alberto, but the Master put up a fight and told me that there was always something very positive in learning from the failings of others, and that I should learn as much from the shortcomings of others as from my own.

Finally, he said assertively, "you should never, for any reason, waste time accusing someone who was not even present to defend himself." The master was right. In fact, the Master always had the most perfect understanding of all things and all beings. I kept his lesson and promised to learn from the imperfections of others, just as I swore to the Master that I would never again waste time dwelling on matters that were petty and frivolous.

"Still water in a watertight puddle, however, is still water," said Professor Benedito, thus ending the subject once and for all.

And because Master loved that I told him one or another episode of mine, I reported to him that after being excommunicated by professor LAF, I was no longer a renegade, but was declared by the holy priest as an outcast. The Master stopped his march full of jubilation. He did not move because of his belly of joy. Considering my discernment was absolutely hilarious. Excited, I confessed to him that I was currently occupying the garage of the student residence. Making it my studio, and that it was there that I lay with my guest. As I was her host.

The Master opened the door with his paternal smile, revealing the age of his teeth. He immediately understood the reference to my play—*The Guest and the Host*. Finally, I exaggerated the drama of the missing mattresses from the garage. I lamented that I still did not know how I would house my entire theatre company. The Master was delighted with the number of my cast. Assuring me that on the opening date he would be there.

Then I went back to my studio. I went back to a world still without a feature. I went back to a configuration that only I could possibly arrogate. I turned off the lights and lay down on the only mattress that had survived. It was cold in the annex. But I ignored the incorporeal cold of that moment. The butchery of my current world now fits all in that utility room: plastic terrace chairs, a grocery cart, a stepladder, and things and thoughts piling up for who knows why.

After opening the daylight to see where I was, I found in the annex the exact place where I was and where I was piling up the material goods of my poor existence. My present world fits into a formless garage and the form that occupies my present studio. My experience fits in this existential room of mine, where I have been camping and fornicating on December days with Neida, Góis' friend. Especially since my housemates have tried to open my office door. When they encountered an opposing force on the other side, they tried harder to open it.

In that back-and-forth struggle to maintain the positions or to move forward the speculations and confirm who was doing what, I increased my pleasure more and more. I remained, however, firm on the other side, on the inside of the room. Containing myself within the roof of her mouth. In any case, the battalion of curious colleagues on the other side of the room gave up, and I, unable to resist any longer, I cum myself. Keeping the castle door, yet, closed.

The residence is still almost empty. Only the young resident from Madeira has stayed to put on a few more pounds. He is the youngest resident and the most overweight resident. All he does is agree with the other residents. He never disagrees. When he disagrees with one of them, it is because he is part of a majority. His older brother studied at the University of Évora. And, like him, lived in the Vista Alegre residence. Only, in the meantime, he dropped out and went to Lisbon to wash dishes.

I went this week to return the books to the municipal library that I borrowed. Neida came with me. I followed further ahead, so that I would not be associated with her. After all, I was a worthy outcast and she lived in a building with another social exclusion greater than me. I despised her. Not because she is nothing to me. But for being so submissive! Often she tells me that I could have had her without showing her that long, drawn-out black and white film. So too intellectual for her taste.

I entered the library and before I entered, I said, "Stay!" And she stayed.

Mrs Eugénia saw me and immediately came to tell me her news—she had started her Master's degree—while I was peeking through the second-floor window to check if Neida's ugly shadow had moved. Neida's shadow was ugly. Not even the sun beating down on the Roman temple worked magic on her. After Mrs Eugénia heard my encouragement, she wagged her tail and happily returned to her assistant coach seat, dragging the ladder with her. Then she went up to heaven, with the mission of tidying up the books that had been messed up by some very lazy god.

Later, without me having any need, I passed by the Espírito Santo College and told Neida to wait for me beyond the gate. Entering the merchandising store alone. Merely to make time or because I couldn't think of anything more interesting I felt like doing. The lady in the store had her head stuck in the monitor. She didn't even say good afternoon. I grabbed a sweatshirt with the university logo on it and left with it in my hand. Not without first saying very politely: "good afternoon, thank you."

And I left, as Belchior would have done, not caring about losing another bit of his honour. But deep down in the tank of my conscience, that thoughtless gesture of mine had a vital relevance, much more so than if I had forgotten a lit burner. Because I felt something burning inside me. in a violently simmering fire.

After this irreparable moment, I continued through the streets of Évora with Neida walking a few metres behind. Finding, further ahead, unfortunately, more helpless mattresses on the street. I don't know if they were waiting upright for someone or praying that the next ride would save them. I wish I could sleep with them tonight on the street.

In fact, I wish I could rescue all those mattresses that I often find abandoned in Évora. They are prescribed mattresses and they are as outcasts as I am! Poor mattresses that creak softly for knowing that it was there, that they were abandoned forever.

On Christmas Eve, Neida came to visit me. It was a purely sexual visit. She thought, possibly, that I needed the orgasm of her company. In the end, it made me feel even more alone. We had nothing to say to each other, no common ground we could talk about. Except that we fornicated during the December days, and I occasionally projected another movie from another season that only I was interested in watching.

She ended up going with me to buy beat up hashish from the Cruz Picada neighbourhood. From whom? From her brother! Who lives on methadone. He used to live on heroin, now he's moved to methadone. He was another former zombie soldier, an ex-combatant still struggling to leave the drug war. He has a son with Neida's gypsy friend! Top! And we talked for a few minutes in a ring omitted by the progress of the years. Top!

No one turned around. I was relieved. But I was even quieter when I entered the Malagueira neighbourhood and found a hundred rolled up euros notes lying outside a house. I quickly picked them up off the floor and continued walking. Once again, no one had seen me, however, the simmering fire of a stove burner in the kitchen of my soul continued to burn violently inside me. But I kept walking as if it were another day in the consciousness of Belchior's wheel of life. Perhaps, I was impelled by his spring of survival. And I didn't do what I once would have done without hesitation.

Curiously, when I arrived at the residence, I received a message from Francisco telling me that he had transferred a few euros to me and that it was my

Christmas present. After I called him to thank him, I did not mention it to him. Also, about these latest misaligned events of mine, I will say nothing to Marcus.

Marcus believes that money rules the world and that without money there is and can be no hope. But he also believes that honour and morals can never be lost or misplaced. He believes that it is better to lose hope first and that only in the last case does morality capitulate. But honour is never surrendered. Never! Or, in Marcus' case, is it the other way around?

Neida came back with me to the garage. Although, I call it my studio. She came there so that I could randomly flip through her body. First, I ran my hands over the pages of her breasts and after a quick prayer, I plunged into the pornographic image of her sex.

After spending Christmas alone, I have made the decision to return home for the New Year. I will return not exactly as a returnee, nor as a renegade, but I will return as a prescribed and outcast son. In fact, more specifically as a parasite son! A guest! Or a host? I don't know yet. What I do know is that I will possibly stay in the old house that my mother inherited. And in the new house, my blond and blue-eyed brother will be climbing the stairs to heaven.

He will go to his room on the second floor and hit the wall as if I were still on the other side of the wall, in my old room, and I would cascade back. Perhaps at that same time Marcus will knock on the gate of the old house, and I very sceptically, doubting this very possibility, will question, "Who is it?"

And Marcus will say, "It's me."

Chapter 3
The Guest and the Host

(December 2013 to February 2014)

I leave the town of Avelar and return to Évora. I keep parking in the same places where the bus stops, until it does the last stopover in Lisbon. Each day I distance myself more and more from the son that my mother seeks in me. A mother's love is a superior love. It is a love greater than the consideration of a guest or the devotion of a host. It is a greater affection than the brotherly friendship between comrades who refuse to belong to another group.

Last week, I subtracted myself between the house my mother inherited and the new house where my mother lives with my stepfather and my brother. I didn't know if I was going from one side to another, looking to get something that I already knew I would not get back, or if I was looking to write about what I had long known, that I would never find again.

The task of writing and living are not found in one exact place. The house we constantly live in is a place of transition, which lies between the life we dream and the life we have, and which, more or less, we choose every day to live. I left Avelar, however, without the town having left me. I was a guest between yesterday and today. I will be a host between today and tomorrow.

Meanwhile, Francisco called to inform me that the bus he was on, had docked at the station pier! Soon after, I arrived in Lisbon. I got off the bus from Pontão and walked excitedly over the crowded ground. I ran towards my friend Francisco to hug him. But he promptly gestured loudly for everyone to hear, "Wait a minute! That's a little too queer for my taste!"

Then he laughed at me. But I didn't laugh at him. We greeted each other from a distance and waited for Miguel, each one sitting on a bench in the station. Without me, in the meantime, excluding the last meeting in Lisbon, being able to remember the last time I had met Miguel Murtinho. Without Monsieur Francis being present. It would have been, eventually, one night in 2010 when Miguel and I crossed paths at the beginning of Rua dos Mercadores. I was going home to Débora. I had finished my shift. He was coming from the *S.H.E.* and going home to meet Cármen. Or was it 2011 already? And had Cármen already left him?

Shortly after Francis called Miguel for the second time to ask where he was, Miguel Murtinho suddenly arrived at the bus station. And the three of us, already reunited, made a small crossing in the rain that was falling indifferently on us. We ran to the nearest café. The town alarm sounded uninterruptedly in danger. It was dark. The dirty floor of the cafe was an extension of the city floor. The Francis who trod the cafe floor and the city floor, was not, however, the Francisco I knew and who truly existed beneath his skin. He was only the reflection of another Francis; he was mostly the mirror of what his friends wanted him to be. Whatever they saw reflected in him, he would be that.

Miguel is calling Francis a companion, and Francisco, naturally, is copying Miguel Murtinho. I am not allowed! Because it is a buddy thing… Francisco is the protagonist of the group. And, besides being a guest and a host at his parents' house, he will soon also be a guest at the student residence at Vista Alegre. Therefore, it makes more sense that he, and not Miguel, be the main hero of my play. Not least because Miguel Murtinho is a guest son at the home of his loving mother, and an awkward host at the home of his father who can't stand him.

I am a university resident at the Vista Alegre residence, but I still don't know if I am more of a guest, or if I am more of a host. I also don't know who of us is the parasite, and who of us is in fact the real virus. Soon we will be two guests, or two hosts on our way to Évora. Because Miguel will return to his parents' home. He will only come next week. To be one more to occupy Vista Alegre's student residence.

As the bus pulled out of the garage, Francis promptly pulled out his pocket bottle. It rattled like chocolate milk. After shaking the valuable elixir, he stubbornly urged me to drink it. I took a sip. Finishing it off with the rest of the *aguardente* he had in the container. After sucking on it, he wiped his mouth and justified himself, "I didn't want Miguel to know that I had it with me. Otherwise, I would be left high and dry!"

The driver took the wheel while sitting at the front of the bus, and Francis and I were cruising unhurriedly through the night landscape, sitting in the backseat, and it was at the end of the bus that Francisco told me that Débora was loose in Santarém.

After finding one last drop in the jar and only then, when the divine liquid was totally emptied, he put the bottle down, in the secret pocket, sewed inside his coat, by his mother Ana—in order to omit to the other simple mortals, that he always carried with him, the nectar of the gods—and very solemnly stated that Débora had run away again from her parents' house, now sleeping with Lara's ex-boyfriend. Lara, who was a former high school classmate. His and Viegas.

She was an archaeological figure still enduring in the history excavated from the fresh soil of his present. Lara was as fascinating an existence to him as Kurt Cobain's had been. The narrative of Francis' and Lara's lives were entangled, intertwined, and the more they wrapped themselves in the same web, the more Francisco licked himself with satisfaction.

We arrived in Évora intoxicated by the stars that shone in the living bed of darkness. After getting off the bus, we walked along the razor's edge of the night. Francis followed me. He did, as Miguel usually does. And just as I had come to Évora looking for the Master, Francisco had taken a vacation to find his path and the Master of his dream.

Just before we reached the residence, Francis stopped. He took a step back and parked. Remembering something, he took another crabby step and smiled satisfied. It dawned on him that that was where he had lived. Pointing in the direction of the house where he lived during his last years of university with Bernardo, who was an agronomy student during the weekdays, and a dedicated *forcado* at the weekend. He reminded me that he moved there after I left him. He smiled even more satiated, showing me once again the yellow of his teeth, to remind me that I had only been there to visit him a dozen times.

Now, in the middle of the intersection, reincarnated in the small role of a tour guide, with a youthful kind of sarcasm, he indicated to me that on my right-hand side was the street where I had been handcuffed. Absolutely delighted, and already satiated, he moved forward impetuously. As if he knew the rest of the way, and knew exactly where his future lay, and that he didn't need me—for anything else.

***

We promptly settled into my office. My fellow residents were now even more suspicious. They mistook Francisco for someone they knew. Or, perhaps, they saw him as a wanted criminal who was my associate. Francisco and I had too much knowledge for their young apprentice professions, too much novelty and technology for them to absorb so quickly. They didn't know who we were. Nor did they know who they themselves were. But they knew from the day they were born what to do with their college lives and their still young existences.

Maybe they thought they knew who I was. But they were completely unaware of who this Francis was, who now was invading their residence and their student lives. When Francis entered the residence, it was as if he had come home. He always knew socially what to say and what to do. He always knew how to seduce a woman as he knew how to deceive a man or someone with no gender and no opinion.

And because the mattresses once held in the garage had mysteriously evaporated from there, he would sleep contentedly on a strange little bench. Which was exactly his size horizontally. Francisco called the thing a "coffin." He rested one night in the coffin I had found next to the garbage can and asked to sleep the rest of the week at the house of his old classmate. She had once been our neighbour, now living relatively close to me.

Whenever Francisco talked about Rute, he would respectfully mention her colossal ass, "I will never be worthy of her majestic ass! Oh, that imposing, magnificent ass! One of the seven wonders of the world… And the other six, I don't know, and don't care to know, what they are."

It was good to wake up and know that Francisco was in Évora again. It was as if nothing had altered. I hadn't changed, neither had Francisco, and the city definitely hadn't modified at all! Not a bit.

He got out of his coffin around eleven o'clock in the morning. He appeared in my office, the day had long since drawn in. To Francisco, my office was just a room with a table, some chairs and a closet. But the student residence was to him, undeniably, a grandiose headquarters.

"Good morning, my general!" He said, as soon as he arrived, next to me.

"Good afternoon!" I said in a harsh, dry tone. Simulating Father Calé's voice.

Electrician retired very early from *EDP*. For simply having too many years of service, performed mainly during childhood and adolescence.

Father Calé was the son of a gypsy mother, who had once been a famous circus performer and actress in a variety theatre. Father Calé was also one of the great descendants of a family of itinerant fishermen during the famous floods in the Alviela River. And I was a mirror image of that boat, or an echo reflection of the voice of the barge that carried Father Calé when he was still a baby. And, of course, Calé's son always heard his father Calé's voice, no matter how much he covered his unconscious ears.

"My general, I dreamt about you!"

"Did you dream about me?" I asked him incredulously.

"We were at the bottom of a well that was continually filling up with water. We couldn't get up! We couldn't get out of there. And you, very calmly, told me, 'Don't worry! Our ancestors were sailors.'"

Not only would I have my Francis in Évora, I would also have a theatre consortium, which included Sebastião dos Santos, my classmate, who had recently finished his degree and with whom I had crossed paths earlier this winter. Precisely, by the water tank in Rua Nova. Not in the village of Avelar, but in the city of Évora that was the same name. And it was there, before we said goodbye, that he answered yes. That he had, in the meantime, nothing to do, and that he would accept my invitation. My consortium would also embrace Miudinho… Because, at the end of December, I invited him.

Only because I needed Mariana. In fact, I needed his girlfriend's contribution more than I needed his presence in my theatre company. Mariana would be very happy. Revealing by cell phone that I had guessed. Stating that was just what she needed right now and this was the right time. Plus, she emphasised that she was completely free and available to be my girlfriend. Correction, assistant. But perhaps she would also be available and free later on. It would be a matter of days, weeks, months, years, centuries?

For now, I would have an entire corporation not only to keep me company, but also to make art, or so that I could simply play theatre with my friends, and their friends. In fact, not only did I have a theatre company, I had an infantry that would fight by my side. They would fight against Luiz Alberto, against Raul Cancelo, and against any teacher, president, as well as against any other kind of octopus, whose tentacles are spread over the city of Évora, and whose suction cups stuck to everything and anything.

After lunch, Francisco and I went into town. We went reconnoitring where the procession would pass. Signalling on which battlefield our war would be fought. Each one took his legionnaire's knapsack. We returned home in the late afternoon.

After we had gone to buy wine and pizzas for dinner Francis insisted that what we needed was alcohol in our blood and that we didn't really need to eat. But what was vital and indispensable was that there were two or three bottles for each of us to drink. He stated, very categorically, that wine was the primitive fire of men. It was the inheritance that Prometheus had left us. And that we had to honour his will! As well, we had to aspire to be greater than the gods of Olympus.

He repeated his favourite thesis, "We cannot deviate even a millimetre from what you and I are. And that we always, always will be! You and I know where we came from. It was alcohol and drugs. You sometimes forget!"

I stopped in the middle of the sidewalk, imitating Professor Benedito, when we were walking on the greenway. Usually, he would interrupt his walk and I would suspend mine to pay attention to him. I did the same with Francisco, and emulated the Master as best I could. Stopping first and then speaking very objectively, "Tell me something that is pure and innocent… Like you! That long ago you were… When it was you! And not another version. Before you were the scum of the earth! That you are now. That which you have become! Tell me, tell me something new, again."

Maybe I overreacted. But Francisco kept quiet. He was distressed. He was bothered by not knowing what his next line was and not having any guidelines. Until I couldn't contain myself any longer…and I laughed. He laughed too. We both laughed like two friends who were accomplices in the crime that our friendship had committed constantly and since forever.

Yesterday, before Francisco went to Rute's house, which is somewhere between the Malagueira neighbourhood and the municipal swimming pools, he confronted me again with the fact that I was a bad friend. Complaining that I had abandoned and betrayed him in the past, but that he was still my friend. Even after all that I had done to him.

Then leaving with a big smile on his face. His sense of well-being was promoted for three reasons: one, because he knew that I recognised that I had failed him; two, because I immediately admitted to him that, and that I could never, ever be completely forgiven; three, because he knew that our friendship would last forever, and that he could continue to punish and punish me, forever, with the loyalty of his friendship.

I stayed behind in the darkness of the night. Watching him cross the road from one end to the other. Never turning back. Walking fearlessly through the night mist. With the collar of his jacket pulled up. Laughing, still slightly intoxicated. Speaking very softly. Just so his subconscious could hear him and I wouldn't have access to that most intimate conversation of his.

He went away always pretending that a large portion inside him was still hurt, and that he still resented the scar of my disloyalty. But the truth, was that another fraction, made him feel viscerally amazed, that it was I who betrayed him; and delighted, that I was such a great friend, and yet able to strike such a deep blow. Still another chunk or portion of himself would be fascinated, that we were still friends, and in awe of the possibility that we would most likely be friends forever. And just like before! Against everything and everyone, and against all odds. In the end, there would remain the strength of a friendship, which unfortunately for him remained intact.

As a rule, after lunch, the company would meet in a room at headquarters. There was no more room for so many people to be part of the same revolution. Belchior often showed up. Only, because he knew that there were new people there now; every day for him to meet. He came, because it suited him. And, just as he appeared, he would disappear, whenever he felt like it. Usually, in the early afternoon the company moves to the ring to rehearse. During each move, a hymn is heard, consisting basically of a collective whistle, intoned by a herd of souls, who simply walk along, side by side. Marching between the sphere of private space and the sphere of public space.

We usually left the student residence to occupy, preferably, a garden, which was quickly transformed into a theatre room. Most of the time, we rehearsed near the hybrid ring in the neighbourhood next to Vista Alegre. Which, curiously enough, had a house in ruins. With ephemeral walls and windows, preserved for posterity.

Besides the preserved facades, there was a ring with goals and basketball baskets, and also coloured lines marking the limits of what was a multipurpose sports arena, in an area where shrubs and fragrances erupted from the neighbours' houses and the streets that converged in that small enchanted forest. Nature was fighting to occupy the concrete ring, and the ring was fighting against the expansion of nature. It was one of those gardens where progress and disorder reinvented the outer landscape of my inner Alentejo.

Next to one of the goals, an orange tree was bursting on the floor of the concrete ring, not only an orange tree, but also an indoor garden. One of those with small cloisters that are hidden in the houses of the illustrious Eborenses that live within the city walls. As well as there was a theatre as big and as vast as the

Garcia de Resende Theatre. If the holy priest didn't want us in his church, I would make the street the place for my meeting with god.

Meanwhile, Francis continued with his zeal night after night, reminding me that I was a bad friend. Invariably, after each work session is over and we have dinner, he goes to Rute's house to sleep. But first, he always tells me what a bad friend I was and am. Then he puts his hand on my shoulder and tells me about his biggest dream, "Do you know what my biggest dream is? Huh? Big boy! My biggest dream is to one day be able to fuck Rute's ass! What an ass! It's one of the great wonders of the world. Nothing in the world is so big. As monumental as that ass. Holy shit! What an imposing ass the world has seen born."

The next day the couple of amateur musicians—my classmate, Simone and her boyfriend—arrived, predictably, another day late. Francis was opening his eyes. Today he opened them even wider. Almost blowing out his eye sockets through his nose and ears. Shaking his head. Sawing his hands off and then sticking them inside his mouth. Finally, he couldn't help himself, "What a shame. Fuck! I hate people who are late. I hate them! What the fuck, but don't they have any responsibility?"

I was their leader, their general, their spiritual guide. And not one of those three complains. Not a single one protests. Only, they take notes and process opinions. Only then do they apply measures, if necessary. So, I listened, patiently, to his criticism and listened carefully to the groans of the remaining infantry.

When the company marches out of the headquarters to rehearse in the neighbourhood ring and goes whistling and humming, I feel that I have a real mission in the world. And that I am responsible for these actors, these musicians and dancers who want to be soldiers. They are young women who follow me to make art. They are men, still reckless, who accompany me. Not to start another war, but to provoke, at least, a life on the stage of a square, or on the stage of a street in Évora, or in the rivers and streams of another city in the world.

Last night, Francisco faithfully fulfilled his ritual. Yesterday, however, he was superlative. Naturally, before going to bed at Rute's, he accused me of being a bad friend. This time it was precisely of being a disloyal misery that deserted him. He got drunker than on the other nights and went staggering off to Rute's mother's house. Not at the beginning of the night, as usual. But zigzagging past midnight. Throwing up on the sidewalk on the eve of opening day. He did it when I was no longer looking. Then groping for the way to Rute's mother's house. The next day he appeared to me, hoarse and wearing sunglasses. Announcing in a grave enough tone.

"My general! I am finally ready for my role!" I consented. I said yes. Simultaneously shaking my head no.

He asks for chicken soup. They bring him the chicken soup now. Smoke comes out of the bowl. He spoons the soup spoon into the chicken soup and stirs. Puff! Smoke still comes out of the soup spoon, and he sips it without patience. Soon after, he protests. Saying it's too hot. He blows again. Not satisfied, he complains. This time, it doesn't have enough salt. He pours a jar of salt into the soup and stirs. He blows a little more and sips it happily.

We are in an ordinary cafe-restaurant where, shortly afterwards, Francis remembers that he had once gone there for a snack with Lina. He immediately comes to the conclusion that losing Lina was, for him, one of those events that change an entire life. Consequently, it crystallised into something quite different.

At the end of the meal, he asked for coffee and brandy. In the meantime, I told him about the nightmare I had last night: first, I was walking through a wasteland and kept finding scrap metal. All kinds of junk. Then I passed by a cemetery where the dead had been buried in no particular order. The slabs of the tombstones and graves were worn away by time, spent in the sun and rain. I then spotted a cluster of cars parked in front of a living room window.

When I finished my dreamlike account, he stuffed his belongings into his usual backpack. But he only got up, after I administered him a placebo brand confidence injection. Which convinced him that not only was he a true champion, but he was my best spearhead. He also came to believe that I was his coach, and that what I told him was to be done, unquestionably.

Before he joined the company, he told me that some guys had tried to rob him yesterday. On his way to Rute and Rute's mother's house. Only the wretched man wasn't carrying his wallet or his cell phone. Nor did he have anything valuable on him that could be stolen.

They felt sorry for him and let him go. When the story was over, the bum burped, rubbing his belly full of satisfaction.

It was only five minutes before the procession started. I was holding in my hand the licence that authorised the premiere of the play. Still in the distance, I raised my arm. Just to triumphantly show that I had with me the role that confirmed, that I had the power to make it really happen, what I had previously projected in my imagination. What's more, I had the power to pour from my imagination to a sheet of paper and from a sheet of paper to a leaf on a tree in the Theatre Square.

Nobody could stop me anymore! Not Luiz Alberto, not the police. Nobody! Nobody could forbid me anymore. It was really going to happen! And somewhere in me, something was also going to happen and come true.

The company jumped and jumped with one voice. Thinking I was as real as their ideal.

January 11 was due in the year 2014 and I was due somewhere specifically during that January day. I was due somewhere when the play, *The Guest and the Host,* was literally passing through town in a performative procession, of the allegorical and dreamlike kind. Somewhere it was being acclaimed by even those who didn't understand why there was a child lying on a bed and being carried from street to street and square to square.

I could finally cross my arms. I could evaluate the final puzzle of my creation and watch the spontaneous movement of each piece that was presently being played. Regardless, of the compartment each piece was designed to act with the whole, which constituted the chess train already in motion. Each piece of my chess was now autonomous and unpredictable. Old Antero Peçanha even took his half dozen dogs by the leash, mixing his personal disorder into the confusion of the crowd of spectators. Old Peçanha was also part of my concept of the unpredictable, part of that imponderable performance that ran parallel to the other that was happening in the street.

The stage and the audience of the passing city, the showcase of spectators and the squares and squares of people, were one single moving stage. The top street, the side street, the cul-de-sac and the boulevard, were just another costume in my concept of the unexpected, acting out my moving fiction drama.

The whole company believes in me and my vision. I am their staging prophet and they are my congregation. They are the congregation that meets at headquarters and to whom I preach the religion of the sublime. My religion has only the dogma of the unpredictable.

The unpredictable often happens. But the more we plan and prepare, the less we have to wait. To capture it more often, we have to anticipate the potency of each larval moment suddenly turning into the volcano of what we most want to see materialise. This visible effect often succeeds in a metaphorical flapping of wings.

The procession is advancing towards Giraldo Square. I follow the funeral procession of the dream. And behold, when I reach the square, I reach a strange magnetic centre. Suddenly I feel that I am not only in the historical centre of Évora, but also in the centre of Alentejo. More! I also feel that I am in transit, with the people who follow the procession, and with those who simply aim and go their way. Beyond what I feel, I also know that those who sit on the benches in the square and look at the procession, and those who follow it to infinity are connected with something greater than the unpredictable moment of the present in which they are. But that in that very instant, I am walking a quantum path.

In the curve of that quantum path, I recognise the centre of the Alentejo. I know where the path is and the invisible portal there. I learnt it today, on January eleventh, 2014. I know where the centre of Évora is and where the centre of Alentejo is, and I know where my centre is. I already know in part a very small part of my dream, the dream of the South. Finally, I have found the magic door that leads to the underwater cave!

The play ended. Master came to watch and congratulated me. Professor Quaresma still came in time and caught up with the procession as it left the Praça do Giraldo, and headed for the Praça do Sertório. A few other people dragged themselves to the end of the procession. Some of my colleagues from the residence attended. Eduardo came with Belchior, or the other way around. When the company turned and thanked the audience, I realised that the only legitimate theatre is life, or something as important as impalpable camaraderie and individual immaterial courage that keeps us going when others can't see an inch of what lies ahead. Be that, a tremendously glorious and grand future, or just something that is simply human.

The play is over. My mission was over. I was filled with emptiness. The round of applause did not repay those who gave everything and were left with nothing. Now that the show was over, I felt naked and alone, but the soul of each one of us would continue anyway; *The Show must go on…or blah, blah, blah, whiskey bags!*

Francisco wanted to celebrate. But more than celebrating, he wanted to party. I just wanted to go to the dorm and wake up early the next day. He convinced me, however, by insisting that it was important to laurel the pebble after we had achieved something. I didn't believe him. But I humoured him. He promptly arranged dinner in a restaurant that opened next to the Bank of Portugal. And so, it was agreed that we would meet at 8.00 pm.

Francis went to Rute's mother's house hitchhiking. I don't know with whom; Belchior, inexplicably, went too. Supposedly, because he was tired of walking. The bed that had left my room, hitchhiked back to the residence. I just had to put my hands in my pockets and head home. Eduardo accompanied me. Then he went on to Belchior's house. He would meet us later at the *Sociedade Harmonia Eborense*. Belchior, naturally, would make a point of coming. Although, he had not been invited.

Before Eduardo said goodbye to me, he came with me from the porch of the Garcia Resende Theatre to the Vista Alegre residence, asking questions to which I answered somewhat apprehensively. I couldn't tell at the moment if Eduardo was that colleague that I remembered from the Philosophy and Psychoanalysis classes, or if he was Eduardo, Belchior's friend. A friend, not because of any affinity, but because he was extremely similar in temperament. Which would be another Eduardo, completely different. Maybe, it was just Eduardo from whom neither he nor I could remember in which exact fog of the cosmos our friendship had arisen.

***

My troupe of friends awoke after the sun had peeled, and in parallel, a mysterious and indecipherable signal appeared in the form of last night's hangover.

"Yesterday you were handsome! You looked like a big cat! Perched on top of *Harmonia's* roof," Francis said to me, squeezing my face.

While Miguel Murtinho nodded yes, shaking his head up and down affirmatively. We could barely hear what he was saying:

"I took pictures so that later we could remember the friends we had. And how beautiful everything was when we were young and the world was still conquerable." Then he shut up and meticulously wiped the lethargy and fingerprints marked on the lenses of his glasses. Insistently maintaining the tie of his thoughtful air.

My hangover was so heavy that I didn't feel the head or the weight of the saying that wrote somewhere in me the guilty feeling that I didn't know about my wallet. I didn't mind not knowing where it had gone, because all I would have to do is rewind the tape back and I would know where in my mind I was when I lost it. I could just rewind to that moment, or simply review the pictures Miguel had taken during the hazy of last night.

I clearly remember pretending to be more drunk than I was supposed to be even then. I remember consecutively falling out of a chair until I got tired of pretending to be completely out of my mind. I remember that André Monte's friend, Gaspar, persistently criticised my behaviour. I remember because I made a point of showing him how sincerely I didn't care about his opinion. I know and am sure that I was not drunk enough yesterday to create a fuss. I was just drunk enough to strut around in the guise of my chaos by the order that reigned on the *Eborense Harmony Society*.

I was surrounded by a troop of friends, enough to defeat thirty thousand battalions of people, of whom I have serious doubts that they were actually harmonious… My retinue of friends was a valiant platoon of thoughtless spirits. The only legionnaire we lost was Eduardo. He went home early because he was drunk as a skunk. He ended up dying sadly on the beach at night. He vomited, however, gloriously through the window of the cab that picked him up in Giraldo Square. He only stopped regurgitating when he finally arrived home. He was immediately resuscitated when he got out of the cab and quietly entered the house. He went to his room and fell asleep with his duty done. Peace to his soul! Noble soldier who will be posthumously decorated by me.

For majestic acts of bravery on the battlefield, rendered during the war in the trenches of the *Sociedade Harmonia Eborense,* heroically defending the Southern dream. Peace to his soul, he will never be forgotten!

The rest of Sunday was spent with monumental melancholy that had the company of my hangover. Shared by the solidarity of all my friends, who once again gathered in the barracks dormitories. Today, we had the same Évora. We were together again in the same living room, which had a more or less concrete division of time. Certainly, it would be a matter of space of abstraction until I found my wallet in another division of my being…

Each of my friends slept where they could fit. They were true legionnaires. If necessary, they slept on the floor. If necessary, they slept hanging from the ceiling. I slept in the garage. Neida insisted on sleeping on the floor with me. Refusing to go home. Even though she had a fever and was shivering with cold, she still wanted to satisfy me. The more I despised her, the more she showed me what a fearless soldier she was as a woman. Love is also a pitiful war. There are winners and losers. And of the losers no one remembers the name. Neida, however, was hers.

Another new day imploded. Monday woke me up and I got up still not knowing where I got yesterday's hangover. Ignorant of why it had disappeared along with my wallet that had also disappeared the day before yesterday. Strange shadows and shapes danced among the small rays of twilight and had no entity. It was late Monday afternoon and I had no choice but to find the wallet! Not least because I had decided to go to Lisbon. I was hitching a ride with Mariana and Mário. Francis and Miguel were also coming with me. So, I was really, really going to need my wallet to be found today.

Only today was I truly worried. However, I had a feeling that she was not so lost. And maybe that's why I thought I didn't have to worry too much. If only it wouldn't hurt me. Surely, someone must have found it and kept it. And he would have already tried in vain to call, to tell me that he or she had found it and to put my mind at rest. Only I hadn't answered right away, because the number was unknown.

I and what remained of my initial army were now walking through the scenery of the city. Passing where the procession and the parade passed. We went from street to street and from square to square. Finally, we wandered through the association *Sociedade Harmonia Eborense,* which I still don't know if it is for-profit or not for-profit, or if it has any other kind of purpose. Anyway! It doesn't matter. I don't want to know. I asked for my wallet and promptly they gave me a wallet soaked by the rain that had fallen during the weekend.

It was mine! They said that someone had seen it on top of the roof and that they managed to get it out after the fourth or fifth attempt. I was relieved. I could now go to Lisbon and fortunately I would not have a minute to self-analyse and consequently self-criticise. However, the more Mariana proved to be my accomplice, the more Mário disapproved of my sense of responsibility. Anyway! It doesn't matter. I don't care.

Mariana drives now. She is looking at the road and swinging her gaze towards me. She's continuously looking through the centre rear-view mirror. Mário is watching every suspicious movement in the side mirror. I sat in the middle of the back seat. I'm discreetly looking at her. Sometimes I turn around to see the ideas and dreams that are being kept in Évora. And that, with it, they are getting further and further behind. However, I am extremely happy that the Évora that I temporarily leave behind remains forgotten, forever, with Neida.

When we entered Lisbon, Miguel instantly disappeared into the ornate landscape of the night. Francisco took off later on a train bound for Santarém. There was still time for Tiagão, Miudinho's brother, to try the role of the host. But he failed. I was now the one orchestrating the group, not him, nor was Francis anymore.

I was heartbroken to see my friends return from the war and return home leaving their general behind. I dragged myself through the Lisbon night. I kept postponing my departure. Mariana and I ended up in Rua Regueirão dos Anjos wallowing in the puddles of water that still had some of the illusion of rain that had fallen on the asphalt yesterday. Mário disapproved of our behaviour. To Miudinho, I was just the vision of the Poet's program that he had formatted, never to be updated. I was not his metalhead comrade. As was his brother and his brother's friends, who were basically also his best friends.

I stayed for the third time at Mário and Tiago Silva's parents' house. This time, I had to share the mattress with Mário. He insisted on building a barricade of pillows between him and me. Maybe it was a trauma he had acquired in military school… He didn't explain, and I was too sleepy to ask him or ask for an explanation that made any sense to me.

Two days later, Mário and a friend of his took me to Parque das Nações. So that I could go from Oriente station to Pombal station by train. At Pombal, Inácio and Marcus would pick me up and take me home, after first stopping for coffee and refreshments. I would tell them how the premiere of the play went. But I would omit in between, the whole blasphemous and bohemian narrative. I wouldn't even dare to describe a single episode in which the lack of decorum of my soldiers, as well as their general, was evident. Which would be unquestionably unforgivable to Marcus, even if it had happened during the truce interval of a war.

Driving was the profession of Mário's friend. He drove the cars for the TVI soap opera productions. He took me to the Oriente station in no time. He drove like someone playing a rally game on a computer or console. I was in a big rush through the streets and roads of Lisbon. I was going even faster than a speeding high-speed train. The cars that were being overtaken were like buildings perpetually forever parked. I thought we were chasing something or being chased by someone. But no. It was all excitement and continuous lines of adrenaline and not one of cocaine.

Now, I am in the village of Avelar and I am already divided between my mother and stepfather's house, and the somewhat antiquated house that my mother inherited. I add trips to the café; I accumulate returns to home. I multiply the times I opened and closed the newspaper and the times I opened and closed the book of this day's routine, and try in vain to ascertain the meaning of what I dreamt on one of the nights I spent in Lisbon, which coincided with the night of my mother's birthday.

In the dream, I kissed two women in the same street, that street of my childhood and adolescence, and where I, today, went to drink coffee in a pastry shop, looking there for the meaning that my dream had. But I didn't find it there. I only saw from the window of the pastry shop, across the street, Marcus' father's factory. The factory of another time!

The first kiss in the dream was with a stranger. The second was with Adriana. I think that was the reason for the sudden dream disorder. It's that the same place where I kissed the first woman, was also where I kissed Adriana afterwards. But when I kiss her and open my eyes, who do I see? The face I see again is not Adriana's face. Instead, the face I find, after sealing the second kiss, has the feature of a holy apparition.

Oh my! So, but I kissed our Lady of Fátima on the mouth? However, the sensation I had when after closing my eyes, thinking I was going to kiss Adriana, I supposedly kissed the venerable one, was not such a satisfying sensation, as the one I had during the first kiss. Francis and Miguel also appeared in the dream. Just as, appearing in the middle of the dream stage, was Henrique's companion, Anabela. There was certainly a parallel dream event that caused the respectable image to appear in Adriana's place because consequently, before my dream ended, I decided to move away from my friends instead of continuing with them.

Today I had an even more extraordinarily expectant dream. I dreamt of horses that were speeding down the dreamy blue of my dream sky. Each one of them was parachuting down into the sky. They were surreal parachutists that were falling from the abstract sky into my concrete dream. And they were not only parachute horses, they were also huge trees with colossal roots and canopies as sturdy as the hips of the Venus of Willendorf.

To me, the great adventure of human life on planet earth, is scientifically more daring and complicated. Colonising Mars is just another excuse for man to fly a flag in space. It is just another reason to invade a planet, exploit and deplete its resources. Murdering entire galaxies and worlds, on which trillions of species unknown to us live peacefully. Sadly, our world is insufficiently vast for the unbridled ambition that is man's insignificant size.

Probably, being a colonist on Mars will also be the same as being in the village of Avelar today. It will only be a possibility to return to childhood or adolescence, and everything will once again be infinitely vast and infinitely small.

I spoke today with Edgar, who is an architect and lives in his parents' attic. He is my neighbour in the obsolete house that my mother bequeathed. Now he works in a factory. After having temporary and unstable experiences in his field of work. Late in the afternoon, I sprinkled my art project on him. I told him about together creating a virtual scenario through software that would interact with the spectators and the actors. But he did not see me as his leader, he did not accept me as his Messiah. My preaching about art being the salvation of man had no effect on him. He was not interested in redemption.

Nor in the condemnation of his spirit. He just asked me, "How much money is involved?"

I then went back to the old house and opened my mail and read. And, it was really him…

17 jan2014; 12:33:27 AM
Dear Simão,

It was a pleasure to be able to attend the presentation of the first act of your play. As I had commented to you—and I am well aware that comments often ignore the reasons that hinder their author—I hope that my words were not understood as a "pointing the finger at the error," but rather the curiosity, and enthusiasm that I actually wanted to put into them; that's why I asked you about the continuation of the play.
I also recognise the privilege of being able to talk to you after the premiere—I am grateful to you.

Cordially,
Eduardo Parreira.

Chapter 4
The Ping and the Pong

(February 2014)

Everything is aligned—Francis is going to Brazil, and before he leaves, I will go to Santarém, to say goodbye to him. Our friendship progresses. At least, it survives. Because in the middle of January I wrote him a dissertation, for him to apply for a master's scholarship. And by the end of January, he knew he had won it. Just as, both he and I, learned that I would continue to Évora, to complete the same degree. Being a resident at the Vista Alegre residence and, later, a guest at Francisco's parents' house. After, being a guest or host at my stepfather's house. However, now I am just a ping-pong ball bouncing around.

I go to Santarém by train. My mother is apprehensive. She believes that I am heading for a journey without a destination. She worries about the direction the spirit of my existence will take. Not after I arrive at Santarém station, but after I leave Vale Figueira and return to Évora for another semester.

I'm already on the train. I follow my thoughts quickly ahead of where I am. I'm looking through the window of the train. I jump from landscape to landscape. I don't always sit down. Sometimes I get up and change seats so I don't get too comfortable. However, it is impossible for me to travel and feel bored. Nonetheless, I have changed seats and compartments more than once. Only to get another perspective of the place where I had been sitting before and find the reason why I had changed in the meantime.

Each stop is a new season in this train that is as long as a whole year, in my life as a ping-pong ball, where I am going from one side to the other without comfortably knowing why. The trip to Santarém takes a stagecoach. Time is a compartment of the moment, in which I move from one carriage to another carriage. I ride inside the train and enter the movement of the train. I am a ping-pong ball going from one side to the other. I am no longer a returnee. Nor am I a renegade university resident anymore. I am just and only a ball, a ping-pong ball.

I am on my way to Santarém for one more escape and one more semester of evasion in Évora. I try in vain to save myself from what is left behind and what I think is buried. I make this trip and another adventure to not feel so doomed. Francisco is going to Brazil and it will not be the end. It is still the beginning of something that is in the middle. I feel happy for him. But I don't feel happy for myself. Nor do I feel that I have realised myself. Perhaps I have realised that with the end of the first act of the play *The Guest and the Host*, my life and Francis' life may have possibly swapped places. Possibly, they played ping-pong.

It was my mother who told me and insisted that I bring some cheese and chorizos to give to Francisco's parents.

"You can't go to people's houses empty-handed!" She told me, before I left Avelar.

And, from the reaction of Father Calé and Mother Ana, I realised that, after all, the cheeses from Serra da Sicó and Rabaçal, as well as the chorizos from my region, were something very important in Ribatejo. As remarkable and relevant, as once was the idea of civilisation in the village of the Middle Ages. And that the Middle Ages may not have been entirely the world of darkness that we imagine, and that, probably, we now live in the darkness of a global village. But before I entered Francisco's parents' house, I arrived in Santarém…

I arrived in Santarém with my head out the window. When I got out, I went into the station cafe to kill time. Until the train to Vale Figueira passed, I kept staring at the blue and white tiles of the station café. It was the simmering of time. Those blue squares had seen more people pass by than I would ever see in my whole life. And they would never leave there! Perhaps, now, I can more easily understand Marcus' reason, never wanting to leave the place he finds himself in.

I also chatted with the owner of the station cafe. Later, I jumped from there to catch the regional train, which didn't even need to stop for me to get on. The trip to Vale Figueira took longer than the trip from Pombal to Santarém. The train was almost empty and humming the lonely sounds that travellers and ghosts make. Beside me was my suitcase.

On the regional train I had a constant ping-pong of ideas. More than those I brought with me, after having stopped at the Avelar valley. All the time spent in the village of Avelar was a long stopover where I was just passing through. The familiar faces looked at me with the same outsider indifference as the faces of the tourists in Évora. Just curiosity, passing and fleeting. I didn't stay long in the Avelar valley, nor will I stay long in Vale Figueira. Maybe, I'll spend my time in Évora. And paradoxically, maybe not! Maybe, I won't have much time left to finish my course. Because, in the meantime, thank God, he himself will extinguish me and make me disappear.

When I arrive in Vale Figueira, the sound of the carriage is revealing of the haste I was in to leave the valley of Avelar, and the haste I was in to reach this Thursday the green countryside that has the colour and smell of the Ribatejo, but not specifically finding or meeting my place forever in it. It is only, and just, a home to which I can always return. Perhaps, I have existed only for the places I have passed through and that somehow, they have found space in them to live through me.

Francisco was already waiting for me at the Vale Figueira station. We were to have dinner with Viegas. As soon as this Thursday's light went out. Conclusively, all my plans changed. Francis wanted to include Viegas in the second act of my play *The Guest and The Host*, and for this reason, or part of it, we were going to go to Santarém today, to have dinner with him, and discuss what can or cannot be done...

Calé's son picked me up at the station, in his mother's car. He was in a tracksuit. The glasses he wore to drive and to be on the computer now had a strange frame.

"It's cheaper that way!" He said. In short. With that deft sense of him to buy at the right value and not at the value of what was initially marked on the item. Always negotiating with time and with the impatience of the world.

I hadn't been to Francisco's parents' house since 2010. Since our second year of university. When we were still in the apartment at Heróis do Ultramar Avenue. In that instant when we drove from Vale Figueira station to *Pai* Calé's house, I remembered everything. Confirming, on the way, that nothing had essentially changed in Vale Figueira. Just like, in the valley of Avelar! Just like, in any valley in the world! Not even the Vale Figueira station had been painted with a different colour. There was nothing different about the shape of that little town in the Ribatejo. Nothing, nothing had changed!

Everything was basically the same. The garage, where Francis had his space for meeting and socialising, was exactly the same as it was four years ago. And both the winery and the garage were part of the rustic estate of father and son Salvador. Where Carlos Alberto's bullfighting posters mixed with Francisco's memories, and the heritage of what he had lived through. These items were consecutively added to his museum of the past. In part, this grandiose collection of what had been lived by Francis had also been experienced by me.

Including the poem that after being written I had deposited inside a bottle, the cork of which had been put by Francis. Thus, sealing that article which to this day contained the leftover wine in the bottle of my poetry, for which I had drunk, such a manifesto. There it was! And it was guide Francis who was describing that historic event to me, in the museum of a present and a past in common, partially, forgotten by me. There, there was my altar! And, there, I was still the Poet and his eternal promise.

We were surrounded by home-made purple wine and by the picture of little Francisco dressed as a *campino,* we were flanked by a familiar smell, rustic and typical. Mother Ana was an aromatic being no longer smelling, but Monica was an aromatic young herb, with the smell of a young teenager. With the table set, it was certainly a Portuguese house. Yes, there, I was not just another one of son Calé's friends. Now, there, I was also a close friend of the family. And, how good I felt, there. I felt at home! In that modest little house as immodest as I was.

We are all somewhere viruses and parasites of each other. We all need each other to survive in this ping-pong world! Francis is greased with the influence of Zé Pedro Viegas, as eventually Eduardo will be with the influx of our Lord Belchior. If I find the connections and associations they have with each other strange, perhaps Eduardo would consider my friendship with Marcus to be more unusual, as well as any other friendship relationship where one is the guest and the other the host, or else one will be the Ping and the other, necessarily, will be the Pong.

Francisco goes to Brazil because he is just another maladjusted person. Having failed to succeed in his own country, he turns to a country where Portuguese is spoken. So that his integration will be easier, and his adaptation will be faster. He still doesn't speak English, doesn't know how to express his ideas correctly in writing, makes too many mistakes for a university student, and reads very little, compared to Viegas or even Murtinho. But what he does and always did exemplarily well, besides begging and borrowing favours and things, was to imitate and copy the masters. Like Hunter S. Thompson did, whom he likes so much, and for this reason, one day, he will either make it, or bleed it, until he dies.

He returned home after finishing his degree in theatre. Meditated at length on the emptiness he felt and how empty it all is. Going to the gym daily. Practising his version of Buddhism. Putting aside alcohol and drugs for a moment and turning his focus to what was important and essential. Until he put an end to the nonsense he was doing. Staying, only, with the common sense of the gym and his increasingly frequent readings on performance. Exercising—without having to practise it—a new Catholic way of understanding Buddhism. Accumulating all this with a dosed return to alcohol and drugs. With the flavour and distaste coming together, as the palate of his Roman Apostolic Buddhism that he has earned.

After lunch, Francisco opened half of the ping-pong table he bought to play with his sister. The ping-pong table serves him for his poker game with his gang of cousins, it serves him to put down his junk. Basically, it serves him for everything.

There will no longer be the second act of the play The *Guest and the Host*. Another act will be programmed...we will probably do something new... Maybe we will just waste time making art, because we are incapable of doing anything else. We will make one or another video, recording something random with Viegas. But most likely Zé Pedro will say yes to everything at dinner, and tomorrow morning he will call to say that, unfortunately, he won't be able to come. Because, in the meantime, he had a problem with his car.

While Francisco is putting knick-knacks on the ping-pong table, he tells me about the local association of popular amateur theatre that he has been working with, and shows me the material he borrowed from them. That whole table adapts and transforms. It seems to want to be used. It seems to have a life of its own and not have a single purpose. Driven by the circumstance of my genius, which decided to reappear, I told Francis that the ping-pong table, the rackets, and the balls would be the only things we would need for the video recordings we were going to make.

The night goes on fast. We managed to catch the train from Vale Figueira to Santarém. We didn't pay for the ticket. When the conductor got into our carriage, fortunately, the train stopped at the station and we were saved at the last millisecond. After we left the Santarém train station, I told Francisco that the second act of the play, The *Guest and the Host*, would be performed in part in a spaceship. Which would be placed on a stage. The capsule of the stage that the audience could see, however, would be empty. The scene broadcast on a screen facing the audience would be deferred. Although Francis was walking too fast for me to make him understand what I was really talking about.

"*Puto!*" said Viegas, when he opened the door and saw me.

Viegas always started every sentence with "*puto*" and Francis imitated him: "*Puto!*"

Francis is a variation of ping-pong played by José Pedro Viegas' good-natured game. I assume that every relationship is this revealing result of a game of ping-pong, played between two people or more. I don't know, however, who plays Pong and who plays Ping. But I do know that the two together are Ping-Pong.

End of the first day in Santarém! We are at Viegas' parents' house. In a basement that has access to the garage. This is the room where he mainly spends his time. Plastic bottles with twenty-first century piss accumulate among thousands of books piled up, and all the intellectual paraphernalia of someone who thinks and dreams a lot. But does little or nothing. The plan today is to have dinner with Viegas in the most hidden restaurant in Santarém. In order to avoid the world. I can't persuade them to travel beyond their uncomfortable comfort. They have settled into the desolation of their habits and their fears.

Now, there is nothing to be done. The explanation is easy to understand: they don't want to be seen by anyone. Which means that I won't be seen, see or know anyone either, and that nothing of the evening can later be proven to have really happened. Anyway, to sum up, the two are in exile in Santarém and I am obliged to go into exile with them.

The next day, I woke up with a hangover. I was unable to sleep any longer. Francis slept naturally until after ten o'clock. As he usually did. Refusing to wake up even a minute earlier. Even though I went to his room more than once to make noise to wake him up. But he declined to get out of bed. Not even if I told him it was almost eleven. It was Mother Ana who opened the door for us yesterday. She had no doubts. She knew we were drunk. But there was between the sober mother and the inebriated son, a toxic tolerance and unconditional acceptance.

When he finally woke up, he reminded me of my unusual phone call to the famous Paulo Talochas, who was from my town and had been my neighbour. Trivial occurrences that Viegas disregarded. Concentrating his amazement only on the fact that I had the contact of such a celebrity. What each one said on the phone would only be registered by the waiter and another outcast who clearly hadn't drunk as much as the three of us. And, of course, Viegas, the kingdom's chief outcast, didn't show up to film the next day. He called to say what? He wasn't coming. Why not? Because he had had…what? A problem with his car…

The late afternoon sun slowly sets over the station of Vale Figueira. Vale Figueira is just a piece of the world that I know. It's a small piece of Portugal and Ribatejo that has the genuine green colour of the countryside. Meanwhile, Francisco's uncle drives by in his white pickup truck. Francisco touches his uncle's hand and his uncle touches his hand too, leaving it outstretched. Waving a continuous goodbye. Keeping his hand in the air until it disappears. And all this happens, without him having to stop. Not for a moment did the uncle have to slow down. Moving on spectacularly. After touching each other's hand, each one continues to play his part of the movement, and each keeps moving.

Francis' uncle crossed the train tracks and Francis took three steps, then ceased, like an immortal statue on a page of literature. Stalling well before the threshold, only to see the gate lowered and the woman in the gown at the gate cursing. As if it were a market day and morning. Meanwhile, the bell rings, uninterrupted. The danger warning signal is turned on, saying that the train is about to pass. And Francisco shouts, "The train is coming! The train is really coming!"

And the high-speed train passes within an inch and a half of me. It was the rare beauty of one who passes tremendously fast, without caring where it is going. The train passed and yielded its protagonism to the barn tower. And I felt immediately, at that moment, that I had witnessed a great event. More important than 9/11 or Vasco da Gama's discovery of the sea route to India, who is a distant relative of father Calé.

"She's acting weird, but I'd still give her a good fuck." Francisco said about the female guard at the level crossing. Suddenly changing the subject and tone.

"Let's go now! To the street of the casal do convento de Santo António, number 24, Vale Figueira. We have to go for a snack! Did you hear? That the walk was long! And my belly is already crying, Siamese!" Then he started humming happily, "And I, who am, Simão; help my father, and love my mother…" Until he suddenly fell silent and then said, very surprised: "Look, there's another train coming!"

The wind is blowing, the bell is ringing, and the train is whistling, even before it has arrived. When it passes through the Vale Figueira station it overcomes the incoherent sound that is that triumphantly shrill something scraping on the rails of our ears. It is the simple sonority that has the great diffusion and agitation of the truth that perforates us. It is the freight train! But more than that, it is the energy of life that pierces us. It is 4.00 pm Francisco runs along the station platform next to the train.

However, the train runs slightly faster. And while this is happening, the ping-pong balls that we brought from home are lying on the ground forever. It is just an inconsequential compartment of the great ping-pong game played against the backdrop of this grey day, overlapping with the train of that moment.

The gate finally lifts. Those waiting on this side of the gate pull out to the other side without thinking, without hesitating. Francis and I continue on foot. I go diving into the lake that has the grey of the sky and Francis keeps complaining, "I don't want any of this anymore! I'm done. I'm sick of running. I'm hungry. I'm starving. Where's my cell phone? Where did I put my cell phone? Ah! I have it here, in my jacket pocket. Whew! I thought I had already lost it," and continues with the refrain, "and I, who am Salmon, help my father, and love my mother!"

The grey lake disappears from the sky. Halfway there we found a tavern where Francisco's uncle had stopped to have a snack. We ate a ham sandwich and drank a glass of wine with him. Then we said until tomorrow and found the beginning of the evening sea before arriving home. We still hear the bell ringing in the distance, in the middle of the green field. Which is the colour of the Ribatejo sea!

Mother Ana paces back and forth in a daze. She is a woman in constant distress. Her mission is to take care of the house, the children, and to go to work from nine to five, as a maid in the Amarante family home. There is not much time left for her to dream of being something else.

After dinner, we return to the garage. Mónica joins us. On the garage wall is the footage we made today. Mónica sees Francis getting on and off the trains that stop at Vale Figueira. She identifies who is getting on and off the caravans that docked this afternoon at the Vale Figueira pier. She is happy when she recognises a schoolmate! Francisco talks, meanwhile on his cell phone. He underestimates the train of the moment and its duplicate compartment, which is successively projected on the wall at home, "Hello? Zé Américo! Hello? It's by the gate that has lights!"

What interests us is not always the size of a universe. In each life there is only some space for a ping-pong table and little else. I am filming brother and sister Salvador, capturing on the same screen the trains that used to pass in the afternoon at Vale Figueira station, and which are now projected in the garage at night, directly above the pictures of Spanish bullfighters and Portuguese *campinos*, which overlap the ping-pong game currently played by the Salvador brothers.

"Oh man! What a waste!" Mónica comments, bored with her own move.

Francisco keeps quiet. He plays the game that has my scenic ping-pong, like an action hero. Although, everything is practically played on the same ping-pong table.

"Come on, come on! This is a game that is always rolling!" Francis said, intuited that that line was doubly appropriate.

"So, Francis? You have to give me time," Mónica said, very disconsolate and pubescent.

After the game ended, we left home. Mónica went out with her friends and we went to say goodbye to another cooperative of friends, acquaintances, distant cousins and other mere extras in Francis' life. Day after day, he was saying goodbye to a friend or a group of friends quite different and dissident from the previous one. And I went with him, like a ping-pong ball. Because where the Pong goes, so goes the Ping.

Today, it was Bruno's turn. With whom Francis, in the last two years, had often gone fishing. He was a friend from childhood to adolescence who would not exactly have the same continuity in adulthood. But the flame of friendship was rekindled after Francis left Évora University and Bruno left the army. We went with him to Santarém, to a bar, to mingle with a cocktail of people. I couldn't speak, nor could I hear who was saying what, with the noise of the music and the dimming of the lights. Then Bruno guided us to a ladies' house.

It was basically a huge living room with a bar in the middle, and hidden rooms, which beyond the curtains hid no mystery. The nice ladies walked from one side to the other. One of them was an Arabian maiden with very long black hair and a wide, round face, who would approach the three of us. But Bruno picked her up and immediately took her behind the curtains. Not having much time left to tell her story.

On Bruno's face was a huge satisfaction that irritated me. For some reason I liked her. I felt like taking her not behind the curtains, but bringing her home with me and holding her hand and looking with her at the poster of a sunset on a beach in Copacabana. The Arab maiden had been dragged away by Bruno, mid-sentence. Right in the middle of the moment she justified that doing it was as simple as gathering money to go back to school. It was a dream of a woman, an Arab maiden that Bruno would possess, without money paying fairly for what she was worth.

I advised Francis to resist his impulse to pay for sex, reminding him that orgasm would make him more desperate. I insisted that he should instead try to pay the higher price of someone who wants something else more moral; such as: to be top of the class, or things of that sort. I strongly suggested that he channel his semen and energy into something not so immediate, but into a more rewarding and even more climactic orgasm.

In this way, he would try to resolve once and for all the promise of a life that insisted on not gliding on top of the mountain of self-realisation, because vultures fly from the bottom up, or some other such shit that would certainly excuse life passing him by and would also justify the failure of an entire generation.

At the end of the night, Francis and I returned home. Drenched in alcohol and carnal frustration. I would never see that dream of a woman again. That damsel lady that Bruno, Francis' friend, definitely should never have possessed for any money in this world. The problem is that money not only buys most people, it also feeds, as long as it exists, the clients of the oldest and most respectable profession in the world.

The next day, by mere chance, we met another acquaintance of Francisco. This was a dedicated heroin user, who painted oil paintings as well as walls and ceilings, when he was not busy with another stint in a detox clinic. Francis used to regularly give him a few coins to encourage him to produce his art. We recorded some scenes with him at the station. He only stayed a short time.

At first, he thought we had what he wanted, but soon he realised that it turned out to be a seed of illusion that he himself had planted in his head. This made Francis' acquaintance even more agitated and unmotivated to work. Let alone to make art. He didn't think that creating art had medicinal power. What was therapeutic for him was to give it away! He had lost control of his life's dream, now driving only sideways…driving in the passenger seat…never having access to the steering wheel again. Forgetting that, he who dreamt is living the dream that only each one of us can drive.

***

"Don't you have your seat belt on?" Francisco asked me.
"No! I don't need it."
"And us likewise?" Mónica sighed.
"Huh?" Asked her mother Ana.
Mónica repeated, gently clarifying, "And us without a seat belt too!"
"So, in the back, it doesn't have, it's a rest!" Mom Ana laughed.
Francisco took the opportunity to emphasise, "It's a rest!"
Mónica once again tried to explain herself, "No! It's just ever since I saw that scene…" But she was soon interrupted.
"If we have to die, we die with a seat belt or without one!" Mother Ana exclaimed proudly with her reasoning.
"I don't feel anything!" I said, very softly…
Mother Ana once again took the opportunity to complain about her argument with Father Calé. "Stay there, holding the shellfish! What a sneaky thing to do… Damn, that man!"
"But what was the problem?" Francisco asked, as he calmly made the curve of the road that entered the sea of green, reflecting the green in the Ribatejo sky.
"So shouldn't the crab be seasoned and already in the fridge to have more taste on it?" Mother Ana asked, talking with the machine gun in her mouth, which was firing everywhere.
"But I think yesterday, he didn't notice? I don't know!" Francisco affirmed, relaxed, turning the steering wheel to the side he wanted.
Mother Ana was still rattling on, "I took it out last night. He arrives and goes to put it in the fridge. In a little while the crab is still frozen inside. And then it's there! With no good shit on it."
"Oh, Mrs Ana, so you speak French?"
"I speak all languages when I'm angry!"
"She's a polyglot," Francis said. Laughing after blowing his whistle and saying goodbye to half a dozen strangers.
Mother Ana was still very excited to be able to keep complaining about Father Calé. "Now, if I told him to take it out of the freezer, it would still be

there. Then he arrives in such a hurry. If Teresa Amarante wasn't such a bore, I would have left earlier and fixed the seafood. He thinks he knows how to do everything! That man is so annoying."

A few turns and minutes later, we arrived at Francis' grandfather's house. There was a junkyard there. Strangely, or not so strangely, in the middle of the graveyard of mechanical skeletons, in the middle of the bones of electrical appliances, and a vast paraphernalia of things that no longer serve any purpose, there was an ambulance from Figueiró dos Vinhos, parked there, slowly rotting away. Figueiró was the township where my grandmother lived, as well as Marcus, who lived there.

"What a great coincidence!" Francisco said, assertively. He didn't waste a single minute inventing the reasons or listing the logical reasons for it being there.

It was the penultimate scene that we were going to shoot. Francisco would walk with the dance of the grey wind blowing today in the green Ribatejo countryside. Symbolically burying the ping-pong rackets in the earth. It would be the penultimate, because the last adventure of Pong and Ping, was recorded when Francisco lay down on the railway line. Precisely, when in parallel, a door at the Figueira valley station was being closed. That moment was recorded. The two men with reflective vests who were smoking, would also be part of the circumstance in which the last game of Pong and Ping was played.

As well as the clouds of that day or the sign "Stop at the red light," were part of the filmed scenario. Everything served to disguise my fascination with the small and big nothings, in which a large part of humanity lost by bad luck, the game of a lifetime; these include: the Manuel Mira Salvador Street sign, deceased, in combat, 1974, Mozambique.

Now it is raining, it is windy. The wind is blowing violently outside. We are sitting at the table. It's Sunday and I don't feel so lonely. I lick myself carefree. I take the tiger shrimp with my hands and don't think about the storm outside. I just enjoy the moment. It tastes like the eternal, the one that stays on my ephemeral fingers. Ah, the magic of family is this plate full of people around this table! Socialising together, enjoying, living…

I suck the core of the crab. I am an honoured guest. On television, the teams get on the pitch. The storm continues. Soon after, the referee indicates that the Benfica-Porto game will be postponed. The teams go back to the locker room. People leave the stadium. It continues to rain in Lisbon and in Vale Figueira. I keep eating and licking myself, without consternation, if, outside, it rains! Or if the wind blows.

Nobody sitting at this table cares about it, only with the whirlwind of the conversation that goes on at the table. At this, Father Calé tells one of his stories. Usually, they are always short and far-fetched. Something like two brothers were caught stealing fruit. Or three and two makes six. Or, that time that thing and then foxtrot tango machine zero! Dad Calé is not only a stand-up comedian, but he's also a great stand-up guy. Sunday's day will end and the storm will naturally die down like all things that end sooner or later.

After we had dinner, Francis pulled all the memorabilia and souvenirs that had been attached and hung by him off the garage walls. Because his father wanted the walls to be clean, and only the frames of the bullfighters and the pictures of the *campinos* would remain, at least while Francis was in Brazil.

***

I return to Évora this Monday. Mr Carlos and Francisco take me to the bus station. I follow in the back seat of Papa Calé's van. Francis drives the van. Today, he is exceptionally authorised to do so. There he goes, regaining his father's trust, which had been broken since the time he turned over the first and only automobile that old Calé had given him. The story is quick. His father had offered him a second-hand car, and Francisco did him the favour of flipping it over a week later. The vehicle would be turned upside down.

Francis would be removed unscathed from the car, that would go straight to the trash. It was on a famous night when he was coming from the Golegã Fair, the great horse fair, making turns at two hundred miles an hour. He still talks about it today with great pride. Because it was the first medal of praise for the *pagodeiro*, which he would be doomed to be, until I don't know when...

After the quick and inevitable goodbye, I stayed at the bus station bar waiting. Francisco and Mr Carlos, after leaving me and making sure that I didn't need anything, left. While I waited, I recalled the ancient moment of that ghost place. When Francis and I were waiting in 2010 for Bernardo's ride to Évora, and then the four of us: me, Francis, Bernardo, and Débora...

I returned to Évora after my will to find myself there had already arrived, before I did. Nothing stays in the same place, no matter how long we stay here or there. The delay in leaving brought me homesickness and the delay in arriving brought me the desire to leave again.

What a happy contradiction it is to never realise what will have to happen sooner or later. What a sad joy it is to see the truth of the world too late and there is no other way. No, it is not possible to stay forever comfortably in the same uncomfortable place. Nor is it exactly possible to leave the usual position in which we find ourselves, just by temporarily leaving the fixed place in which we live…

I make promises that I know I will never keep. Therefore, I recognise, my will, will never reach heaven. And, because of the salad that my fickle will have, I will fill myself with more vinegar and olive oil, and pinches of salt with the taste that is to blame. I continue, nevertheless, to make promises at the Ribatejo bus station. I do them, basically, to entertain myself. It helps me pass the time.

"Follow your path. Without ever straying from your objectives, and without ever straying from your principles," I said to Francisco, who quietly consented. Believing, now, even more in me. And, not exactly because of the strength of the evidence that our friendship had, but because I had significantly contributed to his going to Brazil. However, as I told him to proceed, that was how I should do it! After all, I was not only talking to him, I was also talking directly to myself. Anyway, now everything was out of alignment—Francisco was going to Brazil, and I was going back to Évora.

Tuesday was the first class of the second semester. Wednesday, Eduardo met me at the Vista Alegre residence. Eduardo arrived and Neida left, because she thought Eduardo was even more intellectual than I was. The way she walked harmlessly down the street annoyed me. Just the fact that she was near me bothered me.

My good friend Eduardo had read and quickly interpreted the whole situation upon his arrival with the unique naturalness that only he could do. We were planning a five-day journey of Vipassana meditation in the Gredos Colony, Candoleda. It would be an inner journey that would be continued, by both of us, abroad, with an inter-rail across the European continent. But in the meantime, Belchior intuitively appeared. He had nothing to do today but stop off at the Vista Alegre residence and wait for I don't know who.

In the afternoon, we went to the museum. Francisca joined us and Belchior, it turned out, came with us too. He no longer had anything to do, or anyone, to meet at the other supposed end of town. Farting around in the exhibition, and excusing himself, "It's just human nature!"

Francisca shook her head, denying his behaviour. However, the contradiction of Belchior's human nature made her laugh uncontrollably. The four of us walked through the museum, which in another century would have been the museum of the Inquisition. Now it was on display there: Paul Sermon, two *sofas*, 1993. One could see Belchior jumping on the sofa, which was on the other side, looking at Francisca very seriously and amazed at the television that was transmitting them, on the other side. She kept shaking her head in complete denial, and now she was crying with laughter. Eduardo was just looking around scientifically. Calmly wandering around the museum, with his notepad and ballpoint pen in his left hand.

In the evening, I went to dinner at the Luís António Verney College. The coloured students gather at a separate table. I dine alone, discriminating between the blue and the pink. I read about Mazdeism, the religion spread by Zarathustra, and about Mithraism, the initiation-type religious cult that originated in ancient Persia. I ended up getting confused, eating first the dessert, with the soup spoon, and finally sipping the soup with the help of a fork and knife.

But what does it all matter, now, at the end of this chapter? What should matter is that I never thought I would have to come to Verney for dinner again and have to put the rest of today's soup, again in plastic Tupperware, so that I can have lunch later. Will this serve for tomorrow's literature, or will it serve, just so tomorrow I won't be hungry? Or, only for me to lament a literature that never kills the hunger I feel today and always?

In the meantime, I have moved to a room in the Vista Alegre neighbourhood. And where to? To that little house that Belchior did the favour of almost blowing up. The termination of the residence contract was taken care of. After I handed over my keys, it was stipulated that the payment of my debt could be executed in small instalments.

Although, el Belchiorinho defended, beforehand, the hypothesis that I should have a copy made, and proceed, right away, with his robbery plan. I opted to hand over the key. Likewise, I opted to leave the shared room in the residence and move to a room in the attic of the Vista Alegre neighbourhood, where I now live above and Belchior below, on the first floor.

I hear Belchior complaining. "The landlord Rodolfo, did this…because he is this, and because he does that," until, shortly after, I stopped listening to what he was saying, just spurting out of his mouth without thinking. Mostly, he talks about the specific nothing he specifically has to say to me.

"The advent of hatred is a good principle. Hate is an alternative for those who have no alternative. Man, for one, hatred is always abundant. In fact, Simão, hatred is the alternative to hatred. Don't you think so? Why can't we hate the other, as Jesus loved his neighbour? Is hating a feeling as human as love? Isn't it?" He said, laughing a lot afterwards, with that genial jerk laugh of his, which was basically the mixture of the chemistry of his sad life, with the eccentricity that only he had.

He continued, excited to know that at that moment I was paying attention to him, "I personally don't consider that hating someone very, very much is wrong! You see, what is incorrect is to feel so much love for someone! Now, come on, love is better than hate! Don't you think that hate is a much better feeling than love? Love is my pet hate. Love above all things... Oh, come on! Do I have to love the other now? No, I hate to love my neighbour. And it's easier to love than to hate. For example, I hate myself as much as I hate my neighbour! Most people don't know it, but love for your neighbour can only lead to hate. Ah! Ah! Ah!"

Then, very happily he bit his bread carcass with nothing. He bit his bread without opening his eyes. Before I climbed the stairs that led to the attic, and to my room, Belchior threw his last rope in an attempt to change the subject. Only so that I would stay longer to listen to him ramble on in the shabby, sticky room.

"There are girls who look like guys. And there are still guys who look a lot like guys."

To put an end once and for all to all that nonsense, I quickly replied, still halfway up the stairs, "That's right!"

I couldn't believe what Belchior was saying so genuinely. Regardless of whether I felt compassion for him, or a slight complicity. The kind you have for the homeless, for the clingy. Or for those we see in the mirror and don't like the reflection we see at all.

I finally went into my room and laid down on the bed listening to the rain music. It was raining musically on the roof of my room. It was raining on me through the night. Through a transparent tile that is embedded in the ceiling of my room. However, I cannot see beyond the darkness of the universe. Although, one can still hear the melody of the rainwater coming and breaking, on top of the roof of the house that is perched between my belly and my head.

Chapter 5
Man Is a Wild Animal

(March to May 2014)

When I got home, I couldn't justify why I brought from the university that whole collection of postcards, which were resting on a wooden bench. Next to the professors' office in the History Department. Anyway, the said notes were inside a cardboard box. Next to a collection of dossiers. And, I impulsively brought them with me. Just like I also grabbed the dossiers, which contained old summaries of history classes. Just because. Not understanding, however, if all that paraphernalia was based on a change of office. Or if its custodian was leaving the university for good, and if, as a result, its memories would also necessarily change place and consignee.

When the afternoon lamp went out, Raquel was still determinedly glueing the damn collection to the walls of my new room. Her will was simply to help me stick all the blessed postcards, and leave with the feeling of a duty done, and of something in her world being forever settled and finished. Augusto agreed with his girlfriend's designs.

Each postcard that was posted on the walls of my room had the memory of another place. Each postcard was the vivid memory of someone, leading me presently to a certain place, or simply invoking another place. Besides the one in the image of a big city, or the one with a famous monument, or the one with a well-known statue that I know, but can't remember its name right now. What I do know and am sure of is that in my possession is a massive collection of postcards with memories that are not mine at all.

After Raquel and Augusto left, some postcards were falling even more insistently to the ground. Just like, the leaves from the trees on the block in the Vista Alegre neighbourhood are stretching out on the sidewalk at the beginning of this winter night.

The next day, on my way home, with my new routine tucked under my arm, I passed places where I had already lived, and which I never thought I would have to pass through again, today, or that I once thought I would live there. Life is a more or less fixed place that we constantly pass through with the idea that we lead a life today that is so different from the life we had yesterday. But the essence of human life is always equal, fundamentally and essentially always equal. That's what the Master told me in one of our walking conversations.

After it had rained heavily on me, I finally opened the front door. As a matter of habit, I reached into my pocket with my hand. But I quickly realised that I had no keys, and that there wasn't even a lock on the door. All I had to do was push! I was soaked on the outside and completely drenched on the inside. I hit the door with a slight kick and the door opened. I walked in, not getting any closer, however, to my idea of home, nor approaching or getting any closer to the initial concept, which had the South of my dream.

I had marched home with an imperative sense, that of finding a new function in the dream. When I entered my room, I looked more for the practical side, rather than the core theoretical notion that my dream had. Although I retained the concept of mission, it clearly required a real intent of sacrifice and persistent self-denial, to maintain the elevation one feels when one climbs at length up a mountain range in central Portugal.

My plan of incorporeal ascent was thwarted by the fact that each day contained the need for bread, and with that, the mass sensation of having achieved nothing leavened within me. It was the inglorious fight between the gladiator of the flesh and the gladiator of the spirit, with the fight constantly going on somewhere in the arena of my mind.

I meditated on the carpet cross-legged. I tried to remain like that. Not waiting for anything. Just sitting there! Listening to my own breathing, until everything was one continuous stream of consciousness and nothing else. Until night fell and fell on me. I achieved no victory in the abstract, but also no defeat concretely. Finally, I fell asleep torn between the fantasy of what I should be and the reality of what I can now effectively be. I passed out repeating the sleep I had yesterday. When I awoke, I stumbled over myself and the postcards that were lying on the floor. Downstairs, Belchior was arguing with the landlord and with himself.

Maybe, I will never be anything and that is already something. Maybe, I will never be someone important and that too is not the main thing at all. And just like that, the landlord also keeps arguing with Belchior.

The bathroom of the villa where I rent a room is a typical room in a social housing. There, I take my bath without, however, ever feeling clean. Everything seems to be disjointed and nothing seems to work properly. The bare walls display the nipples of the bricks that were left exposed by the explosion that occurred last year. The house is as slovenly, as apparently, is the life of the landlord and Belchior. The upbringing of the two has been continually neglected and carelessed by their parents. Both are children of divorced parents. In fact, so am I?

Belchior suffers from the same deformation, and I don't say this because of the obvious absence of bodily hygiene or the lack of cleanliness that his clothing suffers from. I say this because of his daily dose of hereditary lethargy, which is encouraged by the paucity of his will and the toothlessness of his ambition.

It is fair to say that the water in the bathroom always runs cold from the tap. But even though it is winter and one momentarily lacks what is necessary and essential, Belchior should not apologise for not wanting to bathe on a regular basis. Progressively, Belchior comes to resemble an amphibious species—a slimy batrachian! There emanates from him an odour of alienation that has long since permeated the walls of landlord Rodolfo's house.

It is Monday. Noon on the dot, I push aside the long dust curtain hanging from the plastic pole. I peek through the ephemeral window. Here comes Ana Maria, with her round blue glasses. Always stuck to the tip of the thin cane that holds her thin nose; Ana Maria is coming! Walking with a bag that she is swinging in her right hand. She brings Belchior's lunch summary. It's Tupperware full of food. Leftovers of what was overcooked this morning by her mother.

Let's take a look at Belchior's diet for the moment: his nutrition consists mostly of the leftover lunch that Ana Maria brings to Belchior every day. Besides the leftovers from the lunch that his girlfriend transfers to him, there is the bread roll with butter that he eats in the afternoon. And that is the only thing he buys! He uses my butter or he uses the butter that landlord Rodolfo thinks he bought, but which turns out to be mine. Finally, there are the night leftovers that Francisca gives him whenever she comes to visit him around supper time. They are also leftovers, remnants that the aunt gives Francisca to give to her mother, but that sometimes Francisca leaves with Belchior. And so, it goes! Everyone feeds Belchiorinho. Including Belchior, who feeds himself with the hand of his own apathy.

Ana Maria feeds Belchior, not because such an act became something pure or immaculate. Nor is it due to a feeling of compassion or mercy. Nor is it justified by their dating relationship. Eduardo told me that it is just so that no food is wasted. Which as a rule would go straight to the trash. Speaking of Eduardo! I ran into him at the peak of the afternoon. When I was literally drifting, exploring the Vista Alegre neighbourhood. Eduardo was on his way back from collecting data for his Master's thesis. We talked briefly about how the internship in the psychiatric unit of the Évora hospital was going. He seemed immoderately happy to leave the internship and, equally, to know that the end of his obligation was increasingly imminent.

We parted like two wise men who finished their chess game, each one stalling his time. And yet, satisfied that no one had lost much. The Vipassana meditation retreat in Spain, followed by the European trip, was cancelled. By mutual agreement. Eduardo wanted to finish his master's degree as soon as possible, and to do this he would have to dedicate himself full-time during the summer to writing his thesis. Since Eduardo had gone back on his initial decision, he would force me to think about finishing my degree. We made a pact, however, that one day we would do it all later.

I am now twenty-seven and Eduardo is twenty-two. Belchior is one year younger than me. Belchior, Ana Maria, Raquel—all of them were Eduardo's classmates, and all of them dropped out of the psychology course. What's more, they all have the particularity of being much older than Eduardo. Ana Maria herself is a few years older than me.

For some reason that I can't ascertain, Belchior needs Ana Maria. However, I don't know if it is emotionally, spiritually, or just materially. Maybe, because of that reason, he has made an effort to forget his former classmate from the computer course. It was in this course, taught at the Training Centre of the Employment Centre, that Belchiorinho met Francisca and since then they have become Siamese friends and, of course, cheated on Ana Maria with that other classmate from the computer course.

Belchior told me that he revealed to Ana Maria the betrayal. Ana Maria was not at all bothered by his infidelity. El Belchior also confessed to me that he felt frustrated with the rarity of the sex life that he and Ana Maria had, as a couple of lovers. It bothered him that it was always from Friday to Saturday. That was usually when it happened, and it wasn't always guaranteed. However, although he was dissatisfied, he recognised that Ana Maria provided him with a version of stability, which he couldn't exactly describe to me, because he didn't have that much prior love knowledge to seriously evaluate and compare.

He lamented that it was no longer as it was at the beginning of their love relationship. When Ana Maria was in psychology class and seduced Belchior, and, they would both run home, with the sole purpose of rubbing up against each other.

In the end, we were back to the beginning! Belchior declared to me that it was his colleague who had lost interest in him. Despite that, he would like to see her again, sexually, at least just once more. This was the mental attitude that Belchiorinho headed.

One's originality doesn't exactly come from him alone. It comes to us from someone, or from a bottomless deep tank that exists somewhere in the brain of the universe. However, we will never know how we are able to get there and store that channel of knowledge, nor how what we reproduce through it somehow has the shape of what we know, but does not stick to the appearance of our person, nor does it stick to the label of the person we think we are.

Neida was very pleased with her recently obtained anal sex. She told me excitedly that she had spent the past week looking forward to repeating the experience. I listened to her while thinking about her next lesson, also reflecting on my psychosocial adjustment and the consequence of my present lost paradise. Which was shaped like the moon and had Adriana Espinosa's round face. I was equal to Pluto. Excommunicated from the universe, where she and the moon will continue to shine.

The conclusion I come to is that the world is an illusion that we chase. Perhaps Adriana Espinosa was just a deception of this world that I was chasing; who, like a child, runs around convinced that is following the moon, when it is obviously sitting in the sky.

Landlord Rodolfo sits religiously on the end of the couch every day after coming home from work, playing alone on his console. He does this during his entire evening. Superstitiously ordering dinner by cell phone, without pressing the pause button. Even though he brings free meals from work every day. They end up spoiling, being left in the fridge for weeks or even months.

While the landlord is having dinner, he always plays the same kind of game. When his girlfriend calls, he sometimes goes into the bedroom to talk to her and have phone sex. Then he comes back to resume the game where he left off. At other times he talks on the cell phone with his girlfriend in the living room for hours and hours and continues to play without taking his hands off the remote. The phone is held against his ear and rests on his shoulder. Staying four to five hours in that technical position. Which is within the reach of very few people.

Between his work as a waiter, his rest and his form of leisure, an imbalance occurs that is easily noticed. During his extremely repetitive routine, it is possible to hear him saying to Belchior or even to Francisca, who is always there in the house, "Man is a…wild animal…man is a wild animal, and woman, is too."

As for me, I've been insisting with myself to go to taekwondo training, even though it's raining and I take an umbrella, but it doesn't do me any good. It is more a portion of discipline. Although, I feel more soaked than I consider I have progressed. It is probably due to the imbalance I stupidly maintain between my physical, mental and spiritual activities.

The mattress I sleep on is hard, harder than I am. Harder than the life of a stone. Stones always have an adequate body weight. However, for men with the soul of a stone, it is not enough to keep their backs straight, nor their minds aligned with their spirits. One must persist in the beatitude that has the way of the stone and in abstinence as the pebble. With a vigorous attitude and herculean disposition to maintain the proper irreducible posture. Even if we find ourselves between the sword and the wall of a ravine.

***

Simone, my current classmate and who participated in my play *The Guest and the Host* with successive delays insisted on giving me a ride today, even though I had told her three times that it was not needed. Just as I was about to slam the door, I heard, "You don't socialise much, Simão! I never see you. You leave right away…"

Her feminine spirit had to tell me something that she was unable to keep to herself. Probably, if it were a man, perhaps, it would be the same thing. In the world there is always someone able to comment on the lives of others. Be it on the street, be it on television. There is always someone who has an opinion about someone else, or about what they don't know that well.

Simone left with her canine again tap dancing in the trunk of the van. Both she and the van smelled like a wet dog. On top of the seats and the dashboard was a heaped and messy world. Simone was as nice as a freak can be and as radical as a freak is bound to be. In order to fulfil her stereotype and archetype.

She had at least one dreadlock just so I could understand and identify the cliché referring to her social group.

I crossed the playground of the plaza and walked over the freshly trimmed green lawn. It smelled like cut grass. I zigzagged so that no one would know which door I was entering. And like a snake, I entered the house, without needing to use keys or use my hands.

When the day woke me up, I couldn't remember what I had dreamt about. I got up and went to convince myself in front of the broken mirror in the half-ruined bathroom, that the more resilient my character was, the more I would tear down any wall of circumstance. I repeatedly persuaded myself with the belief that although my life was also in ruins, the face of the moment I saw reflected, would serve as an allusion to one day re-erect the edifice of my being, so that a greater purpose would be leveraged. It would be a matter of waiting. Not of Marcus' fatal hope kind, no! In my case, it would be just and only a heroic expectation.

At the end of the day, Eduardo brought the playing cards. Francisca, Belchior, Ana Maria, Neida and I played poker with him in a room in the attic that I tidied and cleaned myself. Belchior tried at first to help, but quickly gave up in the middle of the afternoon to join Francisca for a walk around the industrial area.

This is not just another simple poker game... It's a life lesson! It is a game that results in nothing—and forever the same game that is played now. We are doomed to exist in a certain way. To gather dust, just as, in this place, even more dust has gathered and will gather. The poker game remained uninteresting and monotonous. Ana Maria repeatedly asked what she had to play. I thought that not finishing this poker game would doom me as much as, or more than, not finishing my degree, which was still to be fulfilled.

Belchior was in a hurry to play. However, he had no urgency to organise his thoughts, or to find out how he could live more comfortably. The only thing he accomplished was to constantly inquire whose turn it was. His impatience usually irritates me. Now that he won't let the poker game flow naturally, it makes me want to slap him on the forehead. But it wouldn't do any good. He would still be in a hurry for someone to play. Not waiting for his turn. He would do his tic—blink his eyes, press his lips together, and tilt his face. Like a dog that doesn't understand its master, or its master's world.

I check out, the game goes clockwise, and I follow the silver aqueduct, which can be seen from the attic of my subconscious, where is my room and this game room that I improvised. Meanwhile, I am swept away by the current of the river that flows within me. I am carried to the waterfall of my subconscious, going through the hidden underground tunnels, between the incorporeal memory and the reminiscence of something else even more spiritual and immaterial.

"Hi! Hello! Well? It's your turn!" Belchior said to Francisca. Being terribly insistent each time. He was a Belchior thirsty for bottle caps and beans.

Ana Maria, after asking if she could make a certain move, suggested that Belchior could write about his life story. Belchior shrugged his shoulders and blinked. He did that tic he always does, when he doesn't understand at all what he has been told, or when he simply doesn't believe what he has heard.

Ana Maria is the opposite of Belchior. Maybe they are one of those couples that vibrate together, even in the face of the disharmony of a game played with pennies and beans. Ana Maria is not at all excited about the poker game. Nor does she take seriously what Belchior does or says. What really excites her and amazes her is teaching children to meditate, that is, to sit for three hours without opening their mouths or going to the bathroom.

Now Francisca smokes a pot joint with Belchior in his room. Neither of them bother with the musty smell. The rest of the group has left. I listen to them from my room, wishing only to hear the armour of silence Instead, I hear something catastrophic in what each one states in turn.

Afterwards, I was still forced to listen to Belchior blowing on the harmonica his father gave him to compensate for the paternal absence of a decade and a half. Before falling asleep, I understood once and for all why Belchior always disappeared so mysteriously. It was simply to meet Francisca in order to do something without mystery. So that they could both talk at the same time about their mutual despair.

The next day I went to the *Sítio Certo* for coffee with Neida. I asked her if she would consider the coffee table where we had sat at was the right place, or if there was another table more suitable… But she didn't understand the pun in the conversation—as expected. She moved her head, however, as if she understood the meaning of the conversation, and agreed with me.

"Neida!" I said. "Simone, my classmate, has a dog named Bugiganga. I…have…you."

She turned her head again. As if she still agreed with me. She did not, however, listen to anything I said. I continued, "You've noticed that two very similar sisters work here. How can they be such twins, without their mother stumbling over the name of one and the appearance of the other? And they work here? In the coffee shop of the *Sítio Certo (Right Place)*? But is this the most appropriate place for them to work?"

Neida kept shaking her head, agreeing with me. Apparently, like one of those bobbleheads placed on the dashboard of a car, or a desk.

Today, Belchior is very busy. I had never seen him like this! With so much commitment and diligence... His focus, this day, is to maintain his minimum income from his social insertion subsidy. Social Security doesn't know that Belchiorinho lives in the Vista Alegre neighbourhood. I don't have much to say about that. I am pushed to agree, to concur, that Belchior's struggle for his survival is fought with the same nobility, or lack thereof, as the indifference and opulence in Marcus' non-existence.

Even if Belchior has almost all his teeth rotten! It is so rare and so sublime that someone with so, so many rotten teeth can play the role he plays so well. Fooling social security so wonderfully well, saying he lives at one address, when he really lives at another. The poor guy being forced to appeal daily to his more primitive instincts, as well as, contracting compassion on others. Being required to stay afloat, to swim like a rat, on buoys from the charity of others.

Surviving in a world where usually only the strong and the powerful and with healthy teeth win. After all, let's not forget that all cheaters are affable people, and that when they want to, they speak in a simply charming way.

"Gals look more and more like guys. The guys neither look like girls nor like guys."

"Yes, you had already told me," I answered him.

He then confessed to me that until very late in life he was confused about his sexuality. Although, I considered that my time was being stupidly wasted somewhere in the living room, or in the confessional, where I didn't belong, nevertheless, I had to follow my vocation as a scribe, as a listening writer, as a historian. Until one day I triumph and a heavenly spotlight, solemnly descends on my head and my spirit divests itself of my body and rises toward heaven.

There, everyone will know that I have spent half a lifetime rescuing fools, and listening to a Belchior in the middle of the afternoon discoursing on his existential doubt at the beginning of his sex life. But in the meantime, just as I was getting ready to go up to my quarters, he came after me, to tell me again on the first floor for the fourth or fifth time during this very day how much he hates his bald, potbellied neighbour.

All because on the day of the explosion, that fatal day that Belchior wants so much to forget, the neighbour had been the only one who told him what he thought. And, ironically, the explosion that followed, was only and only because he had, in fact, forgotten...

That day, he was in the middle of the square crying, babbling, very distressed, and desperate for having committed that little and harmless lapse; and the old neighbour, the bald and potbellied one, came to blame him in the middle of the crowd of still terrified and scared neighbours, for being the cause of what had just exploded. With the firemen, the police, the entire Vista Alegre neighbourhood watching that post-explosion moment, when the bald and potbellied neighbour accused Belchiorinho of being irresponsible.

The defendant Belchior, who until today has not assumed the blame or the burden, still felt humiliated, vexed, demoted to the condition of a manifest criminal, only guilty for the crimes that were only his naivety and his constant distraction.

***

When I woke up, Belchior was playing console in the living room. He still hadn't combed his hair or washed his face. His hair was greasy, and his eyes had more sweat than shine. But he was immediately willing to give up his console game and temporarily press the pause button to come have coffee with me. Provided, of course, that I paid for his coffee. That was his only condition!

Belchior spends his entire days accompanied by the sloppiness of his routine, which refuses to abandon him. Relaxed, he tells me he's going back to university. Maybe this year, maybe later; he'll go back to do another course. It doesn't matter. He tells me that what he will do now is learn to play poker professionally.

Life is not a completely exact science. Eventually, I may be scientifically wrong. The fantasy we project onto the screen of reality is something we are continually filming and representing in the world we live in. This world captured by me is represented by a hungry Belchior licking now in the afternoon, the crumbs of the bread, which he ate today, at mid-morning, without butter. Including the thumb that is swallowed by him. Because it is the one that was used to glue the crumbs that were left on the table this morning. Very delighted, in the evening, Belchior swallowed the splinters of his own misery.

I got up the next day sleepy. But I got up making firm promises, while Belchior was still sleeping in his palace. His ceiling is, however, the floor I walk on. Rich little Belchior who sleeps innocently without caring to fix his poor social condition. When he woke up, he petted the dog Nescia, Nescha or Necha? Then he started talking loudly to her, threatening her, bellowing at her, while filling her plate with food, which he himself had arranged so that he could continue to feed the landlord's constant carelessness.

It could be heard, "It's because of you, 'Néscia', that this happened. Was it because of you, 'Nexa'!" said Belchiorinho, more and more accusingly. Not realising that I was at home and that I was listening to him. However, 'Nechia', or 'Nesha' knew very well that it was his fault, and was only bothering to scrape the bottom of her plate. Which had just as quickly filled up as it had emptied.

For Belchior, progress is not knowing where we are going in a year or two. Progress for Belchiorinho is to arrive at the destination without knowing that we have already arrived there. Belchior simply doesn't care what his next day will look like. As long as he can continue today on his welfare benefit and living as he always has, everything is fine. He doesn't want more than the size of his sheet. Only, he wants to be able to pull the sheet up and be able to cover his head and if possible, wake up with a roof over his head.

After all, Belchior is Belchior when he gets up and looks in the mirror and when he pees, without caring whether he is peeing on the floor or on the sink. He is just a man, a monument of a moment in ruins, of the ruins of the world he lives in, and of the ruins of the house in which he resides. Belchiorinho is not just another wild animal, he is also a decadent star, vehemently fleeting, neither good nor bad boy.

Belchior now tells me vaguely about what he understood, or designates, by his truth.

First, it is necessary to ignore him. Belchior is only a survivor with the finishing works of a being that has his own condition. His whole speech is exactly the size of the body that has the illusion of his so-called truth.

"I don't like unpleasant people. I hate unpleasant people! I prefer hypocrisy. Oh man, give me hypocrisy instead!" the king of the bums, the head vicar said. In that authentic feeling that was his alone, in which only he, El Belchior, was capable and bold enough to feel his reality as the most authentic thing in this world. As if what he felt was always the most just and the truth was only and only his. Which would also include being true, which was not at all.

Then, from that once again clumsy conversation of his, he went to give hard bread to the ducks in the square in the public garden. Until Francisca caught him in front of the Court of Appeal. To ascertain a way of being in conformity with the nature of man. Without absorbing, however, any other nature that was not equal to their own.

Belchior can talk for hours and hours about facts that aren't exactly real. He can criticise for days, weeks, months, the whole world, make far-fetched comments about the existence of things that are foreign to him and suddenly evoke names and situations that never existed. I admire the uselessness of his profound conviction. What a great illusionist you are, Mr Belchior. Man may be a wild animal, as landlord Rodolfo would say. But I say that man is a magical animal, able to have faith, able to feel hunger and thirst, and even able to conceive life and death, and to originate order and chaos. And make the world not a seed, but a snake, in a place that is both fantastic and tragic, or just an extraordinary place that contains millions of possibilities all as favourable as unfavourable.

Where millions more are born and reborn and hide, reproducing new emblems, new species. Then counting billions, trillions of so many more illusions created by the greatest conjurer of all, Belchiorinho. Belchior, who before leaving home put a hat on his head and put on sunglasses so as not to bump into today's grey sky.

***

Francisca was complaining about this year. She protested about the recent ingrown toenail on her middle toe and the broken front tooth. It all happened to her earlier this year. Which means that I still play poker with Belchior, Francisca, Neida and Eduardo who, today, came out of his cocoon to come to the Vista Alegre neighbourhood to play poker with the more or less usual group. I, again, made to lose quickly and went to my room, to give Neida one more lesson.

At the end of the lesson, boredom fell upon me and I became bored with the game of my life, in the attic where I live playing a game without cards with the modesty of my subconscious. Soon after, I fell asleep, blacked out, and let myself go. When I woke up Neida was still there. She was drawing an arabesque with my name on it. I asked her to remove my name from the arabesque and then to leave. Never had my soul laid so harshly unrecognisable on a mattress so inversely soft. I had become a despicable being, my unrecognisable figure was vile. And Belchior was just another abject mirror with the face of my existence.

Neida does enjoy Belchior's company. However, not as much as she enjoys the lessons that I am giving her. She went to sleep the rest of the morning at her father's house, who suffers from heart problems. Maybe I am also a heart patient, or maybe I simply don't have one of those that children and adults easily draw.

Francis, at this hour, must be drinking coconut water, in some esplanade in a big avenue, in Natal. By the sea! Remembering with longing the smell of the colour of the blue Atlantic that carries with it every Portuguese at birth, while the sun gilds the tasty asses of Brazilian women. In the interim, of what I am leaving undone, came 31 March 2014—the day of my birthday. It was written on my calendar by Francis' fist: "and when we did that project in Évora? Happy birthday, Simão! My friend!"

After lunch I went to Pingo Doce, with Belchior. To buy a bottle of wine and drink it in the afternoon with him. When we returned home, we stayed on the terrace listening to the elementary school bell ringing during the bird recess. When Belchior poured out the bottle I'd bought, he left immediately. He went to meet Francisca. He came out excited, showing his rotten front teeth, laughing out loud past mid-afternoon. More than what was usual with him. Putting his face aside like a dog that is smart. When we talk to him, he seems to understand everything. Nevertheless, Belchiorinho would be in an even better mood the next day.

Eduardo came to visit us that afternoon. He brought with him the sun. A sun as high as a building of eternal glory. It was possible to see the spiral stairway to heaven as the three of us walked: Eduardo, who was walking with the knowledge of his contemplation, Belchior, who complained that it was too much splendour for him, and I, who was just happy to see the spectacle of the sun painting the walls of the Vista Alegre neighbourhood even whiter, and to see the divine face revealed through the sun that Eduardo had brought with him.

We had gone to visit the Cartuxa Convent, but we didn't get past the gate. We bumped into it because it was not visiting hours. However, right there in front of us was the Cartuxa Convent, the time inside another time, in the story of *Scala Coeli*. And, also, right there, of course, was Belchiorinho. Complaining, concretely, about everything, in the abstract.

In the meantime, one of the monks was selflessly gathering leaves from the trees that were scattered on the ground. While, the convent's bells rang triumphantly the glorious moment when the spiral staircase disappeared and the silver aqueduct appeared levitating on the arch of the horizon. Moving from landscape to landscape.

And where I passed in my later years, I now pass through the silver aqueduct with the conviction that it will continue to pass forever. Even, I believe, until after the white monks leave the convent of Cartuxa and I am finally freed from the spiral of Évora, the silver aqueduct will continue to carry its silver water to another dream in the South, dreamt by someone, who is no longer me. Because the aqueduct of time is eternal dust falling on the floor of the dream of the universe.

Eduardo kept his notebook in his back pocket. Nothing he heard or saw seemed worth noting. Belchior laughed consecutively with that humour, which only he considered funny enough. Above the aqueduct parked in the landscape and over our three heads passed a cloud. It looked like what was near and familiar, or relatively distant, to us. Its shape mirrored, nevertheless, the unknown faraway place that remains from our gaze, that something that is somewhere at the bottom of the ocean, at the bottom of an ocean of a bottomless dream. And that somewhere has the strange shape and configuration, which takes on our more or less strange way of living.

The bell rings, yet there is no one at school today. At this hour the landlord is not at home either. For now, I am a guest in his house. Neida keeps coming over to play ping-pong on the soft mattress that is my desktop. Not even the fact that I ran away to Lisbon, thinking I could temporarily abandon Évora and leave everything behind with a simple ride, didn't deter her. It was me who distanced himself from me. It was me who became even more distant from me, and with that I became further away from the city.

Consequently, I can only feel out of place, from everything and everyone.

Belchior said to Eduardo, "What is time but shoes with laces? Already our memories are batteries, and the head is a continuously discharging battery! Ah! Ah! Ah! Who needs to wear socks in summer? Ah! Ah! Ah!"

And Eduardo with his *Kairos* listened patiently to the slow Belchior, who spoke as relaxed and carefree as he walked down the street. Eduardo listened and spoke as if he always chose the best moment to express himself. Always knowing when not to speak, and when to do so without saying a single word.

Finally, here is Eduardo reacting, "And who wears winter socks in summer?" Shortly after, he left. Once again fulfilling everything he had come and set out to do for himself. The internship, meanwhile, was over. He still had to collect the last surveys, nonetheless. But he had already started working on his thesis. Without postponing for a second his commitment to finish his Master's degree and to start his other commitment. That of growing his hair and his beard without having to worry about going to the hospital anymore.

For now, Belchior has been forced to go to work. He is more exalted now. He complains about the complaints he gets. Worse, he protests that he can't be the one to complain. He works in the call-centre at Fidelidade Insurance. But he still doesn't know what to do when injured or distressed claimants cry out for help, and ask him on his cell phone for help.

Francisca was supposed to show up at any moment to pick him up...said St Belchior, "I like the moustache you left on...it has a good pinch of salt!"

"I don't dislike my moustache either, Belchior."

"You can see that it's a moustache in tune with the walls and ramparts of Évora. I like to see you with that moustache. It's a very big and sophisticated moustache! It is a simply masculine moustache, like Hemingway's, and it is a feminine moustache, like Fernando Pessoa's moustache."

"It's an antenna moustache that connects me to the earth and is facing Dante's heaven and hell."

After we returned home, Belchior sat stridently in the living room. This morning he had done his four-hour day job and was exhausted. Plus, the walk with Eduardo and me had left him completely exhausted. He turned on the TV and lay back on the couch until his body was completely buried in it, and became one. Suddenly, fearing that I would leave him, he let out a rare pearl. "Statistics is the greatest propaganda weapon of the twenty-first century." That had been his big moment. But blinded by his own brilliance, he went on to talk about a certain Srila Prabhupada.

"Xarila left India in 1965. At the age of 69, more or less. Now, only to fulfil the request of his spiritual master. So that he, Shrila Prabhupada taught the science of karma consciousness in all English-speaking countries. But Xarilas was an influential and unwilling man. Yet he still prepared a prayer that has come down to us to this day:

"I am the sunlight/and the artificial light/turned on at night in the house/I am the daylight and the night light/I am the moon and the light that is turned on at dawn in the bathroom/and that illuminates both the woman's penis and the man's vagina, which are washed in the bidet/where both the stinky feet are washed/washed squatting or standing."

Then he laughed to himself. Saying three times, hallelujah, hallelujah, hallelujah. Down joyfully, and quickly, the stairs to the entrance of the house. He jumped up and down. After complaining at length that Francisca never arrived at the time she had arranged with him.

***

Today, it is Monday and I am in Spain. I am in a casino in Badajoz. I came with my landlord.

"Hagan sus apuestas, por favor. Apuestas a punto cerrar. No vas más."

Chapter 6
A Sad Life in Vista Alegre

(June to August 2014)

Then, after I met Gérson, I came back from my mother and brother and stepfather's house, with my haircut and my moustache trimmed. Knowing that something had to end. However, not knowing exactly what that ending would look like. Nor what concretely to do to collapse once and for all what had to fall. Maybe it wouldn't collapse. Maybe it would end, naturally. And, regardless of what I consider to be the unsustainability of my soul, Neida continues to follow me faithfully. She follows me discreetly through the streets and blocks of the Vista Alegre neighbourhood. She follows me like I followed Gérson's stories.

When I start thinking about what my final destiny will be, I never reflect on the notion that my fate will be when Neida disappears from it. Because I know that she is clearly not part of it. Perhaps I wouldn't think about it so clearly if the Gérson I met on this last trip to the Avelar valley hadn't told me about his noble heritage, or rambled on about the third Weimar Republic, or even told me about the daughter with whom he has a distant relationship and the fortune he squandered in the ports of Amsterdam when he was still a young electromechanical engineer.

What I see at present from the ephemeral balcony of the house that Rodolfo's father left him, is a social condition. We are all children of a circumstantial mother, whether raised without a father, we all have a circumstantial mother. Whether we want it or not at all. Now, in the small grassy rectangle of Bairro da Vista Alegre, a small nucleus of neighbours, with their children, is gathering, playing in the square's playground. And, at this moment, at this very instant, the poet and art critic, Rosalindo, who wrote this yesterday, appears in me:

The creation that needs thinking is a splendid thing of talented people. It can only be ingenious and beautiful people who make art out of their children and make art into something else that I have yet to think what it is.

Rosalindo, besides being an art critic, also owns two stores on Mendo Estevens Street, in one of which his wife sells cosmetics. Rosalindo is a comic abjection that I created, inspired by the extremely nice Mr Ezequiel Carvalhinho, who wears a toupee. And he has a drugstore on the street, where Rosalindo virtually lives and works.

So, he made me write, with his avuncular wisdom, today on the early afternoon balcony:

Thinking has the weight of a medicine ball. Invention is a no and it is a yes. Creation is so-so. It is something between a B flat and the C note.

Rosalindo, poet and art critic, continued to read me what he wrote, with his shrill voice, something between the larynx of Ana Maria, Belchior's girlfriend, and the larynx of Mr Ezequiel Carvalhinho, from the drugstore:

Family and art are two houses integrated through a trapdoor; there, we find stairs and a handrail leading to the end of the floor, where our heart is.

Then he concludes by quoting a verse by the popular poet João Gentil Piçarra—who is a poet who also does not exist, or yes, while he lives in me:

The man is handsome!
Whatever the music,
He does it
With a whistle,
Or a toothpick.

Rosalindo has a moustache, as I currently do. All of the characters and all of my selves, who are hauling themselves around in this summer's attic, wear moustaches. Rosalindo's moustache is the same size as mine, however, less thick.

In the late afternoon, I took Neida for a walk to a far flank of the city. A place that I recently found. It is more of a garden oasis, which is on the other side of town, and from where you can look out over the silver aqueduct passing in the shuttle of the landscape. Going there and then coming back here.

It is a small corner on the edge of the city. It is a tiny Napoleon exile for those who want to come and let his dog shit, or for someone, like me, who simply wants to hide from the world and obliterate what he is doing. Thus, being able to temporarily suspend the constant self-analysis of what he is doing and with whom he is doing it.

Neida was wearing an emerald green dress. It was a dress that her gypsy friend lent her, in order for me to be satisfied. I was still, however, very unsatisfied. Neida, in my eyes, was an ugly woman in a beautiful dress. The dress she wore, could not change the adjectives in my mind, no matter how much I closed my eyes. I could not alter the meaning that had only for me, the meaning of ugly and beautiful. Adriana Espinosa was in my mind a beautiful woman, without me having seen her regularly wearing dresses. Nonetheless, able to point out, of all those times, that she manifestly had one leg bigger than the other.

"Tatiana told me to wear it… She knows you like women to walk around in dresses," Neida said, appealing to the fairness of the facts.

But I was not in the least impressed. Her intelligence did not live in the shape of her body, nor did it hide in the curves of her body, nor in the way her emerald green dress fit. I felt like a double of myself. Although, I had returned from my mother's house with a haircut and moustache trimmed and had met Gérson, and even found, after returning to Évora, another little garden oasis. Still, the cloud sensation that I felt in the firmament of myself, had not yet disappeared. It also irritated me that Neida's shadow had not yet disappeared or melted with the tremendous heat this summer.

The next day, I went alone to the public garden to drink tea and soak up the afternoon sun. I absorbed the liquid nature of that which burns both outside and inside of us. Believing in my need to relearn how to drink tea, or whiskey, as Gérson would do at the end of a day's work. It was the influence of Gérson's tree taking root in me, the voice of his logic coming out through my throat, "How much does a cup of tea cost in the garden? And why does it cost so much less next door? How much do you pay for the need to drink tea in the public garden, while the ducks are quacking?"

Then, having ordered ice, I sipped the rest of the nature of my tea, feeling somewhat drawn to the kiosk lady's geniality. "So, what does the boy want today?" The spinster asked.

It was Gérson's influence! Gérson would be the father I never had! The stepfather I will never have! But besides the law of attraction and the importance of the appearance of Gérson and his constant revisiting, in me, there was also the multipurpose power of my moustache. It was good for everything. From picking up a wi-fi signal, to spreading watermelon jam without having to use my hands!

Curiously, with the lady from the kiosk, a girl I worked with at the Arcada coffee shop was now working in that cramped cubicle. More interesting, however, was that she was currently dating Travassos. In fact, with whom she was currently living, and who I had also met there. Travassos would later become my colleague at the lounge bar and restaurant *Spettvs*. And somewhere, much later, Adélia had ended up at Travassos.

Never had she ever thought, or dreamt, that she would one day live with him, and that she would kiss him on the lips. But Adélia both fits in the cubicle of this kiosk, and in the compartment of a world, which has more than a hemisphere of dream and illusion. On the continent of our smallest ambition, the roads that cross it easily lead us to perdition and bewilderment. But, the loneliness of the journey through the dream that we travel, awake or asleep, is sometimes not so much, when accompanied.

This time, I returned to Évora, looking into the mirror fixed somewhere inside me and I didn't recognise myself. I could neither understand nor define how I got here. I now climb the attic stairs that lead to my room. And I don't even think about why Rodolfo's father abandoned him after winning the lottery. I don't even think about why his father left this house to him and to his sister. And why even that didn't help to fix Rodolfo's life. Nor do I wonder why his father abandoned his mother, or why she later went to the insane asylum.

I climb the stairs to heaven, unaware of the exact rented planet on which I live, or in what way I live, in a rented cosmos. I reject the paintings hanging on the living room wall of my factual universe and avoid the cobwebs that weave the daily intrigue between the tenant Belchior and the landlord Rodolfo. I laugh at the days that pass and leave behind cosmic dust. After all, I am a moustache in the world, just a moustache in the world of the moustache. I am climbing up an invisible rope, the ladder that leads up to the sky, up to the mountain and the snow-filled summit.

I am climbing towards the clouds, which is where Gérson, the electromechanical engineer, lives. I'm climbing the stairs that go to the attic of the sky, and I'm no longer looking for the meaning of the Southern dream, nor for the meaning of what I came to Évora to do, at least for now.

It's just another day on the snail's ladder from the cathedral, from myself, to the firmament. It's just another step of the spiral that goes from the attic, where my room is, to the next day's curve. And on the next curve, we are on our way to Graça do Divor: me, with my moustache, Belchior with his cap, Neida with her generous bust, Eduardo with a beard that gets bigger and bigger, and Francisca with a boyish hairdo and a man's belly. Finally, the couple Raquel and Augusto, who ended up coming too, but much later.

We would meet them a long way from the place we had arranged. Now, no pun intended! But they were in the *Sítio Certo* (Right Place), drinking coffee, and we, like fools, were waiting for them in a certain place...

Early that morning, I discussed Belchior's aloofness with Belchior. Neither he, nor I, knew exactly on what our indifference was based. I quarrelled with Belchior, possibly, because of the abstract filth that he represented, and, probably, because of the dirtiness of life that he, concretely, sprayed around landlord Rodolfo's house, as well as, around the Vista Alegre neighbourhood. When I dived into the mirror of water, the water from the Graça do Divor dam, with Augusto, I didn't recognise myself either. There I was, with my moustache and Gérson's influence, on a summer picnic; eating and drinking.

Just like Eduardo, there he was, sitting next to me, resting under the shade of a tree that was supposedly his friend. But as much as I wanted to talk to Eduardo about Gérson's influence, there was no time or space. There was no space, no time to forget my misery and the influence of an Alentejo that was greater than the radiation effect that Gérson had docked on me. Consequently, I felt the weight of time and the weight of a golden space getting tighter and tighter in the sun's field, which didn't even allow the clouds in the sky to lay their wings on top of the ruined, roofless house on top of the hill of Graça do Divor.

Francisca was sweating profusely through her navel and under her armpits. When she lifted her arms, you could see, on the proper scale, the channel of the stain, which is where the sweat of her anguish came through. Belchior himself was protesting. Neither he nor anyone else knew exactly what he was complaining about. As for my friend Eduardo, he was following the horizon with his sense of smell and laughing with the crown of grass he carried on his head.

As for his notebook for this year, it is still almost blank, but it goes along comfortably in his back pocket. Because where one goes, the other always follows.

Then the herd that had gone to the picnic decided to walk through the field. You can hear a Belchiorinho speaking in his condition as an apprentice rapper; an MC—a master of ceremonies—looking for a message to the world that until now had not found it anywhere. He is just a Belchior with a little hat on his head, complaining about the sun and the world of music for being as unfair as any other universe that is as big as it is.

Maybe that is his message. Who knows? However, Neida's breasts are very prominent, and Belchior walks by, systematically looking at her breasts, and I don't mind at all, because that is nothing to do with me, and even because the farther their shadow moves away from me, the more I feel the golden Alentejo reflecting directly into my soul.

Meanwhile, Francisca is chatting with Neida. "You know, I remember you! You were dating a friend of mine from another time. Albano. And now with another friend." Then they both laughed, while a hypnotised Belchior continued to stare at the same place. I continued without caring about it.

Although, what bothered me was only that Francisca thought Neida was my girlfriend.

As we walked through the wilderness of the field, each one disappeared in mid-afternoon. Eduardo, who was behind me, also disappeared. Dissolving into the frame of a picture, of an interlude picture that he himself was painting.

On the afternoon of the next day, I went to write to the newly found goldfield, which is relatively close to that garden oasis, which is in a corner of the city overlooking the silver aqueduct. I often go there to watch the weather pass by and listen to the cars that blur with the twittering of the winged birds hanging upside down from the trees, which live next to the golden open field, where there is an abandoned soccer field. All that remains are the iron goals, which are from a time that has been crumbling. After all, to live is to collapse completely!

I sat on the carpet, which usually flutters with me. Describing, specifically, what I reach for that is beyond what I see. Because what I see is beyond my vision and my contemplation. It is in the dissipation of the grain of time. It is in the notion of the desert of space before the sand of time, it is in the globule of space-time, it is between what I don't see and the golden beyond of the wasteland that I think I see.

When the noises of automobile engines trample the road, the nature of the wind comes on all sides retaliating. In that instant, the field is my body, and my body is barefoot on the field, and my soul is writing in motion. Writing on the edge of the wheat field sheet, a vast verse. Writing in full on the nameless landscape, and passing slowly with the hand of my spirit on the face of the golden wheat field.

Whenever there is television, and the television is continuously on, and there are always, always people calling on their cell phones, and the busy signal is permanently on, nobody can know if the sun is burning, or if our heart, today, beats faster, and of why, all this is more or less important, and more or less ephemeral.

The ultimate miracle is the exact spot where we get lost. The miracle is the originality with which each one meets himself. But after one has repeatedly lost oneself, the wonder is nothing more than a simple aphorism. And it was while cogitating, reminiscing on the last miracle in my land, from which I got lost, that I came across Eduardo, who, in the middle of the conversation, told me something quite relevant: "reality cannot exist at the same moment we recognise the dream."

Eduardo had told me this when I met him in the neighbourhood square. He had come to collect surveys and had parked his car there. After we had arranged to have lunch, we talked about what I had been writing recently. Eduardo became interested in these little heteronyms or alter-egos that fit inside me. Some don't, because they rather occupy the body of a room, and are figures from my imagination. Some of my recent characters are just fantastical examples of a fiction cosplay. Others are a collection of personalities, which give rise to a more or less complete being.

Still others are mere fragments of what is completely real and human. Not only because of the extent of what could be in me, even more ridiculous, than what I actually am, but because all of us may contain in, characteristics, which come close to the people we more or less know, and which are sometimes, easily, lives that we would never dare to represent on the stage of our daily routines. If some of them wear my clothes, because they are my contemporaries, others are from another century. Still others I don't really know yet; I only know that they are mere extensions of myself, and that others, clearly, are just what I am not.

The night had not yet fully begun when the afternoon departed with Eduardo. But already planted in the firmament dwelt a moon with a belly so gracefully full that it resembled a pregnant woman. It was the dream of the blue of the afternoon, which blended with the dark blue beginnings of the evening sea. For a moment, I found again the bridal cave of the dream that I had been looking for since I arrived in Évora. And it doesn't matter if it's already the end of the day, if there was an exam for Spanish literature and arts in room 295, and I missed it. Nor if I meditated after lunch. Not if I studied today's lesson superficially. It was, indeed, one of those beautiful moments of the once dreamt dream, this time experienced awake.

Meanwhile, Raul Cancelo, one of the villains of this story, has unoriginally taken another mandate. This time, in another association. He may not be extremely original, but I give him credit for that stroke of creativity. He is now the octopus president of the *Círculo Eborense*, the club where Eça de Queirós entertained himself during his stay in Évora. It was there that I took Neida for one more lesson. Today's lesson included listening to a talk by the writer João Tordo, accompanied by the town's councilman for culture, Eduardo Luciano. Who looked at me, very interested, more than it was my interest to be noticed. Maybe it was because I didn't allow Neida to sit next to me.

Neida's lesson today was wandering from side to side. First, she dragged herself with one sandal in her hand and another on her foot. While, I was criticising her poverty of spirit and the attitude of her numb and bewildered soul. Then, I was the one who threw her out of the *Círculo Eborense*, where I quickly got bored with the litanies of writer João Tordo, who was as indecisive as I would be, without, however, knowing if I was in the middle of my life lived in Évora.

After all, what I wanted was to listen to someone who knew where I was and what I wanted out of life. Someone like Gérson, who knew who he was and where he was going. The world and literature need more electromechanical engineers.

Five minutes after we were late for the talk, we left. I left first, Neida came timidly after me. Again, with one sandal in her hand and another sandal on her foot. Until she took it off and walked down the Évora sidewalk.

"We have no time to lose, Neida!"

"You're going too fast..."

"Life is not for the indolent, who wearily dream the dream of life. Don't be lazy!"

"Go slower!"

"You are too young to feel the fatigue of reality on the sole of your foot."

"But I'm barefoot…"

We went to the cabins. So, they wouldn't see me with her. She was bored since she had left her father's house. I raved about the dances of Rajasthan. Wishing one day to go to India, wishing to know Rajasthan, which is next to Pakistan. Obviously, leaving Neida in Évora, adrift, like a boat with no direction. This being her last instruction, and so I would go alone, also aimlessly, like a boat adrift, sailing on the sea of the world, after having also learned my last lesson.

Yesterday, I went with Belchior for social food. More in the name of art and literature, than actually moved by an urgent need. I went only to acknowledge his sad existence and his sad path, which was taken, now, almost every day, from the Vista Alegre neighbourhood to Rua dos Penedos…meanwhile, we talked about his fake address, in which he fictionally resides. As well, we talked about the money he receives, while pretending to be looking for work. Initially, he was disinclined to openly confess what he was doing.

But after my insistence he explained his scheme to me. It was then very difficult to get him to shut up. On the way home the conversation with me and him was, "Aren't you interested in talking about the fado of soccer? But Belchior, it is possible to talk to almost anyone about the soccer fado. The fate of the life of our Lusitanian soul can be discussed or sung, like in a soccer game, if decisive throws are missed…for example…"

"Well, it's all about the soccer fado! Everyone knows about soccer and the fado. There are many subjects that are not talked about or discussed! It's the other side of soccer. What matters is history, and what goes down in history will be that Pedro Álvares Cabral, the greatest Portuguese player, who left with his head down and his shoulders shrugged at the end of a losing game. In Portugal not everything is fado! Not everything is soccer!" Said Belchior, immediately trying to indirectly blame the rest of the world, although it was the voice of his personal dissatisfaction that predominantly spoke now.

The saintly Belchior continued, effusively, "Not everything is Fátima! Not everyone is happy. For if some are happy, others must be unhappy, and if some are unhappy, others are so-so."

"Misunderstood?" I asked.

"The so-so are the ones that are neither meat, nor fish, nor vegetarian."

"In the old days, not everyone wore earrings like you, and the greatest! But now everyone does, right?"

"Yeah, the guys are more daring now. The greatest?"

"Vítor Baptista," I replied.

"Was he a fado soccer player?" Belchiorinho asked. He, who didn't know a thing about soccer.

"He was the greatest," I answered.

Meanwhile, we were already at home. Where he quickly recharged his battery. And, after sitting on the sofa in the living room, possessed by the moment, he took up one of his occasional occupations—he called an unknown number from the home phone, and on the other end of the phone line, someone believed Belchior to be João Silva or Gervásio Pintassilgo. Belchior wanted what everyone wants and craves; for a little bit of attention. And, therefore, I gave him what he wanted.

"Let's do an interview with Belchior, Belchior?" His eyes sparkled, promptly going into a trance. "How many heteronyms or alter-egos do you have?" I asked him.

He paused for a long time and, after listening to himself, he confessed in a serious tone, something rare to observe in him... "Pseudonyms: João Silva, a preppy, well-behaved; Gervásio Pintassilgo, when I feel like being rude to people. I only have telephone heteronyms. They don't have a face. They are my two sons! They don't know each other and do everything to get to know each other. They cannot exist at the same time—they are antagonistic!"

"Belchior, is Belchior antagonistic?"

"No, but João Silva and Gervásio are. João Silva is a sensitive man, not in the faggot sense. He is a controlled person. Mister Bright! 32 years old, well dressed, civil engineer/informatician/programmer. He is someone in life! Good student in maths, physics, computers. He is a handsome, intelligent man. A mama's boy, grandma's boy, wife's boy. He is a well-spoken person."

You said, "he is a well-spoken person, is that important?"

This is important to you! To be João Silva, I had to be talking to you on the phone. Also important is the name João Silva. It's a little boy's name. It's a Portuguese name. It could be Sousa, or Mendes. Silva, also refers to Jewish names. João is more elite!

"Do you have something against the Jews?"

"Hey, man! I don't like some Jews... Namely, the ones who control the financial markets. That Jewry! All religions bother me a little bit."

Suddenly, he had the home phone in his hand. Calling, at once, to a number at random. A middle-aged man answered. The talented Belchiorinho began, "You know;" pause. "Your wife is with…" Again, pause. "The bitch is with him." And he hung up. Laughing with an invisibly sinister scream, which came out of his gaping mouth. Displayed with satisfaction and without complexes, his rotten teeth.

"Is there nothing in religion that you admire?" I asked him.

"There are certain things about religions, inside, that interest me."

"Where were you born?"

"In Lisbon! At the Alfredo da Costa maternity. It doesn't exist anymore. Until I was five, I lived in Olivais, Malveira, Cabeço de Montachique. Then I lived in Santo António dos Cavaleiros… And then I went to Sines. There I lived from five until twenty-two. When I was twenty-two, I came to Évora."

"Lisbon, Sines or Évora?" I asked, as I thought about the coincidence that we both came to study in Évora at the age of twenty-two.

"Malveira brings back pleasant memories. Santo Antonio brings back bad memories. My father beating my mother. The biggest cattle fair in the country was in Malveira, 22 years ago! There were flies that never ended."

"Did that impress you?"

"At night, you wanted to sleep, they were on your head! You wanted to eat; they were on your plate. I also have fond memories of my house in Malveira. It was an old house."

"Do you like old houses?"

I like the big old houses. But well-priced. A house from the mid-nineteenth century. You're sure of the space. You have the TV watching room, then you have the living room that's just a dining room. With well-defined rooms. Cigarettes in my house nobody smoked. Only pot! But in one room, and there weren't even books in that room.

"Is space and space definition very important to you? Do you organise better?"

"Maybe I would make a good architect! But I don't have the patience to study architecture."

"You have already studied psychology. Are you going to study again?"

"Yes, tomorrow I'm taking the national exams. I'll take one tomorrow and the other one next week. I haven't even checked the room yet; I have to go tomorrow…"

"Shouldn't you go today?"

"It could be tomorrow. If I get too upset, I'll call the school."

"Are you tormented by something?"

"Sometimes I'm afraid of getting into some situation with nothing. No job, no house. That torments me a little bit. But I think being in shit torments everybody. It worries me, not me, it worries others. It torments me, where the world is going to end up. Most people don't give a shit about others."

"Where do you want to be now?"

"I don't know, I'm fine here. If I could go somewhere else? So many places. I'd like to have a caravan and money for diesel and food, and just take off. Where does a guy go by car? To Spain? Not to the sea! To Europe, maybe even Holland. Poland doesn't interest me. Ukraine? Not now!"

"If you could have a mental keyboard with a button to eradicate someone, that is, eliminate some public figure, who would you erase?"

Nicolau Breyner is annoying. Not Fernando Mendes. The politicians that are in the assembly, all of them. I used to like João Baião; I used to like Malato, but not anymore. Did you know he is a Jehovah's Witness? I can't do sects, man! I would delete so many public figures! Bóinas—Luís Filipe Borges, the guy with the berets... I wouldn't erase Unas, although he's no longer funny. But I would erase five times, Quimbé and Nuno Eiró.

But I would leave Goucha! I have respect for Goucha! Goucha is a guy I've seen being arrogant at parties, but he used to have integrity, before he came out of the closet. I would banish Santana Lopes. I wouldn't ban Guterres and I wouldn't ban Sócrates. Sócrates gave us computers for 150 euros. Mine was free!

At this, the great Belchior, who the world saw being born for who knows what reason, looked at the television and pointed with his index finger. "Look, ah, it looked like Nicolau Breyner! And I'd like to spend a night with Manuela Moura Guedes. But there was nothing between us."

"Could you be on TV?"

"I could."

"Would you be a priest if you were paid?"

"No."

"What profession will you be in in a few years?"

"Right now, I'm focused, or I'm starting to focus on playing poker. I like so many things... I'd like to do two or three things: I'd like to play poker; I'd like to use music in some way; I'd like to, I don't know, so many things. But a specific profession: psychologist, sociologist, translator; I don't know!"

"Are you afraid of going crazy?"

"Since I read *In Praise of Folly*. That one, yes. But man, going crazy in terms of senility, I wouldn't like that very much."

"How do you imagine yourself 10 years from now? In one sentence."

"Wealthy. And wealth, to me, encompasses several aspects."

"Are you a fan of something?"

"I'm a poker fan, just a fan of music, of cannabis. I'm a fan of trees, nature in general, and animals."

"Do you have phrases that you use in your dialogue? In Gervásio or in, such, João?"

"The dog that barks, doesn't bite, by Gervásio Pintassilgo."

"Would you give me the focus of that sentence?"

"That's when there's nothing left! There's nothing left to do. It rained, it rained! I don't have much patience to talk about the weather."

"Are you a patient person?"

"Sometimes. In general, no. But I'm more patient than I was a few years ago, and I hope to be more patient in a few years."

"And bullfighting?"

"Bullfights are a disrespect to others. Any rational being should understand. In one sentence: it makes no sense. It's like religion, they didn't say the sun goes around the Earth? In bullfighting it's very nice to stick the iron! It's all an excuse to make money. There you go, we're back to talking about 'they don't give a shit', and the state financing it. I mean, they suck the money to build the bullrings and then they ask us for the money for the tickets! The *mongos* applaud... Most people are *monga*! Orwell already talked about it..."

"Bullfighting and soccer, Belchior, both have an arena..."

"Both function in the same prism—the spectacle. To alienate. But this is a secret! Everyone sees soccer. I like soccer, the sport. Just as I like basketball, volleyball. Personally, I've never been inclined to team sports. What do we have here? Soccer, roller hockey, cycling. What sports are here to watch? Canoeing? We have surfing, we have Nazaré. We have beaches that are good for surfing. Like Ericeira, which is world renowned."

"Why do you like to make those phone calls?"

"It is communication. You use your voice. I have to imagine and anticipate what the other person is going to say…and you always have to have a counter-argument. It's being one step ahead. It's controlling what the other person is going to do. Whoever asks the most questions, controls the speech. I always try to interrupt people on phone calls. On the phone, it's not me! On the phone, nothing is seen. On camera it's visual, on the phone it's auditory. They are two different things. No, I don't know why, but with my image, I can't. I think it's easier for me to let go with phone calls."

He opened the phone book and improvised. It was his real talent. Fooling others. Pretending to be someone he wasn't. I laughed at Belchior with Belchior. Until he left and went to Francisca, who caught him in the square. When I got out of bed the next day, I opened my eyes slowly and instantly closed the dream page in my hands. I was dreaming about my friend Marcus Matalonga and his mansion in Ribeiro Travesso, between Lâmpada and Caparito.

***

Today, I stopped by the St João's fair in the afternoon. To get lost in the carousel of my thoughts. I felt the vertigo of thinking viscerally about the things I saw and the things I didn't see at all. While the afternoon carousel spun around me, I orbited around the memory of my second summer spent in Évora. The music of the bumper cars served as a soundtrack to the surreal event that I could exist on the edge of society. Easily forgotten by the edge of yesterday's day that flashes as intermittently as the lights of today's empty bumper cars, and that keeps company with the sellers of snacks and churros who stare alienated at the future, perched somewhere just ahead of them.

I live in a neighbourhood called Vista Alegre, where I lead a sad life in my own way. Yes, I recognise that my life has a sad background. But I also recognise that there are many and varied ways of being sadly cheerful people. For example: there are cheerful people who have just entered the afternoon carousel. They are very different from those who wake up and fall asleep in the Vista Alegre neighbourhood and who never, ever, shudder during a single ride on the merry-go-round of their lives.

There are people in the Vista Alegre neighbourhood who get sick just seeing happy people and when they see people who are not so happy, they get absolutely overjoyed, which is what happens to my next door neighbour when she sees Belchior arriving at the square with his hands in his pockets.

I live between Tapada and Vista Alegre and the café that goes by the name of *Sítio Certo*.

It was there that I returned, still in the middle of the afternoon sun. Leaving the Feira de São João and Rossio. Crossing the public garden. Looking from the walls at the people and cars that passed by, far below. I shook my head in disapproval. Although, without having any reason against who was passing by me at that instant. I felt like it. That's all.

Feeling immediately better for being able to judge others so lightly.

I got so excited that I counted the trees that are in the shade and the ones that when they are in the sun, you can't even see them. There is something about the Vista Alegre neighbourhood that is comparable to the tired vision. Perhaps, by the billions of cars parked around the square. Nevertheless, there are park benches to sit on, that are worth more than all the money kept in the vaults of the Banco de Portugal. Sometimes I sit there and rest my eyes. Until you see it, you don't have to pay for it. And as you can see, it is written on one of those benches in the square: "J.P + Cláudia Cambeiro; C=∞; I love J.P, by CláudiaCambeiro."

Also, I hope sitting down, and it's all about seeing to believe that they still love each other. However, it is clear that the Vista neighbourhood may not be so sad, as I am, because it has a more or less joyful view.

I wrote, today, just for myself, a chronicle of how the professional politician António Costa, more government, less government, is going to be the next prime minister. I did so, believing that I could be paid to write for a newspaper, and could have a life here in the Vista Alegre neighbourhood, or elsewhere. Yet, I doubt that will be possible for me.

I left home today to search for the history of post-modernity, as if looking for someone I know. Just as I had snuck out of the house to listen to the song from the street, which corners the drag of inspiration, where people of action live, full of illusion and human contradiction. But it was after I met the statue of the dead man, and noticed that it had been moved, that I started to think about writing a novel—*Preparing for Death Before Dying*—about someone who spends all his time worrying about preparing for his own death. Since he doesn't know on what date, or how exactly he will expire, and that is what bothers him. Because he absolutely does not want to perish with unresolved issues.

It would therefore be unthinkable for him or her to pass away in the middle of the day. But my mother is asking me to get a job, and in the meantime this idea for a short novella will remain in the drawer of what one wants to do. But one doesn't know when it will actually start, or if it will ever get started. That is, if I don't finish it in the meantime, and the idea ends up with me.

I met Eduardo on the way home. He was collecting more data; he had come to the elation that he still had insufficient data at his disposal. He hasn't been showing up to play poker. Since his internship ended, he's been very happy to be rid of it. As if he had something else in life to do, more important to him, than to go to the hospital, ascertain the mental illness of patient xis or patient zê, diagnosing xis and zê, finally putting one label on xis and another on zê.

Meanwhile, a plane tore through the sky, leaving a white furrow. While, the aircraft passed above our heads. For me, that event was, eventually, a singular moment. However, he promptly told me in his usual calm, logical tone, "It's just an aeroplane, carrying passengers. Going from one point to another point. Just that."

The next day, I ran out of the house, with no need to know where I was going, and I came across a drunkard carelessly lying on a park bench by the Misericórdia square. He was contritely healing his hangover. Today, he had no more bottles to empty. On the ground were the fallen flowers of the Jacarandas that painted the sidewalk of this station with lilac, filling with a certain colour, the uncertain tone that had the anguish and despair of that beautiful and abject moment. A little later, old Ricky would pass by me. He was wearing his leather jacket, which had already settled into its shape. Hanging from the corner of his mouth, a rolling cigarette was burning brightly.

Once again, he spoke of going back to Mozambique, and once more he consigned 1969 as one of the best years of his life. And not once would he mention the bill he owes in all the cafés in the historic centre, or the money he owes his friends and acquaintances, who no longer remember that they lent him some change to continue his life. But now he has run out of credit. Nobody gives it to him anymore. This is old Ricky, the one who will never leave Évora, the one who will never return to Mozambique. Not even by swimming, let alone on foot!

But every year, around this time, the lilac flowers of the Jacarandas in the Misericórdia square will continue to fall without ever needing to lie or deceive. I, most likely, will also be another old Ricky, who will never go where he says he wants to go. And in spite of that and of who is arriving and who is actually leaving, the poor decadent drunk will continue to breathe in the hangover of another day, accompanied and supported by the empty wine bottles that stand beside him.

When I returned home, Carmona was standing in the driveway of my landlord's garage, who rented it to him. It serves as his paint warehouse. He was with his employees. One of them was his son. A dull guy, more fat than muscular. A very masculine type, but without any sense of sophistication or introversion. Carmona is a small man. Thick eyebrows and curly hair. A house painter who likes to tell me easy trigger jokes. However, they are too simple to shoot for my taste. But Carmona waved to me and I reciprocated, raising my hand at half-mast to him. Belchior doesn't speak to him, or, he doesn't speak to Belchior.

Lately, I too have avoided speaking to him. Although, I don't disown him and even accept the nature of this sad martyr that hovers around the Vista Alegre neighbourhood. However, there is something in me that makes me inclined to ignore and even despise him and the place in the world where he resides. No matter how much I know that Belchior lives in the same place as me. That is, that the world in which he exists lies beneath the ground I walk on every day and night.

At night, Neida went with me to a Sérgio Godinho concert. I imposed that we didn't hold hands. But we stayed close enough to each other for me to be desirable before the watchful eyes of possible interested parties, who in any other disposition would not be captivated. Nevertheless, during the concert I gave her good advice. But she didn't want it. As generally nobody ever wants advice. Especially when they are not asked for. She was annoyed. But I continued to sprinkle her with my opinions, adding one or another exhortation. Just to see when she would leave. But she resisted my wise torture.

Something, which even if she thought about it, could be tremendously useful to her in the future. Although, when we each went home and she said goodbye to me, she left me feeling frankly optimistic. She made me believe that this would be the last time we would see each other.

Three and a half hours after I went to bed, I awoke from a dream involving her and her friend Tatiana, her gypsy friend. The two were in a house that in the dream possibly, I think, belonged to Tatiana. I must have dreamt about them, both of them, because lately I had been negotiating the sensible clauses of a threesome with her and her friend.

Only the negotiation was dragging on, because Tatiana was currently involved with a market vendor's wife. Besides, she had to take care of Neida's nephew, who was too young to understand the business his mother was involved in. So, the ideal moment was not found, one that would be useful to me and would marry with Tatiana's agenda. And now, of course, it will be more complicated for the business to happen.

***

Around 7 pm, I took a walk with the peacocks that usually hang out in the public garden. They were placed in little niches of nature scattered around the city. Sadly, nature doesn't have much space in the technical and commercial nature of urban man. But fortunately, the dusk had the moth of wood. Not directly seeing, however, that invisible something that occurs beyond our understanding and our ignorance. Every time the sun leaves for its rest, the eternal farewell is repeated, and we slowly learn to internalise it. And, we get used to looking at things without ever seeing them.

During my little pilgrimage, I took some standing notes, for my *Species Observatory*, I share two, as an example, "seagulls are beautiful women, they always look good in the picture; birds run marathons in the sky, and never get tired."

But when I was on the esplanade at the public garden, I still struck up a conversation with Maria, who was also sitting there. She was as smiling as she was reticent. It was the strange Maria Mortágua, who had once come to have lunch with me in the apartment I shared with my friend Francisco on Heróis do Ultramar Avenue. It was also the same Maria Mortágua that had later come to dine with me and Mariana, and Vânia Velez, André Monte, and Mário; and who else...right: Débora; when at my first stay at Maria de Fátima's house. It was curious that she suddenly appeared as she would quickly disappear. Eventually, it was a kind of Belchior but one kind of with greater power?

I invited her to sit with me. She smiled with complicity, but said no. Always behaving in a way that was so mysteriously strange to me. Something about her was truly bizarre to me. As a rule, the most unique things frighten and repel us, sometimes as much as they attract us. She left her table soon after, without saying goodbye. She left through the gate leading to the municipal market. A car from Diana's driving school stopped and took her away.

I continued, the next day, to take notes for the *Species Observatory*. I wrote, first, in the attic about the animals that people are. Then I went to write at the *Palmeira* coffee table. I spent a couple of hours observing the daily crawl of the people who frequent that establishment every day. Its name is obviously due to the palm tree that they stuck in the cloister of the shopping centre.

On the other side of the cloister is the *Sítio Certo* coffee shop and another coffee shop that is also run by another couple, but which is almost always empty. Above all these cafes, there are apartments. And every day, at the same time, I, or any other curious person, can smoke, meditate, protest looking into the air, or simply observe the neighbours, the employees, or the mere *habitués* of the neighbourhood, with their routines, easily distinguishing which are the preys and which are the predators that roam the Vista Alegre neighbourhood from Monday to Sunday.

And, Lo and behold, the meteorite El Belchior, out of nowhere, appeared on the horizon, in spurts. He was outside the stationery store, which is also a tobacco shop. When he passed by me, he had the air of someone very confused. He was not at all expecting to run into me there. However, he also did not know what he would say to me today, after our previous social short-circuit.

Still, it was extremely vital to be able now to summarise the realisation of those who live in the same house but would rather live away from each other. By the way, it was a blessing, to which we should be very grateful… For having argued the morning before the afternoon picnic at Graça do Divor. Afterwards, everyone realised that it was best not to cross each other's social electricity wires, since they cannot actually touch each other.

On the hot afternoon of the next day, a few minutes before the French oral exam started, Professor Ferreira Gomes very elaborately told me, "Don't complicate it." Seeming extremely annoyed to be there. Professor Otília, who had taught me comparative literature studies, was part of the jury. She was full of pimples. At forty-something she was either entering puberty again, or she had another allergic reaction. Clarice considered her limited.

The last time Professor Otília and I spoke was at the university bar. On that day, what brought Professor Otília closer to me was only because she realised that I was friends with Daniel Filipe Mansilha, which made her, at that time, much more condescending towards me than she was today during the exam, or even before it started.

Once she talked with me about Daniel Filipe, who had already finished his degree and he was teaching as a guest lecturer at the University of Évora. Then Daniel Filipe left the University of Évora to go to Lisbon to teach, because he hadn't finished his Master's yet. Was it a year and a half, two years ago?

After the French oral exam, I went shopping at Pingo Doce. Just to walk around. I walked around, however, without finding a place to park my head. I walked around without being able to land in a single place. Without finding a single space that I could occupy or stay there, serenely parked forever. I wanted to do everything, intuiting, although, that I would still accomplish nothing. It was with that devotion and conviction that I returned home.

At the end of the day, Belchior was caught lying by the landlord, who leaned back on the living room couch playing his game. Naturally, as he would do during any day of the week. Eating chicken legs with one hand and holding, with the other, the remote. As much as he had both hands busy, he easily perceived Belchiorinho's ruse. All because Eduardo, while waiting in the living room, unintentionally commented on a narrative that discredited the one that had been previously told by the one who was given the name of Saint Belchior.

Rodolfo had thus realised that his tenant had deceived him. And when the innocent of the sin of the world, our Lord Jesus Christ Belchior returned from the musty catacombs of his room, instead of Eduardo just shutting up and letting it go, or quickly thinking of saying nothing, he was more than resolved not to accept that his name be slandered, nor that his person be pinched. I was even more impressed by my friend Eduardo. That brave gesture of his did not go unnoticed by me. It was a noble gesture, more and more rare in a world of men and women who live without experiencing for a single day the importance and unwavering courage of always telling the truth. Sadly, honour is an increasingly rare jewel.

And when we find it, here and there, it is impossible not to feel dazzled by its brilliance.

After all, what happened? Our Belchior had taken a puppy that was still being suckled by "Néscia." The dog that was frequently neglected by the landlord, and sometimes well treated, sometimes poorly mistreated by the tenant Belchior, who was now feeding with another type of explosion of disorder and confusion, that house in the Vista Alegre neighbourhood; whose residents' lives were, to say the least, sadly absurd.

Here, the philosophical and ethical issue under discussion was that, even if Rodolfo didn't care about those little creatures, who were born with their eyes closed to the truth and illusion of the world, even if Rodolfo didn't care about anything, not even himself, a lie was a lie. It was like that, for Eduardo, as it was for me and even for Rodolfo. Except, perhaps, for Mr Belchiorinho!

Yet, no, not at all. El Belchior, like all liars, would be bathed in the power of the truth of everything sooner or later being known. Who did he think he was? Barabbas? No! Nothing gave him the right to do whatever he wanted! That included not being able to give the cubs to whomever he wanted, without Rodolfo, above all, knowing and agreeing. Not least because, first, the little ones would have to finish being suckled. Something that Belchior, one of those animal lovers, had forgotten of such relevance.

Very surprisingly, the afternoon of the next day, I walked, after lunch, around town talking on the cell phone with Marcus. His voice transmitted an unusual enthusiasm to me. His spirit sounded less defeated to me today. When the cell phone conversation ended, a dove from the sky landed on the awning of the *Terra Fértil* (*Fertile Earth*) farm store. He had already hung up, and so I could not comment to him on how extraordinarily ephemeral it was from Eduardo's point of view, just a very non-special moment. Anyway, every man is a compass tracing his circumference within another circumference. The previous one having nothing similar to the other, nor to the next.

Before the end of that afternoon fell, I visited the carriage museum, which is part of the lego empire of the Fundação Eugénio de Almeida. Since yesterday, I had decided to go in and look for places that I had never visited or frequented, or, which, by some stupid excess, I couldn't remember the last time I had entered there. At the reception desk was Maria do Rosarinho, my former classmate. She was someone I ended up losing touch with. When I saw her, I felt like not only talking to her, but also hugging her.

However, my ego stopped me. On the one hand, I wanted to recover the chest of lost time, but on the other hand, what I really wanted to do today was to count carriages. Maria do Rosarinho was doing her internship there. She was happily progressing with her life as a young woman in a neighbourhood overlooking a completely different part of the Alentejo. I started counting carriages and Maria do Rosarinho continued counting the number of visitors. It was part of her job. Mine, today, besides writing was to count the carriages that came from the past to the present.

Before entering the house, I found in the Vista Alegre square, next to the garbage can, a formidable white desk that had recently been restored, only to be inexplicably abandoned there later. Possibly, because of the excess of things that we insist on wanting to keep at the same time.

However, there is no more room for so much to want and so much to have. This is how I found happiness at the edge of the end of the day, at that exact moment. The sky of my imagination fits on that small surface. I felt connected to that object so light and somehow, there, parked waiting for me. I transported the writing table effortlessly to my room in the attic, and shortly afterwards I would use it to conduct correspondence with Daniel Filipe Mansilha. This time I offered to do him the favour of spending a few days in Oeiras with him and Beatriz Gorjão, his partner.

When I entered the house, I would find an exalted and very angry Belchior. Belchiorinho had discovered that cans of tuna fish had been stolen from him. Precisely, after he had taken my food the day before and I had confronted him. I am now interested to know how long it will take Pinocchio to find out that he or the landlord could only have stolen the tuna cans.

***

I went to change the home address on my citizen's card. Knowing that sooner or later I will have to do it again. Because, quite naturally, I will end up moving house, and consequently I will be forced to change my life. I will keep my clothes, just because I cannot change my skin, jointly. Then I passed by Zorra's house. Which is yet another cultural association run by a couple. Were it not for the culture in Évora, being the daughter of a marriage, or the result of a de facto union.

I went in search of the knowledge and the necessary preparation that my travelling artist residency required. However, I didn't know what precisely I was going there to look for, nor what I would concretely want to find there. I didn't know yet what it was that I was seeking to decode during this artistic project of mine. Zorra's house would be, eventually, a door with a secret passage to another end of the bridge where the ribs of the lost paradise lay.

Through which I and my new writing table could cross. I am referring to the table I found next to the trash can in the square in Barro da Vista Alegre. Next to the same trash can, where Belchior and Francisca found a mattress that they dragged up to the second floor, so that later, I could put it in the attic on top of my bed, where a soft mattress already lived.

Felício, Francisco's former classmate, was doing an internship at Casa da Zorra, Elisa Calçada was also there. She was drawing on the wall when I arrived. She is a plastic artist that I knew from the time I lived in the Senhora da Saúde neighbourhood. She currently collaborates with the couple whose divine power of culture it has brought together.

Shortly after, she went to show me the catacombs of the building, revealing to me the side of the city that I didn't know existed. It was also Elisa who pointed to the fan that had been painted on the wall, across the street, with the inscription, "For the sailor with a desire for the wind. Memory is a starting point."

Today's blue sun was a fire as hot as the version of the sun from my first summer spent ironing in Évora. The indigo heat was everywhere. In Praça do Giraldo, in Largo de São Vicente, in Rua do Imaginário, in Rua São João de Deus—formerly Rua Ancha. The bath of blue I speak of was a cloud shaped like a blue aquarium that flooded the Alentejo. A whole sea of air with torpedoes of blue, a whole trip of unforgettable blue, buzzed with a white cotton brush. Whose indigent grey of the Blessed Beato Salú, that maximum figure of the Eborense society had not yet been able to transform.

Wherever we go, we find what we are looking for, or what we really want to see and find there. That happened to me. I took the wrong road to get to a certain point, where I am now. Somewhere between the blue sky of good and evil that makes my sea of air. There is no right, no wrong. None at all. Just the blue ocean of my life in Évora. It is only the blue air, in the dream of the South, that makes the sea in Alentejo. It's just the blue heat in Alentejo's summer. Évora is the blue city, and in Rua Cinco de Outubro it is possible to find there that proof of blue that I chased from home this morning.

It was possible to read another advertisement for that blue. This time, on a slate board written in chalk by the octopus' partner… "Life is so short. We serve our food with vegetables. We forget the fries. Our menu is inside."

Long live Raul Cancelo who turned to catering! Long live this great Raul, who is not only an octopus president of all the cultural associations, profit or non-profit, of Évora and Alentejo, but is also a political animal, a fortune teller, an upper-middle-class police fireman, whatever he is, he is everywhere and nowhere. Long live Raulito! He is the father and the son, and everything,

everything who is in our midst. Blessed be! Blessed are his pots, which will probably also be included in the menu...

Soon after, the blue of my day was done. I had stopped by the *Art Café*, spoke to the owner; who insisted that he remember me from working at the *Molhóbico* bar and restaurant. Besides that, I had passed by other establishments and commercial surfaces, whose owners had authorised me to do my poetic blue propaganda there. That is, to design what I supposedly thought I was doing. Which basically consisted of carrying around my new writing desk, the one I found in the trash, and wearing a swimming cap and goggles. But my cerulean mission didn't stop there. Because today I had posters printed at the university office and I also went around the city promoting what would be the travelling artistic residency of my travelling blue.

***

Before I literally walked around the traffic circle and under the wall tunnels, wearing shorts, a cap and swimming goggles, and very quickly passed by, like one of those cartoons in a silent movie in blue and white, and everything was recorded, Belchior got tired and suddenly dropped everything to go and meet Francisca. This is how the travels of the Travelling Man through the blue began. This is how *Homo Viator* began, a term coined by Master Benedito Pio, in a mini-biography, which accompanied a couple of my poems that he had selected, in order to see them published in a magazine.

The week began and the artist residency opened with me and Belchior behind the wheel on a Monday afternoon, drinking coffee on my writing table. We each put our coffee cup down on the wooden table painted pure white. It was sunny and Belchior would not take off his cap. He complained that the heat of the blue sun was too strong for him and that the world was too unfair for him. But, there was Belchiorinho accompanying me since I left home. Dragging my writing table with me to the cafe.

He wanted to be part of my saga. Possibly, because he smelt the frenzy of adventure, the fresh air of novelty, which reaches those who dare and who make the boldness of the dream a path of action. He would be done by the time we reached Largo das Alterações. His laziness would force him to stop, preventing him from continuing there, or anywhere else. However, well done to Belchiorinho who appeared at the beginning of my comic itinerary.

After all, a poet can become a great prose diver, and even a writer can become a reasonable explorer, able to observe with his nose and ears all kinds of species, as well as understand the daily life of those species. He can, perhaps, perform and fill balloons on Saturday afternoons, and he can even make others laugh and even feel good about himself. But as for Belchior, he will always remain our little Belchior. He will always be the one who cultivates the routine of the field with his wonderful negligence, with such negligence that the ears themselves recede. Nothing in him can expand and grow.

Regardless, Belchiorinho can, like me, aspire to be someone better, and even, like me, or, like Eduardo, practice in the world the blueness of good. Yet, the desire to be someone better doesn't always accompany the artists of this life, be they, Belchiorinho, be they, other examples of ice sculptors that are carved on a summer day in Alentejo.

It was three o'clock in the afternoon when I smeared sunscreen over my face. Transforming myself into the itinerant character I had created, with intentions of who knows why. I continued my recordings. Belchior left after wiping his indigo sweat from his forehead. It was too much effort made in a single day.

I dragged the table alone across the blue tarmac and continued my recordings and inquiries through the *Mar de Ar* hotel. I went into the pool and dived in as I have done so many times in the past, when I would take my weekly newspaper and lie in the sun on my stomach pretending I was just another occasional tourist. But today, I dived in with an umbrella.

Some children laughed aloud. The whole world is increasingly global and foreign, not just in Portugal. I dived into the hotel pool like an astronaut with the task of making people laugh, besides having the precept of swimming in the sea of blue air that has the golden summer in the golden Alentejo. However, it was also my duty not only to film that moment, but to capture the sapphire essence of the moment.

At first, not everything is clear, like water. We don't really know what we are doing. We don't know if art reveals a part of life, just as we don't know if life repeats the formula that our art of living has. We don't know if we copy others, if we transcribe models, if it is just us, or if it is us and the inspiration given to us by friends and mere acquaintances who dive with us into a bottomless pit. Never foreseeing the conclusion, never knowing the one that truly tastes like the final flavour.

In the end, we let go, we go without resisting. Until we eventually come to the surface, quenching our blue thirst.

There is no sea or tide, in the Alentejo, there is only a silver aqueduct, which is a river flowing to me, and I flow to it, to navigate in it, as it navigates in me. More than a river, it is a channel through which the water from the fountain of life keeps flowing to meet the golden harvest.

After the first day of my first itinerary through blue was over, I had left my writing desk at Zorra's house. Rute Margarida, former actress of the Cendrev theatre company, who is now an actress in the association she runs with her husband, was not interested in my work, nor was she interested in the reason why I walk around wearing a cap and swimming goggles, nor the artistic reason why I drag my writing table mostly alone through the squares of Évora. No, what she really wanted to know was if I would give her my writing table, in the end. Anyway, love for art doesn't necessarily link love for artists.

When I arrived at the attic in the Vista Alegre neighbourhood, the blue of the sun had another colour not so blue. I opened my mail and read an email from João Plácido Rocha, a banking guru, whom I had met when I went, once with Ana Maria and Belchior, to meditate in one of his full attention meditation sessions.

"We live in a society that enslaves and hypnotises people. Imagine that half a dozen people control the lives of millions of people. That is what happens. And for this to happen, it requires people to accept the *status quo* for lack of an alternative and out of fear. Or out of fear of doing something different. The way to imprison people is through time and money. With chronological time, we are trapped in the dimension of time-space that doesn't really exist. Just a false perception of the mind. False is perhaps strong, let's just call it "a form of perception of the mind." In reality, the infinite and the absolute and the ephemeral is just the perception of forms. You know that image of peeking into a room through the keyhole? You can look straight ahead and see a part of the room. You can look to one side and to the other. Down and up, by moving your eye. And then you will have different perceptions of the room. But the room— the whole room—is always there. It's you who move around to see different perspectives of the room. In that sense, life has the same nature as a dream. When you dream you don't choose when you can leave the dream. You may have the notion that you are dreaming, but you don't choose the moment when you stop dreaming, when you leave one dream and go to another. The notion of eternity is immensely liberating. Our essence is eternal. Our form, our body, mind, ego are ephemeral. When we die, only the forms and names die. Since we are totally identified with these (form and names; nama and rupa)—that which makes up the ego—we have a natural fear of death, of finitude. But if we jump beyond this ephemeral reality and connect with our true essence, we know that it is eternal. We are not the form or the names. That is ego, that is circumstance."

Eduardo came to shoot with me the next day. It was a good moment. It seems to me that he was happy to walk the halls of the Espírito Santo College with his skateboard. And for doing it without permission. I think he also enjoyed himself, because he also tried on my swimming cap and goggles. Having left a temporary moustache at my request. Losing the beard in my favour. Maybe Eduardo believed in me, and that was essential. He probably saw with his own eyes, the same blue deluge that was evidently flooding everywhere. He saw the evidence of blue that is the invisible iodine moving through the air. Moving that sea of air through the city's ducts and canals.

Surely he has seen that we are that blue ring, or part of it. We are all those vertical and horizontal signs of blue eternally written and transcribed, in the sky and on the earth, in this and that and another golden summer spent in the Alentejo. Eduardo was probably also pleased that we moved the landlord's pendulum clock, which was in the living room, to the middle of the lawn of the square in the Vista Alegre neighbourhood.

On Sunday, my walking art residency came to an end. And, it was not as I imagined. On the last day I ended up not going to the public garden. After having walked around the city for a whole week harvesting the daily cerulean, I decided that the best thing would be to drag my writing table to the artificial lake in Malagueira to shoot the last scene where I would dive into the putrefying lake.

When I got home, I had an enormous loneliness waiting for me. I took a bath in bleach and sat on the living room couch talking to Belchior's mother. A nice and friendly lady who was sometimes more, sometimes less, dependent on heroin. She was already a wrinkled woman. With the typical aspect that her future corpse would have, which had been in life designed by the doses consumed from the last fifteen days to the last fifteen or more years.

The week is over. It was a journey of local self-discovery. Not only of myself, but also of the globality of those around me. Because existence is a locality that is not always in the same place we live. Maybe, it's not even really a place? Perhaps, the narrative of our existence is a journey through the journey of history. In it there is no heritage of humanity, what exists is an invisible mirror of the monuments of the moment that traverse the spectrum, leaving only small particles as they enter space-time.

***

They parked in front of the square in the Vista Alegre neighbourhood. I went to meet them. I got in the car and sat in the back seat and we went straight to the historic centre. We wandered around the city. The ceiling of the dark night was lit by the moon lamp. Viegas, essentially, was not interested in seeing anything, and, mainly, was committed to doing nothing; Miguel would gladly accept whatever Viegas decided. If it was Viegas' will to drive into a wall, at two hundred and fifty-something miles an hour, Miguel wouldn't object, either.

We missed all the great events of fado and Ebcrense soccer that night. In the afternoon of the next day, we lay thoughtfully on the grass of the public garden. It was a hot August day. Even today, I can still remember the genuine warmth that friendship had that afternoon, which suited all three of us perfectly.

"Look, I think that girl is interested in you, Poet! I think you should do something about it. Don't you think so?" Asked Miguel, meticulously rolling another joint in the sheet of his shroud.

"Maybe later, Miguel," I said.

"Invite her to come out with us to *Art Café*," said Viegas.

"And bring friends for the rest of us!" Miguel immediately added. Laughing soon after. I quickly identified that laugh. It was the drum of my old friend Miguel, from the beginning of a great friendship and the beginning of a great storm. That careful laughter could only belong to Miguel Murtinho, the city prophet, the capital's saint, who, when he finished scientifically rolling his joint, bowed like a young Arab in the springtime of his maturity. Thanking Allah for another opulent summer divinely spent among friends.

Then he called the little birds. They flew from the band of trees to the desolation planted in the palm of his hand. Even Viegas was impressed, almost feeling a mild happiness with the breeze that rubbed his trunks. After all, the great illusion is to pretend to live!

"I like it!" Viegas said, after Murtinho had farted and smelled like gladioli. Or some other literally similar shit. It was right after Viegas pretended he had tripped. But it was so forced and so serious, his pretence of falling that he had failed miserably. It was a forced fall. Which summed up José Pedro Viegas' entire existence and non-existence, that when he walked, the ground generally shook with bowing, at his passing.

"And when I went to do montages at 40° in Avis, for the Festival Escrita na Paisagem! Once, I went there with Carlos, 45°! Fuck! There wasn't a moment you could stay in the shade. Not even a small tree. Because there, trees, if you find one, you're already lucky…" Miguel said, about nothing, which is the theme of everything, in a conversation among friends.

"I see," Viegas said, rubbing his hand across his stomach after almost breathing in all the beer in his glass. Concluding, and then noting, "…I'd like to film in Avis! But I need a better camera…"

"José Pedro is now living for the cam," said Miguel excitedly.

"Sincerely, my friend Simocas!" Viegas said. Looking around as if his life would make a good movie and enjoying that rest of beer with the foam of the moment, which had the value of friendship, and still somewhat satisfied that there would be a home recording that would later prove what he felt now. Although, he would later deny everything.

I asked him, "So, Zé Pedro, that play of yours, *O Mordomo*? The one you wrote, when you still thought you were going to be somebody? Where is it?"

"Is your life not enough for you?"

"Still… Are you recording, poet?" Miguel asked.

"No, no, I'm just capturing the aura of this moment," I replied.

"Here! Oh, my God! Wait a minute, I have to do my look—my look!" Then, there he replied, "The title is no longer *O Mordomo*," affirmed Zé Pedro Viegas. Knowing not that life had passed him by, but that it was he, with his terms and conditions, who had passed her by.

Three days later, Miguel and José Pedro, went on with their lives outside of my plans and frames, and behold I already knew… After three consecutive days of drinking beer and smoking pot joints in the public garden and listening to the purr of the sea of air, and the car engines, and the winged birds that flew by us, when the three of us were sitting in the open field that I showed them, there was still some time for Miguel Murtinho to perch with his spirit in the iron goal of another time, and for José Pedro Viegas to contemplate the golden rest, listening in vain to the direction that the wind takes his destiny.

In those final minutes that preceded the farewell, each of us understood that we were destined to suffer, and to take pleasure in suffering. But also to have to navigate a single thread of the path that constituted the same wrapped ball of thread that was common to everything and everyone.

Possibly, because the thread of a path makes a ball of yarn, and even more than one.

And low and behold, I already knew I was going to move, and I even talked about it while Eduardo and I were running on the maintenance circuit. It was a race among friends, each one following his own pace and the rhythm that had the music on the way. Belchior, that one, had already given up and had not yet left Francisca's car. Complaining about the blue sun and the loose muscles in his legs. It was a race of about four almost at the edge of a hot afternoon, when I was running next to Eduardo, and I told him, "Yes, I have made up my mind. I'm going to move house and maybe, change my life. I'm going to live in the countryside."

And Eduardo agreed with me. He also expected it to be a good decision. But insisting, now, with me, that I run faster.

**Book 3
Garraia**

Chapter 1
In the Preface to the Garraia

(August 2014)

Once upon a time, in the beginning. No! From the early beginnings... Definitely not; the preamble of my move to the Garraia was a kind of... Not like that, either. But anyway! Before heading to the Évora bus station, and catching the express bus that would take me to Pontão, I left, in the landlord's attic, all my belongings tidied away. A whole collection of memories and other unimportant things that had moved as many times as I had and were waiting for me inside cardboard boxes sealed with tape. With my soon-to-be move to the Garraia, there would have been no less than seventeen times that I had moved house, during the last seven years and a few months and weeks. Interestingly enough, it was Francisca who gave me a ride to the bus station that day. The same Francisca who will be my neighbour in the Garraia.

At the Évora bus station, some passengers were giddy with excitement and good humour at the news of their departure trip. Others were less excited. They were less effusive, because they were arriving again, and because nothing great was about to happen to them. It was that wonderful amazement of optimism or pessimism generated by each arrival and departure. And that I could witness once again, that afternoon, before adding another return to the village of Avelar.

Meanwhile, I am passing over the 25 de Abril bridge; I am almost arriving in Lisbon. Down there, everything seems smaller than it really is. I'm crossing to the other bank. The river has the edge of another day. It reflects the echo of another trip back to Pontão. Last year, on this same paradigmatic day, after returning from Epidaurus, and spending the night in Évora, I was returning to the Avelar valley. Crossing the Vasco da Gama Bridge. I was uncertain, not only as to the future's face, but also as to the present.

Now, in *hoc tempore*, I cross the bridge. The truth of who I was and who I am no longer has the sure compass to indicate the best path to follow. At this moment, what is left behind, will only have one or another kilometre of perspective, will only have one or another extension and dimension in the road I will travel, the day after tomorrow. But as I pass over the bridge, the small boats and small ships are of the same preponderance and relevance as the big cruise ships on the high seas.

So what does it matter, who was yesterday or who is today? What does it matter now where childhood is? What does it matter, where was the exordium of adolescence and the prologue of adulthood? What matters is to reach the bridge! To reach the end of the bridge. Everything else is not large enough, to feel the invisible manifestation of that greatness, which can only be seen after reaching the other side.

The express bus landed in Lisbon and fifteen minutes later I got on another. Just before, I came across the monster of the crowd. Anyone who tried to pass through it was devoured by this adamastor of the terminal. No one was moving. Not a soul was moving. Anyone who wanted to find their family member, or friend, who had arrived in the meantime, would be lost forever, if, by chance, they took one step forward. I got on the bus, but only after being regurgitated by the crowd.

And, before I even had time to count to three, I sat down next to her. Although, I had hesitated which wing of the bus would be best.

"No, I don't mind sitting next to you." That was the first thing I said to her. The second, was eventually something like: "You're not another serial-killer, with a nice smile, are you?"

After corresponding with the brightness of her smile, she replied with the innocence she decidedly did not have. "I don't know? But why don't you sit over there. Next to my sister?" She asked, believing with conviction that she could suddenly turn the situation around, and win me over in the liveliness of my own game.

Her name was Carina and she worked in Spain. In a large multinational company, in which she was currently director of marketing. And, I am temporarily fascinated by her. Essentially because she appears to be a determined and independent woman, but also because between men and women feelings are born that give rise to great dramas and great comedies, and sometimes, at the end of the plot, a baby is born.

A little later, the girl wearing an ankle bracelet and summer sandals feels free to chatter away. And now she tells me that she and her sister, who is sitting just opposite, are going next weekend to the *Bons Sons* music festival in Cem Soldos, on the outskirts of Tomar. She already wanted me to go with her. But I will not go. Not for lack of will, but for the practical impossibility of being able to easily go anywhere. I assume that Pascal, my countryman, will drive there. I, however, as much as I want to, will be temporally in the Avelar valley, waiting for my life in the Garraia, being still relatively far from it.

After the two sisters left in Torres Vedras, I clearly realised that I should have sat next to the other sister, the one studying cinema in Covilhã. Anyway, every decision has the effect of the medicine one takes. Some find side effects; others just find the cure.

Carlos Caetano, Francisco's friend recently became the father of a little girl. He currently works at a supermarket checkout in Lisbon. But it's all good! Because his father-in-law is rich and pays for everything. That's what Francis told me. I don't have children, but I have a rented house in the country. Where I will be in exile, just like Napoleon was in Elba. I will not be living the dream yet, but at least I will be residing in the field of the dream. And so, again, I will be forced to change my address.

After I found my little writing table by the trash can, and from it triggered in me, the sudden desire to make art, or to simply parallel a mysterious artistic path, that in my naive hope would transport me to the meaning of something greater than the worm of my ambition. Interestingly enough, it was during one of the afternoons of my walking quest for the blue that the landlady's daughter asked me if I wasn't interested in moving to the country.

I met her at the door of the electrical appliance store that my former landlord, Mr Sertório, had in partnership with his brother, on Rua João de Deus. She had a tiny dog on her lap that kept barking and yelping at me, excited, because of me, or because of this ambiguous something that I was looking for and that was still a cloud with an incomprehensible shape in the yard that day. Yet in that inexplicable moment, everything made inexplicable sense to me.

I now follow in this paragraph my journey back to Avelar. I return not to my origin, but to the origin of the myth factory. I follow in hope for the future. The future has an unknown face. Just as much as it had the face of the past, and so, naturally, what was left behind and what is yet to come, will shape each time with the countenance that reflects the mirror of the present.

Before evening, the next day, I accompanied Marcus to the place where we had become accustomed to go for coffee. Once again following the same route and the same pilgrimage, which occurred more and more occasionally.

Inácio drove silently. Commenting, Marcus, in the back seat, relatively, indignantly, "Look, it's the police in plain clothes! There are two of them inside the car, with the device on the dashboard…"

"They're not cops, Marcus!"

"Ah, they were just like them! They really looked like them." Then, he pointed ahead, amazed, while Inácio drove us in the old car that was still from a time when everything was easy in the life of Marcus Emanuel de Monsalude e Matalonga. Nevertheless, nothing he owned had been effectively conquered by him. Everything he owned was part of the inheritance he received from his grandparents immediately after the factory went bankrupt and his parents' divorce was finalised.

I took the initiative and changed the subject. "You see, I consider that…"

But Marcus, once again, decided not to pay attention to the script. "Is that your grandmother, the lady we saw when Inácio stopped the car to pick you up? But she's from Figueiró, isn't she?" He asked somewhat sharply, in contrast with the rhythm of his nature and with the speed that Inácio had been maintaining since we left the Avelar valley.

Although he had picked up the signal from my previous comment, yet the antennae of his mind, driven by a wave of greater force, would completely ignore me. Marcus, who was now next to me, would be closer to yesterday's pessimism and despondency of the road leading to the next hairpin bend than to the actual bend in the journey we were currently making to the usual café.

Naturally, he would still be attracted by the idea, which I had of him, when he was until then, regarded as a great prodigy doomed to success. Being much closer to this opinion of who he was in the past, than he would be presently there with me. Yes, my friend Marcus would be effectively far away from there. I kept forcing my presence, trying to recover the previous subject. "As I, I was going to tell you before, I think…"

"But before that what were we talking about?" He asked, interrupting me for the second time.

"We were talking about that place, which we used to go to, before the café we currently frequent…"

And without any connection to the current course of the conversation, he fired back. "Ah, it doesn't represent anything. That's just the point. It doesn't represent anything! Eventually, if the world outlook changes, gradually, very gradually, I might think about reintegrating. But it's very complicated. It's difficult. And in the *milieu* that is! It's not a *milieu* that I enjoy at all…it's all bad! There's nothing that's circumstantially good…

"I have on average sent a few letters to close family friends during this past year. They don't even bother to answer me. Meanwhile, friends become simple acquaintances, others, to total strangers. That's just the way it is. We are at the stage of every man for himself. I have lost the influence I had. I lost the power that my influence had.

"I recently went, for fun, to a meeting. Inácio took me there. When I got there, they asked me right away, so you're the grandson of the late Monsalude, and I knew right then and there that they would give me a position, if I accepted their proposal, and invested part of my inheritance. I came relatively close to accepting the offer of these well-known friends of my grandfather, to make a huge investment in a good company in our district…with guaranteed doubled earnings…but I had to reject them, because they were clearly guys of a very doubtful moral."

The conversation lasted longer than the way Inácio drove us there and back. During the trip from the town of Figueiró back to the Avelar valley I was measuring the invisible edge of time and enumerating every little change of the plough in the landscape. Somewhere in the middle, I asked him, "Since when we haven't, seen each other, Marcus?"

Even Marcus couldn't answer quickly, when was the last time we had met. Before Inácio stopped to drop me off at home, Marcus and I said goodbye. As we always did, after a trip to the usual café or a more or less usual pilgrimage.

When I got home, I put on my pyjamas and lay down on the bed. I closed my eyes and went backwards, until the moment I went to Évora for the first time and had to stay awake waiting at the bus station in the early morning for the first bus going south. It was a summer night in the year 2008. Marcus had not yet announced to me the prophecy that would foresee the beginning of something that would forever change his life and consequently the conception of mine.

He had not yet told me about the oracle of a world crisis, nor had he yet confessed to me the bankruptcy that was weaving another textile time, nor that his parents had divorced, feeding the cross of his personal crisis. He had, however, already dropped out of medical school and was studying architecture in Porto.

I believe he was genuinely happy, that summer of 2008, that I was going to Évora, to study literature and arts. But in the following year, or two years later, he would make a sabbatical trip through Europe, which would include, a brief passage through Vienna, two or three properly interpreted concerts, but no opera; he would also strut through Zurich, a spa, and continue his tour through the refinement of another great city in the history of humanity, where he would delight himself with the pleasures of the world. It would be the last great trip of Marcus Emanuel de Monsalude e Matalonga, because afterwards, nothing would be as before.

***

I left home not knowing exactly why I had to escape from my mother and stepfather's residence to enjoy a small cup of coffee, which in the end, I hadn't even appreciated. I also didn't understand why I had to come to Avelar once again, when in the middle of the visit everything tasted like nothing. Perhaps, I would have returned this time to the valley of Avelar for a few days, not to explain the reasons and circumstances of my beginning, but the cause that would determine the last living poet.

Perhaps, I would have convinced myself that by doing so, my going to the Garraia could have another beginning. But a good part of me couldn't believe that it was here, where I supposedly grew up, that I would acquire the calm and encouragement necessary to ascertain the real provenance of the last living poet. Knowing where he came from, however, would help me understand what it was that I had become. For that matter, *alas*, who needs self-discovery? After all, what is needed is chairs and tables and beds, and more than one side table because of *Feng Shui*. Exactly, like the living room and bedroom furniture that are on display above the sidewalk on Rua das Cinco Vilas by *Rainha da Sucata* (*Queen of Scrap*), the used furniture store.

Nobody in the Avelar valley suspects that I am the last living poet. Except for a few, in Évora and in Alentejo, who have heard about the myth of the last living poet, nobody else knows. And that's just as well, because this way I can walk down the street with the excuse that I only came to the pastry shop to drink coffee and read the newspaper, after having given up on being locked up in the old house.

Supposedly, because I have not been able to find a position to feel comfortable there for the time being. I am, perhaps, also a piece of furniture in the house that is overstuffed and that is moved around until it is recognised that we no longer need it. And what we need is the space it occupies.

When I arrived at Avelar, I already wanted to leave, once again, for Évora, and pluck as soon as possible the prelude to my life in Garraia. So that I wouldn't have any doubts, my mother, after I arrived for a short stay, quickly made me understand, with my stepfather, more or less neutral and more or less silent, that I shouldn't have come, and that it's been a long time since I've been part of this landscape, which is still, however, quite familiar to me.

Therefore, when I left the pastry shop today, I was already regretting having left home, and before I left home, I was already contemplating the contrition that summed up another return to the village of Avelar. But fortunately, tomorrow, I will return to Évora, and what is left behind, will not be transported or accommodated. Simply because there is no more space in the scenario that I intend to take with me.

Already on my way to Lisbon, and back to Évora, I am reading the latest version of José Pedro Viegas' play, which is now called *Maria Margarida*. Beside me sits a small, beautiful brunette from northeastern Brazil. Her skin has become even smoother and velvety after being anointed with a cream that smells of vanilla. Meanwhile, she has fallen asleep. Her head is now hanging on the side of my shoulder. In her hands, she holds a tiny red case with her lipstick, mascara, a coin purse, two or three secrets, and four hair pins to hold her long straight hair.

With each kilometre I travel I am peeking over my copy of Viegas' piece. I follow more and more uncontrollably interested between the dialogue that Viegas has written and the curiosity to see beyond her dress dug into her shoulders and bust. I read another page without looking, getting excited at the possibility of being caught up in the writing of the moment. I read one more page, and all I can think is that looking is not enough for me. I bend the handle of another page and surreptitiously confirm if her eyes are still closed.

Yes, she still sleeps! She sleeps like a little Indian princess. She sleeps innocently. Not caring about the trepidation of civilisation, nor about the theater piece Viegas wrote, after he changed, like, a hundred and fifty times, the fucking title. As well as, basically, all the content of the play.

The empress of northeastern Brazil continued to sleep, while I read another page of *Maria Margarida*. The volume of her head, however, was sliding more and more to my side, until her weight rested completely on me. When she awoke, she smiled at me, embarrassed. I smiled too, with my reading covering up for me a small initial reaction that had suddenly increased exponentially. Happily, she didn't even notice that I had my reading copy turned upside down, otherwise she would have thought that besides me being a fool I was also abject.

Then, smiling generously at me, the brunette princess, a native of the Brazilian Northeast, squinted. And without any plausible explanation the protruding mole she has between her nose and upper lip blinds me. I indecorously embrace the chimaera of her existence. At the whim of the moment and without any forewarning, I long more and more to touch her everywhere and nowhere.

That is, what I want is to caress her vulva, without having to explain myself to her before or afterwards. I will just say: it was only a dream. Reading afterwards, nonchalantly, the end of Viegas' play, but, bam! Uproar! Scandal! With the other passengers in the bus kicking me and I only begging, "Please, not in the head! In order that I may keep my genius and preserve my intelligence!" And she, the indigenous brunette, the princess of the Northeast ordering them to stop the beating.

Finally, I, the vile culprit, being safe, provided I marry her and agree in return to reside with her in a hut and make her children once a year. And to say good morning to my neighbour, Mr Gauguin. But no, none of that will happen. But I ask myself: what will she do with her life? And what will I do with my life without her in it? What will I do, after having to proceed alone on this bus, coming from Pontão with a bound for Lisbon? Only to then catch the bus that will take me to the beginning of my life in the Garraia?

After all, where will we go? Where will each one of us go with this love that never happened and that in another location would not happen either. Where will she go when she leaves at the next station and I have no option but to continue sitting and reading the play that Viegas will never stage, the most plausible being that it will be obliterated in a drawer in his parents' basement, or even disappear. I, too, will end up, in my own way, forgetting and being forgotten.

It is now 7 pm and my belongings are already inside the house. It is the happy end of the afternoon, of my first day spent at the Garraia. It is, however, still the beginning of my life in the large estates of the dream. Behind me are sixteen times that I moved house and of course some personality changes; some more than necessary than others. Besides all the other changes that occur that we don't notice or account for. Behind me is my room in the Vista Alegre neighbourhood, without windows. Even more behind, the village and the valley of Avelar. As well as the Indian princess and the (*Rainha da Sucata*) *Scrap Queen*. And, of course, also behind are all the things I forgot to bring, as well as what was lost, and what was impossible to move from its place.

A new life began in Garraia when my neighbour's nephew picked me up in the Vista Alegre neighbourhood and, in a single trip, transported me and all my things in a pickup truck that belonged to the landlady, driving me to Garraia with his girlfriend sitting in the middle seat, while I kept looking ahead in the side mirror, seeing what was left behind looking smaller and farther away.

His girlfriend was much older than he was, or so it seemed, because her face and belly were swollen. She was that age of a woman who had never regained her physical shape after giving birth to the miracle of her life. Like Mrs Justina, my neighbour, she had the same kind of belly, but already in her late sixties. It is possible to see this female form repeated on many sides; both in the slouch of age, of an already tired body, and in a spirit only long married and conformed.

Rolando usually does odd jobs for the Córdova family and also lives at Quinta das Pimentas, in one of the five houses that make up the estate. His aunt, Mrs Justina, is the neighbour who lives in the main house of the estate; and this was how the beginning of my coming to Garraia it premiered... No! No! What I mean, it was like, in the debut of my coming to Garraia; also no!

Everything came at once in the landlady's van, at the launch of my life at Garraia. Including the mattress that was found next to the garbage can by Francisca and Belchior, where later I would also find my small writing table. Sounds better; still, no. But ah, whatever; because at the beginning of my move to the Garraia, everything sounded wonderful. And, at the end of the trip, after my bags and other bundles were unloaded, I gave Rolando a generous tip. As those rather fortunate men do when they arrive at a big hotel.

At first, Rolando said no. That it wasn't necessary. But I insisted. Thinking that the men, unfortunately fallen by the misfortune of a forced exile, would do the same as me, they would stubbornly pay, both the messenger and the freighter.

The landlady filled my house with freshly painted furniture and the smell of the memory of the first day experienced in the Garraia lingered for the first week. The garish colour of the purple tone and the warm presence of the sun contradicted the coldness of the floor paved with concrete cement.

I placed each piece of furniture where I wanted it. My life matched the decor of the house. I had the essentials. I didn't have what I needed, and that's enough for me to feel the blue heat of the sun in the sky of the Garraia, which has another kind of blue, very different from the one I tasted in the middle of summer. When I walked around the city, sometimes inside, sometimes outside the walls.

During the blue of my day, there is a sermon from work, at the Garraia. And at dusk, the wind comes in the form of a prayer. No one calls, no one answers. It is a constant crossing the desert, and any deserted place at night gets colder. The magi and other neighbouring magi without a king and without a kingdom, drink tea with me, looking at the stars planted in the unpopulated sky, watching the caravan of stones, olive trees, sheep, cows and Andalusian horses pass by on the main road; the descendants of the Sorraia horses and the Berber horses.

The landlord, Mr Norberto, came to visit me on the weekend. We went for a drive. During the short drive we took in and around Garraia, he was pointed to the place where Napoleon's army had camped. During one of his invasions. I don't know if it was the second or the third, where he gave up, deciding that there was nothing worse than staying in Portugal.

***

My first impression of Quinta das Pimentas is external. I have the feeling that I am not too far away, but that I am far enough away from the city and the city walls. I also have the feeling that I am relatively closer to myself and closer to the sun.

In the South, the dream horizon is bigger than in the North of Portugal. Each day is confused with yesterday, which is not exactly the case in the mountains and valleys of central Portugal, which is where the centre of the world is. In Garraia, the sunlight imprints a blue grandiosity that I understand.

Yesterday, I took a short walk in the vicinity. I found no small houses, only large estates. When you couldn't exactly find a farm, there was, in the company of the plain, a large residence, living on top of a small hill. Day had not yet fallen on the horizon when I returned home, coming across a horse and a mare on the farm next door chewing with their ivory jaws on the golden straw and the fruits of paradise once lost and now found.

They neighed as I passed them. Each of them moved their heads down and up, and I did the same, greeting them, effusively. Soon after, my mother called me. We argued. That's what happens when we try to talk. My mother was worried about me, and so she argued. "You have to understand that I am your mother!" That was her one and only maxim. Basically, her infallible argument was that because she was my mother, she suffered no counter-argument.

I tried to explain it to her with the analogy of trees, which grow towards the sky. But my mother wouldn't go with such a comparison. She didn't believe that I would expand upwards. She would only accept to repeat that I had bills to pay, not accepting to incorporate in any way, in the conversation that was more discussion and altercation, anything that involved branches, twigs, leaves or roots.

None of that was able to persuade her of my genuine will to progress. Although, my desire was to enrich myself spiritually, and not, strictly speaking, materially. I remain, nevertheless, optimistic about my decision and the prelude to my life on the Garraia, or if you simply prefer it, in the beginning of my coming to the Garraia I kept quite confident.

The next day, the sky awoke vividly blue, and I found in that indigo of the sky, the blue that had the beginning of my exile. It was the Lazuli of the island of the Garraia. It had the form of reconciliation with me and my past, regardless of the argument the day before with my mother. I found shells of hope and whelks of enthusiasm in that blue firmament of the island of Garraia, as well as in the sea of air of the Alentejo.

In the middle of the afternoon, I walked around looking at the blue scarf in the sky. Wherever I went, it went with me. I felt the influence of the blue being exerted on me, yet I felt no pressure. My spirit was going in the same direction where that vividly and warmly blue form was turning. Notwithstanding, I had to find a job that would pay my expenses, and where I could be a slave to that little bit more of nothing.

The sooner I got a job, the sooner I could think, not about how to free myself from it, but how not to let myself be imprisoned by it. At least I could devote my time off to keeping my inner peace and devise an escape plan. Certainly the colour of reconciliation with my mother would not be blue, but it would involve finding as soon as possible the tone of a job that would pay my bills, regardless of whether it had no colour.

When I woke up the next morning, it was six thirty am I went to the bathroom, and then I passed by the kitchen window and saw the celestial vault of the infinitely blue. Then I went into the living room to inhale the smell of the purple paint still fresh on the furniture. Not satiated, I peered in one last time to confirm the infinitely blue firmament. And, yes, that indigo was the sky blue of the Garraia and the Southern dream, where even in winter, one remembers the blue of eternal summer. I was now a man washing himself with the blue water that flowed from the source of the sky. Praying for redemption and preaching my own redemption.

Small are the marks of the divine signs that are engraved on the skin of man, who reinvents himself from the moment he wakes up and walks with his head and soul in the sun, and finally falls asleep on his belly. So, today, when I had a very small breakfast, I went out the door, determined. I marched like a soldier with a foreign legion galloping at his chest. Only, I stopped to contemplate the windmill that could be seen from the middle of the main road of the Garraia. Moving on, quickly then straight ahead with the asphalt of my pilgrimage. More flying than walking. Returning with the wings of a missionary's path to the continent of the unknown. Caring only about the cause, never thinking about the corollary of my destiny.

My badge would be to rise above the water level of the sea of my banality and not let myself be drowned by the river of my vulgarity. But I was late for the job centre and the other appointments I had imagined myself fulfilling. Through the fault of my own insolence; a characteristic no man of my condition can predispose himself to. Well, my mother in our last conversation, that is in our last discussion, hammered me a dozen times that I should be humble or at least learn to be. Humility for my mother is a profession that one studies and embraces over time. Although, I have no vocation for it.

When I returned home, the sky was still blue. It was still infinitely blue, the sea of air seen when reaching the main road to the Garraia. There was, however, no sandy beach. Just a golden field into which I plunged. I could lose myself in it forever, or I could gain something more from it, without having to justify to myself what it was exactly that I gained or what it was concretely that I lost after all. I returned home infected by the bales shaped like cobblestones that temporarily occupied the landscape. Each bale of straw was a sign of the dream. The green tractor stopped at the top, which I spotted before reaching the Garraia halt, was an even greater sign. It was the sign that I had already reached the field of my dream.

After the ruins of the Garraia halt, I cut right and went straight through the ocean with waves tenderly dressed in blue, and was escorted by the property wall with a wide window, which emulates the front of a house, but which is a landmark, a boundary symbol, which marks the beginning of Garraia and of my life on Garraia.

In the meantime, I received my first visitors: Belchior, his girlfriend, and his faithful squire. I didn't want to receive them. But my exile probably shouldn't allow me to exactly select visits, which have a kind of authorisation and invitation that is alien to me. So, it doesn't depend exclusively on me. But distance, time, and the natures of each one will eventually contribute to no longer doing so, at least, so often.

The path that brought me to the Garraia was made up of a herd of events that accumulated in the drawer of the Lost and Found section, and of meeting and missing each other. I recognise that Neida is part of the path that brought me to the Garraia. Just like Belchior and many other magi. They were the ones who did me the favour of pulling or pushing the door of the Garraia, and for that I will be forever grateful to them. To all of them, many thanks.

In the second week of my stay at Garraia with no deadline, I am realising my existence. I am a director projecting onto the living room what he wants to see, as a spectator of his own life. My only and sincere desire is to transform my existence, and that of those who cross my path, into a work of art. Only, to contemplate later, each event and each fiction of that illusion that our eyes fixate on, pampering the beauty of a tenderly ephemeral moment, but which is still real. Like the poignant punch out stomach feels when it is crushed by the force of its truth.

During the week, I went to a workshop at the Dom Manuel Palace. The workshop was conducted by the Swede Linus Sundqvist, who presented himself there, through the *Amphitheatre* Association. I did not, however, have much interest *per se*, in doing such an activity. My interest was in attending, on the spot.

To write the experience of what I lived, but also, to transcribe, the inexperience that I was sometimes forced to live with. And, of course, I would also have the profit of seeing Adriana again, of running into her and greeting Henrique, Anabela, and even Linus, whom I met in Sifnos last year. But my presence was to no avail. Linus barely spoke to me. He probably didn't even remember who I was. The Henrique I had once thought I could learn something from was now just one of those revisits to the past we make, thinking we can somehow recover the time we lived through.

Nevertheless, the space-time train is in constant flux and movement. When a passenger leaves, he or she no longer enters that previous compartment of the past, occupied in the present with the circumstances of another memory, which in the future will have only the vague memory of a trip that was relatively distorted.

I left the Dom Manuel Palace, unaware of how many knots of indecision and what length of resolution the cord of my life had, which, however, clearly still pursued me, and would possibly accompany me, even beyond the Portas de Moura. So much so that when I crossed over in the future, so many more times on my way home, that same cord of consequences would go with me, until I found another route, another alternative path.

Except that the landlady's daughter, Mafalda, saw me and offered me a ride home, and I promptly stopped caring whether there was more light or more darkness resonating within me. Her loose hair and summer dress flew out the window. She laughed as if she were still a young teenager. She was a beautiful stereotype of an aunt from Cascais, originally from the Alentejo. She had a son and was divorced. She drove fast from the city to the Garraia.

I said goodbye to her. She gave me a kiss on the cheek and offered me the music CD that was playing on her car stereo. On the cover of the CD, it read Blue Desire. I thanked her for the irony and got out of the car. Believing, very seriously, that what my life needed was more women. Giving priority to those who like to take dips in the sea when the tide is high, or when the sea is very rough. Certainly, Mafalda would be a good candidate and would even have the right profile.

After slamming the door of her car and marching to the square, just to be different today, I thought about the exact number it would take. Then, suddenly, I moved on to the belief that my life and the lives of those around me, like everything else, are interconnected. This is explained in a very brief abstract way. Eduardo would now say, if he listened to me, that such a thought with such a range of action is quite improbable. He would then feel his scientific necessity to separate the multiform mass of my thesis. First by isolating it, and then by analysing it.

Finally, he would thoroughly untangle every part and thread of my idea. Surely, he would be dazzled by its own process. But the outcome would be something like that plane we saw tearing through the blue sky in the Vista Alegre neighbourhood, going from one point to another. Me considering it to be a sign from the gods, and Eduardo categorically showing with his index finger the light of that revelation. "Yeah, just a plane."

Eventually, he would at least agree with me, that it would make a good story and that it would serve to tell the saga of these crew members going inside the plane that the two of us saw tearing through the sky. Could they have their lives affected by that trip, that would leave them, forever, entangled, one in the other.

At the beginning of the last week of August, I went to the city to leave resumes in supermarkets, offices, stores, and factories. All for the sake of sportsmanship. For me, such a task, was just a moment of disgust, of non-acceptance. Nevertheless, getting a job, at the very least, would give me another reasonably well written chapter. Although, very poorly paid.

Then, wandering from one place to another, towards the end of August, I ran into Romeu and Simone, and Abrantes, a friend of theirs, a hippie freak from the Alentejo who sells weed and usually carries a bag made of wool around the historic centre. And, because I later accepted a ride with them both, I learned that Romeu was my neighbour, that is, he was temporarily living in the house of a friend who let him stay there while she was on a trip. It was through this accidental encounter, in the afternoon, that I learned more than I would have wished for.

If I hadn't left home, I wouldn't have had dinner arranged with Romeu and Simone. I certainly wouldn't have learned that Romeu's girlfriend, or Romev, which is how he is called by his gang of friends and his social group, had made peace with him once again. Because the last time I saw her, she was just pregnant and angry with him. Which is quite funny, because the second last time I saw her, she was not so full of grace! But she was still angry with him.

The second-to-last time I remember seeing her was when she gave me a ride to the Vista Alegre neighbourhood, and she definitely had no beer belly. And the preantepenultimate must have been during the premiere of the play, *The Guest and the Host*, where there was still no one pregnant and no one angry. Just a constantly late little couple. Now, in the protophony of my life in Garraia and the beginning of their life together, as well as in the beginning of the life that will be born a few months from now, our existences and our circumstances crossed paths.

It was late in the afternoon that I went to Romeu's friend's house for dinner. I found him in the vegetable garden, next to a water tank that reminded me of Coutada—a small place in Figueiró dos Vinhos, at the bottom of the mountains, where my grandmother lives. He walked barefoot, watering with buckets of water. He wore his usual yoga pants. He was like that today as he would be any other day. He was an Eborense hippie freak. He was dressed in the stereotype that was the norm for his group. I helped him finish the watering, and together we tied the tomato plants to lift them off the ground.

Perhaps this is why Romev later showed me his cannabis plants. Which made us now more friends, more buddies, more comrades, no matter how much I refused such an obeisance. Just as, without me being interested, he revealed to me that he had broken the back window of his house because last week he had forgotten the keys inside. Now only Simone and I knew about the fandango. Whether I wanted to or not, I was temporarily now a Romeu's friendly neighbour.

However, the dinner did not take place. Because Simone, fortunately, had not remembered before, that she had to study for the special season exams, which were scheduled for mid-September, and which would eventually dictate the end of her degree. I didn't mind that they had cancelled the dinner. It was as if I already knew intuitively that there was not going to be dinner. Before returning to my house and leaving them to their life as a couple, I sat in the living room for a while talking to Romeu about what he wanted to talk about.

In the end, I asked him a few joints, just like the great pasha, the magnanimous Bordalo, the father of the Eborense hippies and the Alentejo freaks, that small-medium master of nothing who once left Francisco in the middle of a beach in the Algarve and took off. And what I would have given to have seen the guru disappear into the van, leaving Francis behind, with no wallet and no cell phone. And Francis, very innocently, not knowing where he was, nor where Bordalo had gone.

I'm talking about Félix Bordalo, who had more wicks than sense in his head and who, surprisingly or not, would convert an entire Évora with his pearls, poor rice pearls and would date one of Francisco's classmates. I don't remember her name now. I do remember that she would abandon her degree in theatre. And the guru, the leader of a spiritual brigade of something that doesn't grow on the ground but is hollow, would constantly do to her what he had done with Francis that time in the Algarve. She was usually left behind without honour and dignity. But regardless of all this torture and suffering, she would always come back to him. Which, I don't know if it's because there are men who make women act like dogs, or if it's simply because there are women who behave like a man's best friend?

What I know, it was when Romeu filled my pocket with pot I immediately set out on my way. Listening to the music of the nocturnal animals that echoed through the country auditorium, and remembering once again, that if I hadn't left home looking for work, I might not have missed anything. Because the next day, I text Neida a message, "Are you busy?" I asked her.

"No," she answered me right away. Before I changed my mind.

"Would you like to come and see my new residence?" I questioned. Eager, that she would tell me no. For having learned, finally, her lesson.

"And how do we do it?" She questioned.

"You meet me at Giraldo Square and from there we go to my house," I replied and realised that after all there was one last lesson for me to learn as well.

"I'm going to take a shower, then, okay?"

"You'll sweat... Don't you want to take it here?" I suggested, wanting to get our last lecture over as soon as possible.

"Ok, I'll get dressed. Are we going to walk a lot?"

"Just a little bit," I summarised, knowing full well how much weight the truth would carry, in her final decision.

"Okay, I'll hurry. I'm just ironing my pants; damn, I've already messed up their zipper."

"At 5:40, I'm at the fountain," I said, finally.

I was in the lead; she was falling further and further behind. She could never keep up with my rhythm. Naturally, the world has a cadence that only it can play, and there are people who sing and dance, and there are people who only complain. They don't really know why they complain, or why the world is moving faster and faster, or why it is getting harder and harder for them to keep up. Naturally, the distance between those who are left behind and those who are moving forward increases. And, generally, those who are ahead set the pace of the world.

Neida will never again walk to the Garraia. Tomorrow she will take a ride with her father, the father who never liked me and whom I never knew and never wanted to know. Tomorrow, he will take his daughter home and I will no longer receive visits from his daughter, whether I want to or not.

Chapter 2
Grey September

(September 2014)

After the blue of August's canvas dripped onto the floor of September's studio, the Garraia was filled with a greyish deluge. Somewhere between the Colégio square and the top of Rua do Cardeal-Rei one could stare with conviction at that dark grey sea that had submerged Évora and the Alentejo. Meanwhile, the landlord Norberto Córdova came on the first afternoon of the September grey to pick me up to go buy a new reducer for the gas. Before returning home, we took another ride in his car, so that I could take a second look at the surroundings under his gaze. He always conversed very calmly and his slow gestures accompanied his thoughtful speech without exception, "Look, Mr Simão! You even have some pine trees there, which must remind you of your area, the central region."

We went back to the farm a little later, and even before the octogenarian landlord took off, he told me how he and landlady Maria Eduarda had met. Besides explaining that the farm was his wife's inheritance, he informed me, for some inner reason, that his oldest son was living in Brazil, and that that was where he conducted his business. However, he did not reveal to me why he had settled there. What he did tell me bluntly was that he, too, had been to Brazil. More specifically when *the Ongoing Revolutionary Process* began. Returning, of course, right when the party was over.

The landlord Norberto Córdova seems to like me. Also, Mrs Maria Eduarda seems to like me a lot. I think they have convinced themselves that I have more money than I actually have. They seem to have been persuaded by the way I articulate language and the consistency of how I combine it with my extremely refined manners. This, however, bothers a certain type of people, but it stupefies another kind. Nevertheless, my good manners do not match my current condition, nor the authenticity of my social origin.

One of his sons, the one who lives in the family building at the Portas de Moura and occupies the floor above his parents, came to the house once with my landlady Maria Eduarda. He was perplexed that I was listening to Bach. He was not only astonished, but also suspicious. Possibly, it was not comfortable for him to accept that I lived in that house and listened to Bach. To him, the two premises were not an acceptable part of the mass of the ensemble.

On her last visit, Maria Eduarda came alone. She parked her car next to my front door and got out with the help of her cane. She was getting closer and closer to the age of eighty and didn't shy away from dragging her arrogant and authoritarian pose. She was, however, always very condescending to me. This time she came to bring me the inventory of the house, for me to sign. We had a cup of tea in the living room and she was complimentary, "The house is very well decorated, Mr Simão, what good taste you have!"

She seemed as overcome with wonder and amazement as that son of hers who accompanied her on one of her visits, when she came to confirm that everything was in accordance with my wishes. When shortly afterwards, Mistress Justina knocked on the door, the landlady would hurry her, so that we could have privacy. She did this as if she were the landlady and I were someone superior to her historical tenant, still in her late sixties.

Mrs Justina, on the other hand, whenever she spoke about the lady, she spoke with reverence. All her sentences were adorned with "Mrs Maria Eduarda" this, "Mrs Maria Eduarda" that. When my landlady spoke of Mrs Justina, she invariably implied that she liked to meddle in the lives of her neighbours. Suggesting that I take my precautions. However, I had already incorporated a strategy, somewhat analogous to the distance between my country house and the city walls. When Rolando, Mrs Justina's nephew, a resident of Quinta das Pimentas, a kind of handyman, came to fix the shower, and asked me if I would tutor his daughter, until then, I maintained a sufficiently circumscribed and rather distant social interval.

At the beginning of September, still at the beginning of my life at the Garraia, I met Elisa Calçada, in the cloister of Inatel, where the *Art Café* terrace is. I was sitting on the esplanade contemplating the ashes in the ashtray left there by someone. The encounter with Elisa was not unexpected. It was a predictable consequence of our frequenting the same place on the same day. There was no theorem, no coincidence or conspiracy theory. Just an equation of connivance and convenience or the influence of Eduardo's thinking, taking root in me.

I tried to explain to Elisa why I went to Garraia and how I was currently living in an exile. Living in seclusion. More or less, like in a convent. And that it would be there, that the conclusion of my cycle would take place, the conclusion of the Southern dream, according to my humanistic calculations. Elisa listened to me attentively. She had been seduced by me. Somewhere without my knowing exactly when. That's why she listened to me with such consideration.

Not because she was interested in hearing about my banishment to a country house and how I thought I saw it. It was irrelevant, to her, whether or not I would discover the subterranean path to autognosis, to the cave of knowledge that we have possessed since we were babies, but which we parted from a few years later, after tearing open our mother's womb. Still, the more we know ourselves, the wider is the map of our humanity and the deeper is the cavern of tolerance and kindness that is regenerated by this important rediscovery.

Elisa is also part of an association of plastic artists that meets in Praça do Sertório. And, according to her, she's friends with the president of a music association, which also functions as a music producer company. At this moment, Elisa is helping him to set up an art fair. And it was following this conversation that she invited me to present a performance. Even because Felício, that great fado singer from Évora, from the Alentejo, wouldn't be available.

Elisa told me, "Although we are on top of the event, I believe that you will have an opportunity to make your work known. In an environment that is all about closeness and conviviality, with the population, and sharing, among those involved, for future collaborations and partnerships."

However, what I needed was to get a job, although the sincere desire to make each day an art story was greater. My only predisposition was to search for the grail of each day living and each day making art. Just like when a man makes love with the heart of a woman.

Before returning home, I passed by the Sé square, where the art fair was being set up, and where the afternoon grey dance was taking place, with the usual cineral faces that regularly attend the same nucleus of activities. Some were the artists' friends, others were the guests of friends of those huge gladiators and swordsmen that are the fado footballers of the region.

The fado singer Lara, or, if you prefer, the soccer player Lara, with whom I have been running into a lot lately, either in the street or on the stage of life, is now, of course, at the afternoon ball. Because her girlfriend is part of the Association that participates in the fair. The great fado soccer player, Lara, is a friend of the great soccer player Felício, and so, obviously the fado singer Felício also dances at the afternoon dance, and everyone dances with him.

Before the end of the afternoon fell completely over the horizon, I wandered around the Sé square, not exactly looking for work, but rehearsing my performance poem, dedicated to my friend Marcus Matalonga, who refuses to embrace his own existence. I spoke with some of these local artists and athletes involved with the fair, including the referees and the sound judges.

Always acting as if I didn't have any arms or hands to grasp my destiny. Walking from side to side, always with my hands behind my back, or simply tucking my arms inside my t-shirt. Constantly asking for favours, and frequently giving directions on the best way to do this and that. Insistently asking questions, "Can I give you a hand? It costs me nothing."

It was still early when I went home. I still had to get used to the idea of the path I had to walk back home. Because the path I had to walk was bigger than the size of this or any other day. The distance from me to the city is, right now, getting longer, while the distance from me to home is getting shorter. I am simultaneously accumulating a whole new sense of time. And, by progressively walking the same path from home to the city, and from the city walls to the field of dream, I am making this same path increasingly greyish, and, consequently, I am better understanding the reason for the grey causes of this day in September, just as I am accepting the consequences of the molecule with the same colour as the colour of the decision I made along the previous blue path that, quite naturally, led me to this one.

I went into town escorted by a slightly grey sun the next day. I met up with Mara and Silvana at the Sé Cathedral to choreograph their participation in the performance of the ungraceful, inelegant, and armless character I would play. Mara works in one of the associations that performed at the Arts Fair, which is taking place next to the Sé square. She was recommended to me by Elisa Calçada. And Mara herself dragged along a friend, Silvana Cautela, a veterinary doctor. Initially, they both thought I was a research fellow, which was more a notion of a certain status I held, but which did not coincide faithfully with my academic situation. Then they probably thought that I was just ridiculous, and that the performance they were going to co-host was just silly. But I didn't care how grey the reality of their belief was. The power of me making art enabled me to ignore the grey liquid of their true humanity. Basically, let's face it, I appeared to be something I wasn't yet, or wasn't at all. Essentially, I was just the mirror of that thing, which I apparently reflected; just the mortar of the September sky.

The performance began with me being carried by Mr Januário in a wheelbarrow, which I had borrowed from him, one of the association's plastic artists, whom I had met through Elisa. He was already retired, yet he looked younger than his age. On the day of the performance there was a wheelbarrow waiting for me. It is increasingly rare to find someone who honours his word. Whether it is by keeping his commitment not to forget to bring a wheelbarrow or for another great cause.

Francisca and Belchior went to see my performance. Henrique Raposo stopped by and stayed a few minutes to see what the hell it was all about. He was as sceptical as an old man who thinks that younger people are a threat to the quality of his existence. If my arms weren't tied because of my character, I would have hugged him. But instead, I gave him a kiss on the lard on his cheek. Because that was the script. Henrique was very disconcerted.

The text that I wrote when I was still the self-styled last living poet, and which was printed for free today at the City Hall reprographics office, with an exaggerated font size, led to the poem, already fulfilled, being transformed into a huge rectangle the size of a stage. And, after the show was over, it would turn into a big ball of paper, which, disappointed with the failure of my vain and consecutive attempts to give birth to the work, I crumpled.

September is a cement wall that surrounds the city and town where my gloomy spirit resides. As grey as the moment when the yellowish Raul Cancelo, because of the illness that had left him convalesce, went to congratulate his friend Silvana Cautela. He ignored me. Worse, he despised me as if I was eternally to blame for his opinion of me changed. Maybe it was because of the desolation he felt that at any moment he might die. Being prevented from continuing to smoke and drink moderately as he had always done. When I saw them chatting, I quickly remembered that Silvana Cautela was the friend with whom he regularly had steak dinners when I worked as a cook at *Spettus*.

Two days later, João Plácido Rocha came to dine with me at my country house. Even before I recognised him, chased by a cloud of grey dust that galloped up the main road to Garraia in greyish September, he was already there, in the distance, on the horizon, driving with his tongue out and grinning from forehead to chin.

Before dinner we walked around the farm. I showed him where I was meditating. Basically, I pointed in the direction of a pile of stones, next to a swarm of grey olive trees. Again, he smiled. Nothing he said to me was a yes or a firm no. Nothing he told me had a conclusive answer. If I asked him a question, he would ask another question. If I raised an arm, he would raise both, smiling invariably at the end.

We sat down at the table, and each one served himself. This was imposed by João Plácido, who refused to be served. His portion was distinctly small. He told me that he always did this. Justifying himself that he didn't need so much food. Adding to his pantagruelic thesis that we were used to having more eyes than belly. However, he repeated it about five or six times. And, of course, in the end, he smiled with a full belly.

After finally being satisfied, I told him about the training I reluctantly had to undergo to work in the PT call-centre.

I would tell him, "It is not enough for me to kill first the Lion of Nemesis and then the Hydra of Lerna. I also have to clean out the stalls of Augeas, which, in my case, will be working as an operator at the PT call-centre."

"It's an illusion," said João Plácido, who was divorced and worked in a bank, besides being a meditation guide, or a group meditation technician? "It's all an illusion," he repeated. As if I hadn't heard him the first time.

Then he assured me that I should be patient, because it was a demanding job. Despite his apparent calm and tranquillity and his permanent smile, what he was telling me was not at all harmonious or convincing to me. Everything he said had the digestion of a Paulo Coelho book or a philosophy that both warmed and chilled me. I shrugged my shoulders and he, of course, smiled from his heels to his ankles.

It was one o'clock in the morning when I closed the door. Since ten o'clock pm he had stated that he would not stay too late. He proceeded as he had at dinner, repeating himself half a dozen times, and always smiling at everything and nothing. He said goodbye, finally, once again showing his exaggeratedly bright teeth. They had never experienced anything other than the crunching of the crust of happiness. The poor bank employee knew no other emotion on his palate. Laughing was as normal to him as breathing through his mouth and meditating deeply through his nose.

I left home walking towards the sea of the unknown this Sunday afternoon. Wading into an ocean of people who are not looking for anything, but end up finding the foam of something or someone, or else, coming across these small interior gardens sprayed throughout the city of Évora. Some with small cloisters, fountains, others with exotic bushes and antique tiles. They are interior gardens just like those found in the Middle East. Which persists, possibly, only in my head. A kind of fantasy island that is not real.

But that we constantly dream about. Like I dream that I discover the buried treasure in Lapa da Moura. These small gardens that I daydream about, omit majestic lives that are lived very discreetly in Évora, as possibly in other unknown propugnacles, where the great mysteries of civilisations that lived centuries of peace and harmony are recorded.

And for those who, like me, walk in the middle of the afternoon without any sense of direction, can still see one or another half-open door that reveals one of those magnificent small gardens and interior oases.

When I arrived in the historic centre, I ran into Felício, that formidable singer of soccer and fado, who was rehearsing his performance in the Sertório square. He danced on top of a huge vase, around a small olive tree that was a little bigger than he was, being applauded by the bulk of his audience, which was made up mostly of the illustrious footballers of his generation and the fado singers who greatly appreciated his lycra pants with a flower print pattern.

Sandro França, who was in the cast of *The Guest and the Host*, was watching the rehearsal. That's why I stopped by. We chatted for a few minutes. I even arranged to have dinner with him at the end of the afternoon, and then go see Felício's performance at Praça do Sertório. Not that I was interested in watching the performances of these great fandango dancers. My idea was just to be seen at the Sertório square. And when our conversation ended, Sandro and the rest of the group of gladiators and fado athletes all went together to the kiosk café, which is next to the Roman temple garden. I returned home.

Sandro would meet me there later. I convinced myself, however, that he would show up by car, but he showed up on a scooter with a ridiculous helmet stuck on his head.

After the plates had been placed on the table, the evening began with my explanation, which was somewhat cryptic, of why I had decided to come and live in the country. Then, I listened disinterestedly to Sandro, who seemed not to have understood at all my explanation of a call for a more rural life. I couldn't be captivated by what he was saying. I listened indifferently as Sandro told me what he had done since we last met somewhere in February of this year.

I didn't know exactly what to tell him now, not having completed my degree, which was supposedly what had prevented me from continuing with more artistic projects and pursuits. Sandro was no longer teaching at André de Gouveia, but had found a position at another school. Naturally, the possibility of continuing as my collaborator had been lost, and the feeling I was now experiencing was like a straitjacket, with the afterglow of a moment that remained unfulfilled after *The Guest and the Host*.

It was the feeling of a fabric that dressed my spirit in grey.

After dinner, we both went on his scooter. I also had to put a helmet on my head and hope no one saw me in those adventures. Shortly after, after a few gusts of wind, Sandro parked and we joined the crowd that had gathered in the Praça do Sertório, to see the marathoners of art, those athletes that no matter how hard they run, never get tired.

After watching Felício Marciano's artistic athletics event, we went for a cocktail with Sandro's friends. I was happy. I haven't felt this happy since I don't know when. I felt happy, not because I had seen Adriana in the crowd, but because I had found her with a new boyfriend, and because her new romance confirmed to me that she possibly had feelings for me. If I wasn't so afraid of being just her friend, maybe now I would be the one with my arm around her waist.

At *Páteo*, there was Raulito, currently manager or one of the partners of the bar and restaurant, still pitifully yellow, at the end of the night, of this greyish end of summer. In the meantime, in that conversation of who's who and who does what, I recognised the fringe of the young psychologist, Beatriz Costa, sitting at our table. I had already crossed paths with her, during the walking blue of this itinerant summer. Her godmother, also sitting with us, suddenly asked me if I was interested in older women. I recognised her, too. Not from a street esplanade, but from the group meditation sessions with the banking guru, João Plácido Rocha.

Sandro França dropped me off at home later. I said goodbye quickly, shaking the cold from my ears and the tip of my nose. An uncomfortable layer of grey frost had accompanied us from the bridge of the Xarrama River. Sandro França was perplexed. I believe he was expecting some amorous gesture to happen in the meantime. But I was a poor, openly heterosexual in exile. Away from the city and more and more away from the rest of the world.

***

When I walk, sometimes back home, sometimes back to the city, I am drowning with the questions and the issues that I reformulate myself. With a simple question, more than one pot of doubt is born. The uncertainty of how I will pay the rent next month is a seed that germinates and grows somewhere in me. As I walk in the late afternoon, even greyer edges emerge on Garraia that I can't distinguish, either near or far, what it all is. It is probably the end of summer; it is the beginning of autumn. Therefore, I am already somewhere in the middle of the winter time, and someone has shifted the clock. The day dies earlier and earlier, and recently, I have been accumulating the mild feeling that I am only a tiny part of the water vapour of the sea of grey air that is found in the early morning and late afternoon. Outside, apparently quiet, but inside, tremendously agitated, so it is, this vast sea of air that swallows the Alentejo.

I'm walking forward towards Évora, and I'm rewinding the curves and counter-curves of the itinerary I made until I got here. Each change of house was a stopover I made between the real station and the dream of a new station. Each stop was a graduation. Yes, all my duties, tasks and schedules served to get here. Yes, sir, possibly, Garraia will be my final graduation! And when my final race is finished, when my final race is over, I will run home. I will run with the jubilation of having accomplished the pinnacle of the dream and of having reached the final rung, as well as, the full meaning of the spiral staircase, having climbed to the highest degree of it; being finally allowed to come down from the mountain and return to the valley or to the plain.

Meanwhile, I started training to be a call-centre operator at PT. From 16:00 to 23:00. At 21:00 I have a 1 hour break for dinner. It's 15 days of training. If I get approved, I sign the contract and get paid for the training. If I am not approved, I don't get paid for the training. If I pass and don't sign the contract, I don't get paid for the training either. Just great! Right?

Working in the call-centre is one more of the jobs of a Hercules in post-modernity. Time is money and the more money you have, the more time you can spend. I have no time to waste. It's keeping your head down and agreeing with everything, always saying yes, to everything and everyone. And, in the end, smile like a fool, or like João Plácido who laughs at everything and nothing.

Today, before I went to the training, I met with Anabela Santos Pereira. We met in the middle of the afternoon, after I had hesitated and doubted a lot, whether I should or should not meet with her. My meeting with Anabela was in my mind the last attempt to redeem myself from the *Amphitheatre* Association, after having hastily abandoned it.

All because I had once felt too close to Adriana, having subsequently considered it best to distance myself. It could be that now I would regain the territory of lost time and regain the heart of that place that I deliberately parted with.

After we had walked in the rain and I was drenched in grey, we ran for shelter under the arcades of the Giraldo Square. In the end, we shook hands and arranged to meet again. Deciding to start working on a common artistic project.

After the training, I refused a ride with my call-centre colleagues. Just so I wouldn't have to listen to them talk about their daily drama. I walked. I listened to the sound of the stars sailing high into the night. Hearing each of them much more clearly with each step I took. The stars were the only lit lamps illuminating the darkness of my path.

The automobiles scraped past me, not seeing me. But I kept whistling happily with my hands in my pockets, walking along the side of the road, without a reflective vest and not exactly finding room to move safely. The road belongs to automobiles, and the world belongs to those who speed and run over others. No! The road does not belong to pedestrians, only to drivers who honk their horns at the poor pedestrians who, like me, are walking along the ditch today.

Convinced that stupid people never change their minds, I grudgingly accepted a ride from my call-centre colleagues the following week. I resigned myself to the back seat. The driver, who almost has a master's degree in sociology from the School of Social Sciences at the University of Évora, tells me that she is supposedly fatter because of depression. She complains that the medication that is supposed to combat her depression produces more side effects, and that one of them is that she has gained weight Another colleague takes her place. She speaks without any shame. She doesn't think what she says, but she says what she thinks. And although she has a boyfriend, she likes to tease the opposite sex. The instructor seems to be her main target. She does so, however, knowing that what she says has a certain effect and power.

Meanwhile, on the car radio, you can hear it:

The Swiss Stefan Kung, the last to start on the course at Ponferrada, had the third best time and guaranteed the last place on the podium. A bitter end for Rafael Reis, who saw his third-place finish come within 10 seconds. Argues Rafael Reis—While I was sitting there, I even dreamt that I could be on the podium and only the last runner to arrive robbed me of that dream.—Regrets Rafael Reis, in declarations by the Portuguese Cycling Federation.

The feisty colleague continues to talk over the news. Now she discusses the lives of others in her village. She tires quickly, and moves on to her homoeopathic commentary, dwelling on the parapet of the life of each colleague in the formation. About what goes on inside the imposing PT building, which blends in with another monument of the city of Évora, what she has to say is a solid glass of nothing. She has not made any remark about the immoral debauchery of this private world, which is a state within another state. The spirited Laplander is not bothered by the corporate labyrinth. It is indifferent to its laws and its webs, in which both flies and workers are swallowed up. Not a single comment about the metallic grey of the rooms, chairs, desks and computers, in which everything is sadly equal to grey September.

Over the weekend, Francisca came to see if she could fix my laptop that had suddenly fallen ill. I was hoping she could save it. She wasn't really a specialist, more of a general practitioner. However, she had that authority of a doctor or an engineer, using a more technical vocabulary at her pleasure. And we, the users, of course, just have to respect what they tell us. If it weren't for the life of our dear little laptop.

"Possibly a virus," Francisca said calmly. Keeping a serious air and a frontal and arrogant attitude only within the reach of a class of people. After a formal pause, she added, "I still don't know exactly what it is."

I exclaimed, "Oh, a virus! A virus! Oh, my God. But why? Why did it have to be my laptop, my dear little laptop?"

And suddenly, without me being prepared, Francisca smiled as I had never seen her before. It was as if she had saved herself for that day. Her face was at that moment, the total revelation of who she really was. Her face was now and only that of someone extremely pleasant, and only because she was now smiling. Like João Plácido Rocha would do, when he drinks sparkling water or when he simply flushes the toilet, in a completely genuine and authentic emotion.

Meanwhile, Francisca gave up on saving my laptop. Excusing herself that she didn't have the necessary stereoscope with her. So, my laptop would have to continue to breathe with limitations, it would have to adapt. That is, it had to do as I did, it had to hold on. She couldn't tell me how much longer it would have to live. It could be a month, a year, or just another half hour. Francisca had done what she could for him. What she knew she had learned in the course, taken through the Jobcentre. It was a course she was very proud of. Although, in practice, it hadn't done her much good. Neither for her, nor for her poor patient.

Outside, the weather had sulked. More and more it roared like a grumpy lion, or like a leopard, simply, angry. The late morning torch was hoisted grey. Violently shaking the sea of air, slowly turning itself upside down. Shaking itself the great ocean parked in the sky, bucking on the bed of the sky on its belly.

A giant's stomach rumbled. Somewhat frightened, Francisca ventured out, however, to see with the tip of her hands what it was all about. She opened the door to the entrance and reached out to pick up a piece of evidence from the floor and exclaimed, "It's there! Simão, look at this! This had never happened before," she repeated apprehensively, fearing that the sea of grey would fall upon her and flood her forever with a greyish deluge.

She immediately connected to the world, entering it through the window of her cell phone screen. She read the news, running her index finger over it, commenting, like a president of the republic. "This is serious in Évora! It's here! All the traffic is being cut off in the Alentejo. In Beja, Ferreira do Alentejo, Alvito, Vidigueira, everything is flooded with water. In Moura, trees have already fallen to the ground and onto houses."

When the truce finally came, we learned that the Alentejo was not going to be flooded after all, and Doctor Francisca could finally make her verdict, "I have never seen so much hail stones rain." Then, running zigzagging to the car. As if she were a cat, and didn't want to get her head or her fur wet.

The next day I waited for Jaime Alma sitting on the Sunday wall outside the estate gate. He was on his way back from Bogotá. I knew little about Jaime Alma. Except, that he had created the *So-So Theatre* with his wife. Oh, and I knew what Francisco had already told me. Jaime and Sandra did "that theatre."

Today, it is Sunday, rarely does a sailing car pass by the side of the road. The wind is blowing slowly. As it usually does in the Alentejo. Jaime arrived sometime later, bringing with him the simplicity of his candid and frank smile. Being as cordial as the fraternity of master Benedito Pio. But Jaime's cordiality was more carnal and not so formal, nor so spiritual. However, he made me extremely comfortable with him. Although, I didn't feel as well as I did in the company of Master Benedito.

He was frankly a simple guy. His clothing consisted of a white t-shirt, a denim jacket, and jeans. Which were ratty, possibly, because they had been worn almost every day for the last twenty years. He was an old hippie actor used to being comfortable in any situation on the stage of life. Always smiling at the beginning and end of every sentence. It was a convinced smile of someone who believed in the revolutions of the 60s, in communism, and in the comfort of being something else if it was more convenient. It was, yet a smile quite distinct from the idiotic smile that João Plácido Rocha had the habit of smiling so often for no apparent reason.

He told me about Bogotá and the work of *So-So Theatre* in South America. I then confessed to him that I had been doing a training course in PT for the last 15 days, and that if it went well, I would be approved. But I would prefer to do an internship in my area. I didn't tell him, however, that the *So-So Theatre* would be, for me, only slightly better, than going to work in the call-centre. Which went against the principles that were taught to me by the Master, going more in favour of the draft that had the pedantic pragmatism of Calé's son.

For Jaime, I was already an intern at *So-So*. Although, *So-So Theatre* couldn't afford to pay me the percentage that should be borne by the association. But if I didn't mind, because there was already more than one trainee in the same condition, he would talk to Sandra.

He didn't stay long. He said goodbye with the same clothes of simplicity and humanity with which the essence of his spirit was dressed. In the end, Mrs Justina came to the window to see who had come to visit me.

Late the next morning, I would promptly receive a message:

"Hooray! I've already talked to Sandra. She, at first, agrees. Now we have to check with the third party, which is Mr Mendes, our collaborator and advisor for financial matters. Could you come here to talk to us?"

Before heading to the grey PT building, I passed by the top of São Bento. I was more excited than if I had won the lottery. Sandra was the one who had the last word. She was the one who decided last. Although, Jaime and Sandra divided democratically the charge of the direction. Mr Mendes, the accountant, with the profile of a Roman emperor minted in the coin of the old empire, raised problems and difficulties but Jaime interceded in my favour.

The training at PT ended this evening. I was approved. "The Old Woman" as my colleague, the smart one, and my other mostly university colleagues called her, did not pass. When she heard that she would not be offered any contract, she cried softly. Her younger colleagues laughed at her. Their compassion was a short fuse, in which some of them at first said "ah! What a shame." Then ending the whole group in laughter and hubbub.

The "Old Woman" at the end of the session, surprisingly, invited me to go for a drink with her, and a friend. But I declined. Returning as soon as possible to my exile in the dream field. I headed home, believing that the internship would go ahead as soon as possible. If all went well, I wouldn't have to bring my dinner in my lunch box next week, nor would I have to eat every mouthful in the company of my fellow students.

Jaime called me the next day to stop by the jobcentre. The final decree was that *So-So Theatre* could not pay me their share, but by my free consent, I would get the money that the state would make available to me. I said yes. It was enough to pay the rent and it was almost enough for me to say that I was finally working in my field of study.

It was official, the internship was going forward. And, I was not going to work for the call-centre prison. I was free! Free! So, the following Saturday, I went to João Plácido Rocha's full attention meditation session. He came to pick me up at the Garraia. But it was Ana Maria, Belchior's girlfriend, and her sister, who lives in Lisbon, who came later to drop me off at the square. When Ana Maria's sister asked if I lived in that house, she said "no, no! He lives in that little house."

The big house was the main house of the estate. It was the house where Dona Justina lived with her husband since the PREC (*Ongoing Revolutionary Process*). A combination between the Córdova family and the Espargosa couple, which allowed the estate not to be appropriated. Ana Maria's sister, seemed discouraged, after the great expectation she had for me, was blown away by the petty and frivolous remark made and repeated by her sister: "No, no! He lives in that tiny little house!" As if it would never be possible for me to live in the big house, in the main house of the estate, known as Quinta das Pimentas.

Chapter 3
Internship

(October to December 2014)

All the properties around Quinta das Pimentas are usually fenced in with nets, or walls as high as the ones of the Évora prison, and the ones in the city walls. But at Quinta das Pimentas, there is no fence, nor is there a gate. Just two pillars that delimit and signalise the entrance and suggest something imposing, Roman, oneiric. They are ancient symbols that resist a hyper-significant civilisation, which denotes everything, but tells us nothing.

I wait for Jaime who is naturally late. It is the tendency of his nature. When we understand the essence of people and the essence of things, we more easily accept their inclination and the movement that each nature contradiction has. I gave up sitting and waited standing. Occasionally, walking in circles. Usually, when on the sand of the beach with the sea wetting our feet, sometimes a boat appears slowly on the horizon, and we wonder: where will it go? And who goes there? Now, down the road, way down the road, a car appears, and I have the expectation that it is finally the boss Jaime Sérgio Alma.

It wasn't. It would come much later, as if the world had been at peace for centuries, and there was no more injustice among men. Just fraternity and equality, and plenty of freedom for everyone to decide what is best for themselves.

"Well, hello, comrade." He said, when I got into the van.

"Do you know that sometimes it is possible to have a dialogue only by repeating what others tell us?" I asked him, ignoring his previous hello.

Jaime laughed with his usual calm and puerile disposition, "How so, comrade?"

"Comrade, it's just how?"

"Yeah, I see… Is everything alright?" Jaime asked, always finding what I did and said funny.

"With this comrade, everything is fine! And, with that comrade; well, everything is fine?"

"That's all right! We have to combine one of these…" answered Jaime, contributing to the peddling of the parody.

He only took off after he told me that the *So-So Theatre's* van was in the workshop. Laughing, not caring about such bad luck, or such good fortune. Showing me not only his false tooth, but also revealing the metal structure on which his pontic tooth rested. He had bad breath. It was unavoidable! It was not the first time that breath had permeated the space where only he and I were confined.

I couldn't help but appreciate its simplicity. Besides, it was easy to appreciate his brotherhood, since he distributed it to everyone equally. Always ready to help others and to laugh at everything. As if he were just an innocent child. With fifty-something years of playing.

"In Bogotá, that's how it's done, and it works, buddy!" said Jaime, who had the particularity of entering a roundabout, without waiting, even though other cars had already been circulating there for a long time.

Next, Jaime would tell me how, recently, he tried to enter the *Círculo Eborense* with his friend and former collaborator Damião, the professional clown known as Pantufa. Precisely the one who was my classmate in an optative subject. And they bumped into the door. Jaime Sérgio blamed President Raul and his doormen. Then he told me with great charm about the time of the fat cows and the subsidies from the Directorate-General for the Arts.

"We all had workshops with the great masters. I used to take the *So-So* van and we would all go," Jaime said with great nostalgia.

Because, now the *So-So Theatre* was with his pockets picked, and the Pantufa, was a solo Damião clown. Speaking Jaime of his departure with some sorrow and resentment. Although, he would tell me, shortly afterwards, that he accepted that Damião had chosen to go his own way.

The internship is not yet recognised by the Employment Centre, but I tried to get involved, right now, in the community's activities. I like having a cultural association, of which I am part. The *So-So There* Association, at this moment, is my community, it is my religion, and I am its congregation. Because, to a lone wolf it is more accessible to find faith, in the middle of a pack of sheep and shepherds.

Meanwhile, we arrived at the *So-So Theatre*. Which is almost at the top of the S. Bento hill. If you follow the Piscinas road, it is on the right; and according to Jaime Alma, further down the road, in the open field, there is usually a gypsy camp. When we got out of the car, Jaime confessed to me that *So-So* suffers from being far from the city and not being closer to the historic centre. I thought he was talking indirectly about me. But I soon realised that it was just something I currently had in common with *So-So Theatre*'s van.

My first task was to remove the awning that had been covering the front of the old elementary school since the summer, which Jaime and Sandra had converted into an association headquarters. After the awning was removed and folded, we went up to the small sound booth. The booth of *So-So Theatre* seemed to have waited 20 years for me to put it away. Meanwhile, Jaime is explaining to me his criteria for winding a sound cable without damaging it, while complaining in a venting tone.

"I lend and then return like this!"

Shortly after, there would be a brief meeting with Sandra, Jaime and the future project that is currently inside Ivone's belly. Ivone, who is also doing an internship at *So-So* and signed, somewhere around last year, a mother's contract without a fixed term.

We talked under the warm shade of an olive tree. Sitting on stones arranged in a circle. The meeting started with Jaime. Then it went clockwise and ended with Sandra. The big discussion was about archiving the story of *So-So*. Ivone and Sandra agreed with me on what needed to be done. They both seemed to realise that the *So-So There* Association was as tangled as the cables in the sound booth.

However, Jaime did not want to tidy up the memories of *So-So's* past into dossiers. Nor did he allow the old props to be put away in drawers and the extra stuff to be put in the trash. At the end of the meeting, Sandra went to give a children's theatre class in the small enclosure of the art school of the *So-So There* Association, and Jaime brought me home. But before he did me the favour, to park at the Portas de Moura, by the fountain. So, I could go pay my rent.

Then, after I rang the bell, Augusta, the landlady's maid, opened the door and I went up the stairs from another century and was led into the waiting room.

"Wait here, Mr Simão! The lady will be right out..." Augusta said, before leaving the scene, just like in a play by Almeida Garrett. It was the drawing room, where the lady would receive me. Just like in big houses, where there are big lives to be lived.

Jaime Sérgio waited patiently for me to pay the rent and then he drove me home. I didn't have to walk anymore! My friends were my drivers. Francisca was one, and Eduardo was another, for example. The quality of each driver was based not only on his personality, but also on the character of each trip. Counting the parameters of the trip being done safely, but also the excitement and speed that each trip brought. Jaime is also one of my drivers Master António Benedito Pio doesn't have a driver's licence, but he is the Master and shepherds, in a way, drive their flocks.

Jaime Sérgio told me he was already more than thirty years old when he got his driving licence; and that he only got it because Sandra was pregnant. Someone had to take her to the hospital and to the appointments with the Esperança baby. Sandra would get her Master's degree. Was the supposed agreement reached between the two of them, about family justice and the couple's economy.

Now I always go by car. Not having one, though. Jaime picks me up and brings me to the Garraia. João Plácido also used to pick me up and bring me to the Garraia when I went to his sessions of mindfulness meditation. But nowadays I am somewhat distant from him. As much, or more, than I am at present from the historic centre.

The distance and the kilometres that currently live between me and João Plácido Rocha were not, however, solely incited by the petty remark of Ana Maria, Saint Belchior's girlfriend. But equally contributing to this was when I went to the house of Jéssica, a friend of João Plácido's.

I'm not sure what it was that annoyed me the most. Was it the fact that Jéssica's place was basically an eastern therapy business in a more or less accidental country? Or was it because she insisted that I tell her what I really thought about the whole thing? Maybe it was the overflow of cakes and cookies on the table where they normally were doing shiatsu and reiki.

Maybe it bothered me that João Plácido criticised my observation. Very quickly disapproving of my pedantry. Although, I had tried to clarify that my sarcasm didn't reflect anyone in particular. But the fact is that Ana Maria's cell phone rang before the end of the session, and regardless of whether it bothered everyone, it was better that I kept quiet. After all, the reason is for those who choose to remain silent, when they could have said something.

But none of that matters. It is night now, and in the South, night has a greater charm than the beauty of the East, or of Iran and Iraq, where I often stay overnight with the tent of my imagination.

The next morning, I left home and stopped, quietly, at the entrance to the estate. Thinking that today there would be another friendly driver who would pick me up to take me to the city. But I gave up waiting for such an idea and marched on. I even thought about asking for a ride with my thumb. But I did not pursue such a resolution. I persuaded myself that I was no longer old enough to carelessly ask strangers for a ride. But in this greater inner abstraction, a pickup truck stopped beside me. It was the same kind of vehicle that Francisco's father drove. Tucked behind the wheel was an old man with a beret, graduate glasses, and an unshaven beard.

"Boy, jump in the van! I'm going to Avis Café. If you want a ride there, I'll give it to you. It doesn't cost me anything."

It had already started to rain, so I immediately accepted that generous offer of his. With the premise that life is about not staying with the same idea from beginning to end.

"You live there, don't you? In the house where Justina's father lived?" The old man asked, who seemed ready to die since he was born.

"Yes, indeed," I answered, as briefly as possible. I wasn't exactly interested in revealing to him who I was.

But the old man spoke openly. "I live there, in Sisuda. That's mine. It's right next to that home they set up there. I saw you last week, and a few other times last month."

At daybreak, the old man with the beret and unshaven beard was already sweating the sweat of an early morning's work. Something drunk and hungover and sober. Experiencing everything and nothing at the same time. His speech was intact, although somewhat worn out.

"I hear poorly," He kept repeating it.

Then he continued, "My daughter and son-in-law already bought me a device like this… But I threw that shit on the floor, and told them I lost it…"

"I would have done the same," I said sympathetically.

"What?" He asked, not listening to a word I said.

"It's good, raining like this!" I shouted at him, changing the subject.

"Yes, it's good for the earth," he consented, listening, at last.

He left me as promised closer to the city, but I was still far from the Jesuit College of Espírito Santo and far from the classroom. The poetry of the clouds kept writing over me, and continued to do so for the rest of the week. Continuously dripping the sand of time from one end of the hourglass to the other. If you turn the hourglass upside down it is inevitable that time does not spill out like rain on the ground. Perhaps for this reason, or for lack of a concrete reason, in the middle of the week, I went with Francisca to pick up her mother from work.

"The car windows don't fog up with our breath, if they are slightly open. Because the temperature is colder outside. If cold air gets in, there's no chance," Francisca said whenever it rained.

Francisca drove neurotically, impulsively dodging water puddles and weather puddles. A waterfall was still falling from the sky. Francisca and I were two tiny drops falling from the same cluster, the same flock, the same cloud of the firmament. We both followed one trajectory. Where I went, Francisca went too, and vice versa.

A few drops of water wanted to join us. They wanted to accompany us in our fall, like fallen angels, banished beings, condemned to inhabit the earth, in the form of small tears of water, which one day, by mere chance or because of fate, came together out of love and friendship, or just out of curiosity, or a matter of simple precipitation. Some droplets unite by the temptation to stay together, but others don't even touch the ground. They evaporate during their collapse.

"Finally!" Francisca said.

The entrance door opens automatically and you see Francisca's mother coming out of her job at the hospital. She's wearing a huge feathered scarf around her neck. And suddenly, it's the 1920s, it's Charleston. The tight blouse defines her breasts, which makes them look even more prominent, and the knee-length skirt reveals the firm bellies of her legs. She walks with the strength and volume of her hips. She doesn't mind the rain. In the background, you can hear the drums of the mambo. And she moves like a woman, like a snake, a serpent, from which we can't take our eyes off her for a single moment.

It's six-something, and the traffic multiplies and the city shrinks. We are stuck in the middle of the traffic. Francisca complains about being where she is. When in fact what she means is that she regrets the choice of life that led her to stay there, that is, not where she is now, but where she has in fact stagnated. Her impatience was not born today, nor was it fermented by the waiting generated by the advance of the car ahead, but only by having remained in the same place. Which makes her feel even more blocked and stuck. The mother seems quiet. Whenever she speaks, she does so sibilantly and softly, giving me a hard-on.

Soon after, she left her mother at home and was satisfied that the task was finished. As if her mother was a package that had finally been delivered. Francisca now lives with her godmother who has recently been widowed. She is the one who takes her niece to school in the morning when her sister can't take her daughter to school. And it is she who mostly drives her mother to work and brings her home. But Francisca is not recognised for her work, nor for her position as head of the family.

We left the Bacelo neighbourhood, where she once lived with her mother, sister and goddaughter. After rolling a joint while driving to her next appointment, she was more relaxed. Which basically consisted of talking to her dealer and hypothetically bringing a few grams of her merchandise. Obviously, we would then have to stop by Belchior's house, so that Belchior could test the product.

In the end, she would drop me off at home. Strangely enough, she would then return to her mother's house, in the Bacelo neighbourhood, to drop off the food that her aunt had made too much of. Before going back to the Garraia, she would stop by Belchior's house again. If there was any time left in the routine of her work, she would still stop by my house. Only then, would she go to sleep in the annex, at her aunt's farm.

***

After the end of the morning class, I had lunch with Jaime and Sandra in their den, which is tucked into the hills of the Malagueira neighbourhood. After lunch we drove to Alto de São Bento for the rehearsal. Today I learned that I am going to the Algarve. The rehearsal hasn't even started yet and I still get fifty euros and some peanuts for the trouble of going to the Algarve to turn on and off some lights and put music X into scene Y. Sandra and Jaime argued during the time that the rehearsal lasted. From the pulpit of the control room, I was distracting them, not with sermons, nor with lessons, but with jokes. The control room is a small, separate compartment of my spaceship. It fits, more or less, everything.

Such is my belief and my faith in the *So-So Theatre*.

I remain standing, bent over the ruler, like a dreamer. I control Jaime's and Sandra's temperament. I adjust the stage lights and regulate the sound effects of each one. I fiddle with all the buttons, without, however, knowing what functions and orders they perform. I even move the spotlight around, just because I do. Then, I fiddle with the soundboard and bang, bang! But Jaime interrupts my cheer to tell me, "That's it for today. I'll take you home if you want."

I get the sense that Jaime doesn't like rehearsals. Which makes me appreciate even more the feline strength that Sandra's female form has. Just like, in a BBC wildlife documentary—she is the female. The female left the savannah and went to the office. Jaime, the defeated male, climbed up to my ivory tower. To bow with me in the *régie*. Forming a dreamy pair with me in the cable jungle, and that's how the rehearsal got halfway through.

After the end of the rehearsal, Jaime left me at the Garraia and went home. But he said goodbye without metaphysics. Because a family man has no metaphysics.

"Goodbye, buddy!" Said Jaime Sérgio Alma, before leaving. Recognising that my life obeyed another sphere.

And between Jaime Alma's simple and fraternal life and my complex existence as a trainee and university student or exiled writer is Viegas, living his exile in an obscure cellar in Santarém. A holy hermit embalmed by the putrefaction of his fear of existing. Reading for hours on end, books that contain no explanation for his problems. An idiot full of intelligence who goes around trying to bite the ghost of his own tail. And it is in the exile of the Garraia that I feel compassion for the city exile of my brother Viegas. Because Viegas is the father of all non-existentialists.

The autumn leaves roll on the ground and are part of one end of the landscape of the hourglass of time. At one end, the Garraia, at the other end, some streets of the city where I lived. The sand of time rushes past us. Or, simply, dripping. So organically elemental and essential is the relationship between mother nature and the daughter nature of things. We pass too quickly through the university of life to fully learn nothing in each lesson from the summary of the universe. However, the leaves of autumn, in autumn, they run, or simply slide, roll on the ground, in an infinite sequence, and I roll, too, with their choreography.

But I was going to the Algarve for the first time and that was all that mattered. The rehearsals in Évora with Anabela are a part of my life that ends when my life as a trainee at *So-So Theatre* begins. And my life as an intern ends when my life as a writer in exile at the Garraia begins. My life at the Garraia and all the others don't always end, however, when my life as a writer begins. Still, I cannot continue *ad infinitum to* ignore Anabela, who is not a driver friend.

I myself don't know the reason for my lack of motivation to go to João Plácido's sessions of mindfulness meditation, or why I didn't want to continue with Anabela's project, which, nevertheless, is more and more hers alone. What really happened? Surely, that is what happens at a junction, at a crossroads, when lives go their separate ways. Each one moving forward, because they have priority, or each one waiting their turn to move forward. Thus, never meeting again, never crossing each other, never crossing each other again.

I fell asleep on Sandra and Jaime's couch. Also ignoring why I let myself be lulled by Sandra's plan. Staying the night before the departure parked at their house. Yesterday, when Jaime and I left his office, where his present junk fit and the junk from his past accumulated, Sandra had already packed her bags, and she had already improvised a bed on the living room couch. And before lights out, Jaime was already upstairs, when Sandra came tucking me into the bedclothes and breathing in my ear, "Sleep well!"

I then slept all night, uncomfortably, with my feet off the couch. When I woke up, I couldn't remember where I was. The only thing I knew, for now, was that I was going to the Algarve. Jaime was making toast. The toasted bread permeated the air deliciously, spreading through every room in the house. After the sound of the knife scraping, you could hear Jaime singing a John Lennon song as he spread each piece of toast with butter. Then he served the coffee: one for me, one for Sandra and one for him.

We arrived in the Algarve after having talked about Sandra and Jaime's travels to South America. We also talked about how they came up with the idea of using a sea of newspapers spread all over the stage during their performance. But Sandra was in a bad mood and everything she told me was of little interest. Jaime went on his way selflessly like a relaxed Jesus Christ. Proceeding mile after mile with the cross of his world. And I, in part, being part of that cross hanging on the shoulders of his universe.

It was only when we arrived in the Algarve, in Faro, and began to set the stage, that Jaime lost his good mood slightly. Because Sandra wanted to rehearse some passages of the show, and he thought that during the show they had more than enough time to rehearse.

I was on stage, perched on the ladder. Tuning the stage lights, when the angel appeared to me—the angel of disquiet, who was quietly coming to alter the root of my fear that I was born and could die in the same valley and the same place.

Thank God, the angel was a female being who didn't walk, she levitated. And, I, an eternal sailor, thank God, shipwrecked, not on the island of gold of her caught hair, but on the continent of her blue eyes. And thank God, I saw, finally, for the first time what was the Portuguese blue sea, the sea of *saudade*! The sea of the South of my destiny of being Portuguese! Because a Portuguese knows at birth what salt tastes like in the lost womb of our motherland. Oh, the vain glory of a fifth empire forever gutted. Once the empire of Dom Sebastião's chimaera, the dream and the foam of the dream lost, everything else is now a distorted photo ship of time as it enters adulthood.

There wasn't much time between the set up and the start of the event. We would open the festival and then it was done. The performance hall was a makeshift space in the middle of rocks and dust. The association had moved premises. It was now where the old beer factory used to be. The *So-So Theatre* had come, supposedly out of friendship and complicity. We helped and supported like good Samaritans.

Like, in a social theory of the civil rights movement, change or help occurs, simply because the leaders of the movement give the participants a sense of identity and a sense of ownership. But fuck society because when I saw the blonde angel, I readily intuited that she was my salvation. Her golden wings were composed of a maternal matter. Something invisibly analogous, similar, to what we see in our mother, being the same later in our beloved.

The show was fast. It took longer to set up than the event itself. The blond angel was even more capable than I was of changing the spotlight. If she wanted to fly, she would not need stairs or elevators to get to heaven. Because she was an angel. Obviously with wings, and, fortunately, with sex. She also knew how to work the soundboard and was a talented actress. In my plays and in my films, she would always appear as the protagonist. We would have children, a house, a car and a dog, and I would have no choice but to move, definitely, even further south.

After dinner, Jaime and I had nothing else to do but drink glasses of free beer.

I would ask Jaime, "But what in this life can be more important than being able to drink what you want?"

Jaime, having no answer, agreed with me, by toasting. Our complicity and friendship grew the drunker we got. The more beer there was, the more our friendship and the more the belly of our complicity enlarged. Shaping the shape that my euphoria had.

"Who's a friend, Comrade Pinheiro?"

"It's you, Jaime Sérgio! You are my friend, Comrade Alma."

"You came to spend a weekend in the Algarve, on business, with everything paid for, Comrade Simão!"

"And the hotel paid, Comrade Jaime?"

"Stay paid, Comrade Simão!" We toasted.

"What about food?"

"All paid up, the festival pays the *So-So*. And *So-So* pays the comrade!" Jaime replied, and we toasted again.

"Long live the *So-So*, comrade!" I shouted, as in revolutions, which go nowhere.

"Hail to *So-So*!" We toasted, both of us at last.

Sandra was determined to leave immediately on Friday afternoon, after the show. But because of my will and Jaime's insistence we continued at the festival of life, in no mood to have a definite position. Sandra and Jaime were, however, distant from each other. Sandra, soon, early in the night, went to the hotel. But before she went, she asked, "Will you take care of yourself and Jaime?" Saying goodbye with a simple "Goodbye boys."

The three of us met, already, Saturday. Sandra was sipping her coffee, bored, perhaps with the taste of her dawn, or perhaps bothered by the taste that her life was taking specifically on this Saturday morning. Jaime looked down at the bottom of his sea of his coffee cup, to see if he had enough for another sip. Thinking that we are all water, and the water in the clouds is the same as the water in the sea. And that angels live at the bottom of the sea as well as at the top of the sky. Sleeping if need be, on top of a cloud of absorbent cotton or in the form of another illusion. And with no door or key to get in or out.

After breakfast, the three of us took a walk by the sea. We walked close to the transparent blue, from where we could see Portugal, the African continent and there, in the background, the desert. Sandra and Jaime were walking by the sea. They seemed tired of each other, tired of the trip they had made to get there. As if it was a tremendous effort, to have to continue a path that would be far away from that blue Algarve. It would probably be impossible for the two of them to be happy ever after But I am a storyteller and believe in fairy tales, although I recognise that a certain world only exists, ideally, in our imagination.

On Saturday afternoon, we joined the audience to see the other companies' shows. Jaime and Sandra surprisingly stayed glued to each other in the audience. Criticising what they saw, even before the lights went out and the curtain opened. Until they both ended up falling asleep without holding hands for a moment.

Saying Jaime when the applause woke him up, "Hey, man! That was really good. This is the one I wasn't expecting."

And Sandra, very quickly, added, "Too bad it was such a short time." Spreading out, then. Stretching her arms towards the sky. According to the aesthetics and training she had as an actress.

When Saturday night began, Jaime and Sandra went to the hotel together, and I stayed with my new friends, and the angel with the golden braids, the compass of the night, the guiding star that never turns off. First, we played foosball in a bar. The Chapitô's company against me and against the golden being. One of Chapitô's friends had a moustache and was from the Algarve. The other was a bearded Lisboner, who was married and had two daughters, and managed to be in almost as good a mood as I was. But everyone was in a good mood with me. And the angel from the Algarve seemed, therefore, to enjoy staying by my side in any game or situation.

"Are you always like this?" My new bearded friend asked me. As if what I was, was a rare thing.

"No, that is, pretending. I am not such a positive being."

"Ah, I'm not either, but I have family and friends who are," he said.

During the crossing of the night when you no longer know what stage floor you are on, you go after someone, and that someone in front of you does the same. In this thread of the plot, I asked my new pal, "How do you get to where you want to go?"

But for a moment he thought I was flattering him. However, what I really wanted was to truly learn how I could one day be happy. Would that be too much to ask? I didn't continue to seek advice and no more serious things. I limited myself to telling my jokes and making my observations. The others laughed and were infected by me, unaware of the clownishness of my pessimism.

Sunday lunch was a sea bean stew, served by the *Musicians Association*, on top of the old beer factory. The best *feijoada* is definitely the Algarve one, and we ate it looking at the blue sea. Drinking beer, wine and sangria. Eating, drinking and laughing. Because life is beautiful when there are people around us. It doesn't matter if we chew with our mouth open or talk with our mouth closed.

After lunch, Jaime and Sandra left me at home and went to the Malagueira neighbourhood. Then Jaime drove with the hurry Sandra had to get home. Raising his hand along the way without ever putting it down. Disappearing in the horizon and we could only see Jaime's hand in the background.

Another week went by with another meeting, at the *So-So Theatre* headquarters. This time it was just between me and Ivone. The meeting was brief and I didn't find any answers to the administrative reform I wanted to see implemented at *So-So Theatre*. What I did find out, however, was that Ivone doesn't care if it's a boy or a girl. Her father is a foot soldier, and after Ivone's internship is over, they both march to her parents' home somewhere in the North.

As for Jaime Sérgio, he still doesn't want to archive the past of the company and the association, not at all. In the entrance hall, the walls of the present are full of fungus, just like, adorned with mould on the posters of the plays that were made during the last 20 years, in the time of the fat cows. The air is permeated with the pestilent, sour smell that is so characteristic of things from the past, like products whose sell-by date has expired; and what's worse is not only that they are past their sell-by date, but that they have become completely outdated and obsolete items; overtaken by new trends that are better adapted and updated all the time.

My little meeting with Ivone caused Sandra and Jaime to argue. Ivone agreed with me. There was a lot to do and, in many areas, and I supposedly had a mission, I had a duty to save *So-So Theatre* and to save Jaime, who was a family man. And if I respect anything it is still family men. Perhaps, because I never had an appeasing sense of family. Although, of course, my primary charge is to tell stories. Nevertheless, those who create narratives to tell others, end up lost, in their own fables and myths.

Francisca came out of nowhere. She usually appears at my house when I return from a trip, or when something new happens in my routine. She comes all the way from the confines of the Garraia, where Auntie's property is located, for the sole purpose of listening to my exploits and misfortunes. I suspect that Francisca inwardly senses my own turmoil. Otherwise, how would she have guessed I returned from Algarve? I don't know, but today her eyes shone without precedent. They were lit by the lamp that had their unprecedented enthusiasm.

Which made her company all the more attractive. Today I didn't feel as bored as I often do.

We took a picture for posterity, imitating each other's facial expressions. In fact, couples who spend a lifetime together, their faces begin to draw the same expressions of joy and disappointment. We resemble our friends by resembling the physiognomy of their desires and daydreams. When they get lost in our dreams, it sometimes happens that we become more and more complicit, the opposite, however, is also quite possible.

"Do you remember, Simão? You used to live in the neighbourhood of Senhora da Saúde. It was the first time I met you and Francisco," Francisca said.

For her, Francisco was still wrapping himself in newsprint or kitchen film. Doing his performance, his trick, his old monkey business. She still saw him, in her head, in the same way she saw him when she met him two, three years ago. She also continued to see me, on the couch in the neighbourhood of Nossa Senhora da Saúde, cheering and encouraging Francisco and drinking wine by the bowl of soup I had brought from the canteen without having thought beforehand of the intention to feed the myth of the last living poet...

A few hours later, I would wake up to the blaring horn of the *So-So Theatre* van being played nonstop.

"I'm coming!" I shouted, still dumbfounded. I got dressed as quickly and as humanly possible. I was more than late. As I jumped into the van, I said, "So, have you come yet? Just now?"

Except Jaime, all the others looked at me with a very serious and circumspect air. As if I were guilty of one of the most heinous crimes of humanity. I sat in the back seat with little interest in that morning trial and concerned only with reporting on the trip.

The Pantufa Clown was wearing his ladies' sunglasses and Mexican shawl. Albano Jerónimo, a musician and music teacher from the arts school of the *So-So There* Association, sat next to him, playing an instrument that looked more like a toy. His stomach would invariably shake whenever Jaime passed over a hole. Carlos Daniel was the musician who had come to replace Zé Guilherme. He was quietly in the front seat, sitting between Jaime and Sandra. Without ever saying anything. And, as well as Mr Pantufa, Sandra was also wearing women's sunglasses, besides, both complained about my professionalism. They both did it, indirectly, shaking their heads in turn.

"But what is he doing here?" Pantufa, the clown, from the back seat, asked Jaime, who was holding the steering wheel with both hands, in the front seat. As if I wasn't next to him and couldn't in the least hear what he was saying.

Jaime, because he genuinely liked me or because he was the most condescending of the group, and the most human, didn't strictly care that I was late. It was Jaime who in this case was guiding them to the justice of reason. However, Sandra considered herself a true humanitarian to the causes of the most infamous and an unconditional supporter of the underprivileged and the oppressed.

My job that day was not only to save the *So-So Theatre*, but also to get to know the Alentejo that lay beyond the walls of my world and the walls of the Garraia. Perhaps, it was part of my internship to get to know the inner sea of Alentejo that one can dive into without sinking into it. Possibly, I let myself get carried away by what Jaime had told me last week, of his desire to set out on a cart and go perform theatre throughout the Alentejo. Taking theatre to the people, and taking the people to the theatre.

In this ecstasy of nothingness that is show business, I met Xavier's younger brother in the Alandroal auditorium. Xavier had been my roommate in Ponte de Ferro. Somehow, I was amazed not only that he remembered me, but that the respect and admiration he had for me was so visible. It was probably I who did not hold myself in high enough regard. After all, we, the tellers of fables and myths, we only tell versions of the same story.

Possibly Xavier's younger brother would believe a version, in which the exaggerated myth of the last living poet would have been told to him already in an enlarged size. But I was already thinking only about lunch, and whether it would come with salad or not!

I arrived home after Albano Jerónimo, complaining about the huge detour Jaime would take to drop me off at home. But I didn't think about his musty bitterness. My stomach was full. Not literally, though, as much as he was. Immediately, after I got home, I talked to Francisco. It's amazing how, with so many millions of people in Brazil and millions more in Portugal, we felt the need to talk to each other for hours and hours, regardless of being separated by an ocean. It was as if Francisco had never left Évora.

"Hey, man, I'm worried…my scholarship money, it still hasn't gone into the bank," Francis said, anguishly.

"Don't forget, you swindler, that starving in a foreign country will make you a better artist. But Brazil is a brother country. Therefore, it won't make you a better person, or a better artist; in short!"

"I'm serious. I'm really worried."

"Don't worry, imposters always get away with it. Don't worry, they'll send the money from the bag in the meantime."

"You've always been much more optimistic than I am. I can't be like that. You look good! You look like you're committed."

"Today I went to Alandroal. I now want to tour all the time. My life has to be a continuous tour."

"You've been to the Algarve, now, you've been to Alandroal, and this is how you keep fooling people, and travelling."

"However, I can't like what's being done in *So-So*."

"So, you eat and drink and go for walks…right? Do you want even better?"

"For punishment, next Saturday I have to go to the São Martinho shows in Redondo. But I get the impression that I'm sailing through the Alentejo, hitching a ride with a theatre company that is a sinking plane. And I, as the captain of the ship, have to go down with it. Maybe I'll be the first to jump! What do you say?"

"A plane sinking?"

"A boat! A boat without wings."

"Look, that what is staged, is not something similar to what is seen, in the end, represented. Oh, giant-killer, weren't you expecting this one? Hmm?"

"Well, maybe I'd better jump!"

"Well, maybe it's for the best! But, man, I'm still worried. Ouch, ouch! Oh, my money!"

"You know it's like that, but then it's all good. In the end, they pay for everything. The world needs people who are paid to investigate, which we all already know."

***

Tan tan tan taan, Romeu has returned to Évora! Tan tan tan taan Simone returned to her parents' house with baby Jerusalem; poof, another sketch of Romeu gored. The Mr designer professionally gets a woman pregnant, that woman gives him a child project, they live together for a short indefinite period, and so it goes… Previously, he got his ex-partner pregnant, and that woman gave him the blueprint of a daughter. They lived together until bam! Separation! And so it goes. But in the end, everything and everyone gets along more or less well. Even the previous plan comes to see the father, and Simone's plan will eventually come to see the father too. Until the next one forces him to use a condom and interrupt his pattern. Simple, isn't it? You don't have to be very Catholic, or very orthodox, to work out the Romeu issue.

Before he left his friend's house, where he lived, temporarily, because his parents didn't want him in their home, Romeu told me to go visit them in São Sebastião da Giesteira; him, Simone, and the baby, who is not to blame for being called Jerusalem. Now he seems to avoid me. I learned about the love development, in this case, the love backlash, when after English class, I went to the job centre with Jaime, and we ran into him and his newness. They both knew each other, and they both knew me very vaguely. On and on I went, so-so comfortable and so-so uncomfortable.

I would then accept Jaime's invitation to have lunch with him, Sandra and her two chrysalises in the cocoon designed by the architect Siza Vieira, as well as outside the Malagueira neighbourhood. First, Jaime would put a Beatles album playing on the stereo in the living room and we would sit in his office, which is a kind of pantry, a mausoleum of his past with Sandra. Everything he has lived up to now is stuffed and stored there. I sat in a strange chair that had the design of a ladder. Jaime slouched in front of the computer, unable to move. He could only laugh in front of it. We chatted and smoked a joint, while Sandra, exceptionally, made lunch today. Jaime used to cook, because Sandra usually had other house chores. Only then we settled around the round table, which is proportional to the living room; sipping the satisfaction of a hot soup.

Sandra asked me, while licking her spoon, "But you know I'm a witch, don't you?" She insisted. "Do you know or not?"

I was not interested, however, in that conversation of Hera. "Say it, Sandra. Are you a good witch or are you a bad one?"

"I am neither bad nor good. I am just a witch. Women are born with the condition of being witches. Although men are born and die with the masculine condition of being nothing."

"Do the witches know what we are thinking?"

"Of course," she replied with conviction, stopping to swallow the spoon.

After lunch the three of us went to the old elementary school. I went with my stomach so-so full, so-so empty. Yet, I was committed to saving the *So-So*

Theatre as if it depended only on me. As if there was no one else who could save the *So-So Theatre* from itself.

Today, it is cold in November, the sky is intermittently a palette of blue-grey, regardless, of the kids from the arts school of the *So-So There* Association, running down the dirt ramp and screaming down their throats as if they were going to war. Then they walk over the wall that goes around the Alto de São Bento house. I myself balance on top of it, but I no longer feel the vertigo of childhood, nor do I feel the joy of being an eternal child.

Sandra uses the wall, not as balance training for equilibrists and pessimistic clowns, but as an exercise in self-confidence. I will record these tender moments of companionship and pedagogical growth. Perhaps, these children will one day be more spontaneous, more confident, more creative and assertive adults. In short, maybe they will be better than me and my generation. Maybe, with them, the seed of hope can be born and sprout, somewhere, in a small pot or a large concrete garden bed.

Professor Sandra speaks to the camera, "Not all children like to go to school, the school of results. Our children need much more than that. They need a space where they can experiment as people, where they can take risks and experience what really interests them. In front of the computer it is so hard to climb. You have to roll over, and this is a space where that can be done. Each person grows as the path is made. You don't grow alone. You grow as a group, in discovery. Self-overcoming, always requires effort."

Jaime's turn followed. Jaime is talking to the camera, while I am registering the garish paintings that accentuate the idyll of the woods, which live next to the old elementary school. They are painted on the walls, with bright colours, that have been painted by former employees and by the past twenty years that have passed. As Jaime was pronouncing himself, Farrusca, his dog, with only three legs was licking his hands. Meanwhile, the sound of backhoe machines in the cork oak forest marked the inn that would be built in the middle of the farm, bordering the house in Alto do São Bento. It was an entire landscape, which at that very instant…was changing and disappearing… Trees more than a hundred years old were falling to the ground with a bang, but not a single scream was heard, nor was there a funeral worthy of those illustrious beings who were murdered in broad daylight.

Jaime is the *So-So-Theatre*. I believe in Jaime, who is a Robin Hood without aesthetics. His world is an ideal. The *So-So* School of Arts is his ideal. Right now, it is part of the imagination in which I live and participate. I believe in Jaime's sincerity and simplicity, as I believe in Sandra's pedagogy and the fanatical fire in which her feminism burns. I also believe in the power of art, but I don't believe that *So-So Theatre* makes that art that I believe in.

***

In between my internship duties, the former prime minister, Mr José Sócrates showed up in Évora. He was brought in like a criminal in a police van. To stay in preventive detention. I learned of the measure of coercion when I walked from home to the city. Hearing on the avenue Lino de Carvalho talking about it with great interest. I heard the popular street anchors "in Portugal it doesn't matter, if he is innocent or if he is guilty, in the end he will be released."

The next day, after lunch, Mr Meireles stopped and offered me a ride. Mr Meireles is an old sailor, who now runs an undertaker's business in town. We immediately created a cordial relationship. The speed with which he was moving today allowed us only a brief conversation. There was still time, however, to learn that his wife had died two years ago. She had been wrongly medicated. Mr Meireles had, although, gotten over his wife's death. Because according to his deontology, there was nothing more to be done.

The death of the deceased would somehow not become the main occupation of his life. As happens with those widowers who, when their beloved dies, they are forever downcast, living like Maria de Fátima, my former landlady, wrapped in a shawl of eternal mourning.

Francisca would come Sunday afternoon to see the performance of the School of Arts with the citizens group, which was formed to stop the use of animals as unpaid circus workers. That is, according to Sandra, the kids from the School of Arts at *So-So Theatre* were joined by a social movement, formed by a small community niche. According to what she had told me, it was a group of kids and a group of teenagers from her theatre classes who wanted to join the movement that had recently arisen in the city, in defence of an animal-free circus. And that somehow, they had come knocking on *So-So's* door, and that, of course, *So-So Theatre* had opened the door.

Tomé also participated, obliged by his mother Sandra, although he would have preferred to stay at home playing computer games and blowing out his bangs that are insistently falling into his eyes. Tomé's freedom is after all the same as the café owner's son who has to help his father to get coffees, or to carry the coffee on the tray, and to say thank you to the customer. Fundamentally, humanity all comes down to the same thing.

Finally, the internship has started. But the delay it took to start, meant that I will be late paying this month's rent. I warned the landlady in the meantime, who accepted very reluctantly. She was not pleased with the news, possibly because she only now realises that I am not that funny. Perhaps also realising that I don't have as much money as she initially thought. I don't think she will see me at the Seleiras' house anymore, which is where she stays on one or the other weekend during the fall, or when she comes to the country on vacation in the summer. Therefore, I will no longer drink tea there, or eat cookies made by Augusta, the maid.

The internship moves forward with a list of uncertainties that will certainly never be resolved. In the meantime, I am having to publicise the company's events. Sandra's latest idea is to make a DVD and a book about the 20 years of the *So-So Theatre* company and the *So-So There* Association, because the day before yesterday she found out about a new contest in which she could apply for another grant.

The solution I recently presented to the Alma couple was to turn the old elementary school into a house of culture and conviviality. I proposed to them to open the doors of *So-So There* to the community, creating a habit of having audiences at the *So-So Theatre*. Jaime's conviction is that someone in this way will steal the association from him, if only a large group signs up as members and wants to dispute his place on the board.

In other words, the entrance of new members is controlled, because Jaime needs to keep his and Sandra's place in the presidency. Jaime tried to explain to me the difference between his theatre company and the association, but I still don't understand the difference. Ending up mixing them, in the same bag. As if one existed only to serve the interests of the other.

As for me, I still haven't figured out what my real role is in the *So-So There* Association. Perhaps, it is to do a little bit of everything, doing nothing. Not being part of the association, not being part of the company, not being part of the world. Alienating myself more and more and withdrawing into the shell of myself. Anyway, the internship has officially started. But for me, I think it has already achieved its purpose.

The following Saturday, I met up with the Alma couple in Praça do Giraldo. I arrived slightly first, being able to see Jaime, before entering Giraldo Square with the rest of his troupe and with the scene stuffed in the trunk of the van. I also saw Sandra getting out of the van as a woman at arms. However, without swords or rifles. Our Lady of Fátima without make-up, a Catarina Eufémia capable of breast-feeding her son, Tomé, with her right tit and claiming his rights with her left tit, and still doing a master's degree, as she constantly and proudly said. Unable, nonetheless, to increase her family comfort. Perhaps, because society never reciprocates with the same generosity as a mother.

Meanwhile, I climbed the work stairs to put up the theatre curtain, under the arcades of Giraldo Square. Enjoying the common task of mortal man. To serve the *So-So There* Association was to serve the community. The *So-So Theatre* promoted an integrative theatre. But it was a theatre that gained nothing from it. However, the great ecstasy of life is to open the door of the heart for all to enter, and through it, to pass.

Sandra, a pedagogue, introduced the show over the microphone. The world, which is built at every moment, did not stop to hear what the Catarina Eufémia of this century had to say. What the audience saw in passing were children playing theatre. Children who interpreted according to Sandra's staging. The fantasy world they still inhabited without fear was a world that adults have long ceased to see, leaving the beauty and innocence of when they were children too, to turn themselves into beasts, or worse.

The square continued to fill up with people crossing from one side to the other. Some waited a few minutes, peeking by the fountain, others crowded in front of the stores, wondering what it was all about. Ana Maria, Belchior's girlfriend, also joined the performance. She was the one presenting the numbers of the show. She was a *cabaretier* with a green wig, who talked as if she had long been a professional clown. She was a version of Willy Wonka, but in a feminine way, "Children and girls, gentlemen and carrots!" So began Ana Maria, with her usual rounded glasses falling onto her thin nose.

Yesterday, without me expecting it, the landlady called me…surprisingly, the lady, Maria Eduarda, told me that she needed part of the furniture, which was in my house, to take to the city. To a house that she had rented to a young lesbian couple. I was forced to agree with Marcus, "money, it moves the wheel of the world. And it is not half the world that turns the other half, it is money that turns half the world and makes the other half turn the other way around." And according to him, it is a waste of time to complain. Besides, according to him, it is ugly to do so.

A week and a half later, I was overdressed, because when I climbed to the top of the ladder to put on the stage lights in St Vincente's Church in my overcoat, I instantly felt that something was wrong. I had the feeling I should be doing something else instead, it wasn't my costume that was inappropriate, it was me climbing the wrong steps on the wrong ladder. And, meanwhile, Professor Luiz Alberto, was pacing back and forth, very suspicious. Eventually, he considered that my presence was profaning his church. And the longer I remained on the ladder, the smaller it seemed to me.

Meanwhile, the landlady has already received the rent money. She even came to bring a wood-burning stove. She didn't do it to repay the injustice of her previous vengeful act. She did it, possibly, only out of fear. Because she was afraid that I, with the cold this winter in the Garraia would set fire to the old chimney. Her generosity was born out of fear that I would set fire to the house, as Belchior did in the Vista Alegre neighbourhood. She said it was my Christmas present and Mr Juveral came to do the installation. Mr Juvenal is another resident of the estate, who, like Rolando, Mrs Jacinta's nephew, also works for the lady.

The landlord, Mr Norberto Córdova, found me this week. I was shooting a promotional video in the Largo de São Vicente. He stopped by one of the billboards announcing the winter season of *So-So Theatre*, in the Church of São Vicente, and asked me if I was working. He was accompanied by one of his sons, the one who lives upstairs in Mr Córdova's building, and who has an office on the ground floor. He doesn't seem to sympathise with me yet. Maybe he doesn't appreciate the simple idea that I like to listen to Bach, or the eloquent and captivating way I speak, or the clothes I wear that hide my poor human condition. Perhaps he is still searching to find the justification for his intuition, which, so far, he has not found.

A little later I would run into my friend Daniel Filipe, who was also walking hand in hand with his girlfriend, Beatriz Gorjão, in the São Vicente square. They were accompanied by Beatriz's mother, who was, curiously, my classmate. When I enrolled, initially at evening course. It was in a mythical and mystical time that now seems so far away from me, as Daniel Filipe's life in Lisbon currently seems very far from the previous complicity we had in Évora. I think that we distance ourselves from those we were accomplices with, because progressively we are accumulating other types of knowledge, and to preserve them, we have to abandon what we dominated before.

I still remember that this summer, Daniel Filipe had invited me to Oeiras to visit him and Beatriz and the half dozen cats that walk between their backyard and their house. Or was it me who invited myself to go visit them? I don't remember exactly anymore. But when I wrote to him saying that yes, I was going, he did not return any more mail. And that would be the week that I found the white table that had been left by the garbage bin in the Vista Alegre square. I ended up doing that artistic residence, finding the itinerant blue and the landlady's daughter.

So, it is my duty to thank Daniel Filipe for not telling me anything else. Seeing him, after all, was not only remembering what I lost and what I left behind, it was also the happiness of following through that mysterious blue-grey channel that has the sky of the future, in the uncertainty of time that can be either today or tomorrow.

In the meantime, I am trying to keep the light on from my bedroom lamp, before I fall asleep with the creed of my faith. I have fallen asleep, though. Believing that my life may no longer be a matter of credit and that the season of the *So-So Theatre* at St Vincente's Church may also no longer be a matter of life or death. After all, St Vincente's Church is now an exhibition gallery, a performance hall. This is the twenty-first century! Holy men are now ordinary men. They may be poets working at a post office counter, they may be writers who write their work on kitchen paper, or construction painters who smear their hope with concrete paint in the abstract form of a spiral staircase.

Ordinary men are now martyrs to a profession of faith, which has convinced them to climb step by step, and paint a wall white or draw geometric figures on the ceiling. The holy men of old, however, were neither so holy nor so martyred. They were only men who knew that sin was also part of martyrdom.

Francisco will come at the end of December to visit me in Évora. Francisco's coming to Évora is an act of faith that is also an *auto-da-fé*. With him comes Miguel and Viegas. The three of them constitute my trinity. I will abandon my cause, my crusade of abstinence, for a moment of temptation. Francisco will come earlier than the other elements of the *Te Deum*. He will spend Christmas in Santarém, to say goodbye to his father who paid for his plane ticket. He will give his mother Ana and his sister Mónica a hug of veneration.

Miguel will come later from Olivais. He will come out of his room and gently knock on the door of the building. Still hearing the echo of his father's contempt, who hates him today as much as he loves him tomorrow and, preferably, when he's not around the house. Between yesterday and today, he has called him at least half a dozen times "lazy," and concluding, very paternally, "you are such a piece of shit, my son!"

The great Viegas will appear one day after Miguel. He will be sitting at the bottom of his cave, that is, sitting on the sofa in his parents' basement. He will remain there, more or less hidden, through the pages of the books he feels like reading until dawn. In between he will take another desperate shift at the Pingo Doce in Santarém. Without even once looking at a customer's face. Pulling up with his index finger the glasses of his narcissistic intellect. He will be the last to arrive and the first to leave. Because he is Viegas, is the father, the son, the brother, and the aunt of all of us non-existentialists.

The first thing he will tell me will be:

"So, Poet, I hear you want to hit me over the head with an axe?" Since, in the meantime, Francis must have already made reference to the theatrical reception I have prepared for him. Something like: first, I would give him a tight hug, hiding the axe that Mr Juvenal lent me. Leaving then Zé Pedro emotionally uncomfortable.

Meanwhile, Viegas, the docile one, the one who omits the fat meat of a life made in consequent frustration, will look at the hand holding the axe and smile, and I will hug him full of pity for my confrere Viegas. All of them, coming to Évora on pilgrimage because Francisco, the father of the trinity, wants to spend a few days with me or, simply, because I am the only one who has a house and lives alone.

At this, the Christmas season began. No audience was enough to fill the small St Vincente Church. Esperança, the eldest daughter of *So-So Theatre* said, "no audience, no performance." Lowering her head and continuing to stare at the small screen of her cell phone. Eventually, that was all she had to spew. Jaime Alma agreed with his daughter, not having to say a word to me. He looked at me, however, fraternally Still, as half a dozen people came, Jaime and Sandra had to go up to the small platform where the vestibule is, precisely, under the vault of the church.

At the entrance of the temple was the sea of newspapers. The audience would stand with their backs to the main altar, looking at the place where the women, the crazy and the catechumens used to stand. When I, the light and sound operator and other fungi, turned on the lights, and stopped the music band, Jaime and Sandra looked older than the age written on their faces. In the end, Esperança would hug her mother, and Tomé would hug his father.

I would turn out the lights, just so I wouldn't have to hug anyone. Luiz Alberto would greet Jaime and Sandra, as if he had already seen everything the world had to offer, and was just another version of it. A *Te Deum*, from me, Francis, Miguel and JP Viegas, to the great *pater* LAF.

The season at St Vincent's Church is proving to be a huge disappointment. There is no audience to love the theatre. That is, there is an audience in Évora, but there is no audience for *So-So Theatre*. We are at the beginning of the stage and I have lost my belief in Sandra and Jaime's theatre. We are somewhere in the middle of December, and nothing is as pure as it used to be.

The devotion I had for Jaime is now a compartment before the train of the moment when Francisco arrived in Portugal. My will to save Sandra, Jaime, Esperança and Tomé and Farrusca, has eclipsed. Definitely, the internship is no longer a question of faith. Finishing my degree is also no longer a question of faith.

It is December and it is cold. The Christmas lights in town are really worn out. My spirit is blind. I cannot see with other eyes another light of truth, nor can I even see beyond what I believe. I cannot, therefore, or any other order of things, feel that I am truly an adept or an initiate. Perhaps, I am only obliged to recognise that the *So-So Theatre* is just another couple, in a union of fact. And any belief needed followers, as Francisco, the son of the great Father Calé, would say.

Maybe Jaime Alma's daughter, Esperança, knows more about religion or hermeticism than I do. And, perhaps, it really does take an audience to show man's need to create. Maybe I need the present conviction of a congregation in the power of art. Maybe you do need an audience. Not to make art, but to believe in it and its power. Because every creation is divine, or because man is imperfect in God's eyes, or because we are made in his image and because we men cannot see God. Because God is light, and we can't look directly into the sunlight, without sunglasses, and even then, it is difficult to look directly into the light of the creator.

Sandra today asked me if I wanted to have lunch with her and Jaime. But I said no, that I had things to do at home. It didn't bother me to have the loneliness of Christmas as company. Meanwhile, Jaime said he wouldn't mind tomorrow, after the last performance at the São Vicente Church, to pick Francisco up at the bus station and then drop us off at the Garraia.